I smiled but couldn't ... a cardboard box whic... my college office afte... my ... It contained my books – those which now crumble to dust in my neglected room – and the wooden model of the uranium nucleus.

She smiled, but it was a strain. 'I'm sorry about the rest of your things. Your office was . . . well, it got destroyed.'

'That's OK'. I put my own small prison bundle into the cardboard box and pressed the flaps down over the top. 'I think I should be going,' I said.

'Where will you go?' she asked.

'Far away. I don't know where. You're right . . . I can't come back.'

'For ever?'

'For ever,' I confirmed.

She showed me to the door and I kissed her. We stood there on either side of the threshold as if we were waiting to begin another more important conversation that never happened.

Apart from once reading in a week-old copy of *The Times* that she had inherited the family business – they were in the hotel trade – I neither saw nor heard anything of Marion for more than fifty years. Until that letter landed in my hallway.

Her words sent me away and her words brought me back. But I would never have stirred from my hiding place if I had known that the danger I had run from still lurked in the world. It seems that 'for ever' does not pass in half a century. She and I were wrong to think it had.

David Hood was born in Peterborough in 1959. He studied physics at Oxford and later took an MBA at Cranfield Management School. He has worked variously as a research scientist, racing car driver, salesman, marketeer, business planner and manufacturing manager. He now divides his time between his own company and several others in which he holds directorships. He lives in Northamptonshire with his wife and two children.

The Chess Men

DAVID HOOD

ORION

An Orion paperback
First published in Great Britain by Victor Gollancz in 1999
This paperback edition published in 2000 by
Orion Books Ltd,
Orion House, 5 Upper St Martin's Lane,
London WC2H 9EA

Copyright © David Martin 1999

A CIP catalogue record for this book
is available from the British Library.

ISBN: 0 75283 476 2

Printed and bound in Great Britain by
Clays Ltd, St Ives plc

To my mother and father,
and to my wife

The term 'cold fusion', as reported in the popular press in recent years, refers to the process of fusing hydrogen nuclei at room temperature. It was allegedly demonstrated in a simple laboratory apparatus in 1989 by Fleischman and Pons. Several experiments have been conducted to try to replicate their work, with limited success. The phenomenon of cold fusion cannot be reproduced on demand and cannot be explained by conventional nuclear physics. Therefore, its commercial potential as an electric generating technology is uncertain.

Source: *Energy Aware Planning Guide II*,
California Energy Commission,
December 1996

PART ONE

1

I am a private man and I will not – perhaps cannot – describe the workings of grief.

It is half a century since I gave up on the world. I thought I was safe. But the past reclaims you, no matter how many precautions you take. For me, it slipped into the house through the letterbox, falling on the hall carpet, wedging beneath a copy of *The Cherwell Christian* magazine.

I did not notice it at first. I was shuffling about in the morning routine – a cup of tea made from the milk and teabags the home help had brought the day before, her weekly visit come and gone in a couple of hours. I ate slices of dried toast spread with homemade jam from the village shop. All seemed normal. I put the breakfast things in the kitchen bowl to soak and came out into the hall.

I was surprised to see the Queen staring regally across the envelope as I picked up the post. I could not remember the last thing I had received with a real stamp. Still, it seemed harmless enough, addressed to 'Mr Smith', a name I had adopted but did not own.

Then I unfolded the ivory paper and read its first line. And everything changed.

I slumped on to the bottom stair. My insides heaved and rumbled. I felt faint. The wall I had built against pain, brick by brick, higher and higher, collapsed all at once and I gazed back over rubble into the memories of a life long since lost.

> Dear Hayden,
> I cannot be sure if this will get to you, but I felt compelled to write. I don't know if you're interested or if you care. Your daughter Emily has cancer. The doctor says she's not got long, a week or two at most.

I know I warned you never to return to Oxford,
but I think it would be nice if you came to her now.
Whatever your decision, please ask your God to
have mercy on her soul. You always had a closer
relationship with him than the rest of us.
Yours, Marion.

It would be 'nice' if I came to her. What was crammed
into that word? The world had been compressed and swallowed down to four little letters.

I took several minutes to recover, sitting on the step,
recapturing scattered emotions that ran out like unpenned
sheep. Eventually, I stood up, painfully examining in the
hallway mirror my disrepaired face. The troubles I ran from
back in Oxford fifty years ago still linger in the grey skin,
tucked into folds which mark the passage of time like rings
in a tree. Too old to change – that's what I thought, that's
what I had told myself – and for a while, in that silvered
image, I looked at myself as a thing already dead.

I suppose it took most of the day to pull my thinking
straight. I took refuge in the room I had set aside and never
used. I read along its old shelf of books, on which personal
histories peep into the present. Chess books, physics books,
the works of the great poets – dusty unread wisdoms.

On the windowsill, I noticed a wooden model I had not
touched in years. I reached for it now, coughing as its dust
flew. The model was five inches high, consisting of 236 black
and white balls. I know the exact number because I designed
and constructed it myself – 92 white, 144 black. When you
held it in both hands and twisted, it broke into two pieces
and three loose black balls fell on the floor. In your right
hand, you then held a representation of a barium nucleus;
in your left, that of krypton. You had just split the atom.
The wooden balls at your feet were the three neutrons that
made the 'A' bomb possible.

Now, in the 1990s, my frail fingers could not grip tightly
enough to operate the model's ancient mechanism. Such is
the effect of years on the human frame. My once skilled

hands are practically useless: joints bulge from the bones like notches in dried bamboo and the blue rope of veins winds around like a creeping plant that strangles them.

Silently, I considered advancing age and the limitations of this failing body. I considered the icy cold of the winter outside and the painful stiffness it brought.

Pale excuses.

From the shelf, I took down and wiped off the cover of the Bible. My hands were quivering, but I held it, eyes closed in prayer, and waited – waited for something. I knew not what. Sometimes the answers of faith take a long time, a long slow time.

When I was done, I replaced the Bible without ever opening its leather binding. I had seen then what I must do.

Even a wrecked old man is compelled by duty. And dutifully, I gathered up strength and began packing a small canvas bag with everything of importance I possessed. In the late afternoon, I wrapped myself inside a vast black cloak and set off.

It is a mile down to the village, a hard uneven walk. From there, I took a fishing boat to the mainland. On the crossing, I hung my head, thought of the past, and cried. The last time I stood on English soil was 7 August 1945, the day they released me. It was the last time I had seen Emily.

2

John Harringhay's manager had dubbed him the 'Greatest Young Chess Player Alive'. But then Helen Michaels was like that – pushy, full of hype, forever broadcasting wild boasts. Her brand of PR seemed to work, though. The tabloids used his picture as if they were trying to wear it out. He was famous, even if he still loitered on the borders of real success.

'It's all about publicity,' she explained while leading him into the TV studio that lunchtime. 'Awareness is what raises the ante. This is the best Western network out here these days. Thank God for satellite.'

He didn't reply. He followed her, a scruffy youth in a cheap T-shirt and cut-off jeans. All he ever seemed to look at was the floor.

Out in front, Helen breezed through the foyer and clattered up the main stairs on her high heels. She breached the swing doors with the broken 'On Air/Off Air' sign, stopping just inside, absorbing everything with her keen business eye. The place was in chaos. She sniffed at the local smells of dust on hot lights. 'Hell,' she said, 'I've never seen such a bloody mess.'

Half a dozen technicians were buzzing around the studio like commuters on speed, swerving between the scattered equipment in a vain attempt at preparation. The director's voice boomed instructions, fast but calm, as if he saw this last-minute dash every day.

'Lip mike . . . I need a lip mike. Get that coffee cup out of the shot. Where's Bob? Have you got him the background for the interview yet?'

Bob strolled nonchalantly into the centre of the set. 'I'm just reading it,' he called out, 'trying to decide the questions.'

'This is the "bad boy" of chess. How hard can it be? Ask him if it's true he took a swing at the referee the other night. You know the stuff.'

'OK, OK, I'm reading. Twenty years old. English. Grandmaster at seventeen ... Blah, blah blah – usual shit! Is he gay?'

The director showed a brief patronizing smile. 'Not according to that tart who sold her story last year. She said he was ...'

'She said he was hung like a pawnbroker's balls,' Helen interrupted, stepping over a spaghetti of wires. 'I wrote that for her myself,' she added proudly.

She had lit a cigarette, a long slim menthol, and was waving it like a baton. Everyone turned towards her. Maybe she was over forty, but she was stylish with it, power dressed, the big-name labels displayed like banners. She sucked in a lungful of smoke and held it. When she exhaled, it came out pencilled with a single controlled breath. No one dared tell her there was a smoking ban.

'We've only got fifteen minutes for this,' she said, taking aim on the director. 'I suggest we get on with it. I know Singapore's dull, but we do have other appointments today.'

'We can't do an interview in fifteen minutes,' Bob protested.

'That's what we agreed.'

Bob looked at his director as if he hadn't been told. The director nodded. 'A quarter of an hour. Don't worry, Bob, you're great at these short pieces.'

'Shit!' Bob stretched the word almost indefinitely. He ran his hand back through his hair and zeroed his gaze on his interviewee, searching for inspiration.

His interviewee, the great would-be chess champion, was squatting on the floor near the entrance, wrapping and unwrapping a crêpe bandage around one hand. Against the bare wall, he looked scrawny and inconsequential, and yet there seemed a great weight upon him, something alien. Bob couldn't place it. 'The legendary John Harringhay,' he sneered, shaking his head.

15

The director shrugged and turned to his assistant. Leaning close, he whispered, 'I think you'd better start your stopwatch. This woman's got a reputation.'

With a shake of her head, Helen left them to it. She negotiated the cabling a second time. Reaching the boy, she leaned over and told him to stop playing with his bandage. He stopped immediately. 'Don't worry,' she promised him. 'Three questions and we're out of here.'

By the time they were ready to film, eleven minutes had ticked away. Interviewer Bob actually managed four questions, but that was down to the brevity of the answers. He opened with a simple platitude. 'Second in a Grandmaster tournament is a great result. What are your feelings?'

John shuffled, looked down and muttered, 'I should've won.'

'But it's a great result for a young player in a tournament of this quality, isn't it?

'No.' The word was delivered without so much as a shake of the head.

'How do you ... er ... feel about the up-coming tournament in San Francisco?'

He paused briefly this time. 'I'll have to do better,' he answered.

Bob thought about chancing another. He coughed and flexed a hand that was beginning to sweat. Nervously he asked, 'What can you tell me about the alleged incident in the hotel?'

The boy's eyes rose from the floor in slow motion. 'Fuck you!' he said.

The eyes sucked Bob in and spat him out. He stepped back as if he'd been hit.

'CUT!' the director screamed. 'Jesus Christ, we can't use that. This is supposed to go out prime time.'

The boy was now examining the ground, using his feet to dig up the PVC tape that marked his spot on the studio floor. Grinning widely, Helen shook her head and moved away. Her portable phone was bleeping insistently.

'Helen Michaels,' she said, greeting its mouthpiece.

'Who? ... His mother's what? ... I'm sorry it's a bad line ... In hospital ... No, not now, he's being interviewed ... Yes, Singapore, colonial charm and Raffles, you know ... Yes, the first flight home, I promise ... Thank you.'

Helen pressed the aerial down. Leaning against the wall, she held the phone to her chest and bit her lip. The ghost of a tremble came and went. For a few seconds, she stood pensive, almost regretful, then she put away the phone and pulled out a little compact, hinging up the mirror. She inspected her face like an engineer checking for cracks in a structure. The look was manufactured, built on top of her real face, but it suited the purpose, she thought – much as her hard business manner towered over whatever uncertainty lay within. She clicked the compact shut and regained her smile.

'That's it, we've got to go,' she announced, walking back on to the studio floor.

'But we haven't got a take we can use,' the director objected.

'You shouldn't ask such stupid questions then, should you? Besides, we've got an exhibition to play in twenty minutes.'

'Look, lady, we all got our commitments. We got Joe Beckett booked in later today, a fucking would-be Governor of California ... a real politician's politician. I mean, he knows how to give a decent fucking interview. You think I need this?'

Helen grabbed John by the arm. 'Let's go,' she said.

She was trying to make telephone calls all the way down the corridor and into the lift. Portable phones don't work in lifts, she discovered. Three minutes later, in the taxi, she was still frantically pressing the redial button.

Suddenly she pulled the mouthpiece away from her face and said, 'John, that was a great interview. Controversial. Pithy. I hope they bleep it out and use it.'

He shrugged. Nothing seemed to move in his body but his shoulders.

17

'I should tell you there's been a change of plan,' she added. 'We're going home tomorrow.'

No reaction. After a while, he murmured, 'Tomorrow?'

'I got a call while you were filming,' she continued, 'I'm afraid your mother's back in hospital . . .'

His face dropped.

'Hell, I'm sorry,' she said. 'I'm sure it's not too bad. Don't worry.'

'Can't we go now?'

She turned to him, a scolding look in her eye. 'John, we have obligations – you should know that. I'm going to have to cancel Bali as it is.'

'Can I call home?'

'Sure, you can use my phone, but let me just get these things rearranged, OK? This is going to cost a bundle.' She glanced briefly at the driver and snarled, 'Are you sure this is the quickest way to the theatre?'

The driver's hand gestures were dismissive more than apologetic. This city's always like this, the gesture said, hot and busy. Unless you know how to fly, this is as fast as it gets! He looked at her in the rear-view mirror as if she were an idiot.

Helen swore under her breath, glaring, wondering if it was worth the fight. She huffed and restarted the telephone conversation. The taxi lurched forward.

John seemed immune to it all, detached. He stared out of the window, his eyes dragging vaguely across the passing traffic, cars and motorbikes like an infestation, four to five abreast on superwide carriageways moving at a crawl. His gaze followed groups of them, then lost them; not a flicker showed in his face.

The phone battery went flat before they arrived at the theatre. Helen apologized. John smiled forcibly. He was still curled in the corner, propped like a ventriloquist's dummy between door and seat back.

When the taxi driver looked down at his meter, the digits seemed to tell him something he didn't believe. He exclaimed in his native language. Over a thousand Singapore dollars, something like five hundred English pounds or eight hundred US dollars.

'I don't understand. This is a new machine,' he mumbled apologetically.

Helen offered him a single twenty-dollar note. While the taxi driver looked at it, John slid out through the door, pulling his good hand up from behind the back seat. He had been playing with the wires that ran from the back axle to the taxi meter.

Revenge. He didn't like anyone who was rude to Helen.

'Keep the change. You did a great job,' Helen was telling the driver. He replied with another hand gesture. Slightly more respect.

At the stage-door entrance, Helen and John were greeted by a tall pencil of a man, six foot three with a hairstyle like the pencil's squared-off eraser. He wore blue shoes, blue straight-cut trousers and a pale yellow jacket ruffled with deep creases.

'We are ready. We are ready,' he shrieked excitedly. His voice was high-pitched and disfigured by its hideous accent, a mongrel cross of Eastern European and Asian. 'Come, come quickly, John, quickly,' he added.

'Are all the opponents ready, Karl?' asked Helen.

'Yes . . . yes, in position, and the audience. We are full – three hundred people. A sell-out,' Karl answered. 'Our sponsors have big important guests today. We are due in two minutes. I thought you would not make it.'

'No, it went to plan. We're smack on schedule . . .' She dabbed a bead of sweat on her forehead. 'Jesus, it's hot in here. I thought this place was supposed to have air conditioning.'

'Yes, but it does not work properly back here.'

Helen examined her fingers for traces of smudged-off make-up. Turning to the boy, she asked, 'John, are you OK?'

'I'm ready but . . . I'd like to call home,' he said.

'No time. Straight after, I promise.'

'You know what is expected, Johnny. Ten opponents –

19

good players – not as good as you, of course. You have five white boards, five black. You understand?'

'He's done this before,' Helen interrupted. 'Come on, we're on.'

John got to his position just as the stage lights were going up. A local radio personality was making the introductions. 'Welcome to the YCK Corporation's annual Chess Exhibition Challenge. I'm your host.' He smiled like a politician. 'I hope you're going to enjoy this simultaneous display by one of the world's leading players. Please welcome *the* most exciting young player of his generation, Mr John Harringhay.'

An expectant hand-clapping followed. John wandered out to meet it, still wearing the T-shirt and cut-offs. His bare legs were white and skinny in the lights; ankle-high trainers ballooned from his feet like inflatable boats.

The main part of the house was dark, but in the elevated boxes with Empire furnishings to either side were the sponsors' guests, lit by the faint glow of backlight, important men and women expensively dressed. They were just above the boy's eye level. He glanced at them briefly, then never looked that way again.

On stage, a motley collection of opponents awaited, short and tall, oriental and Caucasian. Their chess sets were at the ready, the ten tables arranged in a horseshoe around the edge. The boy stopped equidistant from all of them. And stared.

'Let's play chess,' the host yelled, as the hand-clapping faded.

The opponent on Board One pushed forward the first piece and John Harringhay exploded into action.

The task was that of a plate spinner in a variety show, attending to ten games in turn, spending less than ten seconds at each board and making moves with a juggler's rhythm. But he was neither haphazard nor flustered: he was transformed. He stalked between the tables like a tiger, all stealth and intent. He tore into each game, moves jerking out of him.

This was the John Harringhay the tabloids wrote about.

This was the face their pictures showed, arcane and angry, unsettlingly beautiful.

'Brilliant, isn't he?' Helen said, as she seated herself backstage.

The man next to her nodded distractedly. All his attention was on the horseshoe of games and the big displays behind each which showed the progress of play. He was closer to fifty than forty, his appearance distinguished, handsome even. His hair had greyed just a little and he wore a jacket with pens weighting down the top pocket. He had intellectual's glasses, the round frames that multiply intensity in the eyes. Across his knees lay a portable computer open and glowing blue from the screen. Now John had begun playing, he ignored it.

'Sam, did you hear what I said?' Helen asked petulantly.

Sam recognized his name and turned round. 'Sometimes he's just amazing,' he answered; the accent was East Coast American. He brought his hand up to his chin and posed like *The Thinker* for a moment. 'He works it all out like it's a war. He reminds me of Bobby.'

'Bobby?'

'Yes, Fischer. I worked with him once.'

'The last American world champion? You think John could be . . .?' She sounded doubtful.

'I didn't say that. I didn't say he reminded me of Bobby when he was champion. Bobby went nuts afterwards.'

'That's not a pleasant thing to say.' Helen rose to her feet indignantly; her face had screwed itself into a scowl.

'Plenty of chess players go nuts, Helen,' Sam assured her, 'especially the good ones. They have screwy kinds of brains. Like no one else has. Hell, some people even think I'm nuts.'

'When I hired you, people said you were the best chess analyst in the business.'

'Don't get the idea the two are mutually exclusive,' he advised. He put his computer aside and stood up. Their eyes met on a level; his were calm and clear behind his rounded glasses. They smiled at her.

'I remember being with Kichnov when he went weird

on me,' he said. 'He was playing some Russian Grand-master ... before *glasnost*. The Russian kept asking for refreshments and Kichnov insisted the opponent's seconds were sending in special flavours of yoghurt telling their man what move to make next.'

'And were they?'

Sam shrugged. 'Do you know how many possible moves there are on a chess board? They'd have needed every fruit flavour in the world. Armies of KGB chefs in the kitchen. *We need him to move his king's pawn, comrade! Get out the bilberry and pomegranate!*'

'You're pulling my leg, right?' Helen laughed uneasily.

'Well, perhaps a little,' he admitted, 'but not entirely. Kichnov was a weird one. He used to spend his spare time doing jigsaws the wrong way up. You know, picture side down. When he'd finished all he'd got was a reconstructed sheet of cardboard. It seemed to keep him happy. The last time I saw Boris he was standing on a chair in a hotel dining room, shouting 'I'm an orange', and threatening to squirt anyone who came near him.' The American smiled as though he had real affection for the insanity of chess. He seemed to understand it. He seemed to wish he had it himself.

The exhibition lasted less than an hour. John did every-thing fast and perfectly. When it was over, the applause was loud and long and even Sam contributed. As it finally waned, he said, 'You know what's really amazing?'

'No, what?' Helen asked.

'He played a different opening on every single board. Most players don't do that. Even other Grandmasters. Ten boards at once – you want them all to be similar, so you've got some chance of controlling it. You know, similar thought patterns for each game. But he didn't do that. He did the opposite of what you're supposed to do. I don't think he even thought about it. I don't think he ever thinks. Sure, he's impetuous, but he just ... sees where to go and goes there. That's scary!'

'That's John all over,' she said.

By now, John had fallen silent and still, planted firmly in the middle of the stage. The unspoken menace of his movements was replaced by detachment. Someone or something had thrown a switch and he had been turned off. Helen walked on to the stage and shepherded him away.

Sam watched her, automatically following the elegance of her motion, but he was thinking of something else now, something John had said to him at the tournament the day before.

'Did you ever hear of my grandfather?'

It had struck him as a strange question at first. 'I don't think so. I would have remembered the name Harringhay. He was a chess player?'

'No, not Harringhay. A sort of chess player . . .' The boy had hesitated for a second, his usual nervous reserve. 'Hayden Zalapek . . .' he said.

Sam had felt something explode inside. He knew it. Of course, he knew it. The thought had rattled in his head all the way to the hotel that night. In his room, he had uncapped a screw-top beer bottle from the mini-bar, and downed the drink in one, still thinking about it.

The theatre crowd was roused to another short burst of applause before the house lights came up. Sam's mind snapped back to the present.

'Professor Hayden Zalapek,' he whispered to himself as the boy walked past him under Helen's guidance. Now there was a name.

A hotel in Boston, Massachusetts. Two women came into Room 516, dressed as if they'd just attended a party. Dinner dresses in blue and green, slits up the leg, one dress off the shoulder. Both women were in their twenties, not beautiful, but not unattractive either. Both showed the glow of alcohol.

The first woman threw the door key on the side table. The second stood motionless by the bed. A little nervous laughter. The first woman moved towards her, hesitated, then planted a sizeable kiss on her companion.

23

In a moment, they were rolling on the bed, clothes shedding like a washing line in high wind. They panted, naked. Noises of ecstasy and of the headboard banging the wall.

The second woman didn't notice the lens poking from inside the wardrobe door. The first woman seemed almost to play to it.

3

August 1945. I suppose that was also a kind of homecoming, a border between the then and the now – a dividing line that cannot be recrossed.

There I was in a prison-issue suit, a little bundle of belongings tucked under my arm, on a bus for Cornwall with the promise of seeing my daughter.

A woman sat down on the next seat – not invited by me – and insisted on talking. She was prim and clinging to a raffia shopping basket as if she ached for the child it represented, wanting gurgles and all the other heart-warming baby noises that never come from shopping baskets. She told me her name which I have long since forgotten. 'What's yours?' she asked with a West Country twang.

'Hayden,' I replied. She waited for me to give a second name, but I didn't.

'Are you from around here?'

'I'm visiting,' I said. I did not mean to be rude, but I'm afraid it must have seemed that way. On the news that morning, they had announced the bombing of Hiroshima. Those few of us who understood what the grave broadcasts meant knew the end of the world had begun. Inside, I carried the sense of time ticking, the world like a chess clock with its red flag poised to fall from the minute hand. Nowhere left to move.

Even so, this woman didn't seem discouraged by my truncated replies. 'You've family here?' she prompted.

'My daughter,' I said, trying to snap from my melancholy.

'Oh, moved 'er out here to avoid the Blitz? We've got a lot of extra kids because of that.'

'No, not exactly.'

'Is your wife here?' she asked.

The question cut suddenly through flesh and into bone. I hadn't thought about Alice. I had assumed there was no pain left, but I was wrong. 'My wife was killed,' I said, as weights piled into my voice.

'I'm sorry,' she muttered.

'A bomb . . . in London.' I hesitated, picturing my daughter – all that was left. 'Emily's staying with . . . with friends,' I told the woman. 'I've been away.'

'Friends' – I didn't know how else to describe Marion. She had come to my rescue when it seemed as though Emily might be orphaned, taken off to a 'home' or something equally awful. Marion was not 'family' as such, but she had been the mistress of my closest friend and, therefore, part of the extended family which Alice and I had enjoyed in our Oxford years.

My wife died in the same house as Marion's lover, their bodies crushed by the same rubble as the blazing roof fell in. Marion took me aside at the funeral and offered to look after my child. Emily was a babe in arms then.

'I'll take her out of the war,' she promised. 'I'll take her away.'

I had a prison guard at my side and a deadline for reporting back to captivity. What choices did I have? And in truth, I was grateful and I know Alice would have trusted her. She always liked Marion; she would probably have thought her more suitable a guardian than I could ever be.

My companion on the bus had continued looking me up and down while I daydreamed. 'The services?' she asked at last, though I think she'd already guessed the answer.

'No,' I said.

'You're of the right age.'

'I don't doubt it.'

I saw her look at my institutional suit and nod. 'I suppose there's nothing wrong with it, if that's what you believe in,' she said.

Despite her faint approval, she got off at the next stop, sniffing haughtily as she rose from her seat.

I suppose some people can sense what you are. Perhaps I

should have been tattooed with the words 'conscientious objector'.

After that, I changed buses a couple of times myself. I was heading for an address on the outskirts of Truro. Marion had an uncle who had a big town house there. She had borrowed it or, rather, taken it over forcibly when she decided to decamp from Oxford. True to her word, she had taken my daughter 'out of the war'.

Marion was living in a road where the street lamps dripped like exotic flowers – Victorian styling that had never gone out of fashion – and great iron gates fronted every residence. I came upon the house by accident, finding it when I thought I was lost. In truth, it was so big, it was hard to miss. Ivy climbed its gigantic walls and its forty-yard drive was lined with overhanging trees, their shadows scooping into the gravel like great skeletal hands. Neither house nor vegetation showed any signs of war. It set me to wondering if the whole terrible nightmare had really happened.

I stood on the other side of the street gazing up the drive at the house. My feet seemed to be planted and I couldn't have moved if I'd wanted to.

After a while, my blonde-haired girl came out of the house with a woman I didn't recognize. I assumed she was the nanny. By now, Emily was coming down the drive on her little tricycle, going as hard as she could.

When she and the nanny reached the end of the drive, Emily looked across at me. But I meant nothing to her. Why would I? I had been away five years, her entire life.

Emily cycled along the pavement and past the neighbours' drive, the nanny now running after her.

I stood there, and waited while she faded slowly into the distance and out of my life. I don't think I realized then how complete that separation would become.

When Emily was out of sight, I walked up the drive to the front door, counted up to ten to still my breathing and pulled at the bell.

I knew it was Marion before she opened the door.

27

Something about the muted shuffle in the hall told me. I was prepared better than she when the oak barrier between us swung away.

'Hayden,' she gasped. Then she said nothing more for a long, long time. She examined me, not the cut of my clothes as the woman on the bus had done, but my face, looking deep; she searched for the soul in my eyes. I think she needed to know it was not dead.

I tried to smile as I gazed back at her. She would have been twenty-seven or twenty-eight then. Still handsome – the tight black curls of her hair, the pearl-black eyes, the Jewish nose she wore so proudly. Her dress was silk; I remember her buying it from some French house before the war. New fashions, at least, were something she'd had to give up for the duration.

'Hayden,' she said again, as if the name emptied her lungs. 'My God, you look so thin.' She had a cigarette resting fashionably between the fingers of one hand, but she held out the other, running the back of its knuckles gently over my cheek. I thought I saw the beginning of a tear.

'Prison rations,' I said.

'I suppose you'd better come in. Don't stand on the porch step. Should I offer you something to eat?'

I shook my head and followed her down the passage and into the drawing room. She called a servant and ordered tea, then she stubbed out her cigarette and reclined on to a chaise longue. She beckoned me to the nearest armchair, smiling in a painful kind of way.

Looking around the room, I couldn't help thinking of its permanence. Half the world was destroyed and yet here the mahogany tabletops remained polished, the china displays were orderly and the stately rooms held their ever-expansive magnificence.

Not that I'm blaming Marion. I'm not tarring her with that brush. Marion was the kindest, gentlest soul I ever knew, and no one could say she had not taken her share of pain from the war.

'I saw Emily,' I told her.

28

'Oh, God, no,' she replied, as if the thought was appalling. 'What do you mean?'

'You didn't tell her who you were, did you?'

'I didn't speak to her. She didn't even notice me,' I said defensively. 'Why?'

'Why?' she repeated. 'Hayden, have you no idea how dangerous this world is for you? That you bring peril on everyone you come in contact with? This war is all but over and Emily and I will go back to Oxford. But you . . . Hayden, you never can . . . You can never go back.'

'Surely . . .' I began, but got no further.

I don't think I'd ever realized that truth until she said it. I'd come out of prison believing I could recover. A strange delusion – I knew the world was doomed, my wife already dead, I knew I was also destroyed, yet I couldn't grasp it. It was an act of denial, born of short rations and too many blank walls and days of staring.

'God, you don't understand what those bastards did,' she said suddenly.

I looked at her plush walls and considered the state of things. Prison whitewash or wallpaper – the reality was the same. I shook my head. 'I know exactly,' I said.

'And you know what they were looking for?'

The answer churned inside me. Of course I knew.

The tea came in a silver pot and she wisely waved away her servant and poured out the delicate cups herself.

'Emily is a lovely child,' she told me.

'You've been too kind. I cannot . . .'

'Nonsense. She was all that kept me sane . . . After Ward. We were good for each other.' She smiled, but it was a smile dragged out from a toolbox somewhere. She used it, but it was not made of any emotion.

'Yes,' I replied gently. 'I suppose so.'

We drank in silence. Though there was so much we wanted to say, we could not say it. Silence sometimes fills with a thousand thoughts that fight each other for expression but end up bound and trapped. So it was with Marion. I owed her so much. Ward's friendship with me had cost her everything she cared about. She never cared for her money. She was casual about wealth in the way only rich people can be; Ward she loved. And that love now seemed to have transferred to Emily, and I was thankful for that. The dizzy socialite – for that's what she had been – had been hardened to life and had become the warmest and best of people.

I smiled but couldn't tell her how I felt. She gave me a cardboard box which she said she had saved from my college office after my arrest. It contained my books – those which now crumble to dust in my neglected room – and the wooden model of the uranium nucleus.

'I saved these too,' she said, handing me a small tin of mint balls with the lid removed. I looked down on to the sharp sticky sweets in their paper wrappers and took one. 'You know I always hoarded things. Junk mostly,' she added.

'My favourite,' I told her, reading the tin.

'You always had this brand. Ward used to love them too – do you remember?' She smiled, but it was a strain. 'I'm sorry about the rest of your things. Your office was . . . well, it got destroyed.'

'That's OK.' I put my own small prison bundle into the cardboard box and pressed the flaps down over the top. 'I think I should be going,' I said.

'Where will you go?' she asked.

'Far away. I don't know where. You're right . . . I can't come back.'

'For ever?'

'For ever,' I confirmed.

'I'll look after Emily.'

'I already know that.'

She showed me to the door and I kissed her. We stood there on either side of the threshold as if we were waiting to begin another more important conversation, but it never happened.

Apart from once reading in a week-old copy of *The Times* that she had inherited the family business – they were in the hotel trade – I neither heard nor saw anything of Marion for more than fifty years. Until that letter landed in my hallway.

Her words sent me away and her words brought me back. But I would never have stirred from my hiding place, if I had known that the danger I had run from still lurked in the world. It seems 'for ever' does not pass in half a century. She and I were wrong to think it had.

4

Sam watched as Helen ushered her young client into the lounge where the YCK Corporation's guests were being served champagne and caviar. When introduced, John shook hands but said nothing. Helen did all the talking, making excuses for John's silence by describing him as a laconic genius. She was a smart operator. She chattered on and smiled sweetly at the guests who confessed to having a wonderful time. She always seemed to work them round to the subject of money.

Sam followed Helen's silk-smooth sales pitches for a while – it's always fascinating to watch a master at work – then he thought better of it and moved off to sample another plate of caviar. He always worked hard to despise this sort of occasion. It was a matter of principle. He took the view that the noble art of chess should be about chess players and not about corporate gate-crashers butt-kissing their way through thousands of dollars of entertainment budget. He was just consoling himself by piling some expensive-looking orange eggs on to a slice of melba toast when an American accent interrupted.

'Mr Stylls?' the voice said, drawling a West Coast laziness across the words.

He turned to a beautiful young woman, a very dark brunette with short hair and primary blue eyes. She smiled and seemed to light up the dull room.

'You're American,' he said in surprise.

'Talk to me as if you know me, will you?' she asked. 'I'm trying to avoid someone.'

'Who?'

'Wave your arms, will you? Look animated like we're old

friends.' She glanced furtively over her shoulder. 'That bottom-pinching oriental over there.'

Sam followed the general direction of her glance. Her problem was a slim man in his forties, wearing a grey suit. He was gazing towards them out of a crowd of half a dozen guests on the other side of the room.

'He's Yoshi Yakamura,' the young woman continued, 'son of Mr Yakamura himself. A fine man if you've got a bullet-proof ass.'

'He seems to like you,' Sam said, noting the man's gaze.

'Fuck him,' she said. 'Do you know the guy? I'm told his mother's a former geisha. That's where he gets those porcelain features. She married the old man when he was forty-three and she was seventeen – can you believe that? They say the old man wants him to take over the company. In fact, I read it in the *Wall Street Journal*, so it must be at least fifty per cent true. "Believe half of what you read" – that's what I was taught. It's going to be a disaster if it ever happens.'

She was looking and sneering in Yoshi's direction as she spoke. Slowly her gaze dragged away from him and focused back on Sam. 'Hi, I'm Kate Morris,' she said, offering out her right hand, while with the other she indicated the name badge provided by the sponsors. The badge announced her as a 'financial journalist'. It was pinned to a light blue print dress, very cool, very thin, very out of place among the dowdy corporate guests. 'Pleased to finally meet you, Mr Stylls.'

Sam stared at her name plate as if he didn't understand the words. 'You know me?'

'Know you? Sure I know who you are. You're the guy who did all that stock-market modelling work a few years back.'

'I don't do that any more,' he replied, shrugging. His voice was hesitant as he tried to figure her out – the bubbling entrance, the beaming smile. Too much at once.

'Really?' she said, continuing the onslaught.

'No, just chess. My first love.'

33

'You're with Harringhay? I don't know diddly about chess,' Kate confessed, 'but he's cute ... in a strange way!' She winked and glanced across the room to where John was uneasily engaged in conversation with a Taiwanese banker. Helen was riding shotgun.

'Want an introduction?' Sam asked.

She considered it for a moment. She wrinkled her nose, licked her lips, then seemed to think better of it. 'Nah,' she said. 'Not my style. He reminds me of one of those Russian gymnasts, you know? Beating the world and stuck in puberty. You feel like you've got to protect them. He looked totally lost the moment he stopped playing.'

'John's not like that.'

Kate shrugged. Sam felt uncomfortable. Half of him wanted to agree, but he couldn't allow that. He spooned up some more of the orange eggs, trying to guess how many dollars an ounce he was about to put in his mouth. 'So, what're you doing here?' he enquired casually.

'A girl doesn't get too many party invitations in Singapore, Sam, if you know what I mean.'

'YCK invited you?'

'Not exactly. Haven't you taken a look around? This is the largest informal gathering of "big-wig" politicos this side of the United Nations. Your young genius has just provided part of the entertainment on the rest day of the Asian Government in Business Conference. All sponsored by YCK, of course. There are a couple of prime ministers, a handful of foreign ministers and US senators. You should be feeling honoured. This is a big day. I'm told even the old man is here today.'

'Yoshi's father?'

'Right. Yakamura,' she confirmed, as if it ought to mean something. 'Kazuo Yakamura. He is YCK. He started it from nothing in 1949 and built it into the largest civil contractor in the world. It builds sixty per cent of the power stations, dams and water treatment works in Asia, and it's been making strides into Europe and the USA for the last ten years. Hell, this is boring, isn't it?' She stopped and sipped

34

her drink, glancing around, looking for something more interesting to talk about; then she turned back to him, her flashing eyes inviting him to speak.

Sam couldn't think of anything. He wondered if she was flirting with him, but decided she couldn't be serious. Just youthful and bored. Her eyes twinkled at him none the less. He noticed the tiny coral atolls dotted in them like Polynesian lagoons. She was a natural masterpiece. A nervous one, though. She seemed to be trying just that bit too hard.

'See that guy,' Kate said suddenly. She pointed vaguely, swinging her finger through the assembled company and stopping on a tall fiftyish man surrounded by the biggest group in the room. 'Recognize him? Come on. I'll admit he's West Coast, but he made quite a hit in Washington the few years he was there. One term in the Senate to underscore his home state credentials – you don't remember?'

'I haven't been home in a while,' he admitted.

'Well, he's why I'm really here. That, my dear Sam, is Joseph Edward Beckett. This time next year, he'll be elected Governor of California. And unless I miss my guess, you might just be looking at a future President. He's on a tour trying to prove he's an international statesman, building up momentum for his campaign.' She hesitated. 'Not doing a bad job of it either, I have to confess. I came here expecting a right-wing loony who wants to ban abortion and bring back the death sentence for petty crimes, but he's not like that . . . I might even vote for him. That would be something of a first for a little old liberal like me.'

'You like him then?' Sam observed.

'I've been trying hard not to, but it hasn't worked so far. The material's too thin. I didn't volunteer to be here, you know. I drew the short straw at the office lottery. No one wants a free ride on this kind of odyssey tour across Japan and Europe.'

'A future Governor not being big enough for you.'

'Listen,' she said, 'Governor of the Golden State is plenty big enough. He may not get the press back East, but this man's going to be head of the seventh largest economy in the world. Agriculture, wine, fishing, films, Silicon Valley – we've got it all and he's going to run it. Did you know that a governor gets to appoint the heads of every damned board and commission there is – thirty of them? I learnt that on this trip. And all the judges. And rules all the militia. Once he's in power, this man's on the right hand of God for the next four years.'

She leaned past him to take an olive from the buffet table. Her gaze wandered across the room to where John was now skulking alone in a corner. He had backed out of the group Helen was talking to and sat examining the grubby bandage on his hand.

'I hear he punched a television. Is that true?'

'Where did you hear that?' Sam said.

'Ooo, here and there. You know what we journos are like . . . terribly talkative. I see he's coming to play in San Francisco next month – my home town. Can we expect him to trash a few local hotels?' She smiled at Sam. 'Before you ask, I read his schedule in the free gold-embossed programme.' She waved it at him. 'Also sponsored by YCK. When Kazz Yakamura entertains, he goes the whole nine yards . . . nine and a half, if you'll let him.' She popped another olive into her mouth and laughed. She had control. She always had control. 'I must be going,' she said. 'Maybe we'll meet again.'

Sam stared after her as she glided away from him. She was not overly tall, but her body was long and sinewy. Hips swaying, she seemed to take hold of the world. The print dress waved and he gazed at the bare tanned shoulders. They seemed to be the fixed pivot of her movement as she faded away.

Without fully realizing, he compared her to Helen, unable to decide which he preferred. No, that wasn't true. He knew which he preferred, he just didn't know why. He shook his head and tried to centre back on reality.

The arrival of Kazuo Yakamura was like that of a god. He came in full Japanese national dress, headed by three or four

36

minions who seemed to double as both servants and body-guards. The whole room turned from their champagne to applaud their host.

He went first to the prime ministers, spending not less than five minutes talking to each. Then he was introduced to the foreign ministers. The crowd drifted back to their drinks and expensive buffet.

Yakamura was in his eighties. He spoke four languages. Small talk was not a problem to him, whoever the guest might be. When he moved to speak to Joe Beckett, it was like parting the Red Sea. Aides and assistants on both sides melted away, allowing the two men room to discuss what-ever private business they might have. Yakamura and his guest clinked glasses together and chatted for a good twenty minutes. Then Yakamura clearly proposed something and they moved in Helen Michaels' direction.

Helen had just finished talking with an Australian busi-nessman, interested – so he said – in taking 'chess to the outback'. It had soon become clear the man was so drunk on YCK champagne he wouldn't have recognized a chess-board if it had hit him square between the eyes. He did seem to appreciate Helen's dress sense, though. He kept trying to feel around the back of it, and she had finished the conversation by grabbing his wandering fingers and almost breaking them off at the knuckles.

'Miss Michaels,' Yakamura began as he and Beckett approached.

Helen straightened her dress and nodded. She had only seen them coming at the last moment.

'This is Joe Beckett,' Yakamura continued.

'Mr Beckett,' Helen acknowledged.

'Helen,' Beckett said, taking her hand energetically. 'I may call you Helen? That boy of yours . . . Hell, I've never seen anything like it. Is he here?'

'Sure, he's just resting . . . taking a sit-down in the corner over there. I'll introduce you.'

Helen turned sharply. In two strides, she was rousing John from his wallflower pose. She grabbed at his arm and lifted him bodily towards her two important companions. 'Stand up straight,' she scolded as she propelled him across the floor.

'You are a remarkable young man,' Beckett said, greeting the reluctant new arrival. He shook hands and looked down at John's ragged clothes, the T-shirt, the cut-off jeans and trainers. Like a true politician, the boy's outrageous image didn't phase him for a moment. 'I've never seen anything quite like the way you play chess,' he continued.

'Thanks,' John mumbled almost too quietly to be heard.

'John made Grandmaster rank over two years ago,' Helen chipped in.

'Really? Most impressive.' Beckett turned to Yakamura. 'Kazz,' he said, 'I have to go. I have an interview arranged. But I'll see you this evening as arranged, OK?'

'I'll send my limousine,' Yakamura assured him.

'Great. Great.' The big American was sliding away. He waved one last time. 'Remarkable chess, young man. Remarkable.'

Yakamura watched his guest melt into a gathering of grey-suited men on the other side of the room. Hangers-on and bodyguards swarmed around the group like bees smelling a honeypot.

'Mr Beckett is a very important man,' Yakamura observed in his perfect English, 'but he has no appreciation of chess. A shame. The tactics of chess are the tactics of business and of war. In fact, they are the tactics of all things.'

'You play chess?' Helen asked.

'But of course. YCK would not sponsor something unless I approved.'

'I see.'

John was edging sideways, moving so his body started disappearing behind Helen's shoulder. The more the grandly dressed Japanese enthused about chess the more nervous John began to appear. Helen, on the other hand, had started to smell money.

'You speak excellent English, Mr Yakamura,' she said.

'True,' he agreed. He nodded his head and laughed. 'It is

38

necessary to speak perhaps not English but certainly American. But as it happens, I did learn my English in England.'

Helen raised her eyebrows, managing a look of supreme interest.

'My father was very unusual for a Japanese of his era. He was what you would call an "aristocrat", very rich, very powerful. But he believed in trade, not in conquest as most Japanese did at the time. When I was eighteen, he sent me to Europe. I studied at your Oxford for five years.'

'Oxford?' Helen said. 'That's John's home town.'

'I was at the university. I studied Physics – or Natural Philosophy as they so quaintly call it.'

Helen smiled and tipped her head reverentially. The Japanese was obviously very proud of his classical education. 'John never quite made it to the university,' she said.

'My grandfather did,' John interrupted suddenly. When they both looked at him, he seemed almost embarrassed by his outburst. 'He was a physicist,' he added quietly. 'A great one. Aunt Marion told me.'

'You never told me that,' Helen said.

'He was,' John insisted. He locked eyes with Helen. She seemed to be scheming, perhaps thinking of a new publicity angle – 'Grandson of the Great Physicist'. How did you put that alongside 'Greatest Young Chess Player Alive'?

'There were many great physicists from Oxford,' Yakamura said. 'Who was your grandfather? Is he now departed? Maybe I know him?'

'I don't know,' John replied reluctantly. 'No one's seen him for . . . like . . . a thousand years. Hayden Zalapek.'

'Ah, Zalapek,' Yakamura said, stretching the name. He stopped suddenly, and his eyes rolled in his head and took a moment to come back straight.

'He disappeared in the war. He's supposed to be dead,' John added weakly.

'John does have an imagination,' Helen interrupted.

'Not at all,' Yakamura said. He smiled. 'I knew Professor Zalapek. In fact, for a while, we worked in the same building. But then . . . the war came and I had to go home. Back to Japan, you understand.'

'You knew my grandfather?' John asked, suddenly losing his reluctance to talk.

'Yes, young man, I knew him. He was a genius, a genuine magician. In my country, we say there are two kinds of genius: those who do things better than everyone else, and those who do things and you never know how they do them. These are the magicians. Your grandfather was one of those. He played chess as well, I recall.'

'Yes, yes, he did.'

'I played him a few times, but . . . Hayden was good at everything.' Yakamura bowed, then he turned to Helen. 'And now I must attend to my other guests. Perhaps you would care to join me later? I am holding a little . . . how do you say? "party" is not the right word . . . "get-together" for the more "adventurous" of my special guests.'

'Yes,' said Helen in surprise. 'I'm sure we'd love it.' Thoughts of rubbing shoulders with world leaders in the process of letting their hair down span through her head like a bowling ball skittling its way to a strike.

'Very well,' Yakamura concluded. 'I will send a car at eight o'clock. You are staying at the Oriental?'

'Yes . . .'

'Very well.' He bowed again and before Helen could speak, he was on his way to his next set of guests.

The phone rang on an oak desk, the sound bouncing off the wood panels in the surrounding office. A man in his early sixties picked up the receiver.

'Hello,' he said.

'You know who this is?'

The man baulked. The voice was familiar, but tired and croaked with age even greater than his own.

'Yeah, I know,' he said. 'How're you doing . . .?'

'Don't say my name. I taught you better than that. You're like a raw recruit. Age must have addled you.'

'Perhaps,' he laughed. 'It's a long time since I was your junior.'

'Forty years. Who's counting?'

'My wife. She tells me I should retire. I tell her "no", but she won't listen.'

'Yeah, a wife'll do that for you.' The caller chuckled mechanically, then said, 'Listen, I need to talk to you about something.'

The man grunted assent.

'This thing with Joe . . . the election. It's going to raise an awful lot of questions.'

'Shit, we put those all to bed twenty or thirty years ago, didn't we?'

'Enough of them . . . for then. The world's changed. Freedom of information. People asking other people questions. There's stuff released into public record all the time. Papers that were never meant for that sort of audience. Certain things need to go away.'

'I heard "certain things" already. Something about Boston.'

'That was nothing but smart journalism. I'm talking messier problems here . . . my problems.'

'You're asking for help then?'

'I never asked you nothing before.' A deep breath like this was hard for the caller. 'I lost my connections thirty years ago. Swore myself to sainthood when Nixon was still top of the pile. It's before that that worries me.'

'I don't have . . .'

'Let's be subtle about this. You owe me. And I know you still have the means . . . the contacts . . . to influence things.'

'Not like I used to.'

'Good enough.'

There was silence for a moment.

'Good enough,' the man agreed.

5

Oxford. I walked up past the Apollo Theatre and into the Broad, not really realizing where I was heading. Trinity gates. Blackwell's. Brasenose. The Sheldonian. The passing cars with their lights ablaze showed no concern for me as they splashed through puddles in the icy gutters.

I thought of walking to Marion's house, but soon thought better of it. Instead I opened the letter again and rang the telephone number below the address. A butler answered. Marion was not at home, he said.

I stopped. I couldn't tell him what it was I wanted.

In the silence I created, the butler said, 'Miss Stern's been at the hospital most of the night. I don't know when she'll be back.'

I mumbled my thank-yous and put down the phone.

I set off from the city centre, passing Blackwell's and Keble College. I cut down the far side of the college, went across the churchyard and on to the Woodstock Road. I remembered where the hospital was.

When I asked at the enquiry desk, I found Emily's name was not Zalapek. I tried Stern – a name I thought she might have adopted – but the result was the same. Next I tried Alice's maiden name. It was not that either. I explained who I was as best as I could and something about the distress that welled in me when I could not find my own daughter's name brought sympathy from the woman behind the desk. Eventually using 'Emily' and her exact age, the woman was able to tell me that Emily's second name was 'Harringhay'. I smiled and thanked her, and followed her directions through the mazy corridors to the appropriate ward.

I found Emily after a short search. She was not in the main ward, but set aside in her own room. Her frail body was surrounded by the harsh outlines of medical instruments, bleeping and glugging like scavengers waiting. The sight was terrible – shaming.

In truth, I could not have recognized her without the chart at the bottom of her bed. Death is a simple fact, part of the contract of mortality. Here it lay withered and hairless and expectant, and I sank under its weight, suddenly exhausted, grateful for the chair at her bedside.

Eyes closed, I listened to the sounds of the room. I blocked out the machines. I listened to the effort in the simple process of her breathing. The wasting breath guttered in her throat like air drawing through the straw at the bottom of a child's milkshake, and I wondered how the child I had once seen had come to this. How had Emily Jane Zalapek become Mrs E. Harringhay?

I spent twelve hours at Emily's bedside.

For the first hour, maybe more, we were alone. Then Marion came in, carrying flowers and a shopping bag. It's strange to think now that I greeted her quite so casually, but I suppose my attention was all for Emily. I didn't even look at Marion's face or her clothes, or notice how well or badly the years had treated her.

'Hayden,' she said, seeing the ghost before her.

I tried to stand but found I could not, so she came over and kissed me where I sat.

In the waning hours of Emily's life, Marion talked to me about my daughter, her broken marriage, the wayward chess-playing grandson I had but didn't know. I realize now the only things I ever knew about Emily I learnt while watching her die.

'They gave her radiotherapy, you know.' Marion said.

It took me a moment to realize what she meant. She was referring to radioactivity, the nuclear death. She was referring to that branch of science I had loved and lost, discovered and hidden.

I looked down at the white sheet that covered Emily's faintly stirring body. Hollow needles and tubes carried fluid in and out of her veins, and green traces measured out what

43

remained of rhythm on a distant screen. I sat at her bed and watched the screen and the gently flowing liquid, and I listened to her breathing. I smelt the antiseptic ward with its hard fixtures and sparse furnishing; I smelt too the faint undertone of decay.

When the next spasm of pain came, I held her bony hand in my distorted one and she gave it a desperate squeeze. She never opened her eyes. I softly touched her cheek with my free hand, smoothing over the loose skin.

I tried to hold her, hold on to the core of her. But when her eyes finally opened, she was not there, the pupils dim and shadowed like headlights which have fogged over through too many miles on treacherous roads.

Emily died at five o'clock the following morning, and Marion and I embraced and cried.

I think back now to the first time I met Marion Stern. It was on the Thursday evening of Eights Week in 1936. I was playing chess in the coffee shop in the High, relaxing in the way I knew best. It was one of those special cafés where they provide the clientele with various games – chess, chequers, dominoes.

I had played three or four games before I noticed I was being watched. A man and woman were sitting at a table a short distance away, sipping coffee and studying my moves very closely.

The woman was no more than a teenager – seventeen or eighteen, maybe two or three years younger than I was. She had stylish black hair and clothes no ordinary student could afford. The man, something more than twice her age, was undistinguished, at least in appearance. About average height, about average looks, dressed much the same as the average man about town in those days.

At the end of the next game – we were playing to a five-minute limit – I asked my opponent if he knew them. He couldn't name the woman, but he said the man was Dr Ward Costello.

Ward's name was already familiar to me. He had created

enough of a stir within the university to spread his reputation far and wide. He had arrived a couple of years earlier to work as a post-graduate under Sir Charles Sherrington. Ever since, he had caused ructions in meetings of the various philosophical and religious groups around Oxford by preaching a distorted version of Western Christianity and Eastern Mysticism. He had re-engineered the classical view of these subjects to fit his own theories of brain physiology and psychology. I wrote occasionally for a local religious magazine called *The Cherwell Christian* and my complimentary copy had already featured several scathing articles and letters attacking views that Ward Costello had advanced.

'Dr Costello?' I said, tentatively holding out my hand.

He looked at it and, without taking it, answered, 'Mr Zalapek, I presume.'

'You know me?' I asked in surprise.

'Of course. They say you are the greatest young mind in Oxford. Of course, they say that of half a dozen young men, but in your case . . .'

He pursed his lips as if to indicate that in my case it might actually be true. I nodded and thanked him.

'This is my friend, Marion Stern,' he said.

She bowed her head very reverently, and as it raised again, her beauty fixed me with its smiling eyes. A moment I will never forget.

'Do you realize, sir, you are a bloody genius?' her companion continued, unaware of my fixation. 'I read your latest paper, "The Ingredients of Matter". Incredible. Incredible.'

He gestured for me to sit on the spare chair at their table and I sat, fighting the urge to stare at Marion.

'I didn't realize you were interested in the new science,' I said.

'I'm not,' he replied. 'I'm interested in the workings of the mind. I'm interested in the workings of special minds. I'm interested in you. I was intrigued by the thinking in your paper, and I see for myself you're also a fair player of the chequered game here.' He pointed at the chessboard.

45

'A little better than county standard perhaps,' I confessed.

He turned briefly to Marion. 'The man has such modesty,' he said. 'Sir, I saw your game against Max Euwe printed in *The Times*. It was ... very fine.'

'Yes, but I lost.'

'Ah, but you could have won, and Euwe will sooner or later be world champion.'

I thought for a moment. Ward was confusing, too intense to be easily understood or absorbed, and at that moment, I was distracted. 'Do you play?' I asked vaguely.

'Me? No, not at all.'

I turned to Marion and she shook her head as well. She seemed surprised that I should even ask the question.

'I've worked with a few great men, though,' Ward chirped up. 'I've helped them. I told you, I'm interested in the workings of special minds. Have you ever thought about it? How your mind works? Why it works? What made it? Think of this: two hundred years ago, people lived in ignorance. The average man had less than one per cent of the knowledge we have now. If the mind was created by evolution over thousands of years, how can that be? How did evolution anticipate that need for capacity? Don't you understand what that means? This is God's creation we work with.'

As he spoke, he began to capture my attention. He sucked it in as if drawing it up through a straw. In a minute, maybe two, I understood why Ward Costello had caused such a stir at those Oxford meetings. He expressed himself with a passion that was hard to resist. I noticed the way Marion simply rested back in her chair and watched him. She was proud of him, in love with him, and I realized then how the relationship between the three of us would be.

'Listen,' Ward said over our second coffee together, 'if you will allow me, I can help you. I've seen all I need to know what I can do with you. What is it you really want to do with that brain of yours?'

I thought for a few seconds. There was only one thing on

my mind. Not chess. I think Ward already knew what I was going to say.

'I want to understand the structure of the nucleus,' I said.

'Hmm,' he mused. For a while he simply looked at me, then he cracked into a smile. 'What dangerous dreams you have. Do you believe you will see the mind of God?'

'No,' I replied, 'I believe in God, Mr Costello, but I don't believe that.'

'It's what most of them think, most of the new physicists. They think that if they understood how God built the universe, how He held together its fabric, then they would know His mind. It is a reasonable argument.'

I did not react, detecting some kind of test in his words. We sat eyeball to eyeball and then he smiled again, and then Marion smiled.

I had no way of knowing how important both of them would become to me. 'I think I might help you,' Ward said. 'I think that might just be fun. What do you think, my dear?' He turned to Marion.

'Don't tease, Ward,' she said. 'You know you've already decided. And you know I don't understand anything about physics.' She gave him a look so radiant it would have melted the basest of metals. Marion was a good actress in those days. She played at being second string, while all the time there was something more going on.

'Let me give you a lesson, my dear,' he offered. 'You should understand Mr Zalapek's importance.'

I smiled. My 'importance' was still a novelty back then.

'You see, my dear, until recently, the world's great thinkers believed that matter was a nice, evenly spread thing,' he continued, leaning towards Marion as he began to teach the lesson. 'The stuff was a bit like pure butter, they said. But this was a folly on a par with the flat earth theory.' He glanced at me for approval. 'Do you want to continue this story?'

'You're telling it better than I could.'

'Very well. But I'm only paraphrasing your paper. In 1911, on a whim, Ernst Rutherford had a student fire some alpha

47

particles into a gold leaf. This changed everything. The alpha particles – something like atom-sized air rifle pellets as I understand them – should have gone shooting through the buttery gold leaf. But surprise! Some bounced straight back at him. From this, Rutherford gave us a new theory of matter. It's not like butter at all, he said. Matter, you see, must have hard bits in it. It is more like a handful of marbles shaken in a large empty sack. What mass there is must be concentrated in small dense pieces, in marbles big and hard enough to rebound the alpha particles if they happen to collide. These pieces inside the matter are the atomic nuclei. So now we see Mr Zalapek's quest – what is an atomic nucleus?'

'For twenty years, we've been getting it wrong,' I said.

'So your paper says.'

'I don't understand,' Marion interrupted.

'Many theorists have tried to calculate the structure of this nucleus since 1911. What makes up the marble?' Ward continued. 'But they all got it wrong. And you know why? Because they were missing an ingredient.'

Marion still looked blank. I took up the story.

'Three years ago, James Chadwick, our great rival working at Cambridge, discovered the neutron, a particle no one had considered. The whole question is up in the air again.'

Marion looked unimpressed. 'What difference does it make what matter is made of?' she asked, shrugging in that fashionable dismissive way.

'Power,' Ward said suddenly.

'Power?'

'$E=mc^2$,' he quoted. 'I am right, am I not, Mr Zalapek? I did give your paper only a cursory glance.'

'You are correct,' I agreed, sure now that 'cursory' did not begin to describe his understanding of it.

'You see, my dear, Mr Zalapek believes that by manipulating the structure of nuclei he can destroy mass. This is something the great Albert Einstein has proposed but never proved: that if you can destroy mass you get energy. And then you would have an unlimited supply of power.'

'And Mr Zalapek can do this?' she asked.

Ward smiled. He reached across and took the wooden box of dominoes the café provided. He tipped them out.

'Chain reaction,' he said. He stood a row of half a dozen dominoes on their ends and knocked the first one over. The first tumbled into the second, the second into the third and so on. 'See how they fall one after the other,' he explained. 'That's how you get unlimited power. Each reaction within a nucleus produces a little energy and, if you choose your nucleus carefully, a little something that triggers a reaction in the next nucleus.'

He put the dominoes back on their ends and knocked them down a second time.

'Neutrons,' I said.

Marion looked at me strangely.

'The neutron particle,' I explained. 'If I am right, there are certain reactions of the nucleus which are triggered by neutrons and also produce neutrons as part of the reaction. It is, if you will, the same as a domino in this chain. Its toppling is triggered by the toppling of the last domino and causes the toppling of the next.'

'I see,' Marion said. 'At least, I think I see.'

Ward reset the dominoes on their ends, but this time he arranged them slightly differently, using more dominoes and staggering a number of rows across the table. The toppling of the first hit two others. The toppling of each of them caught two more, so the sequence of falling didn't go one by one as it had before. Instead, it went one, two, four, eight and so on.

'Suppose you find a type of nucleus where the reaction releases two neutrons instead of one. Perhaps more than two, perhaps three. That would be a bomb, wouldn't it?'

I stared at him in amazement. It wasn't that the physics was new to me, I simply hadn't considered a bomb.

'No,' I said, not particularly rationally, 'I . . . I don't believe it will be like that.'

'Why not?'

It was a fair enough question.

'I don't believe God would make the universe that way,' I told him.

'These reactions you talk about, are they possible?' Marion said, butting in. She looked at Ward, repeating her earlier question. 'Can Mr Zalapek really produce energy by destroying mass? Can he make a bomb?'

'No,' I said, 'I cannot . . . And I would not.'

'Maybe not yet,' Ward allowed, 'but surely that is where it will end.'

6

The next time Kate saw John Harringhay, he was standing in the entrance of Papa Joe's casino. The doorman was looking him up and down as if he didn't believe what he was seeing. T-shirt and jeans! Nobody gets into the swankiest private club in Singapore in T-shirt and jeans.

Kate's chauffeur – provided courtesy of Mr Yakamura – had described Papa Joe's as the greatest secret treat on the island. So it was. Green baize on the tables and painted Chinese patterns on the walls, seating for two hundred and mini-skirted waitresses hustling beneath low ceilings hung with dim paper lanterns. The only thing well lit was the gambling – Papa Joe's speciality – while everything else wallowed in a heavy semi-darkness, spiced with local fragrances and the odd whiff of something more exotic.

'Our rules require a jacket, sir,' the doorman said loudly.

Helen was waving her arms frenetically. Kate couldn't hear what she was saying – her back was turned away. She watched as the scene quickly became totally bizarre. In a couple of minutes, the club's management found something to help John meet the dress code, a garish jacket made for fat Americans with fifty-inch guts. It made him look more untidy and out of place than he had in his simple jeans and T-shirt. Kate saw him try to protest, but it seemed to make no difference. Both Helen and the Papa Joe management were smiling and satisfied.

As the evening progressed, Kate noticed other things which seemed to be understood between the casino and the clientele, things that were not exactly 'on the level'. Once she saw Helen slip John a little pack of white powder. She watched him disappear into the toilets in clear view of at least half a dozen of Papa Joe's staff. No one said a word.

Kate was stunned. This was Singapore; they hanged people here. Helen was either stupid or really confident.

Eventually, after Kate had seen the antics of some of the other Yakamura guests, she voted for the latter, deciding that the description 'private club' probably covered both 'shadily licensed' and 'borderline illegal'. With a wry shake of the head she started to let the whole 'Papa Joe's experience' wash over her. It had been a hard day – why not just get into it? A few drinks. Put her feet up.

She talked to the barman for a while. He was a fellow American from Detroit. He claimed to know every cocktail ever served, but naming their ingredients unfortunately proved the limit of his conversation. When Kate saw Helen heading for the roulette wheels with John close behind, she couldn't contain her own curiosity.

She made her excuses to the barman and found herself a booth on the balcony just behind the roulette table. John and his manager were now no more than twelve feet away. Her chosen seating had the advantage of elevation – two ornamental steps of extra height that allowed her to peer down on to the proceedings, almost over the shoulders of the half-dozen gamblers seated below.

'Give me a beer,' she said to the waitress who came and blocked the view. Helen's chips were rolling now, wagered on red, though she wasn't gambling big amounts. Kate found that somewhat surprising.

Helen won once and lost once. Kate's drink arrived in a tall glass. Regrettably, it arrived attached to Yoshi Yakamura.

'The lady's order,' he said ceremoniously as he plonked himself in the seat opposite.

Kate stared at him, danger signals flashing inside her head. Yoshi was attractive enough. He would have got his name in an international *Who's Who*. But she baulked at the thought of him. None of his good points made any difference. It wasn't that Yoshi was unintelligent. It was simply that he was arrogant and treated women as if they were Barbie dolls. It would come as no surprise if he pulled their limbs off when they annoyed or bored him. Kate hunched her shoulders, preparing her best rebuff.

'I thought I told you to fuck off,' she said.

'Ah, but I know you . . . you didn't mean it.'

'Ah, but I did. Not the "fuck" part perhaps, but the general principle was right there.' Kate spat the words. She had always found it the best form of defence, and she had been defending herself for a long time. The world seemed to find her combination of brains and beauty hard to deal with. It handed her pawing uncles and balding perverts. She hated it. It wanted her to be a toy. It threatened to destroy her. At heart, she was still a scared little girl, trying to figure out how she was going to make it on her own merits. She was extrovert and foul-mouthed and 'in your face', and all these were defence against being twenty-three and more talented than was professionally useful.

'Didn't you hear me?' she asked.

Yoshi looked at her. Weighing her up now, she could tell. That's how it went. They moved from lustful bravado to uncertainty. If she held her ground, pretty soon he'd flee like the rest of them.

'You're not very friendly,' he said weakly.

She smiled. 'Not to you, I'm not. Now, if you don't mind, you're blocking my view.'

He lingered a few seconds more, then took a business card from his pocket and thrust it across the table at her.

'In case you change your mind,' he said. He shook his head. Then he got up and left. She'd seen it happen so many times before. The muttered words he threw at her as he left were familiar in tone even if they were in Japanese.

'Red eighteen . . .'

The voice of the croupier suddenly caught her attention, jumping her from the daydream. He was raking chips across the baize top, his practised motions like poetry. Kate swilled a mouthful of beer over her palate – her version of washing the foul words off her tongue – then she gazed down on to the roulette table.

'Madam is very lucky tonight,' the croupier said as he

pushed a stack of chips towards Helen Michaels. He gave a smile his boss would have been proud of. 'Place your next bets, please,' he added.

'John, what now? What next?' Helen was asking urgently as the croupier started to spin the wheel.

The boy looked as if he hardly understood the question.

'Come on, you've been studying these tables for an hour, on and off. It must be time to up the stakes,' she urged.

'Twelve,' he said, pronouncing the word with reluctance.

The ball was thrown into the roulette wheel with the croupier's arrogant backhanded toss. Helen just had time to get a ten-dollar chip down.

Kate craned her neck to track the ball as it kicked and hopped. It seemed to have a life of its own, wanting to be anywhere but in the spinning slots of numbers. Soon, however, it fell down and was swallowed.

'Twelve . . .' the croupier announced in surprise. 'Madam wins again.'

Helen bounced in her seat, something of her normal calm slipping. She took another, larger slug from her drink as the pile of chips grew in front of her. She gazed at them and then at John. He looked at the floor. He must have known her eyes asked the question, and if he knew the answer he didn't want to give it to her.

'Well?' she pressed.

He sighed. 'Do we have to do this?'

She said nothing, but her face squeezed at him, forcing him to give what he'd got.

'Do it again,' he said in submission.

'What?'

'Same number . . . On twelve.'

Helen pushed four hundred Singapore dollars in chips back across the green baize. They fell out of their neatly arranged stack and the croupier had to adjust them so they fitted on their allotted place on the table.

'All done?' he asked as he cupped the ball in his hand and dropped it into the wheel. 'No more bets, please. No more bets.'

The ball ricocheted off the side of the dish. It wedged into its chosen slot long before the wheel slowed. Twelve! The six gamblers sucked in a collective breath so sharply it seemed to leave a temporary vacuum over the table.

'Twelve,' the croupier called.

On the balcony, Kate choked on her beer, coughing as she looked at the boy in amazement. John Harringhay sat without expression. Suddenly she caught his eye.

It was at this moment – later she would recall it – that Kate first realized how she and John were alike. Lost in the big world. Unprotected by whatever talents they might have. She wanted to help, but didn't know how.

Helen was now tapping the table impatiently. Over fourteen thousand dollars of chips were piled up in front of her. Her other hand fingered her neck chain; a muscle ticked below one eye. She stared ferociously at John. His eyes fell closed as if he was being asked to reveal some secret of which he was ashamed.

Kate's thoughts raced. Did he really know the fall of the numbers? Was that possible?

'Five,' she heard the boy say. Then he repeated it more quietly, speaking as if to someone hidden beneath the table.

'Thank you,' Helen said and pushed forward her entire pile of chips.

Kate noticed the croupier glancing to his right. A shady man in a white suit seated at the bar on the far side had suddenly taken an interest in the action. The croupier was trying to catch his eye. Fourteen thousand dollars at thirty-five to one – the croupier was asking the man in white to consider the possibilities. Slowly the man nodded, and the croupier shrugged and turned back to the table.

Everyone else watched the wheel as it started its spin, but Kate stared at John. Something told her he was lying.

Ball and wheel had set off in opposite directions, so the ball was held up in the rim of the bowl for several revolutions. Then it plunged down and bucked off the slot ridges like a rider thrown off a stallion. Unsaddled, it pinged up the slope of the bowl and fell back, pinged and fell back. It settled with the wheel still spinning, Kate couldn't see the number. She waited, swallowing hard.

'Zero,' the croupier shouted. Then he said it again calmly. 'Zero.'

The man in the white suit turned back to his drink and the croupier raked in fourteen thousand dollars' worth of chips, and Kate nodded to herself.

'Shit,' Helen cursed.

'I'm sorry ... I'm no good at this,' the boy said weakly, hanging his head.

'Nonsense, John,' she said, straightening her back. 'Just unlucky. We nearly had it that time ... nearly had it.'

Helen got off her chair and patted him on the back. 'I'm going for another drink,' she told him. 'Play these chips for me, will you?' She handed over three ten-dollar chips she'd been holding in reserve and set off.

Kate tipped her drink, swallowing it quickly for a reason she only half grasped. There he was alone. Compelling. She remembered his eyes when he had looked at her and she stared at the empty seat beside him. All she had to do was go down there, introduce herself and slip right in. He needed protecting; he needed help. But she hesitated. 'This is stupid,' she said, loud enough only for herself to hear. 'I don't need this.'

She lingered for a few moments, ten seconds of see-sawing on the 'will I, won't I' fence. And by then, it was too late. Someone else had stolen the empty seat.

'Hell, I don't need this. Don't need this complication,' she told herself. She hailed down a passing waitress. 'Get me a taxi, will you?' she said.

Sam Stylls was drinking Southern Comfort and feeling depressed. His heart lifted when he saw Helen coming, then fell when he noticed the blackness of her face. He swigged his drink and tried to look nonchalant.

'Success?' he asked as she deposited herself into the chair on the other side of the table.

Helen glared at him briefly, then began fumbling in her handbag. She took a long slim cigarette from a silver case.

'I don't think we'll ever make money,' she said. She tapped the cigarette on the table. 'At last, somewhere you can smoke on this island. I need this.'

Sam gazed at her thoughtfully. 'I told you he's a chess player, not a psychic.'

'He's good at it,' she protested.

'Didn't you just get busted?'

Helen smiled thinly. 'OK,' she admitted, 'but we were doing well for a while.'

Sam watched her, and saw a kind of greed in her eyes. Some chess insiders had told him he shouldn't go near John Harringhay. They said Helen Michaels was evil, and sure enough she did have a Cruella De Vil way about her, but that was somehow attractive, the attraction of danger. Sam knew he had a weakness for people wilder than himself. He had carved a career on his steady attention to detail. Mostly it satisfied him, but sometimes he hated himself and hated the choices he'd made.

She lit her cigarette and he stared.

'John was upset,' she said. 'The news about his mother, you know.'

'Yes,' Sam said. Then, snapping from his daze, he added, 'And this night out was supposed to soothe him?'

'We had to do something. We couldn't just sit in the hotel. It's not good for him.'

'So, you're worried about your investment?' he asked. Sam wasn't quite sure where this was leading. Perhaps he just wanted to feel her reaction – the lion tamer's thrill. He took off his glasses, breathed on them briefly and polished the lenses off with a napkin. He was going to stay calm, he told himself, play her along a little. Aloud, he said, 'That's what he is, isn't he? An investment?'

She stared at him and shrugged. 'You need to look after your investments.'

'No feelings for the boy, then?' he pressed.

'I could chew you up and spit you out,' she assured him.

'Don't try your pop psychology on me. I didn't hire you as a personal shrink.'

Sam sipped his drink, strangely excited by her reaction, by his own bravery. She was Cruella De Vil all right. But the truth was he didn't need the work. She could fire him if she liked. Half a dozen Grandmasters would have given their eye-teeth to have him working in their back-room team. He had chosen this only because he found the challenge of John Harringhay interesting.

'Money's all you care about, huh?' he said.

'As a matter of fact ... My job, my hobby, my passion, all rolled into one.' She seemed proud of it. 'Just lucky, I guess. Is there anything wrong with that?'

'I don't know. What does the boy want?'

'He's with me.'

'If you say so ...' Sam said. Then, more quietly, he added, 'But he's twenty and you've made him a star. Now he's so screwed up he doesn't know what he wants.'

'Star? He's not a star, not yet. Stars make money, big money. We can hardly pay the bills. I don't know why the fuck I took him on!'

'You know exactly why.'

'Perhaps.' She left it at that, a smile spreading slowly through her face. She waved over a waitress and ordered whiskey, pausing briefly to point at Sam, indicating he should order what he wanted.

'No, I'm fine,' he said.

'Come on, drink with me,' she urged. 'If you're going to lecture me, it's the least you can do.' She smiled.

He couldn't remember if he'd ever seen her genuine smile before. He'd seen the business version, but that was all – a pale and overblown imitation. He liked the real thing much better, but why did she finally smile at him just when he was attacking her?

'OK,' he said, with a mixture of pleasure and confusion.

Helen issued an order for a bottle, waving the surprised waitress to fetch it. 'It's such a fucking mess, I feel like getting drunk,' she said loudly. More quietly, she added, 'Do you really think I'm so bad for him?'

'He's not in your normal line of clients, is he?'

She laughed, gazing at him as her eyes sparkled. 'I like you, Sam, you speak your mind. I guess you could say he's a little unusual for a client,' she agreed, 'but then, I've never gone for normal. That's not how I've made my money. D'you know the first client I ever had?'

Sam shook his head and leaned back in his chair, anticipating her story. Helen was in full swing now. The starchy reserve had disappeared quite suddenly. He wasn't entirely sure what to make of it, but it felt better this way.

'Tell me,' he invited.

'Well, she was a lady snooker player,' Helen began. 'Twenty-one, very pretty – you would have liked her. She won the Ladies' World Championship. But there's no money in ladies' snooker. Fuck, perhaps even less than there is in chess! No one would take her on . . . but I did. We scratched round for a year and a half, staying in dives, eating takeaway meals and working in men's clubs for bugger all. I was looking for an angle. I promised myself I wasn't going to be beaten. So at last, I had her pose for *Mayfair*. I even got her on to page three of the *Sun*. All tits and arse. Suddenly, we got rich. She was invited on to *Question of Sport*. I multiplied her appearance fees by ten and we had a glorious year of fame. In the end, she married a fireman, retired from snooker and set up home in Essex. She's happy enough and she's set for life. She doesn't even miss the game.'

She sighed contentedly and Sam looked at her in amazement. For a moment, he seemed lost for words. Then he said, 'Well, there're plenty of women's magazines of that sort these days. Maybe you'd like John to pose for one of them—'

'That's not my point,' she retorted, glaring at him fiercely.

He saw her swallow.

'I'll look after him, you know?' she said. Then, more quietly: 'It's just a case of finding the right angle.'

The waitress came and delivered Helen's whiskey, a litre

bottle and two glasses. She poured it out and took half her share in the first gulp. She took two enormous lungfuls of cigarette.

'And what is your angle, Helen? With John, I mean.'

'Difficult to say,' she admitted, putting the glass down on the table and gazing at the fallen cigarette. 'It seems increasingly unlikely it has anything to do with chess.'

'Did you know his mother was ill before you brought him out here?'

Sam watched for her reaction. She seemed genuinely shocked. She jumped in her chair, turned towards him hard-faced, then softened and waited.

'No,' she said at last. 'I swear to you. I didn't know how ill she was. I'm not quite the bastard they make me out.'

Sam nodded and drank. She drained her glass and poured out another.

He wasn't sure if he was being told the truth. He was only sure he wanted to believe her.

It took Kate Morris half an hour to get back to her hotel room. Singapore seemed a lonely place. Not that she wasn't lonely quite often back home, but there was almost nothing left to do here. She'd filed her stories and her plane wasn't until the next day.

She sat in her hotel room, staring at a big bunch of red roses with Yoshi Yakamura's name on the ticket. Shit, would he never give in? After their conversation in Papa Joe's, she felt like slinging them in the bin, but the flowers themselves were beautiful. They deserved better. They deserved to have been severed in a worthier cause.

She realized suddenly that she had forgotten to eat that day and it was already gone midnight. She made for the room-service menu. She ordered dinner and, when it came, sat down to eat it, watching television.

The first thing she saw was the smiling teeth of Joe Beckett, beaming out of the screen. He was face to face in comfy chairs with interviewer Bob.

'Why are you out here in Singapore?'

'Asia is a big investor in California,' Beckett said, basking in the softened lighting he preferred.

'It might seem like a strange trip to the folks back home.'

'It is not enough to be a domestic politician any more,' Beckett continued. 'Business is global. All countries and states are dealing with multiculturalism. I'd like to think of this as a fact-finding tour.' He paused. 'We stand now at the end of the twentieth century in both the best and worst of times, the safest and most dangerous. The problems of the world now recognize no territorial borders, and it is no longer possible to hold office credibly in any administration without gathering the widest perspective.'

Kate knew the tricks of journalism. She knew when an interviewer was in trouble and, alternatively, when the guest was making it easy. She saw this interviewer's relaxed smile, knowing he was into something that was going to make wonderful television: an interviewee who served up sound bites like twenty-four-carat nuggets.

'God, this Beckett is too good to be true,' she mumbled to herself with a mouth full of cold beefburger and fries.

'Our problems are global – global warming, global trade, drug trafficking, the Middle East question which affects all states and all nations. As we come into the next century, we have an energy crisis to face. Do we continue to burn fossil fuels? Do we concentrate our efforts on nuclear technology with all its associated problems? What about solar power? Wind power?'

'You think these concerns are priorities for a state governor?'

Beckett produced a sincere gaze. He surprised interviewer Bob, pinning him in his comfy chair.

'Do you think we will be here in a hundred years if they're not?'

Kate laughed. He was brilliant: the moves, the looks, the speeches. She reached across for the remote control and sent his image spiralling into the black centre of the screen.

She pushed the remains on her plate aside and got out the notebook computer which had recently become her principal working tool. Since she had a modem for sending her work back home and an Internet account with international access, she could surf at will, gathering information on whatever she felt like.

The subject of her current research was not Joe Beckett. He was just too squeaky clean. She focused instead on Arthur Beckett, his father.

Joe Beckett's campaign made a lot of his family heritage. Arthur had been a war hero, briefly posted to the London embassy at the beginning of the war, but pulled back to Washington when the US entered the fray. Afterwards, he'd moved through various jobs in various branches of the Secret Service. No one seemed to know too much about them. That was fair enough, but even later, when he appeared at the arm of political leaders, no one really understood what Arthur Beckett was doing there.

In his middle years, he amassed a considerable personal fortune, much of which he'd since put behind his son's early political career. So far – she'd been working on this for a couple of weeks – Kate had been unable to find any reasonable explanation for the extent of his wealth.

Arthur was in his late eighties now. No one saw him. He lived in seclusion behind the high walls of the Beckett family home. Kate was suspicious. Maybe that was simply the nature of journalism, but this seemed something more than a hunch. The official Arthur Beckett story smelt odd.

She accessed a number of web pages belonging to the libraries that held public access records back home. Three or four of them came up blank. She couldn't think of a way that could happen – unless they had been deliberately erased.

7

In 1937, I won a big chess tournament in Paris. The play I showed was like nothing anyone had seen before. I put it down to Ward's influence and that was enough to turn me from young prodigy to demon seed in the eyes of many at Oxford. They said my academic papers also showed the same wildness of thought.

But there was no wildness of thought; quite the contrary. It was the prejudice against Ward showing through.

Ward's first 'sin' was to be an American. He had been born in New Orleans in 1891. His father was an Italian, active in the union movement, his mother a Jewish seamstress. His second 'sin' was to take her religion.

In his early career, he studied medicine in New York and specialized in neurosurgery, a discipline perceived as a black art at the time. He came to Europe during the Great War, apparently working alongside the famous American neurosurgeon Harvey Cushing. He told people he was shot in both legs at the battle of the Somme. He still walked with a limp when I met him.

No one really knew where he had been after the Armistice before he resurfaced in Oxford in the early thirties. Neither did anyone really know why Sherrington had taken him on. Sherrington was a big name in Oxford. He was the Waynflete Professor of Physiology and about to be awarded the Nobel Prize for his work on the neuron. He could have chosen anyone. That he should have chosen this unknown Jewish American with controversial views on psychology had caused waves in the department when Sherrington announced his choice.

'Are you really the Antichrist?' I asked Ward once. It was

meant as a joke. We were taking coffee in his rooms at the time.

Ward laughed. 'I like you, Hayden. Always those important questions. You should know the answer. You're a religious man.'

'I don't subscribe to that kind of religion.'

'I guess not,' he agreed.

'All right,' I said, 'but are you a phoney?'

His mood changed, growing heavy and his face drew back into serious lines.

'I don't fit,' he admitted. 'I'm forty-six years old. I haven't done the traditional academic things, yet here I am in academia. I've rolled around the world most of my life and all I've really collected is a reputation. And not a very good reputation, at that. My relationship with Marion is a scandal. She's far too young for me. Her parents object to our ... liaison. Not only that but she terrifies the other fellows' wives by going to college sherry parties and telling them how much she enjoys sex. This is a concept which they are unable to deal with, especially as she loves to elaborate. Why are you asking me these questions now?'

'I'm making progress,' I said, 'but I cannot understand why the world appears the way it does. I begin to think it is all illusion, and dangerous illusion at that.'

He did not reply but simply listened, and I started telling him the point I had reached.

'I was in Italy a month ago. I went to Fermi's laboratory.'

'Visiting the Pope,' Ward quipped.

Enrico Fermi ran the major physics laboratory in Italy. His collaborators nicknamed him 'the Pope'.

'It's about the construction of the nucleus,' I continued. 'Three years ago, he began systematically bombarding all the known elements with neutrons – Chadwick's new particle. He claims to have created artificial radioactivity. That is to say, after bombardment certain non-radioactive elements give off radiation similar to that of the known radioactive elements. He also told me that when he reached uranium, he noticed odd things occurring. He believes that he has created new elements with nuclear centres – nuclei – heavier than that of uranium.'

'And you doubt him?'

'I don't know,' I said honestly. I reached for the coffee pot and poured its contents into my cup. Ward's coffee was always extra strong. 'Ever since that particle was discovered, I have been of the opinion that the nucleus is made of protons and neutrons. It seems logical, though I have not yet formed the mathematics to support it. This means, I suppose, that it is indeed possible to make new elements out of others by adding or subtracting neutrons . . . and even protons. Perhaps all those alchemists' dreams of turning lead into gold were not so foolish. Only their tools were wrong.'

'You are disturbed by his finding, though?' Ward was good at this. He sat back and drew you out – a psychologist's trick.

'There are protons and neutrons floating all over the place. There is a small sea of them. Wouldn't you expect those new elements to exist in nature if Fermi was right? Unless . . .'

'Unless?' Ward prompted.

'Unless all those bigger elements are unstable and do not last very long. Fermi's experiment is not just a matter of addition, there is also the subtraction . . . the radioactivity he discovered. I think it is necessary to consider the construction and decay of the nucleus with one single model. It may be that once the nucleus grows to a certain size, it is inherently unstable . . . Like a soap bubble. One of those ones you blow up. It gets bigger and bigger, held together by the surface tension of the soap liquid, then "Pop!"'

I sipped the coffee, and waited a moment while Ward considered the image.

'The question is, inside the nucleus, what creates that surface tension?' I said. Then, more quietly, I added, 'It is clear from the energy of the radioactivity produced that there are powerful forces inside the nucleus. If we could unlock them, we would indeed have an almost unlimited supply of power, just as I first thought.'

Ward smiled. 'I have read your papers, Hayden. Remember? I believe I almost understood them. You'll agree, my précis of them was impressive.'

'Yes, but think of it,' I said, caught by my own imagination. 'No more need to dig in the earth for coal or oil. Ward, you and I are fond of thinking of the world in terms of God. "How would God have done it?" we say. Perhaps he has left us the greatest gift here. But then I begin to worry what unlimited power would mean.' I hesitated, thinking about the question Ward had once asked with the dominoes. What happens if your chain reaction is not so much a chain reaction as a chain explosion – the number of reactions growing uncontrollably from the first?

'Is that what worries you?' Ward asked.

'It's not the kind of physics that would be safe in anyone's hands,' I said.

8

Mai was a cocktail of cultures, a little miniature of Singapore. Her father had been an American sailor with a false name, her mother a local who, twenty years ago, had swallowed the name and fallen in love.

The product of their brief union had poured herself into a green Chinese silk dress and stalked through Papa Joe's casino bar. She had slipped in next to John the moment he was alone at the roulette wheel, taking the seat still warm after Helen's departure.

'Very unlucky,' she said. Her voice was husky and low, with hardly a trace of the Orient.

John turned towards her but did not reply.

She patted him on the shoulder. 'Don't worry, I don't bite.'

Maybe not, but her assurance wasn't convincing. She pressed her long slim body closer and closer to him as he squandered Helen's thirty dollars in six turns of the wheel. By the time he was broke, she was whispering into his ear and holding him by the hand.

'Don't worry,' she said again, 'I've got money.'

'Why . . .?' he stumbled.

'You're John Harringhay, aren't you?' she replied. That seemed explanation enough.

She rode with him in a taxi to his hotel. They consumed half the liquor in the mini-bar, then she brought her dollish face close to his and kissed him, capturing him and smothering any protest he might have raised. Her black wiry hair fell around her cheeks and tickled against his skin. It did the same against his chest a moment later as she stripped off his ridiculous jacket and scraggy T-shirt. Then she unbuckled the belt of his jeans.

She seemed to want him with a peculiar intensity. She seemed to recognize in him all that she lacked, and she took it.

She told him to make lots of noise.

'I want to remember every sigh,' she said.

Afterwards, she held him in her arms and soothed him into a long and deep sleep. He slept and never stirred.

In the morning, she left him that way.

Upstairs, when she was having breakfast next to the roof-top pool, Kazuo Yakamura himself stopped by her table. He didn't sit down. He leaned awkwardly across a spare chair and handed Mai an envelope. She handed back a cassette recorder no bigger than a cigarette packet.

'How did it go?' he said, speaking his immaculate English.

'I've had worse,' Mai said, looking up, 'but he's weird, very weird. He doesn't say much, does he? I got the impression I had a better time than he did. He was always thinking of something else.'

'A shame. My guests should be satisfied.'

Unperturbed, Mai slit the flap of the envelope with a fingernail and looked down at the edges of the notes without counting them.

'His mother is dying,' she replied, folding the envelope carefully. 'He has to go home to England today, to be with her. That is distraction enough for anyone.'

Yakamura smiled wanly. He took another small bundle of notes from his wallet and handed them across.

'What's this for?' Mai asked. For the first time, her cool face furrowed in surprise.

'Your information is very valuable,' he said.

'I just slept with him . . . that's all.'

'Sleep and death are sometimes great gifts.'

Helen woke up in a bed that wasn't her own and tried to remember how long it was since the last time. She put her hand to her forehead and said, 'Oh, God,' to no one in particular.

Sam was propped upright on his elbow, looking down at her sprawling body. He smiled and she cringed.

She pulled the bedclothes over her breasts.

'Don't worry,' he said, 'I've already seen.'

'Not in the cold light of morning, you haven't.' She rolled over.

'Perhaps I should . . .' he ventured hesitantly.

She heard it, though – his pain, the surprise of being suddenly shut out. Hell, she knew she was putting her armour back on. Somehow she couldn't quite stop herself. 'No . . . No, I didn't mean it like that,' she tried saying. 'It's just that . . . well, I didn't expect it to move so fast . . .'

'So you regret it? I'm sorry. We were both a little the worse for—'

'Oh shit, no, please don't go all coy and chivalrous on me, and start apologizing for taking advantage.' She sat up, dragging the sheet with her. 'I wasn't so far gone that I didn't know what I was doing.'

There, she said it. Now would he be happy? She manufactured a smile. 'And . . . well . . . it's not easy to regret,' she added generously.

She checked the clock at the bedside, sighing heavily when she saw that most of the morning had been lost. 'I'm late,' she said, 'and my head feels like it's been stepped on. Don't you have any kind of a hangover?'

Sam grinned, an obviously hangover-free expression. He picked up his glasses from the bedside table, stretched himself vigorously when he reached the foot of the bed and, without dressing, walked towards the bathroom.

Hangover or not, Helen's mind was working overtime. Life was always full of surprises – mistakes and surprises. You've decided you're going to be independent – celibate – then one unexpected man and one too many drinks and Jesus, it's all gone to hell. She tried to bring some order to her thoughts. She tried to control her emotions.

She got out of bed and looked for her clothes, dressed while Sam was still in the bathroom. She found the full-length mirror, pushing her hair back while examining the damage the night had inflicted on her face.

Sam reappeared, still naked. He seemed to have absolutely no qualms about his nakedness. His genitals hung like tired and empty sacks between his legs and beneath a matted clump of short black hairs. She looked down at them once and then stoically pinned her eyes on his face.

'Do you want to put something on?' she said.

'Do you want me to?'

'Suit yourself.' She hesitated.

He picked up his trousers from the floor and started pulling them on.

She felt guilty, and couldn't quite understand why his silent stares had that effect on her. She put her hand to her neck, found her familiar chain and started to inch it around nervously.

'Look—' she began.

'Look what? Look, I've made a mistake? If that's what you want to say, I can say it for you.'

'No . . . No, Sam, it's nothing like that.' She found herself strangely tongue-tied, not something that she was used to.

'Tell me it didn't mean anything then.'

'I was drunk—'

'It meant something to me.'

'So it has to mean something to me?'

'Tell me it didn't,' he repeated. He waited for her, daring her to say it.

'I'm sorry,' she whispered. 'I can't deal with this now.'

He stared at her blankly. Hurt. Eyes shining, close to tears.

She felt empty, torn, like a woman shunning roses. Memories. Sometimes we are merely the sum of our histories.

Stephen was an architect who had made a pile designing skyscrapers for foreign bankers in the City of London. Nearing forty, he wanted babies. 'Before it was too late,' he said. Already thirty-six, she had told herself that this time it was right. But in the end it hadn't worked out. She had gone away, swearing never again, blood from the rose thorns oozing from her finger.

Sam was still standing, expectant. She could see a tremble in his lip. She leaned forward and took Sam's head between her outstretched hands, drawing his face towards her until it reached the limit of her focus. 'Don't you understand, this would be easy for me if I didn't . . .' She choked on her breath and the words wouldn't come. She kissed him gently instead.

He blinked but without recoil.

'Maybe if I didn't have feelings for you,' she said.

She withdrew her hands, dropping her gaze as she turned. She was waiting for him to speak as she moved to the door. Didn't know what she expected him to say. She was halfway through when he said, 'But I love you.'

She stepped out into the corridor and closed the door without ever looking back.

There was no sign of Mai when he finally came to. She was gone and only the wreckage of the room – bottles and cans and a chair they had toppled in their passion – remained in evidence. John shook his fuzzy head and went to the shower.

The water fell over him and slowly uncovered the memory of his mother's illness. Something he had poured out and then forgotten in the heat of the night.

He slumped backwards against the wall, sliding down the tiles. He sat there over the drain, naked, head at his knees.

He felt no will to move as the water continued falling. None of it washed him clean.

The YCK offices in Singapore occupied the top three floors of a building overlooking the old colonial district. In honour of Kazuo Yakamura's visit, several of the company's more senior executives had been sent abroad so that their offices could be taken over by the old man's entourage. Yakamura himself took a corner office the size of a tennis court with Italian furniture and glass down the two outside walls. There was a perfect view on to the Boat Quay in one direction and out across the Pedang and past City Hall towards Raffles in the other.

Despite its size, Yakamura didn't have much to put in this office except himself and an A4 diary in which he organized his entire business life. He was not from the computer age, and although computers played a large part in his business he had never in his life deigned to use one. The sparseness this policy brought to his office life only seemed to underline the plush excess of the space around him. It was the perfect atmosphere in which to entertain visitors and his visitor that morning was perhaps the most important man on the island that day.

'Joe Beckett is here,' a male voice informed him over the intercom.

Yakamura flicked the reply button. 'Thank you, Shoyo.'

He just had time to adopt a suitable pose around the polished mahogany table that stretched half the length of the room. He chose one of the twelve surrounding chairs and gazed at the door so he would have exactly the right look when Beckett walked in the room. Yakamura was a past master at many things. Dealing with the egos of aspiring politicians was one of his specialities, a necessary one when half the large civil projects in the world needed the green light from some government or another.

'Joe ... Joe,' he said, rising enthusiastically as the American entered.

'Mr Yakamura,' Beckett replied, bowing as the diplomats at the embassy had no doubt taught him; then he smiled. 'It's always good to see you, Kazz,' he added.

When they shook hands it was obvious how different these two men were. Although they were both in Western dress – Yakamura was wearing a suit from Armani's latest collection, Beckett looked as if he'd just stepped out of Harvard – the similarities ended there. Yakamura was over eighty, and five foot nothing in stockinged feet. Joe Beckett was in his late forties, the image of a former all-American sports hero made good, six foot three and iron-chested. He smiled straight and broad, and his hair – now streaked with middle-aged grey – gave you that last mile of confidence. You saw that this politically youthful man was also mature and responsible. You could trust Joe Beckett when you voted for him.

Yakamura had concluded some years before just how important this politician was going to become. He had planned their friendship for years. He had known Joe's father, Arthur, when he was active in politics in the sixties, and he quickly latched on to the son as soon as it was clear he was following Arthur into the family business. Joe had first repaid the faith when he was elected to the state senate, but Yakamura had recognized that Beckett was going to be more than that. He was going to the Governor's residence in Sacramento and he was going to make a difference. Yakamura needed that sort of ally if he was ever going to make YCK a serious player on the West Coast, and, indeed, in America as a whole.

'You want coffee?' Yakamura asked, already pouring the cups from a small silver pot placed on the table.

'Thank you. This is all very formal,' Beckett remarked. 'Why did you ask me to come alone?'

'Hangers-on,' said Yakamura, handing him a cup, 'are sometimes an encumbrance. Did you enjoy last night?'

'I always enjoy your hospitality, Kazz. But I'm afraid I had to send the girls back. I don't do that kind of thing any more. I'm not twenty. I'm pushing fifty and running for office.'

'The family-man image.' His host nodded.

'It's not just an image, Kazz.'

Yakamura bowed. 'I hope I did not offend.'

'Of course not.'

Beckett took the coffee and walked around the room. He stood at the window and looked out across Singapore, his eyes drifting away to the horizon.

'No place like it, is there?' Yakamura said, coming to his elbow.

'America's supposed to be the home of capitalism,' Beckett replied. 'Sometimes I'm not so sure.'

Yakamura gestured to a seat and his guest sat down, head still turned to the window. 'You said you needed to talk business before I left,' Beckett began as he finally tore himself away from the view.

'You're leaving today?' Yakamura asked as he took the seat opposite. There was something in his polite tone that showed he clearly knew the answer already.

'Germany, then Paris, London and home,' Beckett informed him.

'In that case, I will be brief. Joe, I want to contribute to your campaign. You're going to incur significant "expenses" over the next twelve months.'

'I appreciate the offer, but that may not be so easy,' Beckett said with a smile. 'Back home, we don't take kindly to Asian-backed candidates. We don't want to admit quite how much you own of our country.'

'Joe, it's precisely because we own so much that I can transfer funds through any one of a dozen routes.'

'I'm sure. Knowing you, you could make them look so "apple-pie" you'd think they came over on the *Mayflower*. Still . . .' He hesitated. 'How much're we talking?' he asked reluctantly.

'That depends.'

'OK . . . What is it you want?'

'I want to build a nuclear plant.'

'Difficult.'

'In California,' Yakamura added.

'Jesus, that's impossible.'

'OK then,' Yakamura conceded, 'in a neighbouring state feeding into California.'

'Kazz, let me understand you here,' Beckett said. 'No American utility company has even bothered to propose a new nuclear power plant in the States since the seventies. You know why? 'Cos there's no damn chance they're going to be approved, and even less chance they're going to make money. I'm sure you know this, so why the hell are you bothering?'

Yakamura smiled. 'Things change, Joe. The US Nuclear

Regulatory Commission has recently approved several new designs. One is a YCK specification, based on plants in Japan and China. We call it SALWAR – Super Advanced Light Water Reactor. Two thousand megawatts and a fraction of the safety and clean-up costs of the old PWRs.'

'You know how much trouble we've had with Pressurized Water Reactors?' Beckett said. 'I've drowned in committees and inquiries on those. I think you're simply barking up the wrong tree. However you cut it, all this nuclear fission stuff is an environmental nightmare. One hiccup and you've made either an 'A' bomb or a big smoking hole in the ground with a core heading south. More than that, you've got to fence off the waste products for a zillion years. If you want to go nuclear, why can't you guys get fusion to work for Christ's sake?'

'Ah, you've heard of fusion?' Yakamura sounded surprised. Beckett was better informed than he'd expected.

'Didn't I just say I'd served on energy committees?' Beckett reminded him.

'Then you'll know that at its best attempt, Princeton's Fusion Test Reactor produced exactly one third of the energy output required to make it stable. Even then it was running at 510 million degrees Celsius. This is the state-of-the-art, Joe. It is not an art that's coming any time soon. Not in time to fill the energy gap.'

Joe Beckett shrugged.

'So, it's coal, oil, gas,' Yakamura said. 'California is producing twice as much energy from burning organics than any other source, and it's still importing 50 billion kilowatt hours a year.'

'At least it's mainly gas.'

'It's still a non-renewable source and a carbon dioxide producer. What do you want, Joe? You know you need nuclear, not just in California, but in the whole industrialized world. Otherwise ... well, it's either an energy crisis or global warming, whichever comes first.'

'It's a tough call, but that's what the public wants.'

Yakamura raised his eyebrows.

'I want to get elected,' Beckett told him.

'Then you need funds.'

They looked at each other for a few seconds, both serious. Beckett burst out laughing. 'Hell, we've done business together for long enough, haven't we?' he said.

'We have always been friends,' the Japanese replied.

'I'm going to do this cleanly, Kazz.' He hesitated. 'From a moral standpoint, even if my choice of fuel offends you. Are you disappointed in me?'

'No. I respect your honour. But did you expect me not to offer "help"?'

'I expected it,' Beckett admitted.

'You must choose your friends carefully, Joe. You will make a good governor.' He raised his cup as if toasting the younger man.

The truth was Beckett had changed. He recognized that now. He seemed no longer to be his father's son. Arthur would have taken money and flexed his morality to accommodate it. He had been as corrupt as any politician Yakamura had ever dealt with. And he'd dealt with plenty. Yakamura had made a series of very lucrative deals with Arthur Beckett, but he'd always kept him at arm's length, always kept a little something on him in the background, just in case things went wrong. He'd done the same with Joe in the early days. He was glad he'd never had to use it. Yet even so, the Becketts and the Yakamuras were families of alliance, each profiting by the power it held over the other. Joe could be useful, even as an honest politician.

The candidate stayed for another half-hour, drinking and chatting about the Japanese economy and how the advent of digital communications had shrunk the world. International industrialists and politicians have plenty of legitimate things to talk over. Both men were full of smiles. Then Shoyo rang through to say Beckett's car had arrived to take him to the airport. The two men shook hands and Beckett slapped his diminutive benefactor on the back. Five minutes later, he was on his way to the airport.

After his guest had gone, Yakamura sat in his office

looking out over the view which had so fascinated the American. He found a spot where the flow from the air conditioner washed over him as if he were the test model in a wind tunnel. Most of his Japanese colleagues thought air conditioning ruined the body, but not him. He needed chilled air. The particular heat of Singapore did not seem to agree with his ageing constitution. Not that Tokyo was any cooler in the summer, but somehow heat in your own country was easier.

He pondered this absurdity for a while before the light on the office phone lit up. Leaning over to the main desk at full stretch, he tripped the appropriate button.

'Yes,' he said in Japanese.

'E-mail from London office,' said Shoyo, 'and your son is here.'

'Show him in.'

Yoshi breezed in, waving a printed copy of the message. Shoyo held the door, then waited dutifully next to it.

'I'm heading for China, just stopping for a moment,' Yoshi said. He lifted the paper, going straight to the message, reading it aloud. ' "Emily Harringhay died this morning, London time. Await next instructions." What is this about, Father?'

'A private matter . . .'

'You never put private matters through the company offices.'

Yakamura swivelled slowly in his chair. 'I suppose that is true enough. You are asking yourself, no doubt, "Why does Yakamura worry about this woman?" Hayden Zalapek. You have heard me talk of him?'

'I don't remember.' Yoshi's interest was waning. He pulled open the drinks cabinet that was recessed into a side wall.

The old man watched him for a while, then he asked, 'Do you not know that sometimes there are men so brilliant that they jump generations and generations of progress? If there had been no Einstein, no Newton, the discoveries they brought to the world would have taken another hundred years to uncover.'

'What are you on about, Father? Is this one of your flights of fantasy?' Yoshi poured a glass of imported whiskey from a crystal flask. He raised the flask towards his father.

Yakamura shook his head. 'I have just spent an hour trying to bribe the man who may soon become the most important man in America as far as YCK is concerned.'

'Is this something I need to know?'

Yakamura ignored the question. 'Why?' he said. 'Why does Yakamura need to do this? I ask you. I am asking you a lot of questions today ... Because nuclear power is not clean, not healthy. We have all looked for something better but 510 million degrees is a hopeless place to look for salvation.' The old man stopped and cast his eyes back across the Singapore skyline. 'I thought he was dead.'

Yoshi paid no attention, concentrating on the whiskey as he slid it between his lips.

'You know your trouble?' Yakamura said, noting his son's disdain. 'You believe you can inherit the presidency of this company. But really, you know nothing about what makes it run.'

'So you're going to vote in one of your half-dead cronies, is that it? I've heard this threat before, Father.' The word 'threat' got extra emphasis.

'It won't be me doing the voting, my son,' the old man countered.

'Please! When you retire, you'll still be the largest shareholder.'

'But not the majority.'

'You think they'll appoint that arse-wipe, Suzuki?' Yoshi's voice rose. 'You think they'll do that – appoint him just because he knows the company song?'

'My son, they'll appoint him because you don't.'

Yoshi turned and stared at his father.

'This problem we have in China is yours,' Yakamura said, switching his attack.

Yoshi laughed. 'The shit is always mine...' His face

suddenly closed like a fist, anger popping from his eyes. 'I'm already working on it,' he said. 'Why do you think I'm flying around the world? I'm going to sort it out, all right?'

He slammed his glass to the table and stormed to the door. Shoyo held it open and watched him go without so much as a flicker crossing his face.

Yakamura and his assistant were left alone. A small chubby man – no more than five four, immaculately dressed in a Western suit and silk tie – Shoyo was the perfect example of his position. His age was somewhere between thirty and forty, but something in his manner signalled that age didn't matter to either him or his boss.

'Thank you, Shoyo,' Yakamura said when Yoshi was long gone.

'I don't see the connection. I'm sorry, sir. If I may ask about this Hayden Zalapek.' The assistant seemed to be apologizing for his own stupidity, as if the thing must make sense and the fault had to lie with him.

Orlando, Florida. Two dark figures scuttling rat-like against a moonless sky. No one stirred inside Hollis House as the shadow men breached the fence and started up the drive.

Henry Hollis was watching the football game on television. His wife, Nancy, was sewing clothes for their latest great-granddaughter or great-grandson, due any day now. Henry was a devoted golfer – that's why they'd retired to Florida after he quit government service. They lived ten miles from Disney World in a house they'd saved for all their lives. They had heard about the crime rate, of course, but it didn't seem any more dangerous here than anywhere else in the United States. Much better than some places.

So Henry wasn't worried when he heard noises outside the front door. He waited for the Dolphins to fail on 'third and long' and went to see what it was.

The next thing Nancy heard was the shot that killed him.

'Not your typical crime,' the county sheriff said later. 'They never came in . . . never took nothing. Maybe kids.

Sometimes they shoot someone accidental like that and get scared. They can't finish off what they came for ... On the other hand, maybe killing Henry Hollis was all they were after.'

9

Emily's death found something empty inside me. I dredged quite desperately through the wardrobe of memory, finding emotion's tattered robes moth-eaten and stiff. I could not put them on.

I stayed in a hotel in Oxford, unable to take up Marion's offer of hospitality. The habit of solitude, I suppose. The drift of mourners coming and going was more than I could face, so I slunk away until the arrangements were made and I asked Marion's butler to call me and tell me where to be and when.

In the event, it was Marion herself who called me two days later.

'The funeral's tomorrow,' she said. 'I don't know much more.'

'What do you mean?' I asked.

'That Michaels woman, she has taken over. Probably for the best. She seems perfectly competent ... a good organizer.' She sounded sad, a sadness I first put down to grief.

'Are you OK?'

I heard her sobbing gently in the remoteness of the telephone.

'Be there tomorrow,' she said. 'Promise me.'

'I promise.'

'Thank you.'

Even so, I found it hard to drag myself to the funeral. I slid into the rear of the crematorium chapel after everyone else was seated, invited but unwelcomed, like a ghost.

I looked down the aisle, beyond the mourners and their hats and the children who'd rather not be here. I stared at the wooden box, the coffin.

There, in her casket, were all my lost years. The should-have-beens, the could-have-beens that never were. Bones and flesh I should have known when they contained something more than undertakers' fluid.

Then I saw the boy. The congregation had been singing, but suddenly it stopped. I saw him screw up his eyes and I saw him swallow. He turned his head and looked back over the rows of wooden benches to where I stood. Somehow, as that gaze of his jumped across the pews, it jumped also across the years.

I knew him from the look of family in his eyes. They spanned over his poor mother, and in his face I recognized something that carried the callow rage of his grandmother . . . Alice.

I found myself eye to eye with remembrances of my wife . . . Quite unable to cope.

So it was that I slipped in and out of Emily's funeral, and never spoke to a soul. A row of photographers at the door looked at me strangely, but I pushed past them. I didn't like the look in their eyes, but it seemed way beyond the point. All I wanted to do was get away.

History may well judge me harshly for all that I have done. More so if it sees the consequence.

To take no action when you know the consequence of inaction. Is that a sin? If the robbers had still been beating their victim when the good Samaritan came upon them, should he have joined the fight? And would he have been judged so good if he had waited and bound the wounds of a dead man?

I would not join the war. I did not join it, even believing and knowing what I did. As a result, people came to my home looking for the papers of my work. They were desperate men. They seized my wife a week after she'd had our daughter. They kidnapped my best friend. And they killed them.

10

Bangkok. Thailand. A private dining room in a very elegant restaurant.

The barefoot waitresses had gone, taking their smiling servitude and rosebud lips with them. All that remained was American coffee served for two American guests.

'Please,' said their host, lifting the silver pot in offering.

Rich spices and roasted coffee beans wafted on the heat of lanterns and soft light caressed the red silk trim of the room. The decor had a certain Asian authenticity, though the dining table and chairs were Spanish and the crockery and silverware were English.

The host reached out and started pouring for his guests.

The first was Hudson Brown, a long-time civil servant. He had spent years away from home in various far-flung parts of the world, but he was Washington-based these days and he made these trips only rarely now. Truth was he tried to avoid them. He had reached fifty-seven. Too old for life in the international fast lane, he was happy to just coast along.

'It sure is good of you to meet us here. Great hospitality,' Brown said, exercising his usual brand of easy diplomacy. He smiled at their host, the smile as straight and clean as his tie, which was as straight and clean as his suit. Brown was a straight and clean kind of guy.

The host clearly warmed to him. He returned Brown's smile with his own toothy version. 'I was, as I told you, passing through in any case, going on to Europe,' he said. He was an oriental, speaking mid-Atlantic English. 'I was anxious to hear the first news of your findings. As you know, the SALWAR design is the very latest. Our company is keen to get to the bottom of problems and, of course, to do its duty in this potentially damaging situation. We regret that your investigation was ever necessary.'

'It certainly was necessary,' the second guest piped up. 'I don't know what you guys thought you were building there in China, but, my God, you sure screwed up!'

This was Ed Wingate, a keen thirty-year-old, a so-called 'international expert' on nuclear recycling.

The host looked at him. There was no hint of malice, but he gave Wingate none of the smiling approval he beamed at Brown. 'That's unfortunate,' he said.

'I don't want to insult your hospitality. We had a job to do.'

'Quite. And this will be in the report you are writing?'

'Yes, it will,' Wingate confirmed. 'The pipe welds in the containment area have been leaking, I'd say, from day one. The damned operators have simply been topping the water system up. They didn't realize or didn't care that it was supposed to be a sealed system. The whole soil structure under the plant is contaminated right down to the water-table. We found elevated levels of radioactivity up to fifteen miles away. It's not surprising there's an increase of cancer in the population.'

'Unfortunate.'

'Unfortunate, you're damned right. Poor fucking kids!'

'Shall we change the subject?' Brown suggested. 'This is a social dinner after all.'

'Yes, quite,' the host agreed, 'and I have laid on a little cabaret. I hope you will stay to enjoy it.'

Wingate rose. 'I think I've had about as much of this as I can take,' he said. 'Hud, I just don't know how you can sit there.'

Brown shot him an embarrassed look and got halfway through mouthing 'Sit down', before he gave up. Instead he turned to the host.

'Don't worry, I will arrange a car,' the host said.

He rang the silver bell which the restaurant manager had strategically placed in the middle of the table before the meal. A gigantic Sumo-sized Japanese appeared through a doorway.

'This is Stan, Mr Wingate,' the host explained. 'Of course his real name is not Stan, but it is a little difficult to say in English. Stan will look after you. Just tell him where you want to go. Mr Brown and I will stay for the entertainment.'

Wingate guffawed, still contemptuous but perhaps mildly appeased. 'The hotel will be fine,' he said before adding a curt 'Goodnight' and following Stan.

'I'm sorry about Ed,' Brown said when Wingate had gone. 'He gets a bit too involved in his work. He's young. He'll learn.'

The host shrugged and poured his own cup of coffee. This was arrogance, the bad manners of pouring one's own drink – something he had avoided before. Wingate's departure seemed to leave him more relaxed, more carefree. He slid down a little in his chair, unstiffening his back. 'Don't worry,' he told Brown. 'Mr Wingate will be taken care of.'

'Taken care of?' Brown asked.

'Yes, Stan will take him down town. Then he will kill him.'

A pause. Brown trying to calculate what he'd just heard.

'You're joking of course,' he said.

The host wasn't laughing. 'Wingate, I'm afraid, has to go. He will never compromise his report.'

'What the fuck are you on about? You can't sit there and start telling me you're going to kill people.'

'Why not? An accident. Your colleague strays into the wrong part of town, looking for a little "action". In Bangkok, it happens.'

'But . . .' Brown made a show of springing to his feet, but his legs buckled and he grasped at the table. 'Y-you're serious!' His lips continued to move but nothing came.

'Unfortunate,' the host repeated, maintaining the tone and feeling for the word he'd used earlier. It was almost as if he'd been rehearsing it before. 'Don't worry, Mr Brown, I'm not going to kill you.'

Brown pushed himself straight, levering his arms against the table, mouth moving like a goldfish.

The host swung a notebook computer up on to the table, opened it and switched it on. 'It takes so long to boot these, don't you think?' he said. 'Bad design. You Americans are usually so clever at that sort of thing. Ah, here we are.'

He clicked a few keys and used the touchpad to steer the pointer. Then he turned the screen so it pointed at Brown.

'You see, we are in my e-mail system. I am writing a message and addressing it to your boss, to your boss's boss, to the editors of several newspapers, to certain government officials in China and here in Thailand. I write to them because I think they would be interested in your activities.'

'I'm just out here as an independent inspector,' Brown said, genuinely confused. The fear had brought water to his eyes. He brushed it away, sniffing like a snotty kid.

'Indeed,' the host acknowledged. He reached around and clicked another button. A digitized photograph appeared. 'This is the file I am attaching. You recognize the girl?'

'Y-Y-Y-' Brown stammered, 'you sick perverted bastard!'

'On the contrary, Mr Brown, I'm simply doing what I must. Her name is Chi-Ling. Such a flexible body! But then, you know that from last night! You make such a cute couple. How old are you? Chi-Ling is nine. You probably know that too.'

'I didn't know she worked for your company.'

'Not for YCK . . . for me. Everything you have seen or been given since you arrived on your little "stop-over in Bangkok" has been courtesy of me. Now you must pay back.'

Somewhere in Ohio, a fire raged.

The archive storage depot had been built on five acres of land on the edge of a military base. Its site was purposely miles from anywhere. That's why it was chosen – far from the nearest city, but close to surrounding military personnel who could provide the necessary security and back-up.

Even so, the flames were two hundred feet in the air before the first of the army fire trucks arrived.

Ten minutes later, the base commander ate humble pie and called for civilian reinforcements. Because of the distance, serious help took an hour to arrive. By then, the building, the surrounding grass and trees for two hundred yards, and three carelessly parked military vehicles were toast.

The fire burned out naturally just before five in the morning when it could find nothing else to feed on.

'This was not a natural fire,' the fire chief said when he examined the wreckage at first light. How he knew was not clear. The only evidence consisted of a black amorphous mass and two buckled steel struts. Nothing else from the building's structure remained.

Two days later, the chief medical examiner confirmed the discovery of a single victim scraped up from the blackness. 'Body is the wrong word,' she said. 'There wasn't that much left. We're assuming it was the nightwatchman, but that's just a guess.'

11

The death of a mother. A terrible loneliness that somehow the closeness of others cannot assuage. John Harringhay stood with all the people who had been with him and whom he had known since he was a child. Collectively, their sympathy added up to nothing. What was inside him was a hole that nothing could fill.

After the ceremony, he watched the mourners trail back to the house he had grown up in. His Aunt Marion – a title she had given herself long ago – had laid on a small spread of food. Family and friends ate in silence. The deafening roar of it rattled in his head. Until he had to get out. Had to get out. Had to go.

He spoke to Helen. He said, 'I'm leaving before I go mad.'

'I'm sorry,' Helen said uneasily. 'I didn't organize this part of it. I left the reception to your aunt.'

'No, it's not that. I just . . . just have to go.'

'Remember we have a dinner in London tonight,' she cautioned.

'I'll be there . . . Take care of things. I'll meet you. You take care of things. You always do.'

Helen looked unusually hesitant, uncertain. His pain seemed overpowering. Even to her. She nodded.

'John, you're going to be there, aren't you? We have commitments.'

'I need time . . . on my own. I'll take the train . . .' He practically ran out, and no one got an explanation of his departure.

He walked for what seemed like an age until he came to a park he hardly recognized. He sat under a tree. He selected the bench that was furthest from anyone else. Trees and water surrounded him. The trees smouldered red, dying in a late autumn flame. The spent leaves lay brown and crisp on the ground. He felt as if he were just another part of an ageing tapestry where the bright living things had faded until all was grey or rust. He watched his breath wasting into the air; each breath seemed more wasted than the last.

In his pocket, he had a small penknife and his own little pharmacy of drugs. He took out a pill and popped it, hoping – no, believing – there was some kind of escape in such chemicals. He had found it that way before. When all else fails you, drugs don't let you down.

But all the time, even as his bloodstream filled up with the narcotic, there was the echo of his mother. Not of her voice. Not of her face or hands or of any physical part of her. But the emotion of her. The emotion of her presence in the world was now missing. He had to face it alone. He hadn't seen his father since he was six years old. There had only been his mother, and now he was an orphan. It didn't matter that he had hardly been home in the last couple of years: his orphan state started now. Here where he was alone. He took another pill from his pocket, and looked at it lying there, hard and still and solitary in the palm of his hand. He liked the colour of this one better than the last one. Yeah, it would be all right, he thought. Then he took it into his mouth and swallowed it in one flowing movement.

In rational moments, he had argued with himself about his habits. And it was a habit, despite his internal protests of control. He knew it was self-delusion, but he couldn't put the brakes on. Not today.

His head was quickly becoming woozy, a certain floating feeling that somehow put his pain outside his body for a while. In fact, it made everything absurdly funny. Funny in a way he couldn't explain. He found himself walking down the side of the main road and waving his thumb at the passing traffic and wondering if it really was possible to hitch a lift to London.

Of course it was . . . Maybe it took a while these days, but someone will always pick you up.

'Hey, mate, 're you looking for a lift?'

'Yeah . . . er, sure, yes.'

'Get yer ass up here then.'

Up into the big cab. Music blaring. The noise of the diesel.

'You looked like you were freezin', son. And you're soaked through. Is that a suit you've got on? Didn't you realize it was raining?'

Shrugged. What does it matter anyway? He was busy trying not to throw up.

Before John really knew it, they were on the motorway. Moving objects all around and below them. And the cab seemed to be falling, falling, through a tunnel of white studs. He was caught in some insane form of gravity and only the roar of the diesel and the blurred beat of bad rock comforted him. Like womb music. He wanted to be a child again, wanted to sleep, but there was too much junk in his veins.

Getting to London took hours. He didn't know and didn't care how many hours. He popped another pill when the driver stopped for fuel. He considered offering the driver one, but decided against it. He looked the sort that might freak out if he knew substance abuse was going on. Some drivers are very possessive about their cabs. The thought of the driver freaking out was oddly amusing. He laughed to himself, vaguely thinking that he should feel guilt, but he didn't.

His dead mother was now a memory that seemed to belong to someone else, as if he had acquired it on the cheap somewhere and it was kind of second-hand and worn out and detached, so that he could see the pain but not feel it.

Amber street lights joined headlights and tail-lights when they reached the outskirts of the city. Then, some time later, he was standing in the street, cold again and alone, and the cab with the warm seat and loud music and its panoramic view of the world was gone.

Where was he now? In some street, in some suburb. Just down from an overhead motorway. He could hear its roar but not see it. He knew only that he needed a bus or a taxi.

Something that could take him into the city proper. He found something that looked like a bus stop, but it wasn't. Then he found something that didn't look like a bus stop, but must have been because there was a bus. He got on and, fumbling for change, pulled out his stash in front of the amazed bus driver.

'Sweets,' the boy explained with a childish giggle. 'Just sweeties.'

The driver seemed to want to throw him off the bus, and was only placated when the boy produced a five-pound note from his jacket pocket.

'Duzziz go to the middle?' he slurred.

'Where d'you want?'

'I dunno . . . Westminster?'

'It does if you sit on it long enough, son,' the driver said, 'but we go all the way out first. This bus is going in the wrong direction.'

'Izz OK.' Waving his hand, the boy flopped into a seat and the bus pulled off.

Coming down a little bit now. Perhaps he should take another. Perhaps he should wait until he at least knew where he was going. Where was he going? He didn't know. Away from the pain or something. Wasn't he supposed to be playing chess in London? Yeah, but that was tomorrow, wasn't it? Hell, he felt like playing now. Wheel 'em up, he'd knock them down. Where could you go in London on a Tuesday night? Chess clubs? He'd been in thousands of them since he was five years old. He'd been a county player – played for Oxfordshire when he was ten. Been to London several times playing chess. Where was it now? Didn't that club used to meet on a Tuesday? It was no good; his memory had been put through a blender.

The bus ride passed in a blur and ended the same way. He sat down in a shop doorway, parking himself on the one patch of ground the rain had not reached. E4, E5, F4 – he had played a king's gambit. A wild and wondrous thing. That was in London. He was still in short pants then. Where was it now, that club?

A man went by and he called to him, 'Hey, d'you know where the club is?'

The man's face filled with worry and glancing back furtively, he disappeared at an accelerated walk.

'Bastard!' the boy called after him. He looked into his pocket and dipped his hand in. Everything had turned to powder. He laughed. He must have crushed them when he sat down on the bus or on the hard floor, or something. He dipped his finger into the mingled powders and licked it clumsily.

Wait for the rush now. Here it comes, here it comes. Wonderful! Meaninglessly wonderful!

After a while, he found himself at a junction, leaning on a green metal cabinet and watching the cars criss-crossing as the lights changed. So orderly. So boring. It seemed to have nothing of the wonderful chaos he'd seen in Asia. Order had that terrible English stiff upper lip.

But he was leaning on the fucking lights box, wasn't he? He could make it more interesting, if he wanted to.

He reached in his pocket and took out his penknife. He worked it into the crack where the little door mated into its frame. In a few moments, he was looking at a rack of electrical wires and terminals.

'Bingo,' he said, using what he thought was a colonial-style upper-class accent.

First he turned all the lights red. Then, when the horns honked enough, he turned them all green. The traffic screeched to a halt in the yellow-striped heart of the junction. This was more like it.

He would have carried on – he had plans for an encore – but several motorists were getting out of their cars, shouting and advancing towards him. He had to run for it, falling over a litterbin and a curb, and ending up sprinting down an alley with two big men in pursuit. All the time, he was laughing, though there didn't seem to be a joke.

He finally lost them with a double-back through an arcade, though in truth they probably thought better of it anyway. He leaned against the window outside a Chinese take-away, panting for breath.

The drugs were so far into his system, he could no longer remember what he was hurting about. Couldn't remember what pain was anyway. But suddenly, he could remember Curtois Street. It was in Curtois Street. That's where the chess was.

He tried to stand up. That's when another problem came to him: he had only ten quid left in his pocket and he couldn't remember where he was supposed to be staying or going that night. Some kind of sponsor's function. He'd promised. Supposed to be with Helen and Sam. Helen had a new dress. Bollocks to it. Where the hell was Curtois Street anyway?

Eight o'clock and he found it. He could hear a distant clock chiming. All the buildings were on the lean and he struggled to walk in the club because of the stairs. He was sure they went generally upwards, but they seemed to go about it in a very haphazard fashion. He got to the top somehow, pulled out his tenner and waved it about. 'Anyone want to play me for a tenner?'

He vaguely noticed men and women in woolly jumpers, looking astonished at his entrance. Were they all deaf, or foreign, or both? Be an Englishman. Be a colonial Englishman. Say it again louder. That was the way to get through to foreigners. 'Hey chaps, anyone want to fucking play?'

He found himself sitting at the chessboard and up against a burly man with a beard. The man had a tenner which he used to trump the boy's. A woman was commandeered to hold the two notes. She was pretty. Very, very sexy in a blurry kind of way. Legs that went on for at least a million miles, possibly longer – he couldn't tell. He tried to think about his mother, but she had somehow become detached back when the pain and the rest of that paraphernalia had left him.

He glanced at the chess set for a moment. It was the only thing that currently seemed to hold a steady focus.

''R'n't we going to use clocks? I love it when we use clocks.'

'Thirty minutes the whole game suit you?' the bearded man said.

'Fine.' He was looking at the woman, working up from the feet and wondering what was at the end of those million miles. *Hey, we got chess to play. King's gambit. Why the fuck not?*

An hour later, he was sitting stupefied in his seat, holding twenty pounds and thinking that the paper of the notes held her heat, the heat of her hand, but that was enough. The man with the beard was getting to his feet and looking angry. A little crowd had gathered and was applauding. They looked like a great big single monster with many heads and legs and hands designed only for giving applause. For some reason this strange monster was purple. He felt a compulsion to laugh. Then it all receded and he was there on his own, except for the woman. The woman was still there.

'Are you all right?' she asked.

'I'm supposed to be somewhere,' he slurred.

'Where?'

'I dunno. A fancy hotel. Name some fancy hotels.'

'I recognize you . . . I know who you are.'

'I wish I did . . . Who are you?'

'Amy.'

He looked around, and couldn't think of anything else to say now he knew her name. People seemed to be leaving. 'I must be going now,' he said. Then he burst out laughing.

Joe Beckett's campaign manager picked him up at LA airport. His wife came along, standing open-armed to create the perfect photo opportunity. *The great hero comes home.* A quick dash through the corridor of Cyclops-eyed cameras and a short speech to a handpicked TV crew, and Joe Beckett was on his way home. The limousine pulled away with half the paparazzi still clinging to the door handles.

The Beckett family home lay a few miles north of Mulholland Drive, not exactly in that area notorious for its famous homes, but not exactly out of it either. It was a long and torturous drive in the mid-afternoon, even if it was no more than fifteen miles as the crow flies. Beckett took up the notes his secretary had prepared on domestic events of the last week and a half. He was booked on a TV talk show the next evening; he needed to be ready.

When they finally got there, Joe was able to ditch his luggage, take a shower and slide into the jeans he preferred, ten-year-old Levis. He was proud that he could still get into them.

'Your father wants to see you,' his campaign manager had said. Joe remembered it as he was walking back down the stairs and he diverted himself towards the library where his father always spent the afternoon hours between five and seven.

Arthur Beckett's frail body was confined to an electric wheelchair by both age and the remnants of a stroke. The stroke in particular had switched off most of the muscles down his left side. Even so, he retained a clarity of mind and purpose. He had always wanted his son to succeed. Governor of California and afterwards who knows? Now that Joe stood but a year from that goal, Beckett Senior was unwilling to leave this life with the ambition unfulfilled.

'Joe,' he called. His voice was strained, disfigured by the muscles that refused to move to form the words.

'Sir.'

'It's good to see you. We got great reports from Asia and Europe. You made the news nearly every night. Have they showed you the cuttings yet?'

'They told me. I haven't read them. They told me you wanted to see me.'

'Yes . . . yes. I have something for you. I told you I'd get something on Craddock.'

'I told you I didn't want it. I wasn't going to fight that way.'

Arthur Beckett's fingers worked the controls of his electric chair, and he turned it and pointed it across the room, accelerating towards the desk on the far side.

'This is politics, Joey. You're not a stupid boy. You know how it works. Craddock is your main rival. He's making ground on you, son. While you've been away, he's been making hay.'

'People are entitled to vote for him, Father.'

'Fuck that,' Arthur said, spinning his chair on the spot. He held out a brown folder.

'What's that?'

'Papers and pictures ... What does it look like? Read them. Sometimes there's a great power in papers and pictures.'

Joe eyed the bundle suspiciously. Finally, he reached out and took it.

'Summary?' he asked.

His father smiled lopsidedly. 'OK. A summary: Craddock's daughter's a dyke.'

'Oh, Father, please!' Joe exclaimed. 'What's that got to do with the man?'

'Not for us to judge. That's for the people.'

'You want me to get up and denounce Craddock because his daughter is gay. And you think that's going to get me votes?'

'No, of course not,' his father said. 'It would be a serious political error for you to be anything other than very supportive of Mike Craddock when this whole sorry business comes out. There's a big gay community out there ...'

'Jesus fucking Christ!' Joe said slowly. 'You've leaked it already, haven't you?'

'Listen to me, Joe. He has support from the traditional God-fearing white Christians. You're seen as too much of a liberal. But you know what they think of gays.'

'And what about when the mud really starts flying, Father? It's six months to the primary, eleven to the real thing. D'you think we're bulletproof? Do you think anyone is?'

'I've taken steps, son—'

'Steps?'

'I am taking steps. I may be in a chair, but I still got friends.'

'You haven't done enough already? Oh God, what are you doing?'

'You ... you don't want to know.' Arthur Beckett turned so the dead side of his face was towards his son.

Joe Beckett hesitated. 'You're right ... I don't want to know.'

'You're going to be the Governor, son. Nothing's going to stop us. You just have to accept what it takes to get power. Believe me, I know.'

12

After the funeral, I wandered the streets for a time. It seemed I should find somewhere I still belonged in Oxford, but even in the places I remembered, my presence rattled as if I had grown too thin. I suffered the paranoia of the recluse, believing there were men and women following me. In particular, a slight oriental gentleman appeared and reappeared at intervals during my journey. Finally I gave it up. There was nothing here for me.

Back at the hotel there was a message handed to me with my key. It came from a Mr Sam Stylls, an envelope with a note and a ticket to a chess game in London.

> Dear Mr Zalapek,
>   I know you do not know me, but I know your reputation. I thought you might be interested in seeing your grandson play chess. I think you should come and try to help him. God knows he needs your help.
>   With best regards.

I stared at the words. Not those of a natural writer: bumbling but somehow conveying a sense of the urgent, the important. I took the note up to my room and laid it on the bed next to the ticket. *John Harringhay versus Brad Rasatta*. The date was the next day. The time and the seat number stared at me, and I didn't know why it seemed to draw me in. Perhaps something to do with the way the boy had looked at me in the chapel. Perhaps simple and deadly curiosity.

After a while, I took out Marion's ivory letter and read the telephone number and dialled. When the butler answered, I asked to be put through to her.

'Hayden?' she said, taking the receiver.

'Yes.'

'I was worried . . . the way you left.'

'I'm sorry.'

'It's OK . . . now I know you're all right.' She hesitated.

'Who is Sam Stylls?' I asked.

'He's John's coach, I think. Why?'

'He sent me a ticket. He says I should go to London, to watch him play.'

Silence.

'What is it?' I said.

'You should go,' she said at last.

'Why? Is there something . . .?'

'When we were at Emily's bedside,' she began, 'I – I didn't tell you everything about John. Didn't you notice? The way John is dominated by that woman, Helen Michaels. She was the one who made all the arrangements. She had photographers outside, Hayden. She wanted pictures of the grief.'

'Yes, but why should I go to London?'

'Didn't you look in his eyes?'

'Not really.'

'Then go to London and look in his eyes.'

'You're talking in riddles,' I began, but my voice trailed away and the line sounded suddenly distant as if she had moved the receiver away from her mouth.

I waited. Marion said nothing and I felt my stomach turn. I wanted back the life I had adopted, wanted back my old age and my solitude. I didn't belong here. 'No,' I said, 'I'm going home tomorrow. To where no one can find me.'

'Mr Smith?' she asked scornfully.

'Yes, I'm going to be Mr Smith.' Hopeless Mr Smith, I wanted to add.

'I found you, Mr Smith,' she said. She stopped. She let it hang there, waiting for me to ask the question.

'Yes,' I admitted, 'how did you do that after . . .?'

'I've known for five years,' she said. 'It was John who found you. When he was fourteen he had a passion about it. Came to see me and asked lots of questions about you.

Three weeks later he was back. He had your address on a piece of paper. It was strange because it was one of the few times he ever came to see me. His mother and I were never that close after she grew up. I was never part of the family. Emily had your kind of pride. When I offered her money she would never take it; she wanted to make her own way in the world. I admired her for that, though it hurt me. John was the same. I was Aunt Marion to both. Never "Mum" or "Mother". Never "Granny". Emily never even knew Alice, but it made no difference.'

'How did he find me?' I asked.

'I don't know Hayden. Why don't you go and ask him?'

I thought for a moment. Then I said, 'Did I get it all so wrong, Marion?'

'You know I can't answer that.' There was a sob hidden in the strength of her voice. 'Please,' she said, 'he's all alone now . . . an orphan. There's no one else to protect him. You should know what it's like.'

'What do you mean?'

'To have something everybody wants . . .'

I took the train. I watched him play. He defeated Brad Rasatta, a man the programme described as the 'tenth strongest player on the planet'.

It was a great win, accomplished with dash and verve. John's style at the board was chillingly familiar – exploring every avenue; a mind so open, so grasping; plans so deep and far-sighted. If I had not known better, I would have sworn he showed the influence of Ward Costello's teaching; I would have sworn I was watching myself sixty years ago.

I saw but one tiny mistake – he was a little too anxious to accept a sacrifice – but he found a trap to save himself. He seemed good at setting traps for his opponent, nice simple traps, the sort the cleverest men fall to.

But more, much more than this, the boy's strange manner chilled me. The moves – great as many of them were – seemed to wrench from him something unseen yet irreplaceable as if they sucked marrow out of his bones.

And away from the board, he seemed like a light bulb unplugged. I found him to be a lifeless, slump-shouldered boy. He stumbled around with the grace of a stringless puppet. Beneath his flapping jacket was a T-shirt that said 'Fuck the Tories', as garish and cruel as a diamond waistcoat on a trained poodle. He performed great tricks, then took the applause with bemusement, waiting for his tit-bit to be fed.

I do not say this lightly. This was my grandson . . . all that was left of the line.

The doorman stopped me as I tried to enter the theatre through the stage door. I was set on a path – not easy to stop.

'Oi,' the doorman said. He pointed and then barred my way. Even 'set on path', I was too old and weak to push past.

'Yes, it's you I'm talking to,' the doorman continued, wagging a finger. 'Where d'ya think you're going, pal?' He looked me up and down as if I were a tramp. 'Who are you?' he asked.

'I am here to see John Harringhay. I am his grandfather.'

'Family?'

'Yes, family.'

The doorman looked again, disbelievingly. 'Got a pass?'

'No.'

The doorman was now confused. It seemed blood relations asking for access to the star still had to have passes. This had obviously not been covered on his training course. He scratched his head and said, 'I'll phone for you.'

Three minutes later, Helen Michaels appeared. She was wearing the same grey two-piece she had worn to the funeral. I remembered seeing her, but I had not known then who she was.

'I didn't expect to see you,' she said, speaking as though we were old but estranged friends. 'John says come on down.'

She turned on her heels and began leading me away. We walked along a dimly lit corridor, descending rapidly into a kind of underground maze. She walked quickly and efficiently on her business-like heels, and with my own shuffling movements I found myself struggling behind her. Her speed made me weak. It unnerved me. I wondered what I was doing here. Wasn't I supposed to be going home?

Helen had to stop at regular intervals to let me catch up, and each time her stare seemed more reproachful. She seemed to be trying to wear me down deliberately, but once past a certain point, I ceased to get weaker, finding instead a rising passion in my craw. A passion as yet unnamed.

'What do you think of our boy today? Polished that guy off pretty well?' she asked during one of her pauses. I detected the note of triumph.

'Pretty well, as you say.'

'Hell, we got paid a nice bundle too. Those insurance brokers pay well.'

'Insurance brokers?'

'Yes, didn't you see their banners all over the place? They're the sponsors. They love chess, you know. Gives them that air of intellectuality. Yes, intellectuality – that's the word. John's just so marketable right now.'

'I am not sure I understand,' I said, though I understood well enough.

'Well, whatever . . . you know. They pay well. John's got an appeal to the younger generation too – that rebel look. Insurance types like to be seen as intellectual and solid, but they like that little rebel edge. Helps them sign up the younger generation as well as the old fogies. You should be proud of him.'

The modern concept of sponsorship was alien to me, but I had seen long ago what happens when science sells itself to masters uninterested in the science itself. I guessed the same applied to chess.

My lips moved, but said nothing. I sighed and breathed deeply. Suddenly the passion had a name. Anger.

I had not felt such emotion in a long time. I was unsure where it came from or how to handle it and I walked with increasing distress in the wake of Helen Michaels' clicking heels. It all seemed too much, far too much.

I should say, perhaps, that this was a surprise. I hadn't expected the rush, hadn't expected to feel anything for John, and I was not prepared.

At last, the corridor opened into a brightly lit area outside the dressing rooms. A man I had also seen at the funeral was leaning against one wall. I assumed this was Sam Stylls, but we were not introduced.

Helen knocked at a dressing-room door and a woman's voice shouted back from inside, 'Come in, we're decent.'

Helen opened the door.

The brightness of the corridor flooded into the dressing room, catching John in its first wave. He was sitting in a wickerwork chair, staring at himself in a theatrical make-up mirror. He had a can of soft drink in his hand and he had discarded his stage jacket, so the full force of the T-shirt was on display.

He turned his head only when Helen Michaels said, 'This is your grandfather.'

The light was behind me, so as he stood, my shadow fell across him. Although I had not intended it, the shadow prevented us looking one another in the eye.

'Hello, John,' I said.

'Grandfather.' There was a small stammer in the word.

'You are dressed a little differently from the last time I saw you.' I nodded towards the T-shirt, indicating disapproval.

'These are my working clothes.'

'Working?'

'Helen says it's good for the image.' The boy looked uncomfortable.

'The managing partner of the sponsors is a firm left-winger,' Helen explained. 'We try to pander to their little prejudices.'

John gazed at me. He looked as if he was appraising a relic, something dug up from the past. I suppose in that he was right. I stood and waited.

'I see you're dressed the same,' he said at last.

'The only clothes I have. The price of poverty.'

'Too bad. Have I introduced you to Amy? Amy, this is my grandfather.'

'Hello, Mr Zalapek,' she said, as if responding to a practised cue. She was a good-looking woman, with a bright-eyed smile and long graceful limbs. I took in all I needed with the first glance.

'Hello,' I said, while my gaze switched back to John.

'John told me about you,' she added unprompted.

I nodded a brief acknowledgement, but that was all. She shrank backwards and I noted the timid withdrawal. I knew she had no place in the boy's life, but I considered her one line more closely for a moment. Then I said, 'This is the first time John and I have really met, my dear.'

'What did you think of my play today, Grandfather? Grandfather? That sounds odd.' John tried to deflect the conversation. I could see a certain nervousness in his face.

After a moment Helen leapt in. 'Hell, it was impressive, right? And did you see the crowd he drew? I mean, your grandson's going to be a star.'

'Marketable. Isn't that your word for it, Miss Michaels?' I said.

'Sure, he's marketable,' she admitted without apology. 'At his age! He's something, isn't he? We've already got one book in publication, two more in the pipeline. Not a fortune yet, but we're building up.'

It is difficult for me to describe what was now going on inside me. I am a mild man, made milder and weaker by age. Yet here I was, responding to Marion's plea. And responding, perhaps, to that instinct of family and parent-hood which I had never been able to exercise in 1940. It burst out of me, out of my old bones – something immature and oddly energetic.

I looked straight at him and said, 'The way you are going, John, you will never be a great player.'

He stared back in surprise. Something locked us together.

104

'Never be a great one...' I added, as if it were an aftershock.

His face contorted. 'Like you?' he said.

'I never was ... not at chess. Perhaps not at anything.'

'That's right,' he shouted, the explosion coming. 'You were too fucking *yellow*.'

After he said it, he slumped back, out of air like a spent balloon. His eyes fell closed in the shadows.

Perhaps as much as a minute ticked by – I don't know. Just the sound of several people breathing deeply.

I spoke first. But to Helen Michaels and the other woman, not to him.

In a very controlled voice, I said, 'Would you mind leaving us for a moment? We have a family matter to resolve.'

Amy opened her mouth, but no words came out. He waved her away without speaking and without looking at her directly.

I saw Helen appraising the situation more closely. She obviously considered objection, but found no threat in me, not after I had crossed her client and got him agitated. She smiled and turned on her heels, and followed Amy out of the room, closing the door behind them.

Without the light from the corridor, the room was almost dark. 'Do you mind if I turn up the lights?' I asked.

'Go ahead.'

I found the switch and, in the new light, I noticed the twisted slump of the boy's posture in the chair, almost foetal.

' "Fuck the Tories"?' I said, reading the T-shirt aloud.

'You've been away too long, old man. You don't know.'

'Oh, I know you, John. Marion told me you are a chess genius. But you never went to school past fourteen. You don't read too well and you can hardly write.'

'I don't need those things.'

'True enough. You inherited much the same mind as I did. And none of that did me much good in the end.'

'What the fuck's that supposed to mean?'

'I think you know.'

'Am I supposed to thank you for it? Or is that meant to be comforting?'

'What do you think?'

The boy shrugged. 'I have a good team around me. We're making money.'

I said nothing for a moment. I moved forward unsteadily, coming closer to the seated boy. He lifted his gaze and, for the first time, I looked at him square in the face.

His skin was pale as alabaster and the wild strands of hair fought with one another. Only his eyes moved.

'Look in his eyes' – that's what Marion had said.

I looked and the boy's returning stare struck out at me. I flinched but refused to withdraw, gazing back into the angry face, trying to absorb its blow.

Moving closer. I saw the eyes, the detail of them, like nothing I had ever seen. Dark and cratered, moon eyes, sunk deep into their sockets as if pushed too hard into the soft hollows of cheeks. The pupils gaped out at me with dilated chemical echoes. I saw them only as extra mouths screaming.

I reached for him.

Slowly, I said, 'Listen to me, John. You say you want money and that is all right. But I think you want more. You cannot live like this.'

'Can't I?' Still angry. Defensive.

'No. You know it.' I paused. 'Let me tell you where you are, since you do not seem to know. You're not a champion. You're not even a player. You're a pawn. You are in a freak show, John, a Victorian freak show. Helen Michaels is the ringmaster and you are her freak. The freakier you are, the more she likes it.'

'It's not like that,' he protested.

'Isn't it? Stick your great deformed head through the bars of your cage, my son. Look around. It is exactly like that. She can sell you as the boy genius chess player, the peculiar rebel without a cause. Look at your T-shirt. I think you were made to be better than that.'

106

I stopped, surprised at myself, considering the words as if they had been spoken by someone else.

His lips quivered, but made no sound. He started as if to rise from his chair but stopped himself and fell back.

I reached into my pocket and, with some difficulty, pulled out a piece of paper. My arthritic hands crushed it slightly as I held it out and dropped it into John's lap.

I took one last slow look into the boy's face. Thought I saw the beginning of a tear.

Then I turned and shuffled away, opening and closing the door without offering a goodbye.

13

John Harringhay slowly opened out the paper. There were chess moves written on it, scrawled in the old descriptive notation now virtually extinct. He understood it well enough though. '28 ... Kt × QB.' Knight takes queen's bishop. There followed a brilliant combination which he had never considered during the game. He looked at it closely. It would have destroyed the position.

'Fuck you,' he shouted in the direction of the door. He looked down and read the paper again. The words were pain.

Knight takes queen's bishop.

A single drop of salt water fell and hit the paper. The ink ran. He watched it run for a moment. Then he screwed up the paper and threw it against the wall.

Sam Stylls followed Zalapek as he left the theatre. He caught up with him in the alley outside. The old man was breathing hard and trembling, his bony body slumped against the theatre wall. His grandson seemed to evoke some emotion that was overpowering. The ancient eyes danced, staring at Sam as if struggling to focus.

'Mr Zalapek! Are you all right?' Sam said.

'I tried to help him, but I don't think it did any good. He makes me angry.'

'Well, at least you tried. Do you need a hand?'

He lifted the old man into a sitting position.

'That better?' Sam enquired. He squatted down. 'Thank you for trying.'

'I don't understand.'

'Thank you for trying to help him.'

'I have never seen anyone look like that.'

'It's the drugs.'

'Drugs?'

'Yeah.' Sam waited a few seconds. 'You didn't realize?'

Zalapek shook his head and mumbled. 'Apart from a few opium smokers, it was never . . . I mean, I never . . . I never saw it before.'

'Yeah, well it's common enough now. Ecstasy, whiz, speed, LSD – anything he can get in tabs. He won't inject. He's too scared.'

'You? I mean, are you?'

Sam smiled. 'No. I try to stop him. I think even Helen's realizing it's not such a smart idea. But it does no good. She wants him to play chess everywhere and make half a dozen personal appearances in half a dozen different time zones. Sometimes, the only way to stay awake is . . . Well, that's why . . . why he needs help.'

'I didn't know.'

'No, well, I suppose you had no reason to.' Sam examined the pavement for a while, then he asked, 'Where're you going now?'

'Home. I'll find a hotel tonight and then—'

'I am sorry, I thought you and he could perhaps . . .' Sam supported the old man as he tried to stand. 'Let me take you to our hotel. I don't think you're in any state to be alone.'

'I've been alone for many years,' Zalapek said defiantly.

'That's as maybe. But not tonight.' Sam looked at him. 'He has no one else, you know.'

'Yes. But he sees me as what I am, an old man – too ancient. I have no right to help him, no right to tell him anything.'

'He's wrong.'

Zalapek laughed for no real reason and shook his head.

'I'll call a taxi,' Sam said.

He got the reluctant doorman to telephone for him. When it came, he helped the old man get in and they drove away without another word about John or his problems.

*

109

Helen Michaels had crept away along the corridor. An unusual and unexpected smallness had gripped her. She went up from the lower reaches of the theatre with a desperate desire for a cigarette clawing at her chest. Signs saying 'No smoking' were plastered liberally over every available surface in the wings, so she walked out on to the stage.

The chess table and its chairs were still standing just as they had been an hour ago. The safety curtain was up; she could see out into the house with its dark rows of seats, and its carpets seeded with spilt popcorn, crisp packets and paper drinking cups. Corporate logos rolled discarded in the aisles – 'Pepsi' shrouded in red and blue. She took out a cigarette and lit it with a trembling hand. Her lungs clutched in the smoke. She felt her throat tighten and then, a second later, that blessed relief as the nicotine hit.

'God, I needed that,' she said to no one in particular. The vanished audience beyond the stage offered nothing but a faint echo and she slumped into a chair at the chess table. She looked down suspiciously on the sixty-four squares of black and white and the carved wooden pieces of the Staunton Notation figures that denoted the two armies. King and queen, rook and bishop, knight and pawn.

Cheap pieces of wood, she told herself. And yet she lived now in a world where the movements of those wooden fragments were all important, where some people – Sam Stylls for instance – saw whole lives, saw meaning, saw some kind of expression of existence in those same ridiculous fragments.

Fuck! She could not be part of it. Not because she lacked the wit, nor because she didn't see the niceties. No. It was because she lived in a far more solid world. Her reality had a watermark through its core and metal strip to prove its authenticity. She had no need of spiritual comforts. They were nothing but consolations to those who couldn't make material of their dreams.

But would she ever make money out of this bloody chess player? This was the question she kept asking herself. Was he worth the trouble? The latest episode brought her just that bit closer to the edge.

She crossed one leg firmly over the other so that the calf of one leg dangled down as if jointed to the knee of the other. She looked down at her black ladderless tights and blacker Cartier shoes. Two-inch heels – elegant but manageable, chosen to do business in. She thought of examples of deals she had done while wearing two-inch heels. How many pairs of shoes could she have bought for that money? Any number. Any number, she told herself. Why did she need this hassle?

Suddenly her mobile phone chirped up its piercing call tones. A cold feeling went through her and she wanted to hug herself. This was not the time, she told herself; she needed to get back to the business. Calls to make, calls to receive – that kind of thing. Slowly, she took the phone from her handbag, pulled up the aerial and answered.

She announced her name.

'Miss Michaels,' confirmed the voice on the other end, 'this is Kazuo Yakamura. We met in Singapore, you remember?'

'Of course, Mr YCK.' Helen stiffened herself, instantly perfectly calm. The professional instinct cutting in over anything else.

'I was very pleased with the result of our exhibition and very impressed with Mr Harringhay,' Yakamura continued.

'Yes,' Helen said, trying to prompt him to the point.

'I understand his contract is with Helen Michaels Associates . . . Your company?'

'Sure.'

'Then I'd like you to consider selling it to me.'

'What?'

'YCK sponsors several sportsmen around the world – a tennis player, a couple of golfers. My proposal is to buy your company, thus acquiring both the boy and your own management expertise. I would then have you manage YCK's sporting investments as a subsidiary . . . Are you interested?'

'Yes,' she said automatically.

'Very well,' he said, without hint of emotion. 'I am in California for the next two weeks, where I understand you will be coming shortly to our San Francisco tournament. Why don't you fly out as my guests? We can discuss it. I will send tickets . . . first class, of course. A little gesture by YCK. Oh, and please to bring Mr Zalapek, the boy's grandfather. He and I are old friends. It would be good to see him again.'

'I'm not sure that would be—'

'I will send the tickets in the morning. Shall we meet on Wednesday? That would be best for me.'

'OK . . . fine, that would be fine.' Helen spoke weakly, her words faltering, not knowing what else to say.

'Thank you. Goodbye,' Yakamura concluded.

There was a click on the line and her latest benefactor was gone.

14

Sam Stylls woke me in the night. After my near collapse, he had booked me into his hotel and paid for my room. He had even helped me to bed.

That was around four in the afternoon and I was halfway through my long sleep when I heard his insistent knock.

'What time is it?' I said, opening the door in the dark. I was only vaguely awake. I just wanted him to stop shouting in the corridor.

'Early. Very early,' he told me. 'I need you . . . John needs you. This is trouble.'

He didn't seem concerned that I was nearly naked before him – holed underwear and not much else, leaning on the door for support because my bones were too stiff and bent to stand of their own accord. What was I supposed to do? His face and the eyes behind the glasses were much too serious.

'I'll get some clothes,' I said.

He waited for me and then we waited together for the elevator, heading up to the seventh floor. For some reason, it stopped on the sixth and Sam had time to explain what was happening while we walked up the last flight.

'It started at dinner. Amy and Helen didn't get on. Then John joined in. I'm not sure whose side he thought he was on.'

'What happened?'

'Well, nothing right then. The night clerk woke me up. Said he was calling the police if I didn't do something. That was before Helen got up.'

'So what is . . .?' I started, but never got the question out.

We were coming along the corridor on the seventh floor, and there were two hotel staff outside Room 715. Sam nodded to them and banged on the door and assured whoever was inside of his identity.

Nothing happened for a moment. Then Helen opened the door. She was dressed oddly, in the bottom half of a trouser suit and a winter jumper. They were obviously the first things to hand when the hotel roused her.

As the door swung further open, the first thing I saw was a low table lying on its side with a leg broken. The remains of a chess set and a fruit bowl were scattered amongst its splinters. A banana had been trodden on, squashing a queen into the carpet; a baseless knight lay on what was left of the chequered squares. A little further round the room, one of the formal chairs had been smashed through a mirror above the bedside table and glass had spread like flakes of glitter over the floor. I saw Amy huddled on the bed, weeping softly, a coat thrown round her bare shoulders.

'This was John's room,' Sam explained.

'Where is he?' I said. For some reason, I suddenly felt a rod of iron rigid in my back. I hadn't felt so strong in twenty or thirty years. 'Where is he?' I repeated.

I saw Helen cast her glance across the room. The bathroom door was shut. I guessed that was what she was indicating.

'Is he on drugs?'

'On what?' Helen said, as if the question made no sense.

'Is he on drugs?'

'What are you going to do?'

I stared straight at her. 'I hear you're good at publicity?'

Helen thought for a few seconds. I saw the wheels turning behind her eyes. 'OK,' she said finally, and went towards the main door. 'I'll go outside and stop this getting any worse.'

'You want to wake up the manager?' I heard her saying to the two employees in the corridor. She had just the right tone. 'Look, let us deal with this first, OK? Go and wake up the manager if you have to. He knows me. I'm sure he and I can settle this without fuss.'

It took several attempts, Helen repeating the same message in different words, before they got her message.

'Take Amy to my room,' I told Sam. 'I want to be alone with him.'

'But—' he began.

'It's why you invited me here, isn't it?' I said.

He picked up a bathrobe from on top of a cupboard and wrapped it around the young woman in place of the coat. Then he led her away.

'He's mad,' she said. 'He's a madman.'

I heard her protests fading into the distance as I stared at the bathroom door. And I recognized her accusations. I had been similarly accused in 1938.

When I was finally alone and the room was quiet, I walked across to the main door and bolted it from the inside. Then I took the one undamaged chair and sat down and waited. Calming thoughts. I was worried. I had no idea what I was going to do.

About an hour later, the bathroom door opened. John was bare-chested, his bottom half loosely clad in a towel. Glass from the mirror had cut his upper arm, and I could see small shards of it glinting in the dark stains on his skin.

'I feel like shit,' he said.

I looked at him.

'What're you doing here?' he asked.

His eyes followed me as I moved around the bed to a suitcase. I pulled out a clean T-shirt and jeans and threw them on the bed. 'You had better go back and take a shower. You've still got glass on you. Then we'll deal with the cuts. I'll start cleaning this mess up.'

He looked uncomfortable and finally he said, 'I'm sorry.'

'Sorry for what?'

'I dunno.'

I picked up the chessboard and started retrieving the pieces, setting them up on the bed.

'You can keep saying the words, my son, but you don't know what they mean.'

'I'm sorry,' he said again. 'What with my mother and all.'

115

'This has nothing to do with your mother. It started long before then . . . Didn't it?'

'I'm a bad person,' he said, wallowing in it.

I waited for the moment to pass. I waited until it was no longer possible for him to hide behind his excuses. I waited for them to fade from that room and leave him naked. I waited for him to look at me.

'Is that your solution? After all these years?' he asked, looking at the half-prepared chess set. Only then, finally, did he look at me. 'I need help,' he said. 'I want to be straight . . . be a player again. I can't live like this.'

Oh yes, I know what it's like to be broken and misunderstood. I know what it's like to find things you never knew among the shattered pieces. We all walk a tightrope between failure and disaster.

In 1938, Ward Costello made me a chessboard with coloured counters instead of chess men. It was divided into four segments, each of sixteen squares, supported at various heights above the table.

When I first saw it, I was amazed. I muttered some inane exclamation.

He smiled. 'Heaven and hell. A little exercise for you. I said I'd help you. When you think, I want to involve every piece of your mind. Colour. Space. Logic. Emotion. These are the dimensions of the mind.'

I solved chess problems for a month on his strange board. Apart from a headache, I felt I had gained nothing. Friends told me I was insane to put my mind in the hands of this strange man. They said he'd have me babbling; they'd have to cart me away in a straightjacket.

I didn't believe them, but then I lost two games in a tournament very badly, I wasn't getting anywhere with the work on the nucleus, and I suffered a blinding migraine that lasted for two days. I lay in my college room in the dark, thinking this was all a terrible mistake. There were several papers I was supposed to read – the whole question of the

116

nucleus was becoming more and more mysterious with every published work.

As I was feeling a little better on the third morning, Marion came to see me. She wanted to tell me she had bought a new house on Banbury Road and Ward had moved in. She said they were tired of sneaking around his college rooms, smuggling her in and out past the gatekeeper.

'We're having a party,' she said, 'my friends—'

'I'm too ill,' I replied, 'and I have work.'

'Nonsense,' she scolded. 'You'll come. I've picked out a nice girl for you to sit with at dinner. Alice – you'll like her.'

'I'm ill,' I repeated.

She shrugged and smiled that smile of hers, as if she knew nothing. But I never quite believed that. She knew I would be there.

I got up and took a shower and went to the new house in the early evening. It was big and ostentatious – something like I'd imagined – but with almost no furniture inside.

Ward greeted me at the door. He was walking around in an old smoking jacket and dress trousers. He had no shoes on his feet.

'How do you like the house? Not quite finished yet. No chairs and we're sleeping on the floor. These traders never deliver on time,' he said jovially. 'People are going to be able to say I'm a kept man now.'

'Impressive,' I agreed.

I was by far the earliest of the guests, so Ward and I sat drinking in the library for an hour. I was telling him how impossible it was to solve this mystery of the nucleus.

'Maybe you're thinking about it in the wrong way,' he suggested helpfully.

'Don't you think I've tried thinking about it every which way?'

'Think about it in terms of my chessboard,' he said.

I looked blank.

'You should never think about a solution in terms of the problem. Too limiting. Problem and solution are sometimes quite separate. For example, you could describe the game of

117

chess and know nothing about the structure of my three-dimensional board. On the other hand, as a layman, you could look at my board and not perceive the game that was played on it.'

'One of your riddles,' I said. 'I hate them.'

'Well, tonight, dear Hayden, just for tonight, let's forget our stuffy thoughts and get drunk.'

'Is that your solution?'

'Oh, Hayden, there doesn't always have to be a solution for every minute of the day.'

With that he topped up my glass with rum punch and stood like a children's nanny administering cod liver oil while I poured it down.

'Have another,' he said. Then a little later, 'Have another.' And so on and so forth until I was quite unable to control what I was doing.

I met Alice when I was drunk, probably the first time in my life I'd been drunk. She was pretty and not dissimilar to Marion in many ways. She told me they had met at school; their fathers had done business together. When she asked me what I did, Marion cut in and said, 'Hayden doesn't do anything. He just thinks.'

They laughed and I knew I was failing, but the alcohol had taken me to such a point that I really didn't know how I felt about the problem.

Later, after dinner, I was sulking in the corner and everyone was drinking coffee, and the men were smoking. In typical Marion fashion, the women were encouraged to take cigars and join them, but only a few of them did.

I suddenly felt it within me. Inspiration – I don't know what else to call it.

Alice had walked up to me, cigar and brandy in hand. We had barely spoken more than a dozen words all evening.

'What are you thinking, clever man?' she asked in a voice made amiable by the drink.

I looked at her slurrily. Her face focused slowly and I saw the smile. That was the click of it, the pin falling from the fuse.

'How would I construct the world if I was God? That is the question. The problem. You're not interested—'

'Go on.'

I launched: the inspiration – everything that was pouring through the breached walls of my mind. And there I was babbling, just as everyone who warned me about Ward had predicted.

I was drunk and a public disgrace, releasing this torrent of thought on a young woman I had just met. I couldn't stop now. But I realized, as the words tumbled out of me, that I wasn't talking nonsense any more. I was suddenly making sense.

'How would I construct the world if I was God with solid atoms certainly not why would I do that it wouldn't make sense so what is mass then what is space I don't know perhaps it all goes together perhaps it's not supposed to make sense perhaps it's all made of green cheese like children say like we were lied to in the nursery perhaps it's all made of one thing perhaps it's all made of one thing. PERHAPS IT'S ALL MADE OF ONE THING ... Alice, perhaps it's all made of one thing.'

Alice was backing away uncertainly. She turned her head to other guests who were staring. I think they all thought I was having a fit of some kind. A particular woman who was the wife of a rich local jeweller came forward and grabbed Alice by the arm, pulling her away as though it was dangerous to be near me.

'He's mad,' she said. 'He's a madman.'

I remember Marion running from the other room, hearing the commotion. I was lying on the floor, rocking gently on my back on the carpet when she reached me. Ward was one step behind her, peering over her shoulder as they looked down on me.

'Are you drunk?' she asked.

I stopped, a wide-eyed doll with no control over arms or legs.

'Fermi was wrong,' I said. 'Imagine there was no matter.

Just different forms of space. Some with energy parcelled up inside them. It is all made of one thing.'

'Who is Fermi?' Marion asked. 'Do you want me to call an ambulance?'

'A straightjacket,' I mumbled. A madman's smile was spreading across my face. 'Send for the men in the white coats now . . .'

'That won't be necessary,' Ward assured her. 'Enrico Fermi is an Italian.'

'The Pope,' I cried, 'the Pope has messed it up.' I scrabbled to sit upright. 'Ward, I believe Fermi has already split the nucleus. In fact he did it four years ago. He just doesn't realize he's done it.'

'So he's a fool,' Marion said, 'just like you two.'

'No,' Ward said, 'it's more serious than that . . .'

He had a big smile on his face.

Enrico Fermi was wrong all along. He was not creating new elements; he was cutting the nucleus in half.

But until my night of drunken babbling in 1938, no one realized. We drank on into the night in triumph. I danced with Alice, and Ward and I sang bawdy versions of popular songs. Marion said it was a good job the new furniture hadn't yet arrived.

15

Non-stop showers doused New York. Steel-hard rain fell on the cold city and the aeroplane shifted uneasily on the runway after touchdown. She'd thought it would be fun to stopover in the Big Apple on her way home; she hadn't figured on the weather. She looked out of the aeroplane window depressed. Two weeks away and all she'd gathered were three lousy 'called-in' stories on Joe Beckett and the vague promise of a future interview with Kazz Yakamura. 'Certainly,' he'd said, 'we will arrange it the next time I'm in America . . .'

Fat chance – Kate Morris knew that kind of promise. She collected her bags and her composure, rented a hire car and headed for an address in Manhattan.

Margaret Jane Watson, a name she had picked out of various files downloaded from the Internet. Margaret Watson had been Arthur Beckett's PA in the late fifties. Never married, she'd retired in 1987. Kate had called her from Singapore.

Sure, she'd love to be interviewed, she had said; come to my home. Kate thought the woman sounded lonely and old, with not much to do in life. The problem would be stopping her, not starting her. Women like that would talk for ever. A long shot, but maybe she would say something that would help.

Kate's first sight of Margaret Watson was preceded by a strange conversation over the building's entryphone and the sound of six or seven heavy bolts sliding across the apartment door when she finally reached it.

'Hello, dear,' Margaret Watson said.

Kate swallowed. A smell of cat and overwarmed air hit her. The woman was all of twenty stone. Five foot nothing.

No wonder she took so long to come to the door. Kate wondered if she ever went out.

'Are you going to come in, dear? Would you like tea, my dear?' she offered. 'Coffee perhaps?'

Kate accepted instinctively before she realized how much of an effort it was going to be. Watching that overweight woman hefting herself into the kitchen, hearing the noises of toil from within, Kate didn't know whether it was better to sit and wait or rush up to help.

Sitting with the guilt, she found her gaze drawn to a sideboard where two pictures were framed in silver. The first, an old black and white, showed a twenties' couple very much in love. Kate reckoned the family resemblance and pencilled them in as Margaret's mother and father. The second picture was of a young woman, slim and beautiful, perched next to a sports car. The car and the clothes set the photograph in the middle fifties. It took Kate more than a minute to see that the woman depicted was Margaret Watson.

'Jesus, that she should come to this,' Kate said to herself.

As she gazed at the fifties' Margaret, she wondered at the lack of any other photographs. No husband. No children. Not even brothers and sisters. Margaret was alone in the world.

'I was pretty then,' said a voice from behind.

Kate turned, caught by surprise and embarrassed again. The present-day Margaret Watson was coming towards her, coffee tottering on an unstable tray. Kate stepped forward to take her cup before the contents formed too much of a lake in the saucer.

'Pretty like you,' Margaret continued. 'You look a lot like me. Like me back then.'

'Is that good?'

'Not if you go my way.' Margaret laughed and took her own cup and sat down. The chair heaved under her weight. 'Now what did you want to ask me, my dear?'

Kate took out her notepad, and flicked it open so the

pages circled round the spiral binding at the top. 'You were Arthur Beckett's secretary?'

'From nineteen fifty-three to fifty-eight, yes. But he called me a personal assistant. PA was the normal term.'

'Personal assistant . . . right.'

'I'm afraid I can't tell you much. Most of it was classified. I guess that still holds even now.' She scooped her saucer from under the cup, pouring the captured dregs back into the body of her coffee.

'Then tell me what he was like to work for,' Kate said.

'Oh, he was a dashing man. A war hero. Arty, they used to call him. He was so elegant. They based his code name on it, you know? They called him the 'Art Master'. Master by name and masterful by nature. He was a natural leader. He could persuade anybody of anything.'

Kate ummed to show interest, encouraging her to continue.

'Yes. It was a glamorous life in those days,' Margaret responded. Her eyes rolled into some past life. 'Being PA to Arthur Beckett helped me see the world. A girl from the worst streets of New York didn't get to see the world in those days. Travelling was for the élite.'

A cat came in from the kitchen, stalked purposefully across the carpet and sprang into Margaret Watson's enormous lap. The shock of its landing broke the spell.

'Oh, Kitty,' she said and stroked it.

'Arthur Beckett worked on the nuclear programme?' Kate stated a fact she knew, framed as a question.

'Yes,' Margaret agreed. 'He had been at Los Alamos. And he was involved in later testing in the Pacific as a . . . as a military advisor. I'm not sure I should say more.'

'People have accused him of being—' Kate began.

Margaret cut her off. 'People are liars. Arthur was never like that. I don't believe it. It seems these days everybody has filth written about them. Arthur can't defend himself, because everything he did was classified. So they use that as an excuse. Don't you go printing lies like that. He was a great man.'

Kate looked at the woman in surprise. My God, she thought, she's in love with him.

Margaret calmed down, stroked the cat once or twice. 'Have you ever met a man like that?' she mused. 'There's more important stuff going on inside ... Even if you only see him once, you know, don't you? Hold on to him, my dear, hold on to him ...'Course it helps if he's not married. Arthur Beckett'd never look at me. '

Kate didn't know what to say. She had for a moment the whiff of scandal, then it faded. *Unrequited love of the 280-pound woman.* She couldn't see the headline flying.

Kate drank her coffee and folded her notebook. '*More important stuff going on inside.*' For some reason, she couldn't help thinking of John Harringhay, and the questions she had wanted to ask Margaret wouldn't come to her, wouldn't flow like they normally did. In twenty minutes, she was downstairs and driving away.

Margaret Watson bolted her doors once more, finally feeling safe when the last one slid home. She poured milk into a saucer and fed the cat. Then she went to the telephone and made the phone call that would end her sad life.

Tokyo airport. The VIP lounge. Kazuo Yakamura was sipping coffee in an armchair, his carry-on luggage at his side. He had half an hour, maybe more, before his US flight was called.

A small disturbance at the reception desk heralded Yoshi's arrival. He walked over red-faced, exasperation showing.

'Why do we have to meet in these fucking stupid places?' he said, the question and its associated swearing in Japanese.

Yakamura Senior looked at him serenely. 'You are on a flight from Hong Kong. I am going to America. It seems our paths would have crossed here anyway.'

'Yes, but why not a meeting suite?'

'There are only two of us.'

Yoshi glared as if he thought that hardly mattered – the

old man was just too tight to pay out money for a little privacy. He swept up the Japanese newspaper from the nearest chair and flung it aside so he could sit.

'They weren't going to let me in, just because I forgot my card,' he complained.

'It's their job.' The old man put down his coffee. 'Have you news on the problem with our Chinese facility?'

Yoshi smiled. 'The official report will exonerate YCK. The SALWAR did not leak anything toxic.'

'And the children?'

'A statistical blip. Sometimes there are pockets of leukemia for no reason. This is . . . normal.' He hesitated on the word 'normal'. 'They did tests in the soil and found nothing. The plant is less than five years old; it's sealed tight.'

Yakamura's face tensed in thought. 'Their fathers were all our workers. Did they test the men?'

'No, why should they?'

Tension spread into worry on the old man's face. 'I don't know. There have been cases where damage to the father causes defects in the child.'

Yoshi shrugged. 'Not in China.'

'Suzuki says he is concerned at the integrity of some of the subcontractors used in China. You were in charge of this project, Yoshi. What do you say?'

'Suzuki is an asshole. And a troublemaker. You know it's him or me for the presidency. He sings the company song and swears his loyalty to you, then he stabs me in the back. You'd think he didn't realize I was your son. Don't believe you're safe, Father. He would bring both of us down in a blink of a butterfly's wings.'

Yakamura didn't react. He waited for a gap in his son's tirade. 'So, the plant was built cleanly?' he asked.

'It produces nuclear waste, Father. It contains enough uranium to contaminate a million square miles and make it uninhabitable for the next million years, or however long the stuff has to hang around before it stops killing people. I am not stupid enough to allow safety to be compromised in such a plant.'

125

Yakamura sighed, the tension falling, body loose in the chair. 'I'm sorry,' he said. 'Sometimes the business worries me. Soon we will have more toxic waste than we can possibly keep track of. The Europeans want to blast it into space. Create another waste dump up there. Maybe I'm getting old and cautious. I don't like it. One slip . . . one slip is all . . . I hate these reactors driven by fission, yet we have to build them.'

He thought about his conversation with Joe Beckett, almost glad Beckett had turned him down on the California project.

Yoshi stood up, taking his father's musings as criticism.

'I assure you,' he said, 'I tell you formally, I did not cut corners on this plant. This was the first of our new design. I was in charge. I made sure. It is company policy. And now the report has proved that. The affair is over. I'm going to have some sake.'

The old man nodded, content for a moment at his son's certainty. Worst fears are sometimes just that. We see the worst in everything; it is rarely that bad. Of course, Yoshi would not do such a thing. Admittedly he had been wild, the spoilt child underlying everything. You give them money but no attention, no time, then you regret it for the rest of their lives. Even at forty-five, those mistakes of childhood showed through. He blamed himself.

But Yoshi was maturing, the old man could see it – or thought he could. Yes, his wildest years were behind him. Besides, no one would cut corners in a nuclear plant . . . no one. It was unthinkable. Yakamura leaned back, imagining the company safe in his son's hands when he finally handed on the reins. The dream was a good one.

By now, Yoshi was buzzing around the lounge, sake cup in hand, looking confident. 'This trip of yours to the States – why?' he asked, returning to his father. 'The territory belongs to my vice-presidency. You're going on to my patch.'

'Yes,' Yakamura admitted. 'This patch of yours made no money in the last quarter.' He held up his hand. 'But this is not why I go there. It is more a social trip than anything.'

'You? A social trip?'

'Call it a holiday.'

'You've never had a holiday in your life.'

Yakamura smiled, flattered by the comment. Hard work was a code he lived by; he was proud of it. 'I am going to our chess tournament, the one we sponsor through the company,' he said. 'You remember that young man we saw in Singapore?'

'You have no real interest in chess,' Yoshi scolded. 'You pay out only for the image.'

'Oh, but I do. And he is such a player. I am thinking of buying his contract.'

Yoshi was unimpressed. He wrinkled his nose, squinting as though pained by something internal. 'A charity case! At least our golfers get on television. "YCK" embroidered on the shirt of some would-be Jack Nicklaus. I never even understood why that represented us in the eyes of the world. I remember this Harringhay. What is he going to do? Paint "YCK" on his chess clock? Maybe arrange his pieces in a big "Y"? Who cares?'

Yakamura looked at his son and shook his head. The petulance showed through – no calm, no judgement. Disappointing. Some things about your offspring will always disappoint and you will be blind to them. He rethought his optimism of a moment ago. Perhaps his son was more mature, but there was a distance to go. He hung on to the presidency of YCK only because he believed one day Yoshi would be ready to take the mantle. Sometimes he thought 'yes', sometimes 'no'. And now, once again, he wasn't sure.

He sank slowly in the chair. The weight of office and the prospect of the long flight hung on him, and he wondered if it would all be worth it. Why didn't he just sell his shares and retire? Leave YCK on a high. He could pass Yoshi a few million dollars on account and tell him to wait for the rest in the will. Death for Yakamura could not be many years away. Doctors told him to rest: his heart wasn't good. He said he'd rather die in harness.

127

16

I spent most of the month after that party in 1938 ensconced in my college rooms. I ate and drank in there. Sometimes I slept over the work. What I found as I slowly unlocked the secret of the nucleus was something far too hideous to believe. I wandered around like a zombie – all I knew and believed seemed to fight for ascendancy in my head, and I found myself drowning in questions I could not answer.

At the end of the time, I suppose I was close to cracking, a breakdown perhaps. Those people predicting dire things from my work with Ward might have had the last laugh even then.

I had started to talk to myself, to the wooden furniture of the room: the chair and table at which I worked, the hat-stand behind the door, which I had inherited from the room's previous occupant, and, most bizarrely, the walls of the little annexe that held my bed.

As usual, it was Ward and Marion who pulled me back and papered over the emerging cracks.

Ward had been away on the Continent for most of the second half of August, but he came to see me on the first day after his return. 'I hear you've been working,' he said. His manner seemed a little forced. 'Come on, it's still summer. Time to go on the river. Relax a little. I didn't improve your mind so you could burn it to a frazzle.'

'I am nearly done,' I replied, 'nearly there.' I don't think I even looked up. I wasn't ready to tell him. It needed the right moment.

'Sunday, then,' he insisted. 'Marion has Alice staying with us. You remember, from the party?'

I shuddered with embarrassment. 'She probably thinks I'm a madman.'

'At the time. But Marion told her you were a genius and not to be judged by the usual rules of behaviour.'

'I'm sure that went down well.'

'Sunday,' Ward said definitively. 'We'll call for you here at ten.'

By accident or design, Ward had picked the warmest day of the summer. He booked a boat to go punting on the Cherwell. Marion and Alice made up a picnic and iced two bottles of champagne and they were all at my door by 10.15, fashionably late.

'I booked this boat with the man down at Roley's Jetty,' Ward told us as we walked along. He swung the picnic hamper at his side. 'How are you at punting? It can be quite tricky for the beginner.'

'I've never been on a punt before,' Alice said, alarmed at the thought. 'Is it quite safe?'

Her unease made me smile. She smiled back and laughed at herself, and I grasped her hand. It was the first touch we'd had beyond the formalities of greeting and dancing. We walked along, fingers interlocked, and neither of us looked down at our hands.

Our boat was long and wooden, with a flat bottom and a little platform at the back from which you poled your way along. Ward cast us off confidently from one end and the boatman threw the tie ropes in to me as the current moved the boat slowly forward. We slid away with almost no noise.

Ward had taken his shoes and socks off and rolled his trousers above his knees. He poled us along for a while with the long pole the boatman had given him. Then he stopped and let the momentum carry us. He stood and sucked in the day. Willows wept over the gentle river and the fanned crowns of elms cast their shade over the boat. Every kind of graceful tree lined the river's bend, their tips almost meeting in an arch overhead.

The women submerged themselves in the soft seats amidships with their best summer dresses floating stylishly around them. I could not get over how similar Alice and

Marion were in appearance. In many ways, they could have been sisters, both dark and beautiful.

Presently, I got up and went to the back of the boat and took the pole from Ward. I slid the pole down in the water and made a great play of sweeping it across the surface to redirect our drift. The boat needed no redirection, but I felt I needed something to occupy me.

Ward sat down in the boat next to Marion and put his arm around her. 'If you did nothing but work while I was away,' he said to me, 'did you make much progress?'

'Yes,' I admitted, but then clammed shut as to what it might be.

'There's that genius again,' Marion chipped in. She turned to Alice. 'What do you think?'

She nodded, but said nothing.

'Ward, I have to tell you something,' I said.

'What?' he answered breezily. He was full of smiles. Too full – he seemed to be forcing himself to make the most of the day.

'I'm changing my direction.'

'Well, just pull the pole through the water a bit more.'

'No, you don't understand,' I said. 'I mean, I'm not going to work on fission any more.'

Marion looked shocked. Even Alice looked up.

'Did I hear you right?' Ward asked.

'Yes. You see, I've been doing some work. Theoretical work. I need to . . . retune my mind.'

'It's not like a radio, you know.'

I think he saw, even in that moment, what it was that I was not telling him.

I had read a copy of a private letter that week written by a German chemist called Otto Hahn. He was describing an experiment in which bombarded uranium turned into barium. He thought he must be wrong. How could uranium turn into another element so much lighter than itself? How, unless he had split the atom? It had to be nuclear fission, but to Hahn that was unthinkable. His results fitted my theory perfectly, apart from the absence of three little neutrons which I was sure must be leaping out of the middle of the bombardment. Neutrons are hard to find at the best of times. They have none of the normal handles scientists need to grab on to. They are too small to see, of course, but also they lack charge and they don't interact with anything very strongly. I guessed, correctly as it turned out, that Hahn and his colleague Strassmann had simply failed to observe them. It was an omission much easier than Fermi's mistake. But now we had two groups that had split the nucleus of the atom, and neither realized, as I did, what was happening.

Ward looked at me and, despite my reluctance, the story started to spill out.

'I can't believe why God would do this,' he said when he grasped it. 'It's like he's created a second tree of knowledge and dangled its apples right in front of us.'

'What are you two on about?' Marion asked. 'You are always talking riddles. Can I have a turn with that pole thing?'

She got up and started to move towards me.

'I will not take a bite,' I said.

'You already have, my friend,' he reminded me quietly.

'Can I have a turn?' Marion insisted. She was smiling and didn't seem to notice how much more serious Ward's expression had become.

He leaned aside and she came and took the pole from me. I urged her to be cautious.

'I'll be fine,' she protested, setting herself barefooted on the back of the boat. She took a firm stance, stretching her slender feet across the rudely varnished wood. 'This is not as easy as it looks,' she admitted.

'Don't fall,' I said.

'I won't.'

She laughed and slipped at the same time. The heavy pole held at chest height made her top heavy and unbalanced; it gave her no chance of recovery. We saw her petticoat, the soles of her feet, and then the eruption of broken white water as she slapped down into the river below.

'Marion,' Ward shouted. 'Are you all right, Marion?'

He scrabbled front first across the bulwark so he could peer over the boat's stern without the risk of falling in. From there, he saw her head bobbing above the water with her white teeth showing as she laughed. She slicked back her hair and said, 'Give me a hand to get out of here, will you?' We gripped one hand each and pulled her up. Her wet body emerged through the murky veil of the water.

I looked around at Alice. She seemed to have slipped away and become forgotten. I told myself I'd better pay some attention to my guest.

Later, when the champagne had been drunk, Ward revealed his conclusion from the Continental trip.

'There will be a war,' he said. 'There is no doubt. It cannot be avoided.'

'How can you be so sure?' Alice asked him.

His face was black and I saw all at once that I was not alone in straining to hold back what I knew.

'This generation of Germans is vengeful, spiteful and cruel,' he said. 'They are ungodly, and they are led by a man as ungodly as any who have walked the face of this earth. The right half of me is Jewish, and what I have seen done to my people in Europe makes me certain of it.'

'Ward, you're frightening her,' Marion complained.

'If she is frightened, she is the only one with normal emotions among us. Fear is the right reaction.'

'That's not nice,' Marion said.

'Not nice? War is not a thing to be "nice" or "not nice". It is far graver than that. It is the darkest of things. There you sit with your money and your privilege, believing that nothing can dent your world. There sits Hayden shutting away what he knows, because he believes his duty is to God.'

'All our duty is to God,' I told him.

Alice reached out for my arm. 'I believe that,' she said.

Ward sank slowly into his wooden seat on the port side. His face was ashen and I wondered what he had really seen on his trip. It seemed to have roused such feelings within him, as if he was reliving a nightmare he had seen before and knew the end of.

'I thought I had seen the war to end all wars,' he said. 'I was in the Great War and that's what they told us. I believed that somehow, in those mud-filled French holes, the trench foot and blood had taught us well enough.' He paused. 'Do you know what you have to do, Hayden? You have to build a bomb,' he said. 'You cannot uneat the apple. What you know is what you know.'

I gazed at him, lost. At the time, I did not understand him.

'In France, I stuck men back together. I have stood next to their beds and watched them suffer, and wondered if I shouldn't take up their guns and shoot them where they lay. Some of them would have thanked me for it. A few even begged. Even as a doctor, I was tempted. Civilization is not a state we are born to, it is a state we come to after violence. It is both brief and fragile.'

I think I was shaking my head. I could not believe, or rather could not bear, what he was saying. He posed questions too difficult to answer.

Ward pulled at his ear, which was a habit of his, then he held out his hands, one in the form of a fist. He approached me with it. 'Suppose I was to tell you that I held a fly in this fist. Now I know you would not hurt even a fly, Hayden, so when I ask you if I should crush this fly, you would be appalled.'

'Obviously,' I agreed.

'Quite so. But suppose this particular fly carries a deadly strain of – shall we say? – malaria. Shall I release it to bite Marion? To bite Alice? Do I not have a duty to stop it, Hayden? Would you crush it now? Here, you take it in your fist.'

He grabbed my wrist with his free hand, thrust his imaginary fly into mine and squeezed around my fingers so I was obliged to close them into a cage.

'What is the point . . .?' I complained, hoping perhaps his question would go away.

But he would not give it up. 'Answer me,' he said sharply. 'Answer me now, before you have too long to put your template of morality across the question.'

'But I—'

'Ah, too late. Too late,' he said with a sad shake of his head. He leaned back so far I thought he might fall into the water.

'I don't see . . .' I began. 'It runs against my belief.' Something cut me short.

I looked at him and realized he was crying.

'You used to tell me about Göttingen,' he said, 'the great triumphs of German physics.'

'They are weaker now,' I said. 'The Jews have been—'

I never finished the sentence. He was staring me straight in the eye.

'Tell me,' he said. 'Tell me about your belief. Do you believe, weakened or not, that the Germans could build a bomb from the principle of nuclear fission?'

I thought about Otto Hahn's experiment and I knew it was true. Sooner or later, everything I had written in my own work would be discovered somewhere else and by someone else.

He turned to me and my face was as bleak as his. What he said was right, prophetic even. I thought on it then, not wanting to believe it.

Ward's question hit the truth straight on. He knew the background as well as I did, the dominance of German science.

Back in the 1920s, Göttingen in Germany had established itself as the centre of the physics world. It was a small sleepy town, through which passed – either as student or visitor – every major name of the age: Heisenberg, Einstein, Bohr, Fermi, Oppenheimer. The list was endless. So dominant was their science that in 1925, when I turned ten, my grandfather, believing I would one day make a scientist, sent me to be taught German. He considered the language essential.

I thought about that now – what it said about the relative strengths of science and technology in the world.

'Yes,' I concluded, 'they could.'

He shook his head and turned from me. 'I thought so,' he said. I could almost touch his fear, taste it. Perhaps for the first time, I realized how clear his vision of the future could be. It frightened me.

After a while, I looked down and found my fist still clenched around his metaphoric fly. I opened my fingers and it flew away.

The Nazis had expelled the Jewish professors and students of Göttingen as one of their first acts of power, along with anyone else who resisted the change. The heart of the theoretical world was disabled, but the Nazis replaced it with what they called 'German physics', still some distance in front of the rest of the world.

The displaced talent reassembled in other parts of Europe – Fermi's group in Rome and Bohr's in Copenhagen being the most significant – and there was a gradual drift of scientists towards the West in the late thirties and early forties, borne as if on a wave by the advance of Hitler's forces.

Later, well after my small career was ended, it was largely men with Göttingen experience who helped the Americans assemble their atomic bomb. They were exiled Europeans in fear of Hitler and they joined a crusade which, finding Hitler gone, rumbled onwards and eventually slaughtered the Japanese.

Afterwards, Albert Einstein said that if he had known the bomb would be used against Japan and not Germany, he would never have raised a finger to help it get built. It seemed the world of science had been hijacked, conned, by masters who now cared more for power than the purity of the natural world we studied and struggled to understand.

PART TWO

17

YCK laid on a lavish reception for the chess tournament in San Francisco – players, officials, hangers-on. The company took the top-floor ballroom of one of the city's finest hotels and employed a catering staff of over a hundred. Yakamura himself took a suite of rooms one floor below.

It was there that Kate Morris got her exclusive interview. Yakamura gave her an appointment before the main wave of guests arrived. She was surprised. She had never thought he'd keep his promise.

Her only complaint was that Yakamura was late. She had been told 5.30, but when she arrived spot on time, she had to wait in the hotel lobby for a good hour.

Shoyo, the great man's assistant, came and apologetically explained the situation. 'YCK is immersed in takeover talks,' he said. 'A small subsidiary, but Mr Yakamura must attend. Please . . . to wait.'

She sat down and waited in the circle of visitors' chairs backing towards the hotel's fountain, a steel and concrete structure with shiny tubes like pointed organ pipes reaching into the air, one much higher than the others. She craned her neck round and watched it for a while. Water rushed up this main tube and sprayed into the air, falling artistically into the recycling pool with designer rocks below. She realized that, to her great surprise, she was not nervous. Perhaps she had finally paid her dues in journalism, cubbish excitement replaced by professionalism. She looked back on her foreign trip and suddenly it seemed that she had gained all the experience it had promised at its outset. The thought felt good.

She was gazing up at the enormous skylights in the roof

of the lobby when Shoyo finally called her. She smiled at him confidently and followed.

Yakamura wasn't quite as she expected, but she took it in her stride. He was older, not so much in age as in wisdom. Everything about him was so rounded, so formed. He explained the rise of Asia's industrial nations, the advance of technology, the response of the West. She wrote precise summaries of his words. None of his ideas seemed imbued with the normal personal prejudice; none of them seemed contrived or sullied with emotion. Kazuo Yakamura just told you the way he saw things. She liked him and, when they parted, he invited her to join the YCK reception.

As she was leaving his suite, she was surprised to see Helen Michaels going in. She shouted out a greeting, choking herself back when she realized she'd never actually been introduced to John's manager.

She felt suddenly like a schoolgirl again. A teenage crush. She was looking in on the whole Harringhay team. The only one she'd ever spoken to was Sam Stylls.

She resolved to seek him out, if he could be found at this 'reception'. She would, she told herself, somewhat belatedly take up the offer he'd made in Singapore: an introduction.

The ballroom for the reception was impressive, the size of a basketball court – shiny wood on the floor and furnished with purple velvet trimmings. Several hundred people were already circulating by the time Kate was admitted and announced by a bellowing man in a red dinner jacket. 'Imported from England,' she was told; 'used to serve at royal functions.'

Kate let it pass and walked out into the main throng. She took champagne from a stationary waiter, who had a surplus of glasses on a silver tray, and began her search.

Sam Stylls wasn't difficult to find. He was slouching by the caviar, just as he had been in Singapore. He was carrying a notebook computer and a newspaper, as if he'd stopped off on his way home from the office.

'This place remind you of anything?' she asked, sneaking up from behind.

140

He turned and smiled. For a moment, it seemed he wanted to hug her, but realized they weren't on those sort of terms. And anyway he had a Toshiba stuffed under his arm. 'What're you doing here?' he said.

'My home town, remember? Are you always camped by the most expensive food?' She leaned across him and plunged her finger inelegantly into an avocado dip. 'Have they got nothing to dip with? Tastes good, though. I'm getting used to these chess things. It's a whole new world for a journo like me. Is your boy going to win here? Where is he?'

'He's ... er ... doing better,' Sam said guardedly.

'I heard about his mother.'

'Yeah, he took it hard. But his grandfather's with us now.'

'His grandfather?' Kate said it as if it was worse than bringing your parents to school.

'They're over there. Didn't you know about his grandfather? Look, it even got a mention in your paper.' Sam brandished a copy of one of the local dailies. It was turned to show page five. Kate took it and looked at the photograph of John Harringhay and Hayden Zalapek arriving through airport immigration. The same two people were now standing not twenty feet away across the room.

'I'm a freelance, Sam, you know that. Besides, I wouldn't write for this shower if they paid me,' Kate said, then set to reading. '"The controversial English Grandmaster and his grandfather ... blah blah blah ... Their trip is sponsored by YCK." God, they get their name in everywhere. Who is this Hayden Zalapek anyway? Why is he so important?'

'I'll introduce you. Walk this way.'

Kate smiled. She hadn't had to ask him. He had repeated the offer and all she had to do was smile reluctantly and follow.

'John, let me present Kate Morris. Kate, this is John. And this is Hayden Zalapek.'

'Professor Zalapek,' John corrected. He looked at the intruders harshly, eyes staring. Kate noticed suddenly how

141

much clearer his eyes looked now than they had done in Singapore.

'Pleased to meet you,' Kate said formally. She gazed and drank him in. John was shorter than she remembered, but then she remembered him as a seven-foot giant, and he was barely six. He was wearing a dinner jacket for the occasion. She could see it was almost identical to his grandfather's. She looked for a family resemblance in the faces but could find none. 'Did you say, "Professor"?' she asked.

'My grandson flatters me,' Zalapek said awkwardly. 'It is not a title I answer to any more.'

'You're retired?'

'Miss Morris, I retired fifty years ago. If you will excuse me . . .' The old man grasped Sam by the arm and led him away.

Kate watched after them. Was this fate – the grandfather wanting to talk to Sam at that very moment – or something subtle the old man had picked up in her opening smile? God, was she being that obvious? She couldn't stop to figure it out now. She remembered how she had been gazumped in Papa Joe's.

'I saw you play in Singapore,' she told John. 'The YCK exhibition.'

He was gazing at his grandfather disappearing into the crowd. He seemed like a lost lamb for a second when finally forced to look her straight in the face.

Then he said, 'I was terrible there.'

'Terrible? No, I don't think so. Quite impressive, I thought. But then what do I know about it?' she gushed.

'Yeah, really shit.'

'You didn't seem it. I thought you were . . . the greatest player I have ever seen.' She wanted to bite her tongue off when she heard the words come out of her mouth. How could she have said something so crass, so uncool? She wasn't usually like that. Usually so controlled.

'How many chess players have you seen?' he asked.

Kate hesitated. 'Not many. As I said, what do I know?'

'I was on crack then.'

142

She took a step away from him, unbalanced for a second. The surprise wasn't the fact, but merely his admission of it. So bold. He sounded like a born-again Christian telling the sins of his past life.

'My grandfather saved me,' he continued.

'What did he do?'

John shrugged. 'He was there for me.'

'But he's only been with you ... what? It can't be three weeks since I saw you in Singapore.'

'I've not taken anything since I met him.' He hesitated. 'I never will again.'

He looked at her properly for the first time. 'You're beautiful, you know?' he said.

She blushed. She was beginning to think this was a mistake.

Then he said, 'I'll bet you get hassled a lot – especially in your line of work.'

'My line of work?' It took her a moment to see just how clearly he saw it. 'Yes ... Yes, I do,' she admitted.

'I can tell. I can tell by the way you try just a little too hard to be cool.'

She shot a daggered look towards him. She hadn't expected to be insulted. But then somehow he didn't say it as if it was meant to be insulting. It was more a statement of fact.

'Makes you lonely, doesn't it?' He paused. 'Do you know why that is?'

She gazed at him blankly. His thoughts seemed to tumble out lean and skinny. There was no fat on his words. No bullshit.

'They want pieces of you,' he went on unprompted. 'You've got something. It's like an undeniable fascination.'

'And that's what you've got?' she asked.

'I don't know what I've got. I've made money ...' He shrugged again.

'Do you really know why you're doing this?' she said.

'I don't so much play chess as belong to it.'

Suddenly he laughed, and she saw his face light up and laughed with him.

'You were . . . sort of part of the board when I saw you play,' she told him, 'crack or no crack. Is that what belonging means?'

'Come tomorrow,' he said. 'I'm playing Antropov. If Singapore was a revelation, tomorrow I'll be every book of the Bible.'

When Helen came and whisked him away, saying sorry but John just had to meet somebody, Kate thought through that last phrase. *'Every book of the Bible.'*

He was a bag of surprises. And more, much more than that, she was drawn to him and the roughness of his manner – a kind of seasick combination of attraction and disorientation.

Two old men meeting after fifty and more years. Sam Stylls watched them as they went through the rituals of greeting, feeling like a voyeur as years of history turned back. Stiff arms and stiff legs – the rust of years falling from the bones.

At first, Hayden Zalapek did not recognize his friend.

'Hayden, it's me . . . Kazz.'

'Kazz?'

Sam looked at Zalapek's eyes. This pale Japanese dressed in American casuals did not seem to register in the old man's mind.

'Kazz Yakamura . . . you know me,' his host said.

At last, Zalapek smiled. 'It's been a long time.'

Yakamura opened his arms, stepped forward and embraced him.

'You look good, my friend,' Yakamura said.

Sam smiled at the impossible flattery. The old man was not 'good', unless the sheer fact of being alive counted. The pair talked for a minute about their well-being and their ravaged faces, and the gruelling consequence of air travel on the octogenarian. It was all amiable stuff. Sam wondered at the innocence of it, a meeting so filled with unpolitical delight. For a moment, he warmed to Yakamura – a man he had previously regarded with suspicion because of his interest in Helen – but then the conversation turned unexpectedly.

'What happened to you?' the Japanese asked.

Zalapek drew back. 'What happened?' he repeated. 'I don't know.'

'What happened to the work?'

Sam saw the old recluse suddenly in full retreat, the smile sucked in and recanted like a trust given too soon.

'Is that why you brought me here?' Zalapek asked.

'No . . . not at all. Why?'

'You don't know.'

Pain spread across his face as if an old wound had ripped open. Sam watched the muscles tensing curiously, like cracks spreading in a stressed sheet of glass. He thought he knew Hayden Zalapek, thought he was a kind, uncomplicated man who had come to his grandson's aid, thought he was a rational voice who would be the boy's redemption. He had watched him emerge from a London hotel room, arm around the fallen maestro, and he had seen the vacant glow fade from John's eyes since. Sam had positioned Zalapek with those thoughts, but now he saw him turn, saw his face greyed in some more complex, some more basic, emotion. What was going on here?

Yakamura reached out his hand. 'Hayden, all I know is the work didn't see the light of day. The world misses what you had even now.'

Zalapek stared straight through him.

'Hayden, you know I have kept it these years, our secret. And if you say so, I will always keep it.'

'Just as well . . . Just as well.'

Then Zalapek turned and walked away slowly and decisively.

'Hayden, please . . .' Yakamura called after him, but Zalapek never turned.

Sam watched in amazement. 'What was that about?'

Yakamura turned to Sam, looking at him as a young and

145

naïve questioner. 'You don't really know who he is, do you?'

'I know he was a physicist, a famous one ... Not a bad chess player either.'

'As I say, you don't really know ...'

Helen called them together when their taxi was due. Sam and John came crawling from separate wallflower positions in the ballroom.

'Where's your grandfather?' Helen asked.

Sam gave the answer. 'He's taken a taxi already. Said it was the jet lag.'

Helen shrugged and put her arm on John's shoulder, guiding him towards the elevator. They got in and pushed the button for the ground. The elevator chugged down to the second floor, then rebounded through the fifth, fourth, seventh and finally stopped at the third.

'Have you been messing with this thing?' Helen said, this time lasering the question at John.

John looked sheepish. 'It's good, isn't it?'

'What do you mean "good"? It's a waste of time.'

'You couldn't do it,' John answered.

'Don't think that makes it clever.'

She flounced past him out of the elevator and took to the stairs. She was downstairs, waiting impatiently by the taxi door, before John and Sam could catch her up.

'You'd better get in,' she said. A hard look was fixed on her face.

They travelled ten minutes in complete silence before Sam got the courage to speak again. He was buried in thoughts of Hayden Zalapek and Kazuo Yakamura, turning over their meeting in his mind but making no sense of it and finding no new angle to view it from. It was like a chess puzzle to him. What did it mean? *Is that why you brought me here?' 'You don't really know who he is ...'*

'What did Yakamura say to you?' he asked Helen suddenly.

Helen seemed surprised. 'He wants to make a deal. Why? Does that bother you?'

'I thought you wanted to extend my contract. Don't you think I ought to know who I'm working for?'

Helen thought for a moment. He could see she wasn't comfortable talking in front of John.

'It's a good deal,' she admitted. 'He buys the whole of the Helen Michaels company. I get to keep my job and he puts a whole pile of management work my way.'

'You'd still be my manager?' John butted in. Sam saw alarm in his face, panic almost. This was what she had been trying to avoid. She knew John well enough to know what would be coming.

'Sure,' Helen soothed.

'And Sam'd still be with us?'

'That's up to Sam.'

'Sam?' John turned to him.

Sam had listened, putting two and two together and coming up with five or six. 'You aren't so sure, are you?' he said, gazing at Helen. 'I thought only money ruled these decisions.'

Helen didn't answer and John looked anxiously from one to the other.

'Sam, are you gonna be with us?' he repeated.

'She's not going to sell,' Sam said. He was uncomfortable saying it. He couldn't put his finger on her objection, but he knew it was there, some feeling she would never admit to. He felt a wave of triumph. He hadn't liked the idea of John's talent being owned by anyone, and he hadn't liked the feeling that Helen might sell herself.

'No, I'm not going to do it,' she said quietly and sank deep into the seat. 'Yakamura didn't like it. In the end, I – I walked out of the meeting.'

Sam should have felt easier, but he didn't. That was two knock-backs and it suddenly felt as if Yakamura was dangerous. It was instinct rather than something tangible. He knew something about Zalapek, and had argued with Helen. It suddenly struck Sam how much power might rest with the president of a big multinational corporation. It sent a shudder through him.

147

18

I think it was in that hotel room in London that I decided what I must do. I watched him 'coming down' – I'm sure that's the phrase.

He was saying, 'I'm never going to do this again. Help me. I'm never going to do this again.'

I couldn't believe he had played chess in that state. Played and won. Perhaps, after all else, it was the thought of what he might do when he was free from his demon that drove me to stay with him. I wanted to see that.

I can't say the next week and a half was easy. Dependencies are not so lightly exorcized, be they drugs, alcohol or any of a hundred other evils. But I shall leave those ten days private and unsaid. Call it a family closing ranks.

At the end, when John and I emerged – cleansed as we were – Helen Michaels asked me to accompany them to America. I could not fathom her reason, but when John asked as well, I agreed.

I thought my wartime dangers had long since faded and I told myself my exile had become more habit than necessity.

After Helen had helped me with the tedious formalities of passport arrangements, the transatlantic journey itself was accomplished in half a day. It put me in mind of the last time I was in the United States. Not that we made the distance in six or seven hours. We went by ship back then. It was 1939.

Alice and I had married in January of that year and almost immediately set sail for a honeymoon. Actually, I suppose it was as much working trip as honeymoon, though I never thought of it that way. There were universities to be visited and perhaps a pilgrimage as well.

For me, the Holy Grail of science was Albert Einstein. He

had by then fled to America and taken up residence in Princeton. He was the most famous figure in science, a totem, a role model, a grandfather figure for all those who, like me, sought a kind of universal truth in the laws of nature.

I had with me a letter of introduction from Neils Bohr. Bohr had been many times to my laboratory in Oxford and had visited his friend Einstein only a month before. I sent his letter by messenger to Einstein's office at Princeton, adding a note of my own to say I was in New York with my wife for a few days. Back came an invitation to take 'English tea' at his house.

Alice didn't complain too much. She thought it grand to be invited to the great man's house, but when we arrived she became very shy and nervous, and when she shook him by the hand she couldn't find words to speak. He seemed to be charmed by the awe in which she held him.

For myself, I had seen Einstein once before. He gave the Herbert Spencer lecture in Oxford when I was but a faceless undergraduate. I noticed the way he had aged in the years since. His hair was white and as wild as I have seen in the most exaggerated cartoons of his face. His clothes were scruffy. He took my hand and pumped it with an iron grip.

'I have heard great things of you,' he said in his thick German accent. 'Come . . . come and meet my . . . come into my house.'

I believe he was going to say 'family' or perhaps 'wife', but he stopped himself. His own wife, Elsa, had died. Some said the event unhinged his mind. I don't hold to that view.

Absent-minded? Surely. But he was approaching his six-tieth birthday. Why not? But that is not the same as unhinged. His eyes had a focus on nature that seemed to be nailed into reality. He knew exactly what was happening and, in the next few minutes, he demonstrated a scientific overview which no one else managed in those uncertain times.

'Neils Bohr recommends you. This is an honour you should not take lightly. Neils does not recommend many.'

'I am flattered,' I said.

'I have read your work. It is not flattery . . . Have a piece of cake.' He offered a plate of cakes first to Alice and then to me. 'But I notice nothing in the last two years,' he added.

'No,' I admitted.

Einstein shrugged. 'Who am I to criticize? I have not published a paper of significance since . . .' He hesitated, laughing at himself. 'They gave me the Nobel Prize in 1922 for work I did in 1906.'

He bit into his slice of cake, the crumbs exploding across his cheeks and catching in his moustache. I did not know what to say, and when I looked at Alice it was clear she was not about to come to my rescue. There was an awkward silence and I rushed to fill it with the first thing that came to me.

'There are reasons for not publishing,' I said.

He nodded. 'Neils brought me a copy of the Hahn and Strassmann work,' he said. 'In his letter, he tells me I should ask you about it.'

'Me?'

'He says you have a model of the nucleus.'

'I am not working in that area any more,' I said.

He did not look surprised. 'There is a young man at Columbia called Leo Szilard,' he continued, brushing at his moustache with a fingertip. 'Leo warns us all that we should abandon work in the area of uranium. He says it will be the death of humanity. Is he correct, Dr Zalapek?'

I stared at him blankly.

'Come, come,' he said. 'I think you know the answer.'

'Why are you asking me?'

'Because Neils is never wrong about such things. Szilard is irrelevant. He will be forgotten by history, because he feels rather than knows what it is he warns us of.' He hesitated. 'If I gave you a piece of paper, would you write it down for me?'

I shook my head.

'Tell me then,' he said, 'what is it you are working on now . . . instead of this uranium?'

150

I smiled wanly. 'Chemistry,' I told him.

'Chemistry?' he exclaimed. 'Is this a subject for a nuclear scientist?'

'If you can split the nucleus, why can't you put it back together?'

'But surely that has already been done. Fermi added protons and neutrons to the large elements long ago. It was of no value. Splitting the atom releases energy, so it must always, by logic, consume energy to put it back together.'

I leaned over and selected another cake from the plate. I examined it in close detail and then took a bite.

'Have you ever looked at the weights of hydrogen and helium?' I said.

'What of them?'

'If those who measure the weight of the neutron are correct, and if the helium nucleus is really made of two hydrogen centres – protons, in other words – and two neutrons, then the helium nucleus is remarkably light. By your own theory, E does equal mc^2. I can produce remarkable energy from such a transition – a fusion of components where mass is destroyed.'

I could see his eyes ticking on the proposition.

He said, 'The best measurements of such things are difficult to grasp. The weight of the helium nucleus appears to be approximately one per cent less than the weight of its components.' His eyes ticked again. 'The energy released from one unit mass is equivalent to one per cent of the speed of light squared.' He pursed his lips, working the calculation in his head. 'The speed of light is 300 billion metres per second. The energy is of the order of 250 thousand kilowatt-hours.'

'Yes, from a single kilogram of fused matter,' I said. 'With it, I could meet the energy requirements of a whole town for several months.'

'But this is not possible,' Einstein complained. 'People have conjectured similar things before. They say the sun uses such a reaction, but it could only be started at billions of degrees Celsius. There is not enough energy in the world to start such a reaction, unless you propose to make a miniature sun in your laboratory. This is a trick of physics I would like to see.'

'I am not going to do it by physics,' I said. 'I am going to do it by chemistry.'

'Chemistry? This is a joke?'

'Chemists already know how to make heavy water. That is halfway to the goal,' I said.

Alice coughed, focusing on a word she half recognized. 'What is heavy water?' she asked nervously. To her, water was water. The concept that it should be 'heavy' was ridiculous.

'Your husband is a clever man, my dear,' Einstein assured her. 'Heavy water, we should explain, is simple H_2O, except that one of the Hs – the normal hydrogen atoms – is replaced by what is called deuterium.' He looked at me. 'In your model, this has a neutron as well as the normal solitary proton?'

I nodded. He turned back to Alice.

'What he is saying, you understand, is that deuterium is half a helium nucleus.'

'Oh,' Alice said, and returned to her unfinished cake.

Einstein thought for a moment, then he shook his head. 'What you are proposing is "cold fusion". You may be as clever as Neils says, my son, but you cannot do nuclear reactions with chemistry.'

'Why not?'

'Is that what your nuclear model tells you?'

He smiled. He had me. He was beginning to glimpse what I was trying to hide. Perhaps he knew it from the beginning. He just needed to hear me say it: *I had stopped work on the fission of uranium because of what the model said. That's why I was now trying to do fusion by chemistry.*

I thought for a moment, his eyes watching me. I wanted to tell him. Oh, how I wanted to tell him! This was Albert Einstein and I wanted to tell him what I had found.

Slowly, I took from my pocket the little wooden model I had constructed of uranium-235.

'Two hundred and thirty-six balls,' I said.

He raised his eyebrows, his attention focused like a magnifying glass upon my words. He leaned forward with a nod.

'The neutron is absorbed into the structure,' I continued. 'It doesn't split the nucleus, so much as render its mathematics unstable. This is fission.'

Einstein pursed his lips a second time. A residual crumb fell from his moustache. 'That would explain how it is possible to break apart something which withstands the most brutal attack by other means.'

I took the model in both hands and twisted it. A barium nucleus came away in my right hand; one of krypton remained in my left. Three black wooden balls fell and bounced on the table. One lodged in an untouched slice of cake.

Einstein looked down at them. 'Bang!' he said ruefully. His eyes rose and focused on me. 'Szilard is right then . . .'

I tipped my head towards the floor.

He stood up suddenly and walked to the window. Looking out, he hummed a tune to himself as though alone in the room. Alice and I gazed at one another. After a minute or so, Einstein turned and walked back towards us, and sat down as if nothing had happened.

'I urge you to forget your chemistry,' he said. 'This is not a time when we scientists can choose our subjects. Perhaps we never can.'

'I thought you were against war.'

'Everyone is against war,' he replied. He sat looking at the fallen neutrons. He knew as well as I did the chain reaction they would trigger. 'If you will not use it, you must guard it well . . . and guard yourself.'

He nodded in sympathy, but never gave me another word of advice.

A few months later, on 2 August 1939, Albert Einstein signed a letter to President Roosevelt. The relevant text read:

> Some recent work . . . leads me to expect that the
> element uranium may be turned into a new and
> important source of energy in the immediate future.
> Certain aspects of the situation call for watchfulness
> and, if necessary, quick action on the part of the
> administration. I believe therefore that it is my duty to
> bring to your attention the following . . . It is
> conceivable that extremely powerful bombs of a new
> type may be constructed.

Almost exactly six years later, the atomic bomb dropped on Hiroshima.

I consider those few words I spoke to him to be the closest I ever came to publicly revealing the secrets of my work on the nuclear model. Whether I came to his house with the intention of telling him, or at least warning him of what I had found, I cannot say. It seems, all these years later, that it could have been my unconscious intention. Why else would I have taken the model?

Neither can I be certain that what I did say made any difference. There were plenty of others making conjectures about chain reactions in uranium and Einstein had many young scientists arriving at his doorstep to plead their case or seek advice.

In truth, I don't think I really believed in the bomb at that time. That is to say I did not grasp it. It was too enormous, and although I saw the terrible inevitability of the chain reaction – the growing piles of fallen dominoes that Ward Costello tumbled on that café table in Oxford – I could not hold it or imagine its consequence.

No, at the time, although the chain reaction scared me, I would have abandoned uranium anyway simply because of the sheer mess it made. It seemed to me inconceivable that one could control the energy supply from uranium without producing tons of radioactive waste, and although the effects of radiation were little known in the thirties, I had already witnessed the cancers that killed many leading workers in this area.

When my theory of nuclear structure took its final shape,

I began to see the sources of invisible radiation that did the damage and I realized fission could never be the universal energy source it had at first seemed.

It was with that thought that I came to the problem of cold fusion, the attempt to fuse protons and neutrons into helium nuclei. I beavered away on it from the latter part of 1938 through the whole of 1939. I tried to forget the other work.

Even so, Einstein was right: in the end, the bomb was real, and it was the knowledge of uranium and its hideous promise that endangered my life and the lives of those around me.

19

On the television, Joe Beckett stood framed behind a lectern, concluding his speech.

'. . . And I say to you, I am the man to lead you. I am the future.'

Wild applause. A wave of the hand. The picture changed. An anchor man with Joe's smile but lacking his sincerity cut into view.

'Latest polls put Joe Beckett way out front in the early running. Last week's shock announcement by Senator Mike Craddock that he would not run has helped push voters towards . . .'

Arthur Beckett wheeled himself away from the television and picked up the remote control from his office desk. He clicked it, killing the picture. A smile battled with the frozen muscles of his face. His pride dwelt long after the brightness of the screen had fallen back into the vacuum behind it.

'It's going to be ours, Joe, it's going to be ours,' he said aloud.

There was no one with him. He spoke without expecting an answer, but at that moment, there was a knock at the door, and someone shouted, 'Father, are you coming to breakfast?'

'Joe, come in,' he called back. 'I was just watching the recording of last night's speech. You sound better every time you talk about those issues.'

Joe dipped through the door. He was carrying his seven-year-old son, Joe Junior, clasped to him like a baby monkey wrapped around its mother.

'Oh, you too,' Arthur cooed, reaching his good hand out towards his grandson.

'Daddy made the paper,' the boy said.

'He did? Don't worry, Joey, he's going to be in the paper lots from now on.'

The older Joe put the boy down and watched him race to sit on an arm of the old man's wheelchair.

'Big splash. Look at page four,' Joe said.

He spread the broadsheet across the desk. Arthur wheeled himself into position to view it, the boy now leaning on his shoulder.

Pictures of Joe Beckett's day covered three-quarters of the left-hand page. Joe smiling. Joe speaking. Joe shaking hands with important-looking people. It took Arthur nearly half a minute to glance at the opposing page.

'YCK TOURNAMENT KICKS INTO ACTION TODAY.'

'Fuck!!'

'Father, please, not in front of—'

Arthur jerked in his chair and the boy spilled off to the side, confused as he looked back at his grandfather.

Before them was the face of John Harringhay pictured at the airport, and next to him, named in the caption, was Hayden Zalapek, grandfather of YCK's latest prodigy. Sam Stylls and Helen Michaels were hangers-on at either side.

Arthur's face whitened. In that cheek where muscles still worked, a tic jumped sporadically.

'What's up, Father? You look like you've seen a ghost.' Joe said.

Arthur, still gazing at the open page: 'I have . . . I have, son.'

His hand reached for the phone. 'Don't wait for me,' he said. 'Take Joe Junior. I'll join you in the breakfast room in just a minute.'

Of the four games taking place that day, one stood out. Victor Antropov was a veteran Grandmaster, nearly sixty, past his prime in chess terms. John Harringhay, playing black, blew him off the board in the chequered game's equivalent of a street mugging. In eighteen moves, the young man used only eleven minutes of clock time. Antropov used an hour and forty minutes of a two-hour allocation before resigning in abject despair.

John stood at the centre of the quartered stage for a full five minutes while applause echoed around him. He was wearing a pure white suit, and although he closed his eyes, he no longer seemed wholly timid in the spotlight of success.

Sam watched him come down from the stage. He patted John on the back and John smiled and disappeared into his dressing room, already peeling off the jacket and tie he hated.

Sam didn't follow. He waited outside, drinking the echoes of the applause still draining down from the auditorium. He leaned against a wall, blank-faced, wondering about this turn of things, polishing spectacles that were already clean. The old man seemed to have brought a change in John's play beyond Sam's wildest imagination.

He saw Kate Morris scuttling towards him out of nowhere, big smile fixed on a nervous face. She called out a greeting, a little forced and overbearing as if pre-recorded and played back at too high a volume.

'What did you think?' Sam gushed, returning the smile.

'A journo like me? We have no opinion,' she began. Then she stopped herself, acknowledging something real. 'You almost feel his intensity. I've never seen . . . felt anything like it,' she said, the words breaking out of her in a single breath.

'I'm sure I haven't either.'

'And he's so different from . . . I mean, that was amazing, but today . . . Am I wrong? It's like he's not the same person I saw in Singapore.'

'I know,' he said. He looked around as though checking for something or someone. He realized – consciously or unconsciously – he was making sure Helen was not within earshot. 'The old man,' he added. 'He's got John's head straight. I knew – knew as soon as I first saw him. This boy's going to be the greatest chess player alive. That's not just Helen's hype.'

Kate raised her eyebrows, indicating a certain disbelief.

Sam lowered his voice. 'You know, it was me brought them together. I think it could be the best thing I ever did.'

'Can I go in, Sam?' she asked, nodding towards the door.

'Sure, he invited you, didn't he?' he said. 'Helen's away somewhere, handling the press, I think.'

He watched her knock and heard the call from inside. Then he moved away and left them to it.

Helen was coming down the steps from the stage. She was muttering under her breath, something about a 'bloody journalist'.

In a move he thought was unusually bold, he simply stood in her way.

'If you're going to sell the company, we need to talk,' he said.

'I told you I'm not going to sell,' Helen snapped.

'We need to talk anyway.'

Perhaps thrown by his approach, she stopped short. For a second, she was blank, then she said, 'Yeah, maybe we do. Do you know anywhere to have dinner in this town?'

'A few places, I guess.'

'Fine. Let me go back to the hotel and freshen up. You can take me to dinner. Where's the old man?'

'He headed back half an hour ago, still complaining of jet lag.'

'Good, we can be alone then.'

The idea of privacy came like a concession flung over a wall. Sam caught it and pulled it towards him. 'OK,' he said, 'just the two of us – a date.'

He didn't really know San Francisco. When he got back to the hotel, he sneaked down to ask the bellboy to recommend a decent Chinese restaurant. Then he ran back up the stairs and changed in double-quick time.

Twenty minutes later, Helen met him in the lobby looking truly transformed. She was wearing a calf-length dress in black silk, small slits up the side. She had her usual perfect make-up, but somehow in its evening shades it seemed to soften her. He looked from head to toe and her appearance silenced him for a moment.

159

'Gosh! Beautiful!' he exclaimed in a sudden uncontrolled rush.

'Come on, let's go then,' she said. She took his arm and led him outside.

It took him a taxi ride and three aperitifs to rediscover the power of proper speech. By then, Helen had downed an equal number of gin and tonics herself. She was starting on the fourth. It did not occur to him that she might be just as nervous.

'How'd you start into this stupid game, Sam?' she asked. That broke the ice.

'I was a player,' he said, 'before I was an analyst.'

'Yes, but you were a great analyst. I know. I took up references. You had as much skill at stocks and shares as you ever did at chess.'

'Ah, but I love chess. I just wasn't good enough to be a player.'

'Really?' She seemed genuinely surprised.

At that moment, the waitress arrived with the first course – crispy duck – and they busied themselves with the pancakes and sauces. Eventually, when the preparation had reached its natural conclusion, Sam launched a little self-revelation.

'I was thirteen when I met Bobby Fischer,' he told her. 'It was 1959. He was sixteen. I sat down at a chessboard with this wiry kid from Brooklyn. Four hours later, when I was shaking his hand, I knew I would never be world champion. The hardest thing I ever had to admit. When your life has one meaning and suddenly you find that, by some unfair distribution of talent, you will never become what you wanted to be, or indeed what you deserve to be, what can you do?'

He waited, wondering if he'd said too much, if she'd respond in kind. He thought he must be stupid: they were grown adults, not kids playing a secret-for-secret game.

'So that's how you got started as an analyst?'

He nodded.

'You know, I wanted to be a writer,' she said. She had

160

begun the construction of her second pancake. She looked up while he was still considering this strange admission. 'It's true. I studied Literature at Cambridge, and then pow! Out into the big bad world. I was going to make my fortune. In three years, I had one short story in *Cosmo*. I couldn't make it pay. I lived by working part-time for a little provincial newspaper. Hard times. Small damp offices, stuck down a back street where the rent was cheap.

'The newspaper was printed on this press that had seen its best days at the beginning of the century. Half the staff used to chase round on a Thursday making running repairs into the small hours to get the week's edition out on time.' She halted herself, considering something she did not seem to be able to translate into words, and then said, 'I lived in the splendour of a twelve-foot-square bedsit backing on to railway tracks. It vibrated like a tuning fork when the Inter-City torpedoed past. I had an old portable typewriter and I would sit in front of it in almighty worship. Like some naïve asshole, I believed that in squalor I was bound to produce great art. Something profound was going to flow down my arms, out of my fingers and on to the tatty recycled paper. Of course, it never did . . . Don't you dare laugh, Sam Stylls.'

'I'm not laughing,' he said, though he sensed the influence of the gin on her words. He stared at her fiddling frantically with the gold chain around her neck. 'But don't tell me anything you don't want to,' he advised her.

'Like in Singapore?' she suggested. She smiled painfully. He figured she probably wished she could take that back. 'Listen, I'm under control now,' she said. 'What would you like to know? Ask anything.'

'What do you think of John's grandfather?' he asked.

'Below the belt,' she complained. 'I can't say he doesn't worry me. God, I'd be a liar to deny it! But he's good for John, I'll admit.'

'Helps you make money?'

'Now you're being cruel.'

'I'm sorry,' Sam said, seeing that for once she meant it.

'He's no manager though – that's how I figure it. That's

how I keep my simmering jealousy in check, you see. You have to pay your dues to go down that management street. You can't do it otherwise. Together we'll do all right for John.'

Sam leaned forward and put his elbow on the table. 'You really care for him, don't you?'

'You mean, in my hard-hearted way. Did it take you so long to work that out?'

'Everything about you takes a long time,' he said, trying to convey his patience.

She gazed at him for a while, then she said, 'Maybe I've just been betrayed too often.'

'Maybe,' he agreed. 'Maybe you should try again.'

As soon as it left his lips, he knew it was a mistake. Her gaze froze over. Full of steam on the inside. Hot and cold staring at him.

'I have tried again, but it always turns out like the first time,' she said. 'I was in my twenties back then. He was the partner in a PR and management company, a married partner. I'd started writing copy for his company when it became clear I was not about to become Shakespeare overnight. I was good at copy. He offered me a full-time job, offered me something else besides. I turned him down twice, but the third time I was a month behind on the rent.'

Sam held her eyes as they melted, wanting to warn her. 'Are you sure you want to go on?' he should have said. But he didn't.

'One evening,' she said, her voice slurring, 'he told me he loved me. I was ... flattered, I suppose. I fell on my back like a giddy teenager. But it didn't last. I got pregnant, then fired. Betrayal is that simple.' She stopped and took a long slim cigarette from a silver case and lit it with a book of restaurant matches off the table. 'He or she would have been thirteen by now ...'

She dragged on its smoke, tasting the tar and nicotine – some desperate need. Then she held the cigarette out in front of her face. It smouldered peacefully between her fingers, as if she'd said nothing at all.

Sam watched her. He watched the smoke billow and float away when she finally exhaled. Her eyes fell closed and he thought he knew what she saw. She saw her younger self.

'Twenty-eight and just had an abortion,' she said bitterly. 'Overdraft in three figures. I owned a suitcase, enough clothes to fill half of it and a battered cassette deck with three tapes . . . Hits from Mozart, one of Verdi's operas and a 10cc album with half the oxide rubbed off through the recording of 'I'm Not in Love'. That's how I got this way, Sam. How I got into management . . . everything.'

Her eyes were clasped into their closed position, but a little salt tear had leaked out and he leaned over and brushed it away with a thumb, wondering what it was he'd started.

'I'm sorry. I'm sorry,' she said, 'I didn't mean this to happen . . .'

'It's OK,' he told her. But he knew in his heart it had gone too far.

She opened her eyes and dabbed them with a paper napkin. In the few seconds her face was obscured, she sucked all the honesty back into herself. When she put down the napkin, Sam found himself looking at the more usual Helen Michaels.

He reached across the table, trying to put his hand on hers, but she drew it away.

'You don't understand,' she said. 'It's just not going to happen. That one time was a mistake. I like you but—'

'I see,' he said, cutting across. He leaned back from her, feeling his back stiffen against the chair.

'Every book of the Bible.' For Kate, it had been a physical thing. John's promise made real.

When he wiped the floor with Victor Antropov, a man in horn-rimmed spectacles three rows below her had dropped popcorn from his gaping mouth and hadn't even noticed. She had felt the same awe. The same rush.

She had never been caught within an unchoreographed standing ovation before. She was caught in one now – real, spontaneous. The crowd didn't seem to care that there were other games still in progress. Only John Harringhay mattered.

When she got out of the auditorium, she found that her knees were still trembling. The buzzing crowd was filing past her. She caught little snippets of superlatives, overbalanced with excited clichés from the kids, a certain numbness from the adults.

Recovering against the wall, she reconstructed the conversation of the previous evening, YCK's reception, turning it into a backstage invitation in her mind. She straightened herself, smoothed down her clothing and strode purposefully for the backstage door.

She expended a sweet smile and a press pass on the backstage doorman. He let her in. If she had thought about it soberly for more than a second, she would never have done it, but he had intoxicated her, and she was set on a path, impossible to stop.

Just before stumbling into Sam, she nearly turned herself around, nerves jangling, a wave of self-consciousness. But Sam spotted her at the critical moment. He had such a schoolboy glee about John's success that her own reaction didn't seem so stupid or far-fetched. Before she had time to consider it further, she had exchanged greetings with Sam and her fist was rapping on the wood panel of the dressing-room door.

'Here goes nothing,' she told herself.

She heard John's voice calling a muffled response and pushed into the room. Another little tremble ran down her leg.

He was seated on the far side, jacket flung over a chair, sucking Coca-Cola through a straw straight from the can. He said nothing but she felt him looking, eyes frisking her.

She was wearing Levis, a thin cotton T-shirt and shoes with the faintest of heels, but suddenly she felt very exposed. Not so much naked – it wasn't to do with the body.

'Hi,' she squeaked. Where was that sassy act of hers now that she really needed it?

'I told you I'd be good,' he said. His brief smile faded like a spent flashbulb. He drained his Coke can through hollowed cheeks and bubbles snorted up through the straw.

She blinked as though she thought this might be a dream, but she didn't wake. What was happening here? She still couldn't understand what it was about him. She was used to men – older mostly – who dated her for her looks. They wanted to unpeel her clothes in a very physical way. She had dealt with lechers, leerers, men with seven hands, violent men – such is the lot of a single, too-beautiful woman. In all the varieties and vintages, she had found pleasure only fleetingly, like so many wines in a bad cellar.

This boy – this young man – didn't seem to care much about that. She wasn't sure he even found her attractive. His attention focused firmly on the deeper Kate Morris and the nakedness he sought was very different – he wanted to peel away her layers.

Suddenly, she realized it was this test that scared her, that brought the trembles. It was very important that he, who probed her in this deeper way, should like and approve of what he found. John Harringhay was special. His eyes looked out at the physical world as though what lurked within his head was so much more important. It was into that spiritual world he drew her now, there to be unclothed, there to be judged.

She felt her little tremble burst into a shudder of fear.

It was so much easier with those others. She knew what they wanted, and whether she gave or withheld it brought no judgement on herself; it was simply a means of control. Her control. With them, she always had that control. And now, with him, she had nothing and she couldn't even find the strength to fake it convincingly.

'I finished my Coke,' he said. 'Wanna go for another?'

'I thought you didn't do coke any more,' she quipped. 'We journos could get a good story if . . .'

He was looking at her. She realized he had her pegged. She was forcing herself into that false character, pulling it on like a dress three sizes too small, and he was just watching it happen. She counted to ten and reined herself back.

'Is there a Coke machine somewhere?' she asked demurely.

'No, I mean, get out . . . get out of here.'

She stepped back in surprise. 'Well, I . . . I've got my car.'

'That'll do.' Pausing briefly, he said, 'You're pretty, you know.'

As she led him to the car park and opened the door of her VW Rabbit, she wondered why his brief compliments dug deeper than any flattery he could have offered. She felt like replying, 'You're a weirdo, you know?' But instead, she just flushed and smiled at him.

They headed for the tourist traps. She drove them along the Embarcadero and down to Fisherman's Wharf. She insisted on taking photographs when they got out of the car. At the first kiosk they came to, she offered him the Coca-Cola, but he said he'd lost his thirst for it.

'What d'you want to do now?' she asked after they had trodden up and down the boards without finding anything to occupy their interest.

He shrugged. She could feel him starting to slip back into his shell.

'I'll tell you what, there's a new shopping mall opened up. They call it the Glass Palace. It's opened in time for Christmas. I had an invite to the opening last month. Journo perk. We could go check out the decorations.'

He made no obvious objection so she took it as agreement and bundled him back into the car. They drove for ten minutes or so – it was nearly rush hour – and he said not a word.

She screeched into the Glass Palace's underground car park, took her ticket, and started roving the aisles for a space.

'The decorations are great,' she assured him. Still she was getting no response.

But when they took the steel elevator up to the shopping levels and spilled out into the mall itself, her date was suddenly in raptures. He stared at the open architecture, the marbled floors, the fall of the light.

166

'Wonderful,' he said. 'It's wonderful.'

The Glass Palace was like a modern odyssey, quite apart from anything else in San Francisco. It had four shopping levels, all high-class shops, and there was a central ground-floor plaza with simulated Roman mosaic tiling. The three upper floors had balconies overlooking this masterpiece. The roof above them was sheet glass. The shopping may have been 'indoor', but the scale of the roof made artificial light completely unnecessary.

The *pièce de résistance* was a pair of glass-panelled elevators, shaped like gilded birdcages, which rose and fell at one edge of the plaza from ground to top floor.

What fascinated John was the mechanism that drove them. It was all on display on the outside, part of the artistic effect, as if the whole thing was only half finished. He insisted on taking a normal elevator – a steel one at the back of the shopping mall where they'd come up from the car park – right to the top and looking down on the glass-caged shoppers.

'I couldn't stand moving up and down like that,' he said.

'Why not?' Kate asked.

'I don't like being looked at.'

It seemed a strange attitude for someone who spent his working life on stage.

He leaned over the balcony rail, eyes bulging as the polished counterweights dropped to make one of the elevators ascend.

'Look at that,' he said, staring up at the winches lodged underneath the roofline.

'Are you always so keen on machinery?' Kate enquired, her voice edgy.

'I'm sorry . . . No, I guess not.'

She laughed. 'Come on, I'll buy you a coffee. We can sit out on this balcony and drink. You haven't even looked at the decorations, have you?'

The hanging reds and blues, the paperchains, the tinsel, the lights seemed to pass him by. Even when she brought him coffee and he drank it talking stiltedly about how he came to play chess, he was still casting looks down into the plaza, watching the glass cages as they carried passenger after passenger on the same journey.

'I grew up round here,' she said. 'Not in the city, in the valley. My father was a computer pioneer. He didn't think journalism was a serious career.' She looked to him for understanding, feeling somehow that he had it in him to understand.

'I never knew my father,' he said. 'He left home.'

'With me, it was the other way around. I left, and he stayed. I was sixteen.'

'I've always got Helen,' he said. 'She's looked after me . . . until I found my grandfather.'

'Yeah, I met him.'

'I'm playing better now.'

'Why do you think that is?'

He looked at her. 'Are you trying to interview me?'

'Maybe,' she admitted. After a pause, she said, 'What do you value most?'

'Winning . . . No, honesty,' he corrected himself.

'Why does that feel like a dig?'

'I don't know. Haven't you been honest?'

He said it as though he wasn't expecting an answer and she didn't know what to say anyway, so she just let it pass.

The lights in some of the shops started to flicker or fade. Shutters were being drawn down. John fixed his stare out over the balcony and Kate thought maybe he would never move again. He seemed so entranced.

Soon all the shops were shut and the swarm of shoppers had reduced to a trickle. A few straggling shopworkers were taking the glass elevator down to the plaza and wending their weary way through the ornate arch of the main entrance, just about visible from John's top-floor perch.

'You folks wanna get on home,' a voice said.

Kate turned to see a middle-aged security officer. He was thick-set and two sizes too big for his uniform. His belly stuck out comically over his belt.

'It's getting on time to lock it all up. You folks'll have to come back tomorrow if you didn't get what you want.'

'My car's in the car park,' Kate said, suddenly worried that it may be shut in for the night.

'That's all right. The regular elevators are still running, and the car park's open another thirty minutes. It's the front gates I gotta lock. I got rounds to make. Car park gets locked on the next one.'

He wandered off and she watched him go. John seemed to have paid no attention to the whole conversation.

She stared at him until he turned towards her. 'What do you want to do now?' she asked.

'I'll leave it to you.'

'Let's buy a bucket of ice-cream,' she said. 'We could go to my place and eat.'

Somewhere between the corner store and her apartment, she decided what she wanted. And although John seemed compliant rather than captivated, she decided to reach out for it.

She was kissing him almost as soon as she plonked herself on the sofa next to him. For a moment, she thought she saw the frightened boy – the Russian gymnast – she had seen in Singapore. But then came the man . . .

He pushed her gently backwards. And she went back willingly at his touch.

Their first sex didn't take long, completed with one article of clothing still on each body. She had underwear still tangled around one ankle. He never had the chance to remove his shirt.

Their second was slower and more tender. He carried her to the bedroom and she removed his shirt and kissed his chest. Then he took her lacy anklet in his teeth and shook it free. Then he moved up, mouth pressed to her skin as he went.

She almost exploded when his tongue found that point of ecstasy between her legs, and later died into moans as his resurrected member repeated and repeated its earlier performance.

20

I was tired and unprepared for the atmosphere of a big tournament. John, on the other hand, was perfectly ready. He had in some way flicked a switch inside, refusing to challenge his body with anything that could be remotely described as a pollutant. No alcohol, no drugs.

He said, 'Grandfather, keep me on this track.' But in truth, it seemed all he needed was for me to be there.

That afternoon, however, the effort of being there started to catch up.

I left the game as soon as it became clear that John was winning. He didn't seem to need me at that moment. There was a group of reporters backstage who tried to ask questions as I left, but I swept past them and got the doorman to call a taxi.

We were staying at a hotel not far from the airport, a towering building surrounded by acres of car park. My corner room had one view over the bay and another that took in several drive-in establishments and a small cinema complex. On a better day, I might have appreciated the former view, but I was so tired it was painful. I lay down on the bed and the next thing I knew it was 2.30 in the morning.

Jet lag is a strange phenomenon. It affects the rhythms of the body in apparently random fashion. For the next four and a half hours, I was alternately sleepy, awake and constipated. Several times I thought I was on the verge of a heart attack, but it never came.

At seven, I decided on a bath to relieve my aches. This is no small decision for a man of my years and delicate joints. It often involves ingenuity of quite breathtaking proportions. On this occasion, I secured a belt around an overhead towel rail, wrapped it around my wrist so there would be no pull on my hands or fingers, and raised and lowered myself into the water with relative ease.

As my head cleared, I realized I had not eaten in nearly twenty hours. That seemed to explain most of the weakness I felt, so I dressed and headed for the hotel restaurant.

It wasn't so much a restaurant as what might be described as a 'diner' – I think that's the American word. I got croissants and orange juice and a plate of fried food from a buffet. I got smiles from a 'service assistant' who seemed to be amazed by my age and capacity to breathe unaided. I smiled back and ate the food.

Sam joined me first and then, a few moments later, Helen appeared. She was her usual self, that hospital-cornered neatness, the beautifully elegant clothes. Sam, on the other hand, was changed. He looked like he hadn't slept, though he wore a crisply pressed jacket. He kept twitching his nose and readjusting his glasses. He spoke to me, but said almost nothing to Helen. In a similar fashion, she aimed all her questions in my direction.

'I know he's not got a game today, but I've no idea where John is. Have you seen him?'

'No, I'm sorry. I seem to have missed most of yesterday. I can't get back into sequence.'

'You know he went off with Kate Morris,' Sam interjected.

'That's why I'm worried.'

'You don't usually worry about his women.'

Helen looked hurt, which was unusual. It was unusual to see her react to anything. 'She's a journalist,' she complained.

'Not when she's with John, she's not.'

Helen sniffed and turned her head. Sam returned to me.

'What are you doing today?' he asked.

I hadn't thought about it. I had thought only about the weakness of my body. But now it was filled with food, it was beginning to find some strength.

'Why don't you come up to the city with me? I could

show you some things. I'm afraid I only know the tourist traps.'

'I think I should wait for John,' I said.

Helen smiled as if she knew it was a lost cause.

'You think he's gone off the rails, don't you?' Sam said. 'Let me tell you, that's not going to happen.'

'It's happened before,' Helen snapped.

'Yeah, but that's when you were responsible.'

They shot daggers at each other across the table while I tried to work out why. Sam finished his coffee and stood up.

'How about it then?' he said to me. 'We can take a taxi. I realize you've come a long way. Just an hour or so? I promise I'll bring you back when you've had enough.'

I nodded reluctantly and started to stand. 'I just need to go to my room for a minute,' I said.

'I'll give you both a lift,' Helen offered. 'I've still got our hire car . . . I have some business to attend to.'

Sam shot her another dagger.

'I'm going that way anyway,' she added weakly.

'We'll take a taxi,' Sam said.

I was a little confused, I must admit. For the last few days, they had seemed to be inching closer and closer, and now here they were in open hostilities. I wondered what had changed.

I spent ten minutes doing those after-breakfast things that most people take five minutes over and met Sam in the hotel lobby. Helen walked past us as we were checking our room keys behind the desk. She stepped towards us as if she was going to come and repeat her offer, but she suddenly saw Sam looking at her, thought better of it and went on.

I told myself that whatever had passed between her and Sam would eventually become clear. Perhaps he would enlighten me once we got in the taxi.

Sam and I walked out into a beautiful crisp day and stood on the front steps, waiting for the taxi promised by the bell captain. The car park spread out in front of us on the other side of the access road and I watched Helen flouncing angrily towards her hire car some fifty yards away.

When she got inside and fiddled her key into the ignition, the blast knocked me over.

I'm not sure how I got to my feet. But I remember the flames licking out of the skeleton of a car. I remember Sam sprinting towards it. I watched him trying to get near, but he couldn't.

I followed after him, being overtaken by people running out of the hotel who were younger and fitter.

When he turned towards me, his clothes were scorched and so close to flame that smoke was rising from the arm of his jacket. He staggered, almost fell, then reached out to me. There was a white contortion to his face, madness seizing its muscles.

Behind him, the billowing clouds raged orange against the pure sky.

I turned my head. I have seen death before.

21

Circumstance and bad timing sometimes strangle new-born love, its breath lost against the wind of tragedy. His mentor of the last four years had been murdered. While he was making love to Kate, he didn't even know.

John Harringhay finally heard the news on the mid-morning bulletin. He was sitting up, eating toast in her bed. Kate had the TV on.

The bulletin started normally enough. 'First reports of an explosion . . .'

Then he saw the pictures. He dropped his slice of peanut butter on wholemeal.

The 'Kate and John' love affair turned from new-born health to cot dead in a matter of moments.

Kate bundled him into the car. The bulletin gave no detail as to casualties, but John was crying and shaking and talking wildly about his grandfather. She kept saying, 'You don't know what's happened . . . You don't know.' It reassured neither of them.

The drive to the hotel took twenty minutes and a further ten passed while they tried to break through the police cordon. They found Zalapek in the hotel lobby, slumped in a chair as if he had collapsed rather than sat in it. John ran to his grandfather, grabbing him, hugging him as if he needed touch to believe what he was seeing.

'You're alive . . . you're alive,' he repeated, pressing his head to Zalapek's chest.

Slowly, the old man pushed him out to arm's length and they looked at each other.

'Oh, God, Helen? Sam?' the boy shouted suddenly.

'Helen,' his grandfather said and shook his head.

*

Sam was treated by the paramedics for minor burns and shock. He refused to get in an ambulance despite advice to the contrary. When he came back into the lobby, there was anger set in his face.

'Fucking Yakamura,' he said.

Kate and John and his grandfather were sitting in a small circle of armchairs and sofas. They looked up surprised from their private ruminations, making no sense of Sam's words.

'Who else?' Sam demanded. 'Do you think this was an accident, for Christ's sake?'

Kate was holding on sheepishly – almost forlornly – to John's arm. Neither of the pair seemed capable of answering such a question. At last, Zalapek spoke.

'We don't know, Sam. We don't know what happened.'

'It wasn't an accident. I never trusted that bastard. I've heard bad things about him, but I never believed . . . It's just 'cos she wouldn't . . . 'cos she wouldn't sell.' He spoke brokenly through sobs as he choked on emotion. 'I-I-I . . .' he continued, but failed to get the next word out.

'You what, Sam?' Kate prompted, reaching out a hand to him.

His eyes rolled upwards and closed. His teeth ground together.

'I loved her.'

A silence. Sam slumped into a spare armchair. That three-word phrase he had found so difficult in life now bled from him, cut from the great gaping wound opening inside him.

'I loved her,' he said again, as if he was quite unable to stem the flow.

22

John saw Helen as a kind of surrogate mother. Losing her and thinking of the loss of his natural mother twisted something within him. Everyone has a support system. Everyone reacts differently to its collapse.

After a silent dinner, he sent Kate away. Unable to cope, I think, with so much at once. She went reluctantly. She looked plaintively at me until I nodded, a sort of family agreement to her departure. She gazed back at him for a moment. She did not want to leave.

I suppose she thought that she might be letting him down in his hour of need, yet she saw the pain that company brought him and sacrificed herself.

'That was cruel,' I said to him when she was gone from earshot.

'It's all I can do,' he said.

By then, I already knew that she loved him. Perhaps better than she knew it herself. Perhaps in the same way I once looked at Marion and knew her love for Ward, even though she thought of herself as a bright young thing, loving nothing and no one. Kate probably told herself the same, and although I knew she loved him, I had no sense that they would ever be together. I had no confidence they would be happy.

My grandson and I sat in his hotel room until gone midnight. We said little. With John and me, the ties of family had become more about time than words. We redeemed each other by simple attendance – the anchor of the past in his present; the reality of the present dragging me from my past. Just as well, for in that aftermath, neither could place the loss of Helen in words, neither could shape understanding around the violence of it. All we knew was that each of us was everything to the other, all that was left. That, at least, was a warm feeling – one I will always treasure.

Afterwards, I went back to my own room and tried to sleep. A couple of hours later, there he was again, knocking on my door.

'I have to talk to you now,' he said.

'Come in,' I beckoned.

He came in and sat on the bed. He was still wearing the bottom of his white suit from the day before and his shirt was half unbuttoned and pulled to one side.

'What do you have to say?' I prompted, realizing he might have difficulty getting it out.

'I dunno,' he said. 'It's like I'm slipping back – becoming a pawn again. I have this urge. I need . . .'

His eyes were screwed tight. His renunciation of drugs had been absolute and sudden and achieved with a will that made me proud. But it was little more than two weeks since that night in a London hotel and I cannot say I would have blamed him much if he had slipped at that moment.

Suddenly, he opened his eyes and stared at me.

'I'm not gonna do it,' he said.

He took a crumpled paper bag from his pocket. He looked at it for a moment, then turned the bag upside down. Coloured pills of various colours fell on the floor.

I tried to smile.

'I'm not gonna do it,' he repeated. He looked at me like someone who had suddenly seen the truth and put his hand on its diamond hardness. He reminded me of myself, how I'd once been, and as if we had synchronized our thoughts, he said, 'Tell me about my grandmother. Why did you leave my mother?'

For a second, the request seemed strange. I did not yet understand the extent of what he had guessed, how wide and how deep it went into my past life.

'It was another world, John. You could not know it,' I told him.

'Do you think that's what this is about?'

'What do you mean?' I asked.

'This is about you, isn't it?' he said. 'You hide yourself away for fifty years. You say exile was the only safe way. You come out of hiding – and suddenly . . .'

Now it was my turn to look at him. Amazement. Shock. That same diamond truth.

Helen's death was something of my past raising its head. I did not know what, or why. But suddenly I sensed that I was meant to die in that car. And it struck me that John was supposed to die as well, and whoever had placed the bomb had not cared. One, two, three other victims – they were no matter.

So it was in 1940 – that's how I should have recognized the nature of it now, even though I could not as yet place any connection between present and past.

Why would anyone still be interested?

I was once the *most dangerous man in the world*, but that was long ago, when the world was at war and what I knew might have shaped the course of it. And what I did put me for ever to shame.

January 1940. The end and the beginning of a long misery. I was languishing in a police cell, hard walls, hard bed, no heating. Winter at its meanest at three in the morning. I was woken, shivering from the cold, by the clank of keys in the lock. The big metal door swung noisily into the room.

I saw the gaoler's face. Then a second, larger man, a shadow who slowly stepped into the light. I knew him even as a shadow, such was the fame of that profile.

I suppose, of all the men I have met in my life – and I have met many of the great scientists and men and women of this century – I met but two who truly mattered: Albert Einstein and Winston Churchill.

It was Churchill who stood there on that cold night. He was wearing a dark overcoat and that style of hat which he made famous. A cigar was sticking from his mouth. At the time, he was the First Lord of the Admiralty, just over three months away from assuming leadership of the war.

'That'll be all,' he said to the gaoler in his low resonant voice. He stooped in through the doorway.

'But, sir—' the man protested.

'I hardly think Professor Zalapek is going to attack me. Give me the lamp, will you?'

The man receded and Churchill came in, holding an oil lamp at shoulder height. He motioned to me with his free hand.

I rubbed my eyes and scooped myself into a ball, huddling at the head of my iron bed and leaving him space at the other end. Churchill nodded and walked across, and sank heavily on to the vacant spot. He leaned his considerable body against the blank wall. Slowly, he put the lamp down on the floor, so that now his face was lit from below, ghost-like as if he were an apparition. I wanted to pinch myself out of the dream, but of course I could not – it was real.

'So,' he began, 'Professor Zalapek.' The title was correct. I had been given the position six months before, though I felt little enough like an Oxford professor in my circumstances.

Churchill took off his hat and laid it on the bed between us. Then he opened his overcoat and offered me a cigar. I shook my head. It was about the only thing I had control of. The rest of my body was all aquiver from the cold and half a dozen other reasons of fear.

'You seem to have got yourself in some trouble,' he said. 'Enlighten me. Did you kill either of them?'

I considered the question for a moment. Neither truth nor lies seemed to fit, and the image of grey bodies leaving dark stains in the carpet clouded my mind.

'I cannot say,' I answered.

'Two corpses are found in your college rooms. You have a gun in your hand. You cannot say?' He puffed his cigar. 'You cannot say because you cannot lie.' Another puff. 'Did you know the men?'

'I knew the college porter.'

'That wasn't what I meant. There were two intruders, I believe. They were trying to take your work?' He hesitated, looking for a response. When I showed none, he continued, 'The dead man ... the other dead man, not the porter ... was a Nazi spy. Not by ideology perhaps. He was an American. He worked for whoever paid him the most money. He never worked alone. Did his colleague get away with the work?'

'What work?'

'Come, come, Professor.'

'No,' I conceded.

'That's good.' I saw him breathe a sigh of relief, his big frame rising and falling against the wall. His voice and his whole manner seemed lightened by the sigh. 'For the last nine months, I've had Neils Bohr writing to me, saying I should recruit you into the atomic project. He tells me about something called fission. I tell him I'm in the Admiralty; I'm not in charge of such things. And he says I'm the only politician in England who can understand what it means. Now his country is torn apart by the Nazis. Maybe I should listen to him, don't you think?'

'I have already been offered the job,' I said.

'I know,' he agreed. He dropped the cigar, now no more than a stub, and trod it into the concrete floor. 'They tell me it could cost millions to build even one bomb. But they tell me it would be worth it.'

I looked up at him reluctantly, then my eyes sank.

'Come now, Professor. I am a politician. Whatever secrets you choose to hold in your head, that is between you and your God. But you cannot think me capable of stealing them away. I'm told even the rest of the scientific world doesn't understand your theories.'

'I stopped working on fission two years ago.'

He took another cigar from his coat. 'Because you had solved the problem?'

'The principle of fission is very simple,' I said, ducking a direct answer. 'It seems from all the evidence and theory we have that one neutron when colliding with a special sort of uranium nucleus releases huge amounts of energy. It also releases three more neutrons.'

'And that is it?'

A knot tightened in my stomach. Of course, I had worked elsewhere for the last two years. I suppose, by continuing down the line of explanation I gave to Churchill, I created a lie, but I merely meant to conceal something I considered totally private.

'I believe they have termed it "critical mass",' I told him. 'It's a simple matter of statistics. If you have enough of the special uranium compressed in the one mass, then more than one of the released neutrons hits another uranium nuclei. Hence, more energy. Then more energy, and more energy. Each successive reaction sets off more and more reactions. I'm sure you can do the arithmetic.'

Churchill nodded and blew smoke from his mouth.

I thought of the dominoes Ward had set up in the café and of the three black wooden balls that fell on Einstein's table.

'Yes, that's all. Of course, this happens very fast. It's all over in perhaps a second. The heat and energy of the blast destroys everything in its path.' I paused, raising my eyes. 'Also there is an aftermath. I believe it will last for years.'

'Aftermath?' he enquired, 'what's that?'

'Radioactivity. A new sort of invisible death.' I stopped to look at him. 'I will not do it.'

'You didn't kill either of them, did you?' he asked. 'You couldn't.'

I said nothing.

'Then who else was in the room?'

'I cannot say,' I repeated.

He shook his head and stood, picking up his hat and walking to the window. He was looking out through the bars when he next spoke.

'You know, I can't let them release you,' he said. 'It just may be that you are the most dangerous man in the world right now . . . But you're not a murderer. I don't know who you're protecting, but you couldn't kill. That's your problem. Yours is a faith too far.'

181

He turned, his face brightening once he had got those words out. They seemed to satisfy him.

'I can lock you up as a "conchie",' he added. 'That'll only last so long. If we're still at war, I'll have to think of something else. You must understand that most people would have you either on their side – or dead.'

'I understand,' I told him.

He called out to the gaoler, who came and opened the door. Then Churchill put his hat on and tipped it in salute.

'I do not have the luxury of your morality, Mr Zalapek,' he said. I noticed my title had been dropped. 'I also have faith in God – yet I am sending men and boys to die.'

He went out and I never saw him again.

My daughter Emily was born that morning, at more or less the time he was leaving. Two weeks later, my wife and my best friend were dead.

23

Kazuo Yakamura received news of the explosion from Shoyo, his assistant. It was a bad day anyway, one on which he did not emerge from his hotel suite.

'Bring me coffee,' was all he said.

He was spending time wading through the accounts of YCK's American operation and did not like what he was reading. In fact, he liked nothing he had heard about this particular subsidiary. The day before, he had summoned Yoshi from Japan and was now preparing for a most difficult meeting with his son.

He had decided against using the YCK office, unable to decide whether the meeting covered family or business ground. Perhaps he expected raised voices. And it is never good for such things to be heard by junior staff. Instead, he took his usual entourage – his personal assistant, Shoyo, and a pair of local bodyguards he always employed when in the United States – and set up a temporary office in the outer lounge of his hotel suite. Everything and everyone now had to come to him.

He took a cup of coffee and, after his first sip, telephoned the hotel where John and his entourage were staying. He could not raise them.

He telephoned the organizing chairman of the chess tournament, instructing him to cancel play for two days. It was an unusual step, but in the light of a sponsor's instruction, the chairman conceded. Yakamura put the phone down, feeling a little appeased.

He replenished his coffee and went back to his deliberations. He had papers spread like a patchwork tablecloth across the antique desk. He said not another word to Shoyo and he dismissed his bodyguards, sending them into a back room. He was thinking, so deeply it was almost meditation, and he needed to be alone.

Yoshi breezed in as the daylight was fading. By then, the newly-made office with its balcony and bay windows was lit not with the natural light of the day but by an enormous crystal chandelier hanging over the table. Yakamura had positioned three or four important papers next to his right hand; the rest had been arranged in piles so that wood now outranked paper as the most visible surface.

'Nice office,' Yoshi said in their native Japanese. 'Our downtown building not good enough for you?' He smiled, referring to his father's supposed meanness over such lavish expense.

'That is not relevant here,' his father said harshly.

'You're not going to ask me if I had a good flight?'

'No.'

'This is serious, then,' Yoshi quipped.

'Do not underestimate how serious,' Yakamura said. He picked up the first of his selected papers. 'I have seen the final report on China,' he began.

Yoshi stepped back. There was a chair ready for him next to his father, but he shunned it, stalking the room, brooding on the indignity of his father's summons.

'Is that what you brought me here for? But the report was good. Hudson Brown and his team did a fine job. He inspected the place thoroughly, and gave us a clean bill of health.'

'There were two investigators on this project.'

'Oh, Wingate?' Yoshi said, his voice lowered. 'The police think he strayed into a "bad" area in Bangkok. Looking for women. They think he was mugged. Unfortunate.'

'He was not, then, using our hospitality?'

'Father, that's an old trick of yours.'

Yakamura's eyes flashed. 'I never used it for blackmail. Only favours.'

'There is a difference?'

'There is a difference,' Yakamura affirmed, 'and anyway it was a long time ago. YCK was a little company.'

'You still do it now. You collect the tapes! The data!'

Yakamura shook his head. 'Mere insurance.'

Yoshi's face tensed, but he didn't snap back. He took a moment to consider.

'Father, let me tell you,' he said. 'This guy was so straight. Even if I'd wanted to, he would accept nothing from us. He was off on his own in Bangkok, just unlucky. But the work he did is included in Brown's report, so we can be sure ... there is no hint of bias.'

'Very well,' Yakamura said. He laid the paper aside and took up the next two. 'I have here two sets of accounts—'

'Is this a trial?' Yoshi interrupted.

'The two sets are thus: in this hand, the American operation's quarterly figures as filed with our Tokyo office; in this, as I gathered them from the accounts department in San Francisco yesterday.' He paused, as though he expected Yoshi to comment.

Yoshi still hadn't sat down. He stood defiantly at the far end of the table, glaring at his father. 'I don't think there's a discrepancy.'

'I suppose that depends on how you read them. To Tokyo, you are reporting a small profit. Not a great performance, but I suppose enough to convince the board that you are running things half well. However ...' Yakamura switched his gaze to the second paper. 'In this, I see, a stock excess of three million dollars and an undeclared bad debt of a further million and a half. Why have you not reported these?'

'The debt is not bad ... And the excess stock will sell,' Yoshi said, but with only partial conviction.

Yakamura was shaking his head solemnly. 'I checked with the accounts people. The bad debt is nearly a year old. Your debtor has serious problems and will probably go into administration within weeks. Your excess stock? We are a constructor. Normally we have very small stock, so I would say this is at least half obsolete. A prudent accountant would have shown a loss of, say, three million dollars in the last quarter.'

'Is that what Leibnitz told you?'

'No,' Yakamura admitted. 'Your finance director – I should call him your "financial puppet" – was quite loyal. It was I that told him, just before I wrote him a cheque and asked him to leave.'

'You did what?'

Slowly, Yakamura put down both the papers.

'I am flying Suzuki out from Tokyo. I have asked him to assemble a task force to save the American arm of YCK.'

'But, Father, you can't do that!'

Yoshi slumped into his appointed chair. It tilted back smoothly under his weight as though it had been expecting him. He hesitated a few seconds, lifeless until he leaned forward suddenly, pleading open-handed to his father.

Yakamura held his gaze. 'I am afraid, my son, that my dream for you is at an end.'

Sam Stylls could not let their story end this way: Helen and Sam . . . Sam and Helen. He could not leave Helen unrevenged. He loved her.

It had taken the shock of death to burst those words out through his mouth in public, but they were out now. And anyway, he had never held any doubt inside.

Standing in the shadows outside Yakamura's hotel, he broke the gun for the tenth time and checked the bullets in the chambers. All filled. Double action, no need to empty the chamber where the hammer rested. He snapped it back together and cupped the cool metal in both hands.

In the blackness of her death, after the flames had died and the echo of them made charcoal of his emotions, he'd thought of sucking on the barrel, sucking and pulling on the trigger at the same time. But that wasn't right, that wasn't justice.

Helen . . . This was for her.

Oh, he'd tried to speak to the others but they weren't listening . . . More interested in quiet grieving than action. Sam was a man who wouldn't stand still once set on course. And in his own version of grief, his conviction hardened into stone.

186

He closed his eyes and rehearsed. He was on his own now; this was for Helen, and for himself.

Lifting the gun. The aim. Quickly. Don't look him in the eyes. It's not easy to look directly at anyone and fire. There will be a small recoil, a jerk back through the arm. Remember to prepare for it. Then, squeeeeeeeze. Yes! The explosion ripping. The head of the bullet faster than sound. The shock waves forever like a scream in a bottomless well. And finally, in the rising waft of spent gunpowder . . . justice and revenge.

This pound and a half of metal was all and everything. He brought it up to his mouth, kissed the barrel lightly. Justifying the sentence to himself: death to the culprit, the murderer.

He looked at it one more time and then slipped the gun back inside his jacket. He licked his lips. They were trembling and tasted now of metal and metal polish.

He decided the direct route was best. Just go up and bang on the door. Why not? Who would suspect a chess analyst?

His first obstacle was Shoyo. It was he who opened the door in response to Sam's banging. All Sam could see beyond the diminutive Japanese assistant was the labyrinth of rooms behind. No easy access.

'Who are you?' Shoyo asked.

'Samuel Stylls. I want to see Mr Yakamura.'

'I'm sorry, he is with his son now. You have no appointment, I think.'

Sam was not a physical man, but he was roused. Perhaps he had lost the balance of his mind, tipping beyond that point where the truly insane take on extra strength. He pushed forward, shoving Shoyo back like a toy. Shoyo protested in Japanese, but Sam was past him.

Once inside the suite, Sam ran through the rooms, taking two wrong turnings before he found Yakamura.

The old man was sitting at a table, accounting papers still in neat piles before him. His son, Yoshi, stood to one side. Yoshi was sipping brandy, speaking plaintively in a language Sam could not comprehend.

'You killed Helen,' Sam yelled.

Yakamura looked up in shock. He raised himself from his chair, unknowingly creating a larger target.

Sam's hand went to his jacket and grasped the metal. He felt the desire to look down at what he was doing, but resisted. No need to look, he warned himself. Surprise was everything.

'Wait,' shouted Yoshi. 'What's this about?'

Sam was thrown for a moment. Yoshi had not been at the rehearsal.

'This man tried to buy John Harringhay,' Sam said. 'He wanted some sort of hold on Zalapek. I don't know what.' The words tumbled out, running together in a strangled voice as though Sam's throat had constricted into a needle's eye of breath. All the time he was telling himself, 'Fire, fire.' But he couldn't pull the trigger.

'Can't we talk about this?' Yoshi said, trying to draw his anger, almost like he'd done this thing before.

'You don't understand, he killed Helen,' Sam wailed. His head twisted to one side as he raised the gun.

The target had one hand on the table now, standing as if trapped by that tunnel down which the bullet would pass, and frozen there, a rabbit in headlights.

Suddenly, a stinging shock of alcohol hit Sam squarely in the face, brandy covering his glasses and attacking his undefended eyes. He pulled the trigger, but it was a blind shot. A flying Yoshi tackled his father, knocking him over a chair. Both of them landed beneath the level of the table.

Sam wiped the liquid away, but by the time he could see again, he could hear commotion in the corridor. Yakamura's bodyguards, summoned from their rest, were dashing through the suite of rooms.

Sam panicked. He fired again, a shot that only splintered the antique wood of the table. Then he crashed through the nearest of the balcony doors, gripped suddenly with a panic about getting away. He was running blindly, desperate for a fire escape, or something.

The leading bodyguard had him in his sights by the time

Sam reached the parapet. Sam looked over but there was nowhere to go. He turned, gun still in hand. Then a bullet hit him and he fell, feet above head as he tumbled over the rail.

The bodyguard hurried forward to examine the result of his handiwork. There was a black shape still in freefall below him. Twenty-six floors is about a four-second fall and he caught the last second and a half of it. Against the background noise of city streets, the final crash of glass was lost.

The bodyguard looked down incredulously. The whole of one panel of the lobby's frosted roof was missing. Framed below was the hotel's grand central sculpture. Sam's body had fallen on its centre. The point of the longest steel tube had skewered through the chest and the recycling system had begun pumping pink water through the fountain. Sam Stylls was dead, a cocktail sausage on a stick.

Behind the bodyguard, Shoyo was now shouting hysterically and Yoshi was lifting himself away from his father, crushed in their tumble over the chair.

'Fuck,' he said in English. Then he addressed his father in their own tongue. 'Are you all right, Father?' he asked.

Yakamura's face was pale and growing paler. Yoshi could see he was entering shock. But the old man fought it, as he fought all the frailties brought about by age.

'I seem to be having some trouble moving, my son,' he said, 'though I thank you for your help.' His lips quivered and his eyes flickered and finally closed.

When they finally took Kazuo Yakamura to the hospital, his doctors found a broken arm and a broken hip among the bruises and lacerations of his body.

Sam's ruined corpse went to the morgue.

189

24

That night when he came into my room, John had begun to understand the truth that lay behind the blood which joined us.

Tell me about my grandmother, he had said. Why did you abandon the family?

These were simple but tearing questions. I had tried to avoid them in exile. Now I faced the one person who deserved an answer to all I had kept as a private hell.

I do not think he quite realized what it was he asked of me, how the shame of my whole life was tied up in that short year of marriage. Still the questions came from his lips and I moved to answer him. How did I end up in prison? What could possibly have led to that?

Step back to 1939. The year started well enough: the wedding, the trip to America. Alice and I were happy for perhaps five or six months.

Then several experiments published by other scientists in other countries proved many of the contentions in my papers of 1935 and '36. Those who had scorned me as a dangerous renegade were forced to recant. Letters praising my achievements were printed in *The Times*. Bohr and Fermi were among the signatories to testimonies in my favour.

'England has the foremost young theorist in the world,' they said.

This vindication happened to correspond with the retirement of an old professor at Oxford. As atonement for their wilder denouncements, my former detractors threw their weight behind my candidacy for the vacant post. You might describe it as an international campaign. In June of 1939, I was installed as the youngest Oxford professor in a century.

This turn of fortune reminded me of Einstein's words. They had given him a Nobel Prize for work that was sixteen years old. They made me professor for the beginnings of a theory which I no longer wished to place on public display. In fact, I had palpably hidden the later fruits of my work, burying it shamefully, and started out in a different direction.

The taste of success was therefore already bitter in my mouth, but far worse was to come. The published version of the Hahn and Strassmann paper showing barium produced by irradiating uranium was beginning to ring alarm bells in the Western scientific community. In July, I was approached to join a secret group looking at uranium for the British government. Scientists on both sides of the Atlantic were being advised not to publish work openly in this area, but circulate it only in an approved group. Governments were becoming involved even before Einstein's letter.

Of course, I turned the approach down, but almost immediately, I was approached again by a different group, offering me an appointment in another weapons programme. I was honest with them all – as later I was with Churchill – but I grew increasingly concerned. War seemed unavoidable and, as the country primed its scientists to join in the effort, I realized how untenable my position would soon become.

Then Alice announced her pregnancy, a baby due in the following January. And in early September, Britain declared war.

Ward pressed me hard to join one military effort or the other. Ever since his Continental trip the previous year, he had propounded the case for confrontation ever more vocally. He had completely abandoned his own pacifism, believing quite genuinely that the world could not allow Hitler to 'eradicate the Jewish faith'.

In the end, I couldn't talk to him.

Much as I loved her, I couldn't talk to Alice either, not about the dilemma I anticipated, since she was in the middle of it. I had the choice of boffin or soldier, but I could accept neither and that would automatically destroy me in a country at war. I turned for help to Marion.

I sent her a note, inviting her to lunch, and she agreed by return. We met in that small café in the High where the three of us – Ward, Marion and myself – had first come together.

'It's strange you should choose this place,' she said as she shook out her umbrella and sat down.

'Can I get you something?' I asked nervously. Somehow this already felt like a betrayal of Alice, even though all I intended was to gather a little advice: Marion's counsel on how to proceed.

'My God, you look so serious,' she said. 'No one's died, have they?' She swept the paper menu off the table and started reading.

'The situation is serious,' I told her.

'I heard Alice is expecting. That should make you happy.'

I didn't answer. I tried a smile that didn't really work.

Presently, a waitress came and took our order – the pie of the day and a simple jug of water to wash it down.

'You usually have these conversations with Ward, don't you?' Marion said. 'Why are you picking on me?'

'I need advice.'

'My dear Hayden, my advice is hardly worth a bean to a man like you.'

I looked at her. I had long since realized that Marion was something more than she pretended, that she was a frivolous heiress only by birth, and not by nature. I think she knew instinctively that her act no longer fooled me.

'OK,' she agreed at length. 'Ward's pretty mad at you, isn't he? You know, he's talking about enlisting. I don't think they'll let him, not with his limp and his age.' She paused. 'Fire away then. Tell me the problem.'

'They're going to conscript me.'

'Who are "they"?'

'The British.'

'Into which service?'

'Ah, there's the rub. I have my choice.'

192

Marion looked down at the table. 'And there's your problem,' she said knowingly. 'It's a choice but no choice.'

'Exactly what do I say to Alice?' I asked.

'Tell her you love her. You do, don't you?'

That seemed a strange question, and it seemed strange that I had to think about it. I did think about it. 'Yes,' I said.

'If you'd have said no, I'd have thrown this table in your face. Alice is my friend. Remember I introduced you.'

'Alice likes being the wife of a professor,' I said, 'and when I refuse service, I'm not sure what will happen. There's no future in Oxford.'

The waitress returned, placing our lunch before us. Marion used the interruption to consider the problem.

'You're committed to what you believe in,' she said eventually. 'I've never met anyone with your kind of faith. Alice married you. She knew what you were. I believe she will accept the consequences.'

She seemed so sure of herself, and for once in my life, I was not. I could not solve the problem rationally and I could not see how Marion had reached her conclusion. I looked straight into her eyes.

'Would you?' I asked. 'Could you accept that?'

'For Ward, I could,' she said.

I am sure that, for Ward, she could have. Maybe that's why she misjudged Alice so completely.

A few hours later. Alice was standing indignantly in the front room of our home. The furniture was new; the curtains had been hanging less than six months. There was the faint smell of new paint and the unheard crackle of a fuse burning down as I told her my position.

'Hayden, you cannot seriously want to do this. I am pregnant. Pregnant! A baby is due. Do you realize what that means?' she exploded.

I shook my head helplessly. A man trying to hold back a bomb by simple denial. 'I know. I know. But I will not . . . will not do it.'

'They are not going to ask you to fight, damn it! They only want your expertise.'

I was so weak, holding on to faith that drained the strength. For a moment, I groped along the edge, hanging on by fingertips. I could only turn my head to the floor, as if assessing the drop.

Alice started crying. Big tears fell on her dress.

'I love you,' I said. But it brought no reply.

She sobbed on and, as she sobbed, I felt a mechanical click inside my head. Something died; some deep resolve stiffened to replace it.

'It's not fighting,' she wailed. 'I understand your belief. I've tried to understand it, haven't I? It's not fighting ... There are others doing intelligence work, code breaking – Milner-Barry and Alexander at Bletchley Park. That's where they're sending other chess players, other clever men.' She was waving her arms accusingly, fists balled as if she would hit me.

'Alice,' I said. And there was a long pause while her attention settled. 'I am no longer a chess player. Do you not realize what I have become? They want me to make weapons. It's to do with what I know. I will not do it. I cannot do it.'

'They'll force you into the army. And what will we do then? Think of your child ...' She paused, but only for breath. 'Don't you realize what that'll mean? Everything will be ruined. Do we mean so little to you, Hayden? Does this child mean so little? Don't you realize you'll be ruined?'

'But to ruin the lives of others—'

'Don't play word games with me. Not now ... We'll be ruined.'

Alice could cry. The tears flowed in her eyes when in need. And I thought they would never stop. And of course, she was right. What I did next, storming from the house, ruined it all. It led me to that gaol cell. It led me to my life of exile.

25

For the next couple of days, Kate threw herself into work. It was therapy as much as anything. She couldn't sit around and think about her own life, about John, about her own position. That was too scary.

She started trying to finish the Beckett piece. She had been struggling on and off with the research ever since she got back from Singapore. Some of the papers she had wanted were supposed to be stored in a warehouse in Ohio, but when she enquired, she found that 'Those papers are not yet open to the public, ma'am.' And on closer questioning, 'Sorry, ma'am, the warehouse went up in flames a couple of weeks ago.'

Kate's whole project had ground to a halt and she had abandoned it to write up her interview with Kazz Yakamura. Now, she took it up again.

The best 'researcher' she knew was Esther Prime, a balding black woman of wild eccentricities and indeterminate age. Esther was strange. Along with the baldness, there was a single one-inch round birthmark that stood out chocolate brown in the middle of her black forehead like a toasted target. Her eclectic taste in clothes ranged from army fatigues to full-length ball gowns for supermarket shopping. She lived in the gayest part of the Castro district, though Kate never knew her sexual orientation. Esther didn't seem to have any fixed sexuality.

She rented a four-room apartment, but only used the two rooms facing north. She said she hated to see the shaded sides of the nearby trees. She couldn't stand all that moss. It reminded her of decay, and Esther was big on decay. She took vitamin pills against her own personal deteriorations, at least a dozen of them every day in all colours and sizes.

She rubbed barrier creams into her hands, sunblocks into her skin on the bleakest of days, and kept a thin coating of Vaseline over her lips at all times.

She had helped Kate on a number of occasions. Lots of journalists went to her. When you wanted to crack something totally impossible, you went to Esther and gave her a couple of days' work. She nearly always came up trumps.

Esther's working habits were as unique as the rest of her life. She locked all her doors and turned classical music up to full volume while she tapped her way into computer files around the globe. Esther was an ace hacker. Mozart and Beethoven accompanied the breaching of bank securities, the rifling of Pentagon files, the reading of confidential corporation documents and – eventually and inevitably – the angry knocking of her neighbours trying to restore peace to their building.

That particular morning, Kate was lucky to find Esther in a good mood. She didn't always answer the door when you knocked and there was no chance of calling her first as Esther would never have a telephone in her home.

'Esther,' Kate said as the door stretched its double chain, 'it's me.'

The head of the balding woman appeared. 'Katieeeee,' she drawled as she struggled with the chains and pulled back to let Kate in. Esther liked Kate. 'Come in,' she invited, 'though I don't have that long. I'm supposed to be lunchin' with a gentleman.'

Kate smiled at her quaint way of speaking. 'I won't keep you long,' she promised.

She was led into one of the two occupied rooms. It had an old sofa, a mismatched armchair that had lost half the stuffing from its cushions, and about twenty thousand dollars' worth of computer hardware strewn across the floor and joined by a tangle of cables.

'I see you've cleaned up since the last time,' Kate said.

A bad joke. Esther didn't laugh. She had no sense of humour if computer hardware was involved. Kate felt suddenly nervous. She sat down on the sofa, which promptly sagged and seemed to grab at her.

'Come on, Katie, let's have it,' Esther said indulgently. 'You want me to do work, I can tell.'

'How's that?'

'You got that look in your eye. All you journalists got it. It's that "oh-fuck-I-don't-know-where-I'm-going-with-this-story" look. Who are you working on? As it so happens, I have a day and a half free in my schedule.'

'Joe Beckett . . . Or rather, Arthur.'

Esther sucked air through her teeth for a full second and a half. Eventually, she asked, 'What you got so far?'

'Zip,' Kate told her.

'Well, that's a start.' Esther laughed.

'I'm sorry. This guy seems to have never existed. It's as though he got this great reputation, but no one ever recorded what he did.'

'So you think he's a crook?'

'I think someone's covering something.'

'Beckett's a dangerous place to go,' Esther said.

'But you'll try for me?'

'Will you pay me double? Only if I deliver, of course.'

'If I can sell a story on Arthur Beckett, I'll go sixty-forty on the whole thing.'

Esther smiled. 'Who's sixty?'

Kate pointed at herself, echoing her new partner's smile.

'Well, you are the pretty one,' Esther agreed. 'And you're sure looking good,' she added with a purr. 'Have you been getting any?'

Kate winced. Esther saw her mistake immediately. 'Sorry . . . carried away,' she said. 'I heard you was involved with that chess boy.'

'Where'd you hear that?'

'Here and there. And I heard about his manager. That wouldn't have anything to do with your interest in Beckett, would it?'

Kate shook her head, feeling suddenly sad. For a moment, in conversation with Esther, she had forgotten

John, forgotten Sam, forgotten Helen. Now they were back, right in the front of her mind.

'I – I'd better go,' she stammered uncertainly.

'Me too. I'll call you when I got something,' Esther said.

'You don't have a phone.'

'Oh, Katieee darling, we have ways and means . . . ways and means.'

She shuffled Kate to the door and hurried through her goodbyes. She was coming out with Kate, turning the various locks with a handful of keys so the door was secured at least three different ways as well as the simple Yale that dropped across when the door was shut. 'I mustn't keep my gentleman waiting,' she explained as she worked. 'He thinks my hair is so cool.'

'You don't have any hair,' Kate reminded her.

'Darling, you're always telling me what I don't have. Anyway, it's not my head he's interested in.' Esther grinned.

Kate smiled briefly, then as she followed Esther down the stairs and watched the bald woman disappear along the street, the burden of the last few days crashed back down on her shoulders and she wondered what else she could do to remove the pain.

The Beckett helicopter hovered over the family home. It turned once, twice, picking its spot on the lawns. There was space aplenty to choose from. Acres and acres of grass like a country park, but much of it was on a slope, a long gentle decline bordered with trees and centred by a grand gazebo. At the bottom of the slope was the family lake.

The ponderous helicopter edged towards its selected landing site, easing down close to the main house, a huge mansion in the style of a French château. The grass flattened out in its wind and then the blades slowed and Joe Beckett stepped out, followed by two aides carrying luggage and various dispatch boxes and bags. His father's chair appeared at the patio doors and wheeled out to greet them as Joe led his entourage up to the house.

'Another good trip?' Arthur asked.

Joe was still ducking under the dipping blades and didn't seem to hear.

'Hi, that was a helluva trip,' he shouted against the fading helicopter noise.

'Come in, let's talk,' Arthur said.

'Yes, we have to,' Joe replied. He gestured to the aides, who took the boxes and bags in a different direction. Joe grasped the handles of his father's chair and pushed it into the house.

'This has power, you know?' Arthur said.

'Yes, but we have to go somewhere private.' Joe had accelerated into a brisk walk, propelling the chair dangerously down a narrowing corridor.

'OK . . . OK, what's this about? You only have to ask.'

'In the library.'

Joe wheeled the chair into the library and shut the door behind them. Arthur spun around with a deft flick on the motor control as soon as Joe let go of the handles.

'OK, so what's got you so fired up?'

'I picked this up in San Diego,' Joe said. He was holding out a newspaper, folded to show a headline. 'YCK CHIEF IN MYSTERY DEATHS.'

'Old Kazz has got himself in some trouble,' Arthur said, perusing the story casually.

'Look at the photos,' Joe commanded.

'What about them?'

Joe was pointing to the photographs of the victims, two passport-sized inserts of Helen Michaels and Samuel Stylls.

'These two were in the background of that other photograph, the one that made you turn so white the other day. What the hell is going on here?'

'You're worried I'm involved?'

'Tell me you're not.'

'If that makes you happy.'

Joe stared at him, almost driving him back with the stare's intensity.

Arthur Beckett gathered himself. He moved his gaze from son to newspaper and back to his son.

'I can't,' he said. 'I can't tell you because it isn't true. When are you going to grow up, son?'

'Grow up?'

'You're trying to be the Governor of the state! Do you think I'm going to let my past rob you of the chance?'

Joe shook his head and tried to look away. 'I've asked you not to—'

'Asked? You know ... You know what's going on. You're about to become one of the most powerful men in the world,' Arthur said.

'I don't want it,' Joe snapped. 'Not if it means this.'

The statement left a hole between them, a silence neither could fill. Arthur nudged his chair half a wheel closer. Across the room, Joe had perched on a desk and was holding his bowed forehead in an outspread hand.

'Power is immortality,' Arthur said. 'Corrupting, isn't it? Power is raising yourself from the ranks of the grubbing irrelevant creatures we are. *Carpe diem*. There is no morality involved. When you die, you want them to raise a plaque the size of the Chinese wall. You want it to say, "Joe Beckett lived here." And you want them to be able to read it from the other end of the universe. More than that, you want a future for Joe Junior. You want to make sure he has everything you had.'

'And that's worth killing for?' Joe interrupted.

'Isn't it?' Arthur said. He paused. 'The telephone's over there, Joe. You want to put an end to it, all you got to do is pick it up and dial. Any journalist, any cop.'

'You know I can't do that.'

'For your information, I didn't kill Stylls. The woman was an accident. The one I'm after is Hayden Zalapek.'

Joe looked up, taking his hand away from his head.

'That old guy in the picture,' Arthur continued. 'Something I did in the war. He's still the greatest danger of all ... I thought he was dead fifty years ago.'

Kazuo Yakamura fell in and out of consciousness. His weary body drifted him out and the pain brought him sharply

200

back in. They gave him drugs for the pain, and when finally he slept, the sleep was long and deep and took him on into the middle of the next day.

He dreamt intensely of the past. From his early childhood in Japan, his memories of his father and mother, his year in Europe before the war, he was propelled forward to the problems with his own son, problems which still remained stubbornly unresolved. They turned to nightmares as he realized the helplessness of his present position. Here he was a 'sick king' – perhaps a dying king – with all the claimants to his throne gathering to argue succession while he laboured over every breath and wished they would go away and leave him to his sickness. Yakamura knew that empires don't run themselves. That thought cut deepest through his dreams.

When the drugs began to fade, he woke from a painful attempt to toss or turn. Coming slowly into focus around him were the comforts of a private room in the best hospital San Francisco had to offer. The bed and TV had remote controls, the white linen was super white, the clinical lines of the surrounding chairs and tables seemed razor sharp, and the faintest smell of antiseptic wafted reassuringly between the spotless walls. But as they became ever clearer, so did the physical agonies of his body. His face contorted.

'Are you in pain?' the waiting nurse asked.

It took Yakamura a few seconds to register the language.

'Yes,' he groaned in English. 'What . . . what—?'

'What happened? You fell over a chair. Someone landed on you. You have broken some bones. Please lie still.'

'Pain,' Yakamura groaned again.

'That's the drugs wearing off. You're due some more. I'll get the doctor. She'll want to examine you now you're awake.'

The doctor took less than a minute to arrive, almost as if she was waiting in the corridor. She was thirtysomething, of South American origin and with an enormous white-toothed smile which eased her into a happy bedside manner whenever she addressed a patient. Professionally, she was hugely detailed and fussy in everything she did. She spent a full half minute assessing the room and reading the data on his chart before she even approached him.

'Good afternoon,' she said, 'it's good to see you're finally back with us. Are you in pain?'

'Everyone seems to want to know that,' Yakamura complained.

'Haven't lost your sense of humour, I see.' She smiled and started her examination. 'We're going to need to take you down and operate. Your hip is the problem. The joint and the bone have shattered.'

'How shattered?'

'It's pretty severe.'

'Will I walk?'

'Too early to tell.'

'Doctor, I'm a man in my eighties.'

'It's too early to tell,' the doctor repeated, holding an admirable neutrality.

'I suppose it's a fair swap,' Yakamura said. 'Mobility for life. Dodging a bullet, I think you would say.'

'You remember what happened?'

'Oh, yes, it's coming back,' he said, nodding sagely. It was coming back. He recalled Sam Stylls, the first shot, the pain and numbness when he fell.

'Your son's outside. Would you like to see him?'

Yakamura carried on nodding. The doctor took it for assent.

'OK, but it'll have to be brief,' she warned. 'I'm just giving you a painkiller. It'll take effect in a couple of minutes.'

Yoshi came in with head bowed. He forced a smile when he saw his father. The doctor hesitated in the doorway, then seeing father and son greet each other, withdrew discreetly.

The greeting itself was quiet, Yoshi saying, 'Father,' and the old man struggling to smile with a face of pale leather that had lost all its strength. Yakamura reached out a hand and Yoshi took it and sat in a chair at the bedside.

'Thank you,' Yakamura said.

'It was I who broke your hip. Don't you remember me falling on you?'

'I remember the man with the gun.'

'Stylls?'

'What happened?' Yakamura asked.

'The bodyguard. He's dead.'

Yakamura breathed a long sigh. Yoshi waited for it to subside, holding his father's hand. Yakamura felt a little nervous tremble run through his son.

'Why did he want to kill you, Father?' Yoshi asked.

Yakamura suddenly turned and looked at his son. The question came as a shock and forming the answer brought a greater aftershock.

'He thought I killed Helen Michaels.'

'That's what he was shouting about. But you didn't,' said Yoshi with certainty.

'Of course not.'

'Then why did he think it?'

'She refused to sell her company . . .'

Yoshi looked surprised. He let go of the hand. Leaning back, a deep thoughtful furrow wrinkled the skin of his forehead.

'We've had takeover bids knocked back before. We haven't killed anyone . . . It's not your way. Why would this man think differently?'

Yakamura began to feel the effect of the drug. It took him quite a while to summon the answer.

'Because he knew about Hayden Zalapek. He knew the secret. At least, he knew there was a secret. The most powerful . . . the most dangerous man in the world.'

'What secret? What are you on about?'

'Are you in charge of the company now?' his father asked, slipping towards unconsciousness.

'I don't know. There's not been a meeting yet. Most likely Suzuki . . . This has come at a bad time. But Father, what is the secret?'

'Do you remember your grandmother? How she used to fold paper? She used to make the most wonderful things.'

'Father, what secret?' Yoshi grabbed the old man by the arm. The pain jolted him awake for a second.

'Secret?' Yakamura mumbled.

'You were going to tell me . . . about Zalapek.'

'Zalapek, oh yes—'

'Yes, Zalapek.'

'There was an enamel bath, lots of water. I have no idea . . . I had no idea. He said to look at the meters. There was no power going in. Only the water was boiling.'

'What are you on about?' Another hard squeeze of the arm.

'Cold fusion,' Yakamura said. 'He demonstrated to me a process of cold fusion.'

'But that's impossible.'

'For any other man, yes. This man understood fission in 1938. He could have built a bomb. He worked on fusion instead.' Yakamura's head lolled to one side. He did not quite realize what it was he had just told his son, something he had kept for so many years. The details of that last experiment. Nor did he realize the train of thoughts that now shunted in and out of Yoshi's mind. The fight for YCK. How he might dispose of Kendo Suzuki.

26

The last experiment, December 1939. I was surrounded by a world heading in a different direction. The scientists of my acquaintance were preparing for war and preparing to take their parts within it. My position – my view – was out of line with theirs, out of line with my friends, at odds with my wife and all that was required of an expectant father. The work I was doing was, to quote one of the more generous of my colleagues, 'complete bunkum'.

After my argument with Alice, I never went back to the house. I walked around for two days, not knowing where I was going or why. I visited places at random, creating regret, remorse, sadness. Eventually, my random patterns settled into a regular routine, going back and forth between college rooms and university laboratory, a walk of some half a mile. The purity of physics was still my means of escape from the agonies surrounding me and I set to work, harder than I had ever done before. I wanted to finish one last thing. Time, I knew, was no longer on my side.

A week later, having slept either in my college rooms or on the floor of the technician's office at the laboratory for half a dozen nights, I had something – something incredible – but I was too dazed and too tired to really assess what I had. I had worked through a series of nineteen- or twenty-hour days; I couldn't think straight and I couldn't trust my judgement. I walked down the corridor and called Kazz, the Japanese student in the next laboratory. I knew him as a fine noble fellow, a true scholar. I could not think of a more honest witness to my work.

'Please, come into the laboratory,' I said. 'I'm not sure what I'm seeing any more.'

He complained about my smell, which I will own was

quite ripe by then, but I promised him a sight such as he had never seen.

I led him into the laboratory and let him gaze at the wonders I had prepared.

There was an enamel tank, four feet by two, filled with approximately twenty gallons of clear liquid, a solution in which tap water was the dominant ingredient. I had connected two copper wires wrapped with oiled-paper insulation to a wood-panelled power supply. The wires led to electrodes dangling into the liquid. One electrode was a carbon rod, the size of a policeman's truncheon; the other, of a similar size, was an unusual-coloured metal.

'What is this?' he asked.

I smiled. What he was about to see could change physics for ever.

I turned a large Bakelite knob on the power supply. I stood back, closed my eyes, and offered a prayer.

There is a fable among scientists. It says that when an experimenter tries something truly novel, God is forced to gather together all His angels and take a vote. 'We hadn't thought of this one,' He says. 'Shall we grant the fellow some new physics? He looks a worthy young man. All those in favour, raise a wing.'

On that day, the last of 1939, the wings were raised.

Kazz walked across the room and leant over the enamel tank, searching the depth of liquid. I hadn't told him what he was supposed to witness, and, at first, there was nothing to see.

But slowly, against the sepia-toned bottom of the tank, a blue-grey glow began. A trail of bubbles stretched from the metal electrode. The size and frequency of the bubbles increased until it looked like something thrashing for its life in the bottom of the tank.

'What is happening? What is the gas?' Kazz shouted in excitement. 'Is there radiation?'

'You've read too much of my other work,' I said. 'I'm just an alchemist now. It's simply water boiling.'

As Kazz relaxed, a puzzled look eased across his face.

'You didn't call to show me water boiling, I think,' he probed.

I smiled and moved towards the power supply. 'This is less than a hundred volts, Kazz. Look at the current,' I instructed him.

There was a crude scale marking amps on the front panel. Its needle hovered below two.

'Hardly anything,' Kazz agreed. 'There is a reaction then?'

'Yes, but it is perhaps not strictly chemistry.'

'What then?'

'It's nuclear. I'm fusing hydrogen into helium.'

'That cannot be,' he said.

I spread my arms out wide, indicating the evidence that stood before him. Twenty gallons of water were boiling violently in the enamel tank, whilst the gauges measuring the reaction showed less than two hundred watts of power being applied, roughly the power of two electric light bulbs. Just as I had promised Einstein, I had indeed created nuclear fusion in a chemical experiment. I had not used fancy ingredients. I produced no radioactive by-products. The power was clean.

Before my hand-picked witness could ask another question, there was a commotion outside which halted everything.

A man in a grey overcoat limped through the door. He was wearing no socks and clutching a trilby.

'Ward,' I called out.

'Dr Costello,' said my more formal oriental colleague.

Ward looked at us both darkly. Then he turned on me alone. 'I must talk with you,' he said. 'The war is being lost. You must act. Act now, or I will act for you. You cannot remain still.' He stopped, gauging my blank expression. 'I cannot believe you,' he shouted. 'You hypocrite! You told me how faith prevented you publishing work. My God, you are not worthy of belief.'

'Ward, we ... I cannot talk now,' I replied, though I had already cut the power to the experiment.

'Now,' he said. 'Now!!' He began to wave his arms,

moving about as if he were a toy set into motion by clockwork.

'Come to my college rooms,' I offered. 'I'm staying there . . .'

He looked at me as if he wanted to kill me there and then, but he checked himself. I wondered what had raised his sudden anger. I suppose I should have guessed, but I assumed he thought only of the war, and of the bomb, and of the fate of his Jewish friends.

'You'll be there?' he said.

'I'm there every night. I have results to write up – a new experiment. I will tell you about—'

His blank look stopped me. His eyes worked round the room. Then he said, 'Very well. Perhaps it would be best.' He turned on his heels and was gone.

27

Kate went to the funeral, but John spoke to her only briefly. He seemed attached to his grandfather as if only they could offer each other support.

She expected – she hoped – he would allow her back into his life ... after the mourning, after the shock. But he showed no sign. Instead, when his grandfather strayed from his arm, John mouthed words as if he were a man drowning behind glass and as if she were a stranger trapped on the outside of his world. Fingers outstretched touching the window between them, but never close to touching the man.

Three hymns. A eulogy. The pain didn't last that long.

That evening Kate bought a bottle of gin and bottle of vodka, drank the better part of both of them and passed out naked on the sofa in her apartment.

She was finally woken by someone banging on her door. The light through the window suggested it was well into the day. She looked at the wall-clock. It said 1.30. My God, the afternoon, she thought.

'Who is it?' she shouted, balancing the pain in her head against the required volume. Her front door was four inches thick; most noise died in its wood grain.

'Esther.'

'How'd you get by the doorman?'

'I let him fumble my bum, what d'you think? Open the door, will you?'

Kate draped the first thing that came to hand around her body. It was a blue bath robe with holes in that she used strictly when she was alone.

'You look terrible,' was the first thing Esther said when she opened the door. Esther pushed her way in and glanced around. 'Demon drink got you, I take it. Wow, and you were on about my place being untidy!'

'I feel like I'm living in someone else's body,' Kate groaned, 'a dead discarded one.'

'Sit down.'

'What?'

'Sit down. You don't need to hear this standing up. I don't think you'd take it.'

Esther backed Kate across the room and guided her zombie-like into an armchair.

'Arthur Beckett is trying to murder your boyfriend's grandfather.'

'What?'

'You keep saying that. Are you sure you're awake?'

Kate's eyes fluttered in confusion, trying to shake some life into her deadened brain. 'I'm sorry. Run it by me again.'

'How plain can I put it? You'll have my report typed up and neat tomorrow, but I can précis it for you.'

'Shoot.'

'OK. Hayden Zalapek was the world's leading nuclear scientist in the late thirties. There are intelligence files on him six inches thick. He was a conscientious objector. Five different groups – three American – tried to recruit him in 1939. He turned them all down.'

Kate was looking puzzled. This had no obvious connection to Beckett. Her bemused look asked an unspoken question which Esther moved to answer.

'Beckett was in American intelligence in London at the time. His boss was a guy called Henry Hollis, recently and very violently deceased. The American files on this period have been 'lost' in inverted commas. They went up, would you believe, in the Ohio warehouse fire.'

'So how can you tie Beckett to Zalapek?'

Esther smiled. 'British files.'

'British files?' Kate was waking now. Adrenalin pumping into her body.

'I have friends,' Esther said. 'A little hacking here, a little outright theft there. We have a mutual arrangement. They scratch my back, I pass them a few interesting passwords for American networks. Anyway, I got the dirt.

'There was an incident in Oxford in January 1940. Two men were killed in Zalapek's college rooms. British intelligence got hold of Zalapek and "disappeared" him.'

'What do you mean?'

'He was a conchie, right? A conchie with a rather exciting knowledge of nuclear science. Don't you think he might have been a little dangerous to have running around during a world war?'

'They tried to kill him.'

'No, the British protected him. When they "disappeared" him, they put him in a sort of wartime witness protection programme. The man who tried to kill him was an American agent. They named him the Art Master. The British thought he was a double agent.'

'Arthur Beckett,' Kate said slowly.

'Art Beckett . . . Art Master, that's what I think.'

There was a pause while Kate considered the possibility.

'I interviewed Margaret Watson,' she said at last.

Esther raised her eyebrows. This was obviously not a name that had come up in her own research.

'She was Beckett's secretary in the fifties,' Kate explained.

'I don't recall coming across the name.'

'She was very coy about what Beckett was involved in, but I'm sure she told me he used that code name. I'm sure she did,' Kate said uncertainly.

'You got her number?'

'Sure, she lives in New York.'

'I have to tell you, Kate, this is starting to get very serious. My sources say that the Helen Michaels thing was a hit by the Boulder Brothers.'

'The Boulder Brothers?' Kate repeated.

'Yeah, Rock and Gravel, after the two cartoon characters . . . *Wacky Races*. Maybe you're too young to remember. At any rate, they are big money players.'

'How do you connect them to Beckett?'

'I don't. Except by guesswork, and a shrewd suspicion

that Beckett probably still has his contacts. That unit he worked for in the fifties was known in certain circles as "pest control". They didn't actually kill people – they were a government agency – but they did a lot of "subcontracting".'

'I can't believe this,' Kate said. 'This guy's son's gonna be the next fucking Governor.'

'All the more reason to springclean your past, don't you think? Can we call this chick in New York and see if she confirms the name?'

'Yeah, sure,' Kate said. Her voice was numb as if pounded by the blows of the last few minutes. She went back into her bedroom and sorted through the piles of notes she kept there. She spread the Singapore pile out on the bed and rummaged for the little slip of hotel stationery on which she'd written Margaret Watson's telephone number. She returned to the main room a couple of minutes later, paper in hand.

Esther was studying the bottles on the coffee table. She had poured herself a neat vodka in a chipped porcelain mug proclaiming 'sex goddess' on its side.

'Want a hair of the dog?' she asked.

'No,' Kate said uncertainly. 'I have the number,' she mumbled.

'OK, dial it . . . You want me to?'

Kate shook her head and picked up the telephone receiver and dialled. It was a cordless, allowing her the freedom to wander the room while she waited for it to answer.

It took fully thirty seconds. When it answered, the voice was male.

'Margaret Watson?' Kate said in surprise.

'Who is this please, ma'am.'

'Er. Kate Morris. Who's this?'

'New York police department . . .'

'Is Margaret Watson there?'

'I'm afraid she's dead, ma'am . . . ma'am . . . ma'am, please don't hang up.'

Kate hung up. She was woozy with the hangover and everything else. She only just made it to the sofa. She only just grabbed the bowl Esther handed her before she buried her green face and vomited into it.

28

In the first week of 1940, I wrote the equations that showed the truth of mass and matter. Times were already dangerous and I hid my work in various places, becoming almost paranoid about it.

For all my religious naïvety, I did realize what it was I was writing; I knew the significance of it and the value it might have had in my country's struggle with the Nazis. I knew also that I would have been safer not to write it at all, but there is something born in scientists that makes us write down our experiments and discoveries. So I wrote them.

At six in the evening on 9 January 1940, I was seated at the desk in my college rooms, writing the notes to the cold fusion experiment. I was very tired and cold, and the words didn't come easily.

Jack, the porter, had been in and stoked up my fire. This was not his usual job, but with the war and being out of termtime, the college was empty and he had become almost a personal servant to me. He knew my working habits and my situation with Alice. Sometimes he brought me food and I invited him to stay and we ate together. That evening he had served up a hot potato on a tin plate and left it for me to eat while I worked. He had complained that he had some extra duties and gone away, promising to return later.

When I heard the knock at the door, I assumed it was him, come back for a sit-down and a chat. I shouted, 'Come in, Jack.'

Ward Costello walked through the door with two men in grey overcoats. I turned and stood up and noticed immediately that Ward had his face turned to the floor. The two men were a step behind him.

'What's this?' I said.

It was then I saw the gun.

'Please sit down,' said the man behind it. He stepped in front of Ward and the other man grabbed my one-time friend by the arm.

'What's this?' I said again, this time in panic.

'Sit down,' the man repeated and thrust the gun towards me so I was obliged to sit back down in my seat at the desk. 'You know Mr Costello here?' he said.

Ward's face peeped from behind the man's shoulder. He was sheepish and white, and this was in itself a confusion as I had never seen Ward shocked or lost for words, and it seemed like this must be a dream.

'Ward,' I pleaded.

'I – I didn't do this,' he blundered. 'This is not what I—'

'Shut up,' the first man said. The second moved Ward bodily across the room and deposited him in an armchair in front of the bookcase.

The man doing all the talking pushed the barrel of his gun under my nose.

'Listen very carefully,' he said. 'Mr Costello has told us about your work. He tells us you have some interesting unpublished papers in the field of this new so-called nuclear physics.'

'I have no—'

'Shut up! I hadn't finished.' He grinned, pure evil. 'We want the papers.'

'You're Americans,' I said, judging the accent. I was trying to put the story together. Ward, seeing himself as a patriot, had gone to the Americans, and told them about my discoveries. Thank God he didn't know about fusion, I thought.

But I didn't realize that the story could be worse than that anyway.

The man with the gun smiled strangely. 'I'm an American,' he agreed.

'He's a traitor,' Ward interrupted. 'A bloody Nazi in the London embassy.'

The man turned around and smashed his pistol across Ward's face. Ward's cheek reddened and he spat blood out

215

of his mouth as he tried to sit back straight in the chair. He was dazed and looked like he might throw up.

All of this left me floundering. I had never had a gun pointed at me in my life and I was shaking even if I hadn't really grasped why.

'It doesn't matter who I work for. I want the papers,' the man insisted.

'You're a Nazi?' I said, belatedly dropping the piece into my personal jigsaw.

He laughed a Nazi laugh – I don't know how that could be, but it was. And it all came finally and most horribly to a single picture.

It was then I heard Jack outside the door. I didn't know what to do, what was best.

'Don't come in,' I shouted, the words involuntary.

But Jack was already pushing through the door, carrying an arm full of logs for my fire. The man with the gun, the Nazi, span around and shot him twice in the chest, a noise like a whiplash. I didn't realize guns were so painfully loud. And then, there he was, Jack, lying on the carpet spilling dark stains across its pale threads.

Ward had fought in the First World War and he had seen horror. Perhaps that's why he had his wits about him more than the rest of us, even with his cheek swollen and a broken tooth and the outward symptoms of concussion.

'My God,' shouted the man guarding him. For a moment, he gaped at the fallen body, taking his eyes off Ward.

There was a steel fire bucket full of sand that rested by the bookcase. Sometimes visitors used it to stub out cigarettes. Ward rose and swung it against the man's head. The man crashed across the room, bumping against his colleague. Ward flung himself in the same direction, realizing – I suppose – that he had only one chance to disarm the murderer.

Together they clattered into my hatstand, and three bodies and two pieces of splintered wood landed in a heap on the floor. The gun landed at my feet.

Ward was on the bottom of the pile with a body motionless on top of him, its skull beginning to ooze. The other man rolled clear, looked for his gun, then gazed straight at me when he saw me pointing its barrel towards him.

For a moment, he simply assessed the situation.

'Are you gonna fire?'

'Shoot the bastard!' Ward shouted from the floor. He must have known I couldn't pull the trigger.

I cannot tell you what I thought of as that man backed away, but I will never forget his face. For all that happened afterwards, I should have killed him. But he kept on backing away, and I kept on not firing until there was just Ward and me and a couple of bodies in that room, and I slumped in the chair and let the gun fall loose in my hand.

'Why didn't you shoot?' Ward asked, but I knew it was a rhetorical question which needed no answer.

I looked at my friend, wondering what was left of our friendship.

Ward picked himself off the floor. Blood and half the fallen man's brain were stained down his front. He didn't seem to mind that. He had, after all, been in neurosurgery during the last war. He strode across to Jack and leaned over him and tried as best he could to do something. The shots had ripped through the porter's chest, one puncturing a lung, the other nicking the heart. Jack was dying. Ward worked and worked, but got nowhere. Finally he gave up.

Slowly, he sat down, facing me across the room. I could sense the weight of his breathing. A sort of closure had come across his face.

'I have made a dreadful mistake,' he said.

29

Kate dressed haphazardly. All the time, her head throbbed with Esther's warning: 'The Boulder Brothers never miss.'

'Can't we go to the police?' Kate had asked.

'You think we got a case?'

No, of course they hadn't.

Jeans buttoned at the fly, a baggy jumper, Nike trainers, the key to the Rabbit: Kate was on her way.

She drove without caution, reaching the tournament venue in record time. Then she struck an obstacle: she had forgotten her press pass. She spent twenty minutes persuading the doorman. There was a different shift working and the doorman was a different nameless face from the one on her last visit. Arguments running 'I've got in before' didn't work. She was about to scream when it hit two o'clock and the shift changed. The new doorman recognized her, but the afternoon's play had already started by the time she got inside.

She found Hayden Zalapek in the wings of the stage, feeling a wash of relief when she spotted him. Perhaps there wasn't a clean shot between here and the hotel, not with the baggage train of reporters trailing behind. Thank God for press harassment.

'It's good to see you,' he greeted her, smiling.

She said, 'I couldn't believe it when they announced on the radio. What's he doing playing? After Sam, I thought . . . I thought he'd never play, that you'd be on your way back to England.'

The old man looked towards the stage.

Of course – it hit her. Chess is a game you belong to. John belonged. She should have known. Hadn't he told her that himself?

'You've got to get out of here,' she told the old man abruptly.

He didn't seem to understand.

'Your life is in danger,' she continued, trying to hold her pace even.

Still no understanding, just a look as if Zalapek thought she was insane.

'Does the Art Master mean anything to you?'

This time his face changed as if a paint-roller had run across it, the grey folds of skin turning back through old fears, contorting in tension. This he understood.

'Of course,' he mumbled. He leaned back against the wall.

'You must leave here.'

She tried to grab him by the arm.

'Wait. Why does this put me in danger? That was a lifetime ago. It can't be of interest to him . . . to anyone.'

'It's not what you have, it's what you know . . . and who he is,' Kate said.

He didn't seem to understand.

'Don't you know who he is now? You can't have been in San Francisco this long without seeing his son. Joe Beckett is about to become the Governor. His face is everywhere.' Kate's voice was rising, almost incoherent by the end of her sentence.

The rising voice jolted through Hayden Zalapek's mind. 'His son?' he said, as if those two words could make sense of so much if only they were true.

'Yes, his son,' she repeated.

Of course, Zalapek had sensed he was the target, but only now did he grasp why. For a while, he didn't speak. He remembered how his life was endangered in 1940. He remembered also how that danger had later killed his wife and his friend.

'We must disappear from here,' he said at last. 'We must take John.'

'John?'

'While I'm alive, everything I touch is in danger.'

Kate nodded, took a step back. 'Me too,' she said. It was

219

not a question; it was a statement. Margaret Watson was already dead for talking to her.

Kendo Suzuki arrived on the morning flight from Tokyo. He had a mandate from the YCK board to take temporary charge while its president remained incapacitated.

Suzuki wasn't a particularly creative or dynamic leader, but he was solid, and he was smart enough to show the board the fax he had received from Yakamura just before his accident. The American operation run by Yakamura's son – and, by coincidence, Suzuki's chief rival – was in trouble. In the crisis, the old man had summoned him, Kendo Suzuki, to solve the problem. That was enough for the board. If Yakamura was backing Suzuki, their long-term favourite, who were they to disagree?

Yoshi received the news with less than the best humour. Shoyo, who bore the brunt of it, was shoved across the office, screamed at in three languages, and finally thrown bodily from the room.

Then Yoshi hit the booze. He hit nightclubs and high-class brothels. He woke up next morning in bed with one white girl, one black girl and a pair of Asian twins, both female. He paid them each a thousand dollars and urged them to depart.

Only when he was alone and the worst of the hangover had passed did he start to think.

Rivals and friends had always considered Yoshi a shark, most dangerous when he was backed into a corner. He was in a corner now. He guessed, quite rightly, that this accident was all the board needed to finally insist on his father's retirement. The timing could not have been worse. The problem in China, the performance of his American operation – they both condemned him.

He made some calls to Tokyo, and tapped into his personal network in the financial sector as well as inside the company. They all said the same thing: Kendo Suzuki had the presidency in his pocket.

He could kill the bastard: that was one cold-blooded

option. He didn't blanche at it, but murder couldn't guarantee him success this time. The finger of suspicion would point straight at him if anything happened to Suzuki. He may have been able to convince his father that he was a saint, but plenty of people within YCK knew how ruthless Yoshi had been in the past.

He thought about his father and Hayden Zalapek. He thought about the things he had learned from his father's lips when the painkillers had washed the sands of secrecy off something that had lain hidden for years: cold fusion.

A desperate long shot took its distorted shape in his head. It made a warped kind of sense. Was it too wild? he asked himself. Was it really too wild?

30

Ward and I watched each other think. We watched each other take in the dead men, each wondering what this carnage meant. Two bodies emptied of life filled the room. I wanted to reach out to Ward, but I couldn't find a way. Instead I sat, breeding questions in my head, saying a little prayer that went unanswered.

'You tried to sell the work?' I said at last.

'Yes. To the Americans, not the Nazis.' He stopped. 'That doesn't make it any better, I know.'

I gazed at him, lost in thought. Doesn't it? Doesn't it make it better? Even in this numbness, doesn't intention count for anything? The questions went around and around until I came back to the starting point more disoriented than I had begun.

In the end, I said, 'What are we going to do?' Emotion came out stillborn in the words.

He dwelt on the problem for a moment. 'You should call the police. I'll make a full statement,' he told me.

I had forgotten, or perhaps not grasped, what he had done. Of course, he had killed a man, smashed his skull with a fire bucket. And another had come into my room and killed Jack. They would have killed me, if it hadn't been for him.

'The work is yours,' Ward said. 'Of course I know it, but you must know why I did it, why I really did it?'

He looked at me, puppy-eyed, and I stared back, still awash with the shock of murder and talk of police.

Then something I had not expected struck me firmly and suddenly: she had told him. That thing which I was most ashamed of, he knew.

Patriotism, principle, belief, all those things we had talked about so academically, holding ourselves dispassionate and logical – maybe we had disagreed, but it was more than that which had pushed him to this, pushed him to match my betrayal with his own.

'Marion,' I said, breathing suddenly the reason.

'Marion . . .' he replied.

'I'm sorry.'

The guilt washed through me, took my bones and unstiffened them. He spoke to me, guilty with his betrayal, and yet it was I who was filled with guilt, rotten with it. For more than a minute I could do nothing, for all the world was numbness and silence.

'Speak to me,' he said. 'Speak to me . . .'

'I can't.'

My eyes rose slowly from the floor. A slow deliberate movement washed through me, toe to head, like the swell after a big wave has passed.

'You want to know how it all went wrong,' he said. 'I called a man at the American embassy. I knew from friends he was a member of the intelligence forces – US intelligence. They gave me his code name: the Art Master. I sent him a letter; he replied. I never thought . . . God, this doesn't matter any more, does it?'

I had listened to him and, listening to him, realized what must be done.

'Ward, are you with me now?' I said.

He sat himself suddenly straight in the chair, holding himself briefly as if he had a washboard to his back.

'You trust me?' he asked.

'You just saved my life. You are . . . you have always been my friend. Promise me.'

The words seemed to hover around us, never landing until he said, 'I'd promise you anything.'

'You said the work was mine. Did you mean it?'

'Of course. I've said—'

'Ward, I have got further than I led everyone to believe . . . further than mere fission.'

'You have? How far?'

223

'Far enough. But I want none of it to play a part in this war. I cannot see how I can protect it ... So I want to eradicate it.'

He was silent for a moment; his now slumping body made no movement. Then he said simply, 'I see.'

'You are the only one I can ask this of ... whether you agree with me or not. I will call the police after you're gone.'

'You want me to destroy the work. Me, who tried to steal it?'

'I will tell you where it is hidden. There are only a handful of papers and these four or five I have here. I want you to take them and burn them – all of them.'

He took a single deep breath and I waited while his head rose slowly. 'I may be a bumbling physician rather than a physicist, but even I know what it is you ask, Hayden.'

I leaned towards him, so I could see his eyes in the flickering reflection of the dying fire in the grate. A little twitch jumped on his right cheek. 'I did not ask you because I believed you would do it with the excuse of ignorance. I would not ask that of you. You understand what it is I want?'

'As well as it is possible to understand,' he agreed. He thought for another moment and then he said, 'Do you love her?'

I made no reply and he did not move.

'We have opened Pandora's box, you and I,' he said.

Finally, after an ageing silence, he stood up.

'All right,' he whispered, 'but I can do no more for you.'

He crossed the room and passed me on his way to the door. He left without either one of us saying goodbye, even though both of us must have guessed it would be the last time we would ever meet. Sixteen sheets of paper and a woman had divided us. Nothing could put that back together.

I never did see Ward Costello again. My papers were never found. He burnt them, just as I asked. I will not deny that half of me wishes he had not. Terrible, awful work that it was, it was none the less everything I had in those years.

I have followed the history of science from afar in the years since. In my exile, I kept track through various journals to which I kept subscriptions. Scientific and religious magazines were all the outside post I ever received on my island until Marion's letter.

I had expected that others would rediscover all I had discovered, the nuclear fission and then the nuclear fusion. I was only half right. Fission powered the atomic bomb in 1945 and, after the war, a series of ever messier nuclear power stations grew up like cancers on the land. In this respect, my dissension only delayed the inevitable. But fusion has only been seen in its crudest form, forced into existence at huge temperatures by the application of enormous power. No one looked at it the way I did.

I suppose it is an indication of the lack of subtlety that spread through post-war science. Its students began to believe big was beautiful. It focused them on big rewards. The war chained scientists in the shackles of multi-million-pound government subsidies, whereas before we had lived and worked at liberty on the minor benevolences of wealthy individuals willing to put in a thousand or two and expecting no return.

Over the years, I have watched my favourite branch of science deal with the question of matter with ever more complex mathematics, leaving reality at a tangent and never returning. Experimenters smashed protons and neutrons – which were the lowest rockbed of the world I knew – into ever smaller 'particles'. They talk now of *quarks* and *strings*, justified by a fantasy of numbers and equations, but these are mere ghosts in a bubble chamber. Their relevance to our reality is lost in the violence of their collisions. If a car smashed so hard into a wall that the loose change in the driver's pocket was scattered over the accident scene, would you conclude that motor cars were made from small denomination coins?

My focus was always on what I could touch and see in

1939. Chadwick's particle had done what seemed impossible. It had crept into the nucleus and caused its split. Before that, so many of us had thought that electrostatic repulsion of one charge for another would render that impossible even using the most fantastic energies. And what I realized was that in alchemy lay the way of bringing nucleus to nucleus – heavy hydrogen to heavy hydrogen – and defeating that same electrostatic force. It's simple when you think about it on those terms. Here are two things that want to be joined. All they have to do is get close enough to reach for one another. Then the reaction is inevitable. Then the fusion happens.

All the modern physics of numbers and waves and things that don't really exist is bunkum. There can be no divisions in mass. It must be all the same, otherwise there could be no general relationship between mass and energy. These scientists should have realized that all that was important was $E=mc^2$.

I still carry the secret of cold fusion like a great weight in my pocket. A burden. A temptation. How heavy was the apple that gave Adam wisdom? In this replay of Eden, which part is played by Hayden Zalapek?

Perhaps I am the unseen and better brother of the serpent with legs. He steals the fruit and runs into exile, never offering to share a bite.

31

Five minutes after John Harringhay finished his game and took the applause of the crowd, a Volkswagen screeched to a halt outside the emergency exit to the theatre stalls. John Harringhay and his grandfather came up through the main body of the theatre, pushing their way through several of the audience who tried to ask for autographs. John leaned his weight against the bar and burst out through the emergency exit, urging his grandfather to keep up.

Zalapek struggled into the rear of the VW and John threw in a canvas bag and ran around and got in the passenger seat. The VW's front wheels ripped at the tarmac, pawing tyre tread over the road surface as the engine powered away through a straining transmission.

Around at the stage-door entrance, a clutch of reporters who were gathering in their now habitual pursuit of the Harringhay news story heard the tyre screams. For a moment, they were frozen. Then they realized what was happening and started running.

But there was no agreement among them as to which direction to run in. Some ran towards the noise like moths to the flame. Some yelled, 'It's them,' and ran forlornly towards vehicles left in car parks blocks away.

In the blink of an eye, the VW was already halfway up the street. One car, a green Dodge, U-turned in the road and set off two hundred yards behind.

'Where will we go?' Zalapek said.

'I haven't thought.' Kate kept her eyes firmly on the road ahead, scared to look in the rear view.

For a few seconds, no one spoke, then the old man asked,

'How do you know these things? How do you know what you say is true?'

'I got a friend to investigate your records. Journalism, I guess . . .' She laughed at herself falsely. 'One of my contacts is already dead.'

'I thought I was safe . . . after all these years . . .'

'John, have you got any ideas?' Kate asked, glancing at him.

John hadn't said anything since the penny dropped, since he knew there were men who would kill them all. He sat brooding, eyes fixed.

'John?' she called again, 'I need you. We need your help now.'

'Help?' he said.

'We need the guy at the chessboard, not the little boy. Can you do it?' she snapped, her voice a little out of control.

'We're being followed,' he said.

She realized suddenly his eyes were on the wing mirror.

'What?'

'A green car, four back.'

'What?' she repeated.

'Make a right turn at these lights. See where it goes.'

She heard the command in his voice, railed against it briefly, then realized he was doing exactly what she'd asked – the guy at the chessboard coming out.

She eased the car to a stop at a red light. Two cars slid alongside on her right. The green Dodge rolled up only two cars behind.

'Shit!' she said. She was suddenly conscious that her legs were shaking. It was hard enough to hold the clutch pedal down. When the lights changed, they kangarooed forward, only just avoiding a stall as the engine bogged and then pulled.

'Are they still there?' Zalapek asked. Sitting stiffly in the back, he couldn't really turn to see.

'Yeah,' Kate said in a tremble, 'they're still there.'

They drove along past the Maritime Museum, Kate accelerating until she was well over the speed limit. She braked sharply as if to turn into Van Ness Avenue.

'No,' John said sharply, 'go for the bridge – the Golden Gate. We don't know who they might be. They could be just press.'

'I don't want to wait to find out.'

'Do it. I want to turn off into the park. We need to see what they do.'

Kate switched lanes. A hundred yards back, the green Dodge did the same. They both turned, ran another mile or so along the waterfront and then headed into the tree-lined tracks of the Presidio. Kate could feel the tension knotting in her body.

'Do you think they know we know?' she asked.

'Who knows? Drive slowly.' John's voice had gathered strength from somewhere. His words had a strange echo of the chessboard, as if he was, in their crisis, talking aloud in the silent voice he used to command over the chequered squares. That persona where all the troubles of the outside world could not reach him, where he became supreme, where he was genius, now shone through into the real world.

Obediently, Kate drove along at a steady twenty. The Dodge dropped back, but every now and again they could see it in the far distance, caught in a mirror, caught by a length of straight too long to hide around the last corner.

'What are they doing?' she asked.

'They're hoping we're going to stop somewhere. If we stop it makes it easy for them,' John said. There was something logical here and his voice delivered it with absolute calm.

Kate looked at him, took her eyes off the road for a moment. 'I'm scared,' she said.

'Don't be . . . We're going to need you.'

'That's my line . . . "We need you," ' she said.

'We're a team, all right. Listen, these must be the men . . . Beckett's goons. If they were reporters, they'd be on our bumper like they've all been for the last two days.'

'What're we going to do?'

John hitched himself around in the seat, looking over into the back. 'Pass me the canvas bag,' he said to his grandfather.

Zalapek leaned across and lifted it painfully so John could reach it.

'Belt yourself in,' John said to his grandfather, then turned back, scrabbling through the contents of the bag. 'Turn left. Let's get back out of this park. Don't speed – it'll only tell them we know. Twenty will be fine.'

They emerged from the park heading east. John had Sam's old laptop opened out on his knees. He and his grandfather had been using it as an analysis tool back at the theatre. Now John saw it in a different role. He had no screwdrivers with him, so he smashed the case against the car's dashboard until he could get enough leverage to prise it open with his penknife.

'I need wire,' he explained. Kate looked at him as if he were insane. 'Just drive anywhere,' John added when he saw her face. 'I need time.'

For the next three minutes, he ripped wiring out of the laptop's guts, taking the individual pieces and biting off the insulation, so he was left with lengths of wire showing bare metal ends. All the time, the green Dodge see-sawed a discreet three or four cars behind them.

'You're going to solder that wire or something?' Kate asked.

'When you pull up at the next red, be prepared to floor it,' he answered.

'What?'

'Listen,' he said, 'I'm going to get out. I want you to make a long circuit of the block. Just keep turning right. Go up above me a block and come back down through this junction. I'll be ready.'

'Ready for what?'

'Just drive fast. As soon as I get out, they're going to realize. It's going to be a chase. Drive safely. I wouldn't want . . . I wouldn't want anything to happen to you . . . or to my grandfather.'

'This is insane.'

'Do what I say.'

By now, they were on a long undulating downslope, lined with scatterings of parked cars, pavements with dustbins empty from the morning pick-up and overlooked by faceless houses which had once been grand but were now sliced mercilessly into cheap apartments. Down the road before them lay traffic light after traffic light as if they were travelling down a hall of mirrors and, instead of light at the end, there was the expanse of water in the San Francisco Bay.

They pulled up at the first red. Two cars behind sat the green Dodge and behind that the rest of the slope which seemed to go up for ever. The road to right and left was relatively flat and built up on both sides with dilapidated commercial enterprises that had seen better days.

'I'm scared,' Kate said again. 'Which way do I go?'

'Straight a block, then right. Don't stop for traffic lights.' John leaned across, kissed her on the cheek. 'When this hits amber, I'm going out of the door. As soon as you see me go, you go.'

John flung open the door, using its momentum to drag himself halfway out. He got a foot on the road and levered himself outwards and upwards. He was leaping for the pavement and slamming the door behind him at the same time. He heard the VW rev and then its screeching take-off as he ducked down behind a parked van. He waited for the noise of the Dodge following.

He needed to hear it. In his part-formed plan, failure was them coming after him, or shooting him as they took off. He was gambling on Zalapek being their only target and that the sight of the old man metaphorically running for it down the street would be sufficiently distracting.

It was . . .

He heard them as they set off in pursuit. He said a prayer

of thanks. Automatic. He found it odd that he should appeal in that direction. No time to think about why.

He glanced around, knowing he had only seconds, looking for the box that controlled the lights. He knew what they looked like in England, and guessed they must look similar in the States. Also he knew how they worked in England, and he was gambling they worked the same here. All of a sudden, it occurred to him that there were an awful lot of guesses and gambles in this plan.

Ten seconds and he had his penknife in the door. He levered it as hard as he could. The blade broke before he realized he was levering at the wrong side. Shit! He pulled it back and jammed the stub in the right side. Paint flaked. The fucker wouldn't open. Shit again ... He'd got this wrong.

Kate and his grandfather were circling to their death. And he'd abandoned them. He glanced desperately down the road, saw the red VW make a hard right and disappear out of sight, the green Dodge twenty car lengths back and already making up ground.

He jabbed into the crack again. This time the panel gave and the access door opened. He only half recognized the circuitry before him, but he knew fully how dangerous this gamble had become.

Kate had never wanted to be a racing driver. An old boyfriend had taken her to a karting track when she was fourteen. The boyfriend was nineteen and persuaded the pit mechanics to let her on the track, even though she couldn't produce a driver's licence. The technique was simple – you went flat out until you came to the corner, stamped on the brakes, and turned. If you wanted to be quick, you had to get enough speed off by the middle of the corner to power out of it under control.

But that's not easy to remember when your pursuers are carrying guns. You don't want to put your foot on the brakes at all. It feels too much as if you're stopping for them, turning to fight. Custer's Last Stand, only here it was an old man and a panicky journo against two trained killers. Not good odds.

She made the first corner only after the front of the car slid wide on the bend. Fortunately the lights were on green and there was no oncoming traffic as she completed the turn. Still she lost a good thirty yards of her lead, and on the next straight, she could see, in her wing mirror, the Dodge's passenger leaning out of his window and brandishing a rifle as if shaping to take a shot. The rifle barrel chopped up and down, never getting steady on the bumpy road. Thank God for the bumps, the broken surface.

'I think you'd better duck down,' she advised her passenger as she glanced back at him. But of course there was nowhere to duck to.

She made a better job of the second turn, although she flashed through red lights to make it. Trying the same thing, the pursuing Dodge got sideways and came within an inch of a Porsche which was coming fast across the junction from left to right. The Porsche veered, its driver standing on the brakes, grinding flat spots on to its tyres as it completed a one-eighty, and ended up backwards in the side of an innocent taxi queued on the opposite side of the road. It didn't slow the Dodge, though.

Kate had her foot firmly to the floor, but the road now rose steeply uphill. The VW engine accelerated in strange fits and starts as the switchbacks made it alternatively harder or easier. The Dodge had a horsepower advantage and, in two blocks, it was nibbling at the bumper.

A forty-foot truck was malingering in the inside lane as they approached the next junction. Kate saw a terrible decision to be made. The lights themselves were green. She could slow and follow the lorry, but that would give her pursuers a clean shot. Worse still, what if the lights went red and the lorry stopped? She had to go left of it, but that meant one hell of a right turn across its bows. Also she'd be gambling the truck wasn't going straight on. In its unhurried progress, it had given no turn signals.

She thought it brave that she didn't shut her eyes as she

turned the wheel. A jink to the left, then right. She kept her foot flat, knowing that if she slowed there was every chance of clipping the front of the lorry.

She got around, the front wheels cocked over as if attempting a snowplough turn and the car describing an even arc at forty-five miles per hour while rubber tore off the Goodyears and the inside rear wheel lifted clean off the ground.

'I'm leaning over,' Zalapek said from the back, 'trying to hold us down.' In truth, he was simply trying to hold his calm, trying to contribute some encouragement.

Kate still had her foot hard on the throttle pedal. She looked back, not at him, only at the Dodge which had chosen the safer option, turning inside the truck as the truck went straight on at the junction. It had lost a good twenty yards but it had a run on them down the next straight. And now the road was flat and relatively smooth.

She suddenly heard a single sharp 'ping' as a hole appeared instantaneously in the front and rear windows. If he hadn't been rocking himself back upright at the time, the bullet would have gone clean through Zalapek's head.

She felt her bladder go just a little. She pressed her foot harder, but there was nothing more. She was already flat out.

The last turn loomed, offering the route back on to their original path, one block above where they had left John, just as he had instructed.

She completed it with an excellence that made her proud. She feinted left, partly to prepare, partly in a vain effort to avoid further gunfire, figuring it would take her away from the side of the Dodge from which the passenger was shooting. Then she braked hard, letting off smoothly as she eased the wheel right, power hard on as soon as she felt the tyres holding their own at the apex of her turn. She belonged to the car as it eased out on to the straight. One and the same. It was perfect. Her old boyfriend would have approved.

But one success bought nothing and she had no time to dwell. She was now on the down slope, a near vertical drop with switchbacks offering multiple opportunities to launch the car at even moderate speeds. One such switchback lay between her and the junction John had chosen. And there she was pushing sixty. She didn't ease up. The lights below her showed green.

She could still see the Dodge in the rear view, further back but still there, still with her.

Why is there never a cop when you need one? What she wouldn't give for a blue light and a year's supply of speeding violations right now. Even arrest seemed a good option.

She closed her eyes as the car dipped into the switchback.

John saw the cars coming towards him – a red Rabbit and a green Dodge. He had already had the traffic lights under control for a good half minute. He was ready.

Kate's car hit the bottom of the switchback, leapt into the air as it emerged and nosedived from five feet up. The fender ripped off as it touched down, a sheet of orange fire sprayed sideways, but it kept on coming. The Dodge took the same punishment a little more elegantly, but it was still a good forty yards back, disadvantaged by Kate's perfect last corner.

John waited until the Rabbit was less than its stopping distance away, then he jabbed the wires he had purloined from the laptop on to two strategic contacts on the control board.

The lights in front of Kate never changed, whilst all those controlling the roads across turned green together. Seconds after the Rabbit sped over the junction, a sixteen-wheeler eased forward from the right, while another began a slow cut-off of the left-hand escape. Both presented wide high-sided walls to the oncoming Dodge.

The Dodge locked its wheels, but down the hill, both cars had touched eighty. Already thirty yards from the junction, the result was an inevitable checkmate.

Whether by design or accident, the skidding Dodge chose the centre of the right-hand truck. Here there were no wheels to hit, just the main goods-laden belly of the truck some three or four feet off the ground.

Momentum took the car's hood underneath at a good thirty miles per hour. The first impact was on the driver's side windshield stanchion, which tore and pulled back the roof like a sardine can opening in a downpour of glass. Metal sparks and flying debris obscured the fate of the occupants.

The chassis and main body of the car appeared from under the truck, running downhill. The roof section bounced back the way it had come, landing in an unrecognizable tangle on the dented side of the truck.

John Harringhay stood up from the crouched position he had adopted over his work. Bystanders were running into the road looking shocked, looking for victims to tend to. No one looked back at John; no one seemed to make the connection between the crash and his interference with the traffic control electronics.

The dented truck had jackknifed to a halt, blocking the left-hand road at the exit of the junction. The other sixteen-wheeler hadn't even bothered to stop.

Meanwhile, the topless Dodge was making its own way down the slope at a sedate ten miles per hour. There was no longer a driver with his foot on the brake. A few of the fitter bystanders were chasing it on foot.

The Dodge arced very slowly to the left, mounted the pavement and nudged gently into a cluster of empty dustbins.

It was too far down the slope for John to even hear the clatter.

Returning to their hotel was too dangerous. Kate drove the three of them south down Route 101, then cut to the coast. They had been going several hours before she dared to stop.

They checked into a motel using names she made up on the spot. She thought about dumping her car, but she was tired and soiled and still trembling. She had no strength to do more.

They ate burgers in the next-door diner. Even Zalapek downed most of his fries and a large plastic tumbler of Coke. He complained of pains in his back from the car's leap, but not of anything else. When the waitress wasn't in earshot, they tried discussing how they could get out of the current mess alive.

But none of them had an idea. And they were zombies that night anyway – zombies who agreed to sleep on it. They said their goodnights and went to separate rooms.

When Kate reached her room, she headed for the shower. She stripped off her clothes – jeans, T-shirt, underwear – and rinsed them, remembering how at one point she had nearly wet herself.

She was cleaned off and wrapped in a towel when she heard the knock at the door.

'Who is it?' she shouted nervously.

'John.'

She had forgotten – suppressed – her feelings. Sheer fucking terror had taken over, numbing that part of her. And anyway, hadn't he walked through their perils as if she was the last thing on his mind? Yes, he'd saved them, but hadn't he put her aside when Helen was killed? 'Kate and John' was a brief affair started on unfortunate timing. Her short life's experience had taught her timing was everything. When it was wrong, nothing could save a relationship. She ought to have run away. Why did she ever go to the theatre? Why was she now stuck like stone in the middle of her motel room?

Just open the door, she told herself. Just open the door! She almost had to say it aloud, give herself the command. It was the only way to make herself move.

'Hi,' he said.

'Hi.'

'I wanted to ask you . . .' he started, never reaching the point.

'To ask me?'

Unspeaking, he ghosted past her, without a glance at her

towel-clad body. Her eyes followed him, still in his chess-player's suit.

'To ask me what?' she repeated.

'You could have been killed.'

'So could you.'

'Yes, but he's my grandfather ... So I wanted to ask you why you did it? Why did you come today?'

She stared at him. He was waiting for an answer. When she gave none, his face contorted and the tears began. She took his head in her hands, holding it so its features stood not six inches from her own, and she kissed his wet cheek. Salt spread across her lips and she licked it away and kissed him on the mouth.

'God, how could I have been so stupid?' he whispered through his pain. 'How could I have ...?'

'How could you have done it any other way?'

His hands brushed across the fine hairs at the top of her back. She sank her head down in his chest and somehow, by a friction that was on neither side deliberate, the towel around her body slipped its temporary anchor and fell to the floor.

Naked she came to him. Peeled away his clothes. Laid him gently back on her rented bed where she kissed every inch of him until all his tension stood erect in one stiffened part of him. She took him inside and shared everything she had, so that afterwards, when he cried again, she lay wiping the last of his tears with her thumb.

And it was not as if she had simply given to him by her tender care, but rather as if the entering had been mutual and she had entered him also, and drawn back into the world that which was hidden within. Pressed to her, she opened him like a flower, a bloom both beautiful and brilliant.

32

My neck and back were stiff in the morning. But I was alive. John was alive, Kate too. There were moments the previous day when that did not seem likely. I thanked God, but good as that felt, we were far from out of danger.

I considered the problem carefully. For fifty years, I had hidden myself away. I had assumed that was long enough. After all, the secret the world had wanted from me was the secret of the bomb, and it had had that long ago from other sources.

I had not realized how the role I had played might continue to threaten others. Men who had sold their morality in that struggle of 1940.

After I was gaoled, a scramble had begun for my papers. The British went through the proper channels, obtaining an order to search my college rooms and laboratory. Arthur Beckett must have already known they would not be found there.

Marion told me their house was ransacked a week after the shooting. I assume my wife and Ward were kidnapped when Beckett's men tried the same ransacking of my own home. Only simple chance saved Emily. She was at her grandmother's for the afternoon while Alice and Ward went into Oxford and tried to hire a solicitor to defend me. They must have walked in on the intruders as they returned.

Alice's body had slash marks across the face when they found it. It was part of the charred wreckage of an abandoned house in London. Ward's body had a dozen broken bones . . . a punctured lung.

Of course, they tortured them both. Innocent . . . But then what weight has morality in the face of war? Men will move mountains for power.

Ward would have screamed that he had burnt the papers. Arthur Beckett would not have believed him. Why would he? Who would expect that a man who only a few days ago wanted to sell the papers had suddenly decided to burn them? Only I knew what tides raged inside Ward Costello. Beckett could never have understood.

And all these things led me to where I was today: in an American state with its next Governor as an enemy. It was a country I did not know and my only allies were a girl and a boy. There seemed few options left.

I showered and dressed and made my way across to the diner where we had eaten the night before.

The breakfast shift was on roller skates, gliding across the polished wooden floors with an awful energy I could not muster in myself. Its *maître d'* scooted me to a table and poured the blackest coffee I have ever seen. I thanked her and ordered an omelette.

John came in five minutes later, pausing to pick up a newspaper before he was rolled over to my table.

'Have you ordered?' he asked.

I shook my head. He unfolded the paper and there on the front page was a picture of the crash scene we had left the previous day.

'No picture of you or me,' he said. 'They describe the VW, but they've got no number.'

'Good,' I told him.

'How difficult do you think it is to spot a red Rabbit with a missing front?' he asked, raising his eyebrows.

'I see . . . John, I'm sorry, I'm not much use.'

He looked at me. I think he understood my despair. Age and fifty years as a recluse were no preparation for this. I felt like luggage, while everyone around me was running or – in the case of the diner – skating.

He said, 'The only good thing is they're saying the traffic lights was simple vandalism. The corner was known for drug peddling. They think it was some kid on a trip. No one seems to have connected it.'

'But?' I heard the word unsaid in his voice.

'Beckett'll connect it. How long do you think it'll take him to find another set of thugs?'

'There's really no way out, is there?'

He shrugged and leaned back in his chair, dropping the newspaper as if it no longer held relevance, or perhaps it just held no more hope. He didn't answer the question.

The waitress came and John ordered a fried breakfast. He even joked with her, seeming surprisingly lucid, somehow changed.

It took time to see it. Perhaps longer for me to make sense of it. He didn't have the fear. He didn't have my fear, or any fear that would be normal. He saw the problem, the danger, but in his head, a problem was all it was. Like two pawns and a king in an end game puzzle. He somehow knew he could work it out.

He said, quite casually, that he didn't want to wait for Kate. He was hungry and she was still asleep, he said. He pointed at me and I found myself ordering toast while I was still completely mesmerized.

'You look pale,' he told me. 'Are you all right?'

'I have thought about our situation,' I said.

'Oh yes?' He seemed eager to hear, but he leaned back in his chair, tilting it far enough for it to rise on to its two back legs.

Suddenly, I found I wanted to ask a different question.

'There is one thing I do not understand,' I said. 'Marion told me that it was you who told her where I was ... I mean, when I was in exile. She said you found me years ago.'

'Ah, your exile. I suppose you think it would all have been all right if no one had found you.' He paused, glanced at me, then tried a smile. 'I will tell you, if you will answer a question.'

He didn't wait for my agreement.

'*The Cherwell Christian*,' he said. 'You were a subscriber. You used to contribute.'

'Before the war,' I agreed.

'There are some changes no one makes. I went to the

publisher's office . . . strictly out of hours. I was . . . different . . . back then – busted twice for shoplifting. I stole their complete list. Even turned on their copier to xerox it.'

He seemed proud of that. He waited a few seconds for it to sink in.

'Then there were scientific journals. They were harder. It took a lot of work to break into those. Of course, as they got themselves on the Internet, that sort of hacking became easier.'

'Hacking?'

'Information burglary, Grandfather.'

'I still don't understand. I was using a false name. I had no connections . . .'

'How many subscribers do you think *The Cherwell Christian* has off-shore? Not many who take *Scientific American*, *Nature* and *Physics Today*. Three in fact, all 'retired academics'. I wrote to them, asking them to reply to a reader survey . . . A chance to win prizes. Of course, you were the one who didn't reply: Mr Harry Smith.'

'Clever,' I conceded. In thirty seconds, he had destroyed my myth of safe seclusion. Perhaps you can find anyone in this world if you try hard enough. In our present predicament, that thought was not a pleasant one.

The waitress delivered his fried breakfast. He took two sauce sachets and squeezed them out on to his food.

'Now my question,' he said. 'You told me about Ward Costello. You told me about Marion. But you didn't tell me it all, did you?'

I thought about this for a good ten, or maybe fifteen, seconds.

'No,' I admitted.

'And it wasn't so noble?'

'No, it was shameful.' I found myself staring at the red check of the tablecloth.

In all the things I have done, I can claim to have followed my faith. All the things, but one. And I found myself telling him – telling him because he deserved to know. No one should look to their ancestors and see them impenetrable and unblemished. They should look and see it all.

I never said my stand against the war was noble. I always said that history would judge me harshly. I always said I was ashamed.

After my argument with Alice, after I had said I would not work for the British or anyone and she threw her pregnancy in my face, I went to Marion's house. I try to tell myself I was looking for Ward, to make up with him. But that is not true.

Marion ushered me inside and I was crying. I was lost and the secrets burned in my insides.

I stood while she reclined full length on a chaise longue, drinking brandy from a crystal glass, beautiful and dark through the sheen of my tears. She looked on my despair with compassion.

'Why did you ever marry, Hayden?' she said. 'You're not the marrying kind.'

'I thought I could make her happy. I thought she could make me—'

'Ward says you're a fool. You won't join the war effort. He says the Nazis will wipe out the civilization of the world.'

'Is that what you believe?'

She smiled. 'I know you better than that.'

I looked back at her, surprised and off guard. The rift with Ward, the split with Alice – I suppose it released all those emotions for Marion which I had chained from our first meeting.

She put down the brandy glass and came across and put one painted hand on each of my shoulders.

Then she kissed me.

I don't know the recipe that changes sadness into desire. I don't know what she saw in me. I don't know why we did what we did when we were both in love with someone else. For a man whose mind was once great, I suppose I know very little. And I suppose that, for a man who gave everything for his faith in God, I was surprisingly weak to the temptation of flesh.

I remember the lace and perfume of the room, the fire burning in the corner. She slipped from her dress like an angel, emerging into this world from another, here for a moment and then gone.

She let down her hair, which was long back then and seemed to be all things.

I touched it softly. Abandoned. Wanton. It did not matter; there was no tomorrow.

So I reached and pressed against her, and she melted towards me, fates sealed and delivered.

Passion has no sense to it, no logic. What were we hoping for as we groped blindly forward? We grasped at passing pleasure as if some antidote for pain could be sucked from its skin before it was lost for ever.

'Oh, God,' she said, turning away when it was done. She sat on her side of the bed, stretched out to the bedside table for a cigarette and lit it with a book of matches. She sucked so hard and long that a pencil of ash formed and drooped and fell. It smashed on her naked breasts, clinging to the sweat our coupling had made there.

'I see,' John said when my tale was finished.

I looked up from the table and realized he had not previously guessed what it was I was going to tell him. Not all of it anyway.

'I should have known,' he said. He had a puzzled, self-questioning look. I think he actually believed he should have worked it out.

'How could you?' I asked him.

'Aunt Marion was always strange with my mother.' He hesitated, assessing the facts as he went. 'Sure, she treated her like a daughter, loved her. But there was something . . . guilt. I figured it was guilt because she had survived the war and my mother was so clearly – well, orphaned by it, I suppose. I never—'

'Of all the things I did, I would do them all the same except this one,' I said.

'Do you think it made a difference?'

'It made Ward betray me. He would never have raised a finger . . .' I said, stopping as I realized that phrase was all too familiar.

'You know she would never allow me to call her "Granny" or "Grandmother", or any of those things.'

'And Emily?'

'She was never allowed to call her "Mother".' His voice drifted away as if it were suddenly worn through and I left him to his thoughts.

I was halfway through my toast before I spoke again. I was weighing the morning in my own mind, turning it over, looking for a way out.

Kate appeared as I munched the last bite. John stood and helped her into her seat, a gentlemanly act I had never seen from him before. She didn't smile; she looked very serious.

'I've thought about this,' she said. 'I think we should go to the police. I don't think Beckett can get to us if we do, and I think – with what Esther has – we can nail Arthur Beckett.'

'All right,' I said. I could see this was the practical plan.

I was surprised when John disagreed quite so firmly.

'We can't do that.'

'Why?' she asked, seconds before I formed the word myself.

'First,' he said, 'we have no evidence that a fancy lawyer couldn't get round. Second, we killed two people yesterday . . .'

Kate looked from John to me. I hadn't considered it that way. From her look, I don't think she had either.

'And anyway . . .' John turned to me. 'We cannot let your secret out. Even if it is only half your secret we reveal, you will be hounded for ever – newspapers, media. You cannot go back to the life—'

'Is that so important, my son?' I asked him.

'To me,' he said. 'To me.'

I thought for a moment. Suddenly something that should have been staring me in the face tripped into focus. 'As I see it, there is only one man we can trust,' I said.

'Who?' Kate asked.

'Kazz Yakamura. He has kept my secrets for more than fifty years.'

'We can't—' she began.

'He is an old friend,' I insisted. 'Besides, who else is there?'

33

Kendo Suzuki had the main office in YCK's San Francisco headquarters cleared for his personal use. His own assistant, a pretty American Japanese woman with dark oriental hair and green eyes, took over the outer office, installing fax machines and portable computer systems flown from Tokyo.

'I'm only here three days,' he said. His office language was Japanese. 'We need a schedule.'

'You will see the old man?' the assistant asked him.

'First,' he confirmed. 'I will go to the hospital now. Then I want Yoshi in my office. Eleven o'clock will do. Then I will talk to the department heads here at midday.'

'I will arrange it,' she assured him.

She bowed. He smiled, picked up his coat and asked her to call his car.

Yoshi Yakamura arrived as called at 10.50. The assistant sat him down in the outer office. It took him less than thirty seconds to work out what Suzuki wanted. When the assistants are not polite any more, you know your star is on the wane.

Suzuki walked in on the dot of eleven, barrelling into his office, ignoring Yoshi's presence. He kept him waiting another ten minutes before he bleeped through and asked his assistant to 'send Mr Yakamura through'.

Yoshi bowed as he entered Suzuki's presence. It was a brief, personally wrenching bow, but even the ferment within did not extend to breaking the normal courtesies.

'Yoshi,' Suzuki said cheerily, suddenly acknowledging a man he had studiously walked past not ten minutes earlier.

'You wanted to see me,' Yoshi said.

'I wanted to tell you personally about the changes.' Suzuki

gestured for him to take a seat on the other side of the main desk.

'Changes?'

'You are in a position of privilege. You should hear of the changes first.'

'Is that what my father told you?'

'No, your father was "very supportive" of me ... of my whole position. He would have preferred, of course, if the board had chosen you to reign in his absence. But he understands.'

'The stock price is falling,' Yoshi said, a smile cracking. 'He has to support you. At least, publicly.'

Suzuki laughed. 'You have always been a dreamer, Yoshi. Perhaps you get that from your father. He dreamt that he could make you the next president of YCK. You? You are a womanizer, a waster. What did you ever bring to YCK but trouble? You killed that American investigator to fix the Chinese report, didn't you?'

'You have evidence?' Yoshi stood up. His eyes flashed with indignation.

'We would not be having this conversation—'

'You gutless motherfucker!'

Suzuki rose angrily, pulling himself up to meet his opponent's eyes. He seemed about to spring, but held himself back, realizing perhaps he had the upper hand. Whatever insults Yoshi might throw, they meant nothing. He sank slowly back down, his stare cooling as he looked at the stranded Yoshi. A young man with nowhere to go. His protection gone. Naked. Abandoned. Yes, Suzuki knew these things well enough.

'I am informing you that you are being replaced as head of the American operation,' he said. 'You will be offered the management of our Scandinavian venture, based in Copenhagen.'

'There's nothing up there. That whole thing doesn't turn more than fifteen million dollars a year.'

'Not too much to screw up then,' Suzuki said.

'You're only sending me there because you dare not fire me.'

A smile cracked on to Suzuki's face. 'Yoshi, sometimes you are a smart boy.'

'You'd never hold the stock market if you lost both my father and me.'

'I could take it if you resigned.'

'Never.'

'Then Scandinavia it is,' Suzuki concluded. 'You may have three days to clear your office and pack your things. I'm told you have a house here?'

'An apartment – about a mile away.'

'Very well.' Suzuki stood up purposefully. 'That is the end of the interview. Thank you.'

He held his hand out. Yoshi looked at it, then turned away. He didn't even bow before leaving the room.

In his study in Los Angeles, Arthur Beckett watched the television with satisfaction. A week to the year's end, his son had a ten-point lead in the polls. This was going to be a good Christmas. Next year was going to be perfect, a smooth glide to Sacramento. The Christmas decorations around the house might have been celebrating the victory even now. All those years leading to this.

The intercom light on the main desk lit up suddenly and unexpectedly. Most of the staff weren't working; the secretaries were on holiday.

Beckett reversed his wheelchair and swivelled it into position.

'Yes,' he said brusquely as he operated the answer button.

'Lady at the gatehouse to see you.'

He recognized the voice of a guard at the front gate.

'I've got no visitors planned,' he said. 'Your job's to keep the reporters out.'

'I know, but this is a strange one. I don't think she's a reporter. Says to tell you she's a friend of Hayden Zalapek. Does that mean anything?'

Beckett thought for a moment. 'Send her up to the house,' he said. 'Better escort her.'

He was trying to think who it might be, pondering all the possibilities until a balding black woman in army green was ushered through the door.

'You want to dismiss your bozo?' was the first thing Esther Prime said.

Beckett smiled. He didn't know who she was, but she had guts. He waved the escort away, asking for privacy. The guard shut the door behind him, probably glad to get out.

'Before we go on,' Esther said, 'I want to tell you I deposited six copies of all I know with various lawyers around LA and San Francisco. It's the usual routine: if I don't show up, it goes to the papers and the cops.'

'What is there to know?' Beckett asked innocently.

'Those boys killed yesterday. They were working for you.'

'Which boys?'

Esther laughed at him. 'OK, we can just forget it if you want. I flew down here this morning 'cos I thought we had something that might be of mutual interest.'

'What's your name?' he asked.

'Call me Esther. Of course, I know yours. Art. Or should I call you "Master"?' She smiled, a row of white teeth punctuated with a gold cap. 'It's a hard word for a littl' ol' *nigger* like me to call a *honky*.'

'You've got a mouth on you, I'll give you that.'

Suddenly, Esther turned on him. 'Listen, you fucker,' she said, leaning over Beckett's chair to stare into his eyes, 'all I want is money. I'll deliver Hayden Zalapek to you.'

'You know where he is?'

'Apart from in hiding from you? Yeah, I know. The girl with him and Harringhay is Katie Morris. You know her?'

Beckett nodded lopsidedly, but the acknowledgement was enough for Esther.

'She's been investigating you,' she continued. 'I guess you knew that, otherwise why would you have had Margaret Watson killed?' Esther hesitated. 'You've got no comment on that, I see. Any road, Kate hired me to dig into your past.

That's how I came by the evidence – you know, that which is now at the lawyers. I just want to remind you of that.'

'You think that's your protection?'

'Don't you?'

'What is it you want?'

'Ah, now we're talking,' Esther cooed. 'I want ten million dollars.'

Arthur Beckett looked straight at her, his good eye holding her gaze for half a minute or more. Esther never blinked. The first rule of negotiation: never blink. Whoever blinks first loses.

'Seems like a fair price,' Beckett said at last. 'Would you like to see the Governor, Esther? Seal the deal?'

Beckett backed the wheelchair to the desk again, leaning over to press the call button on the intercom. The answerer was somewhere distant in the house.

'Is Joe still in?' he asked.

'Down in the garden, I think.' It was a woman's voice.

'Could you find him for me, my dear? Ask him to come up to the library.'

'This isn't necessary,' Esther protested as Beckett let go of the button.

He turned towards her. 'I insist,' he said.

Joe came in a couple of minutes later. He was wearing jeans and a denim jacket. He looked surprised by what he found.

'Father?' he said, mixing greeting and question in a single word.

'This is Esther,' the older Beckett replied by way of explanation. 'Esther wants ten million dollars of our money. You see, she's discovered certain facts about me, and she wants to deliver Hayden Zalapek to us.'

'Ten million?' Joe repeated.

Arthur Beckett waited while Esther and Joe exchanged puzzled glances.

'Of course,' Arthur Beckett said, 'Esther is wearing a wire. You know, one of those tap things. Only I'm pretty sure she's working on her own, aren't you, *dear*? Or should I call you *nigger*, you black bastard!'

He swung up a gun and shot her once through the forehead. The bullet made a 'putt-tuck' sound as it came out of the silenced barrel. Esther toppled backwards, falling over a chair and landing face up on the carpet with an oozing wound plumb centre of her chocolate birthmark.

'Bulls-eye,' he said. 'I didn't know I still had it in me. Good job I'm not a leftie. That stroke would have taken out my gunhand.'

'You shot her!' Joe put his hand out against a bookcase as if he was about to fall. He couldn't take his eyes from the tracks of blood, which seemed to grasp the victim's face and hairless skull like octopus arms extending from that one wound. 'Where d'you get the gun?' he asked in a dead tone.

'Desk drawer. I slipped it out while I was using the intercom. Beginner's stuff. I had it hidden beneath the blanket waiting for the right moment.'

'My God!'

'Check her for the wire,' Arthur instructed. He didn't seem to see anything in the fallen woman. 'It's an amateur job,' he continued. 'I can see it from here. She said she deposited stuff with lawyers. What a fucking pulp fiction idea that is! Came in here like she was some kind of tough guy. I'll call someone and get her out of here.'

'You'll call "someone".'

'Yeah, Joe, that's what I said. Now kneel down and go through her things, will you? We need an address. I'll have to have her place checked out, remove any "evidence" she might actually have.'

'You shot her!' Joe repeated, not making any move towards the body.

'Yes,' Arthur said coldly. 'What else would you have had me do?'

Yoshi leaned back in his office chair and lifted his cowboy boots on to the desk. He cradled the back of his head in his hands. He was searching for options.

In front of him was a small laptop computer. He had it rigged so the modem logged into the stock markets of the world.

YCK had fallen 10 per cent on the Tokyo exchange since the corporation had confirmed the extent of Yakamura Senior's injuries. The same statement was causing lighter tremors in the New York listing.

'It is not expected that Mr Yakamura will return to work for at least the next three months.'

Three months for an octogenarian at the head of a corporation was the end. They were already crowning the new guy. They had already chosen Suzuki. All he needed was to hold up the stock and avoid nasty surprises.

Yoshi thought through the range of possible nasty surprises. All those he could think of tarnished him as much as Suzuki. He was implicated in the Chinese problem. He had been in charge of the American operation as it plunged into loss. Maybe he should take his father's inheritance, live on the dividend income of the YCK stock and have nothing to do with the company.

But that wasn't power. And that was all that counted.

As he was sitting, drawing blanks on all sides, the phone on his desk rang.

'Excuse me. This is Shoyo,' the voice on the other end said.

Yoshi recognized his father's assistant.

'Not now, Shoyo,' he said.

'But I have a call for your father. A man who insists on talking to him. I tell him that your father is still under sedation.'

'Who is it? A reporter?'

'No, sir, I would not trouble you with that. It is Hayden Zalapek.'

Yoshi hesitated. He felt his stomach jump and somersault.

'Put him on,' he instructed. The line clicked. 'This is Yoshi.'

'My name is Hayden Zalapek.'

'I know who you are, Professor Zalapek. My father speaks

often of you. Unfortunately, he is indisposed, and will be so for some while. I am standing in his place. You may consider me as YCK, his company. I speak for him now.'

'I need his help,' the caller said directly, though the voice was weak.

'Where are you?'

'A motel. You know our . . . situation?'

'Someone is trying to kill you,' Yoshi said.

'They tried again yesterday.'

'Sam Stylls thought it was my father. I take it you do not believe this.'

'I know your father.'

'Quite so. You will not go to the police for help?'

'We cannot. We need someone . . . someone with power to help us.'

'Quite so,' Yoshi said again. He paused.

The caller probably supposed he was thinking what help he could offer.

'Very well,' he agreed. 'YCK is powerful. We will protect you. Tell me where you are. Give me the address. I will be with you as soon as I can.'

34

Calling Kazuo Yakamura was my last option, my only option. He was the one who had kept my fusion secret. In all those years of nuclear betrayal, he was the trustworthy one, the one I had chosen to witness the experiment. And he had not let me down.

Of course I had read he was in hospital, so I was not surprised when his assistant told me he was unavailable. Something I said, maybe the desperation in my voice, made him offer Kazz's son as an alternative.

I gave him the name and location of our motel. I even thanked him as I did it. As it turned out, this was as naïve as anything I have ever done. I should have listened to Kate more closely. She argued against YCK, resigning herself to the risk only when John took my side.

After I had put the phone down, I walked back to the diner where we had had breakfast. There was Kate, staring unenthusiastically at a plate of cold croissants. John was nowhere in sight.

'He went to freshen up,' she said. 'He didn't have a chance. He – he spent the night in my room.'

I smiled at her expense. I'm sure she wasn't embarrassed by the act, only the fact he was my grandson. Maybe she thought John should have told me.

'I'm very glad,' I assured her.

'Are you?' she said, surprised.

'You think I'm so straight-laced? That would be the right term?'

'All I know is what I've read, and a little that John told me. You were a great scientist. You could have built the bomb, but you didn't because—'

'Because I was religious. And you think that means I don't approve of you and John.'

'Doesn't it?' It was a strangely innocent question. I would not have expected it of her.

'Tell me, Kate, why do you love him?'

She seemed surprised. She waited a moment, perhaps filtering out the truth she was prepared to offer me. But to her credit, I think her answer was an honest one.

'He looks out at the world like it matters so much less than what goes on inside,' she said.

I considered it for a few seconds. 'I suppose that's right,' I agreed, thinking of that lack of real fear I had seen in him. I wasn't ready for her punchline.

'He gets that look from you.'

I gazed at her, wondering what she saw. I had never thought of the comparison. John and me – sixtysomething years apart. I thought of the loves of my life. Marion? Alice? The pain was too sharp.

'Talk about something else,' I said. Now it was my embarrassment showing.

'Like how the hell we get out of this?' she suggested.

'I called Yakamura.'

She lifted her head. Then I said, 'I only got his son. He's in charge of YCK for the moment.'

'Fuck,' she said. I think the moment I saw her black look was the moment I should have realized how stupid I'd been.

We were all three sitting in my room, small and claustrophobic with one bed and one chair. Kate said repeatedly that Yoshi Yakamura was not the sort of person she'd trust. She never said why. She was in favour of making a run for it, she said, but she could not state her case rationally. She had passion but no facts.

Even so, John spent all his time trying to calm her.

After two hours, he offered to take her for a short walk. 'Let's go and get ice-cream,' he said, winking at her in a way I didn't understand. I think he'd figured he had to do something before she blew her top.

She broke into laughter at his wink and they went out hand in hand.

As it turned out, I have to consider this timing lucky. If it had been any other way, they would have got John too. And if they had been smarter, they would have realized he was the one thing for which I might have given up the secret.

There was a knock on the door. I was getting up to open it, but I was slow in my stiffness. As I got to within a few feet, I heard it being kicked. Once. Twice. The splinters flew towards me and the door swung.

The first through the door was a small Japanese in a grey suit and cowboy boots. The second was a huge Sumo wrestler of a man, maybe six feet tall, at least twenty stone.

'We've come for you,' the smaller one said. 'I'm Yoshi Yakamura.'

'Then why? What?' My speech didn't make much sense. I was staring at the splintered door.

'Change of plan,' he said. 'You can't have the protection of YCK. You can have mine. But there is a price. You must pay back.'

35

Kate chose Belgian chocolate, John plain vanilla. The two small tubs were consumed well before the motel swung back into sight. Just as well because the day was unseasonably warm and the ice-cream had a short half-life.

As they walked, John had his hand squeezed around Kate's. He wanted to close his eyes and pretend he and she were somewhere else.

So it was Kate who saw it first. She pulled her hand away and stopped as if she had been struck.

'What?' John said.

'Look!'

'What?' he said again.

'A black and white – police car to you – over by your grandfather's room.'

John squinted. They were still a hundred yards away, but she was right, the telltale paint job parked not twenty yards from the block of rooms where they had spent the night.

'Shit!' he said. 'What do you think it means?'

'Maybe you ought to stay here, out of sight,' she said without looking at him. Her eyes were staring across, still assessing the problem at the motel. 'This is a journo-type situation. I'll go flash my pass and ask some questions.'

He found a fire hydrant in the shade of a tree and sat down, heart thumping. Kate was gone for the best part of ten minutes.

He couldn't work out if it was her danger, or their danger, or the fate of his grandfather that worried him most. Of course Kate was not in danger, he told himself, not physically. If the police were there, the worst that could happen was they'd arrest her. And for what? She'd done nothing. He was the one who'd flicked the traffic lights on to green.

He was a murderer. His grandfather hadn't even mentioned that. With his passivism, with his unwillingness to contribute even his science to the violence of war, why had his grandfather not mentioned that?

Kate came back at last, carrying the canvas bag which contained the only luggage they had between them.

'They got him,' she said.

'Got him?' John thought she meant his grandfather was dead.

'Snatched him. It's YCK. I knew we shouldn't trust the bastards.'

'Why YCK?'

'Why do you think? Cold fusion. Think of the profits if they had power stations producing unlimited energy.'

'But Beckett's trying to kill him.'

'Yeah, well, it seems like we've got another candidate. A Japanese corporation and a fucking would-be Governor.' She thrust the canvas bag into his midriff. 'Here, I managed to steal this when the cops weren't looking.'

John clutched at the bag idly. His eyes were away in another place.

'You just walked in there?' he said.

'Told them I was a passing reporter. Flashed my badge quick, so they couldn't read the name. Seems the receptionist heard them kicking the door down and called the cops. I interviewed her – "for the newspapers, dearie". She gave me a perfect description of Yoshi Yakamura. The other guy sounds like he was one of YCK's henchmen.'

'Do the cops know?'

'That it was Yoshi? No, of course not. They'll know about us soon enough, though. All they've got to do is run a make on my car. We need to get out of here. Are you ready to walk a few blocks? We'll try and get a cab when we're safely clear.'

'Why Yakamura? Why now?' John said. He got up and followed her, mulling the question over as he stared at the ground.

'Why not now?'

'Kazz Yakamura knew about my grandfather in 1939.'

'He's been in hiding.'

'Yes, but if it's the secrets YCK are after, they had a much better shot while we were their guests. Why did they wait until Beckett started shooting at us too?'

Kate shrugged and tugged at his sleeve, urging him to keep walking.

'Unless Yoshi's on his own,' he mused.

'Yoshi?' she said. 'I'd rather be against the whole corporation. He's a rat.'

'What?'

'Yoshi's a ruthless bastard. He won't quit until he gets what he wants. If he wants cold fusion, he's going to have it.'

'I'm not sure my grandfather even knows how he did it any more.'

Kate caught his arm and swung around to face him. 'John, sometimes you are as stupid as he is. Let's go to the police. Let's make a deal. I reckon now there's half a chance. With the evidence me and Esther have been putting together, maybe we can get out of this.'

'We can *not* go to the police,' John said with emphasis. 'I can't do that to my grandfather. It would betray everything.'

'And this way doesn't?'

'You go if you want.'

The violence of his words stopped them both. She was staring at him a long time as a tear formed in the corner of her eye. Then she said, 'If I'd wanted that, I'd have turned you in back there. All I had to say was take a look at my dented car ... take a look at my fucked-up life, won't you?'

She turned her head away, smearing the tear with the flat of her hand. When he reached out to touch her, she convulsed as if his hand were a cattle prod.

'Leave me alone,' she cried.

'I can't,' he said. He seemed to be searching for a reason. 'I love you. I'm sorry.'

'You what?' She turned back suddenly.

'I'm sorry.'

'No, the other thing you said.'

'Oh, that . . . I love you.'

'Yeah, I thought that's what you said.' A sigh relaxed all the muscles of her body. She threw her head back, brushing away the last of her tears before she came forward in a forced smile. 'We'd still better get moving.'

'No,' he said.

'No?'

'Not till you say it.'

Hesitation. She laughed.

'OK, I love you. Can we get moving now?'

'Sure.' He smiled with her. As much as he could muster in the circumstances.

They walked three blocks along a sunny wide street until they came to a small shopping mall with a large open car park at the front. Kate went in search of a payphone, returning with a can of Coke and the news that a cab was on the way.

'Have you got cash?' he asked.

'Not enough to get us back into town by cab. We need either a BART station or an ATM, preferably both.'

'Money and trains.' He nodded. 'Should we really go back to the city?'

'What do you think?' she asked.

He thought for a moment.

'I think we ought to go and find Esther. Assess your other option,' he said.

'Law and order is my number one priority . . .'

Joe Beckett on a topical news programme, being interviewed for the umpteenth time. Each time he looked so neat. He seemed to have a new suit for every occasion. He seemed to have a sound bite for it too.

'Some people say your policies are draconian. They point to a loss of civil liberties.'

'Enshrined in the Constitution of the United States is the right to liberty. In my view, the administrations of our great nation have a duty to provide a society in which the individual has freedom to exercise those rights. Tell me, is that individual free in a society where we dare not walk the streets at night? Is that individual free when our system of law cannot put the guilty behind bars? Do we promote freedom by allowing drug dealers on our streets?'

'We've been talking about today's news, Frank. Have you got the newspaper there?'

Frank had. He lifted it from the low studio prop of a table that separated them.

'I have,' he confirmed.

'OK. I challenge you to find a news page without a story that threatens the real freedom of our people to live their lives as they would wish.'

'Yes, but . . .'

'No, no. Let me finish my point. Just open it and read.'

' "TWO KILLED IN DELIBERATE CAR SMASH. Tripping addicts blamed for light failure." ' Joe Beckett smiled wanly. 'A pretty gruesome pick, Frank, but let me use it anyway. I think it illustrates the issue. There comes a point when every society – when every individual – has to say, "Just what do we have to do to have the society we want? What do we have to do to get what the Constitution promised us?" Sometimes those things can be hard.'

'I understand that, but are they constitutional?'

'In this century, Frank, we have gone through the two bloodiest wars in history. We have made an atomic bomb and dropped it. When we fight crime today, we have to use that same resolution with which we fought those wars. Can you tell me we are not in a drug war on our streets?'

'This sounds like pretty radical stuff.'

Joe Beckett leaned into the camera. 'I want every man and woman watching to go to the mirror and take a long hard look at themselves. I want them to say, "Some day my kids have to live in the world I am creating." Then I want them to ask themselves, "Who should I vote for to defend those freedoms in this state?" And I want them to remember that my opponents would defend the right of murdering criminals to escape the law on technicalities – on procedural grounds. And I want them to remember that my opponents would tell them this is enshrined in the Constitution.

'I say, "No, my friends, this is not what Joe Beckett is about. Joe Beckett is for freedom. He wants the streets safe. He wants your children safe. He wants to make California the envy of the world, not a toilet for its drugs." '

Joe Beckett stopped. For the first time, he was sweating. He seemed to be having difficulty finishing his sentence. As if somehow it had all begun to stick in his throat.

They took a cab as far as the closest BART Station. Kate thought of calling Esther, then remembered she had no phone. John found a bench to sit on. Kate joined him, falling fitfully asleep on his shoulder while waiting for a train to appear. She woke up only briefly, then fell asleep in the same position on the train.

The BART took them into San Francisco. It was still a fifteen-minute walk to get to Esther's, so it was four in the afternoon by the time they reached her apartment. No one answered the door when they knocked.

'What do you reckon?' Kate asked.

'We've got nowhere else to go.'

'My place?'

'Too dangerous.'

John rattled the door. It bent inwards substantially, as if it was only held on the Yale.

'Strange,' Kate mused.

'What is?'

'Esther has three locks on this door. I've seen her lock it myself. She's obsessed with security. When she's inside, she's got like a million chains and bolts she puts across . . . It's like someone came out and just pulled the door to.'

John scowled and started looking around. There was nothing to hand. He pulled out his penknife, but the broken-off blade was too broad to be of any use.

'You could kick it,' Kate suggested.

'Give me your press card. That's plastic-coated, isn't it?'

'You are not destroying that.'

'It's that or a credit card. Which do you prefer?'

She handed it to him reluctantly. He started levering it into the crack of the door. It wasn't so easy, as the lock was protected by the door frame, but John was an expert at this particular trick. In thirty seconds, the door popped open.

There was an eerie silence. John handed over the battered card and stood back as Kate went past him.

'The place is more of a mess than usual,' she said. Then moving further into the first room: 'Someone's turned this upside down.'

Papers were everywhere. Some of them were ripped in half; a couple had big boot marks on them where they had been trampled over.

'The base unit's gone off this computer,' Kate said, spotting the scattered hardware.

'I don't see any storage media anywhere.'

'They've taken everything.' Kate sank into the saggy sofa. She raised one hand to her head, leaning against it as her eyes sank to the floor. 'Where the hell is Esther?'

John found the door to the rooms Esther never used. The first was empty, just bare boards and damp walls; the second the same, but for a pile of green wine bottles three feet high in one corner. There must have been a hundred, maybe more. He didn't stop to count them. He closed the door softly and went for the last unopened room – the bedroom.

He cried out immediately. Then he shouted, 'Don't come in here.'

But Kate was already on her way to him.

Esther's body was lying across the bed, blood dry and black on her face, legs and arms thrown out at strange angles. He checked – the body was cold.

He caught Kate as she tried to rush by him. His right forearm barred her way to the body. She screamed and when her legs collapsed, he swung her up into both arms and carried her back to the main room. She was sobbing, a huge river of salt, everything suddenly coming out at once.

He laid her on the sofa, held her for a while, then went

back into the bedroom, leaving Kate curled in a ball like a baby in the womb. As he tried to make sense of Esther's demise, there were a number of things that didn't seem right. For now, he simply logged them and passed on. The conclusions came to him only slowly.

When he got back to the main room, he started to reconstruct the hardware. There was no base unit to Esther's computer, but he took the smashed laptop out of his canvas bag and started a reconstruction. The pillage of wire which he had been forced to make during the car chase was mainly confined to the connections of hard-drive, screen and floppy. The motherboard and power supply were untouched. Eventually, he was able to use the monitor port to get an image on Esther's upturned VDU. The laptop was suddenly working again, if a little shakily. It was no problem to rehook its modem into the socket on Esther's wall.

'What are you doing?' Kate asked, emerging from her foetal ball as if unfurling from a cocoon.

'Putting this back together. You know, you're right, she must have been funny. All this technology. She has an ISDN line for her modem, but no phone . . . Weird!' He sat back to admire his handiwork. 'It's OK now as long as you don't want to type anything with a "Q" or "W".' He pointed to show the way the top left edge of the keyboard had been broken beyond repair.

'John, we've got a dead body in the bedroom. We should really get out of here. You're playing with computers.'

'What's your e-mail address?'

'What?'

'Your e-mail address. You have one, surely.'

'Yeah, I have one for work.'

'OK, log in. My guess is Esther didn't go anywhere without e-mailing you.'

'What do you mean? Go anywhere? She's dead in the fucking bedroom.'

'Agreed, but she wasn't killed there.'

Kate looked at him as if he had finally lost his mind.

Maybe he had. He was playing a hunch.

'Not enough blood,' he told her. 'She went out some-where. Someone killed her and brought the body back. My guess is she was going to see someone she thought was pretty dodgy.'

'Beckett?' she asked. Her face stepped through a series of expressions, searching for one that seemed appropriate.

'There's some PVC wire around her neck,' John started explaining. 'I think it's the remains of some sort of bugging system. I think maybe she was trying to record a conversation.'

'Beckett,' Kate said again.

'That would be my guess.'

She came across the room in a single bound, landing beside him, all enthusiasm for his idea. In a few seconds, she had tapped her way into her e-mail system. And there it was – Esther's message.

> Kate,
> I tried to get back to you, but no reply. No surprise.
> I saw your incident on the late-night news. Some car
> crash. I'm glad the Boulder Brothers bought it, but I
> figure you're in danger so I'm going to try to dig up
> some more information on our friend, Arthur. Call it a
> long shot. We need to get enough to nail him.
> Meanwhile please find a summary of my findings to
> date in the attached file.
> See ya, Esther.

The computer screen was offering several options: 'download now' or 'download later'. Kate picked 'download now'. The screen told her that in two minutes they would have everything they wanted on Arthur Beckett.

36

A man as old as I am and feel is very difficult to torture. Wisdom and age have taught me this: whatever we seem as men, we are but simple brief machines. I am old and the future matters very little. Better then to protect the spiritual world. The mask of youth, with its vain gloss of immortality, has long gone and I am all but gone with it. So what if it should be Yoshi Yakamura who pushes me that final inch from this world to the next? My card is marked anyway.

They took me to a house – I don't know where. There was a bare back room with a bed that looked as if it came from prison, and a chair and table that looked much the same.

There they tortured me for a while.

Mere pain.

Not that anyone should dismiss pain as a hurdle easily overcome. The temptation of the flesh is always to make it stop, however that may be achieved.

'I want you to tell me,' he said. And his larger-than-life companion crushed my ruined hand between his fists.

At first, I screamed with pain, then I passed out with it.

One other thing Yoshi should also have known of old men in torture: they fall all too easily into unconsciousness.

For hours, I bobbed at the surface of consciousness. I dreamt. Daydreams. Like a drowning man, I saw my life before me in crazy images.

Once I had questioned the physics of time and space, but that was long ago when I was full of life and belief and curious about the world. And when I found knowledge, all it seemed to do for me was ask more questions and amplify the smallest snags of normal lives into insurmountable problems in mine. Should I help in the war? Should I use what I know or stand back while Germany got the bomb? Could I hold both my wife and my faith?

Oh, God, I hope I've done it right, because in this room I expect to die.

Each time I woke, they produced another torture. My other hand crushed the same way. I heard them arguing with each other as I slipped once again through the divisions of consciousness. Another episode of waking dreams.

If there is one thing I regret it is this: I regret the design of the universe. If God designed this as a test of faith, I do not believe it is a fair test. Life starts in ignorance and for twenty-three hours of its day – I use a day as the scale for all time – it has no knowledge of its own existence.

Only in the last hour does it begin to think. Only in the last five minutes does it begin to realize its ability to make marks upon its world. Cave paintings. Stone buildings. Walls that defend against the sea.

If it takes so long to build to such a pitch, why was there only a single split second to make the decision about the bomb? Why is there so little time to make decisions about all technology? Surely God must have known that hiding these secrets in such a way would release them all too quickly.

One moment, men scratched to understand the nature of matter, the nature of the world. Then, without warning, and in the next moment, we were staring at the power to make and to destroy all things. How could this be right?

The terrible thing about cold fusion is this: if I had given unlimited power to the people of the world, I do not believe that, for some, even this would have been enough.

37

They printed the downloaded file on an ink-jet printer that had weathered the atrocities in the apartment with its cartridge intact. Then they sat on the sofa, reading. It wasn't that they were unaware of the risks, sitting in that place with a body already in decay in the bedroom. They had just run out of places to go.

'There must be thirty pages here,' John said, reluctant to start.

Kate had already skimmed the whole document and was beginning a more detailed perusal.

'There's enough to write a biography. Times, places, his inside leg measurement.' She looked disappointed. 'It's not here though. Nothing we could make stick. Nothing about him being the Art Master. This guy knew Nixon. He's connected. It's not surprising all that matters has disappeared into the ether.'

John said, 'That must have been why she went out.'

'After Beckett . . . Yeah, I guess so.'

'She had a thing for you.'

'What?'

'She put herself on the line, didn't she?'

'I never thought—'

'No . . .'

They sank back defeated. For a while, Kate read the papers and John thought. Then he said, 'I think we ought to go and see Yakamura. If I'm right and Yoshi is on his own, maybe he'll help us.'

'Against his own son?'

'Give me a better idea. My grandfather trusted him.'

Kate shrugged. Then her face contorted and she leaned across for him and they held each other.

'Don't worry,' he said softly, 'we'll get out of this. We'll get my grandfather out of this.' He paused, switching from tenderness to action. 'If we spin back through some news stories, do you suppose we'll find the hospital he's in on the Internet?'

'Probably.'

'Let's do it then. We've got to get right in his face – face to face. I want to be looking at him.'

John slid down on to the floor and shuffled across to where their makeshift computer set-up still lay. He pushed all the power buttons and waited for it to boot.

Kate knew the news pages as if they were family. It was part of her profession to know. In half a minute, leaning over his shoulder, she had fifteen stories on Sam's death and Yakamura's injuries selected on the screen. Two gave partial addresses for the hospital. That was enough.

On another service, John searched for and found a map of the city. It took him only seconds to pinpoint the hospital.

'I already know where it is,' Kate said, blushing with embarrassment. 'I used to date a doctor who worked there.'

John smiled ruefully. 'Why didn't you say?'

She tried to laugh. 'God, John, we've all got history. You don't want to know.'

'I don't need to know.'

'Don't worry, it's a short history,' she added.

He looked down without comment. He switched off the computer and put all the bits except the monitor back into the canvas bag. Then he grasped her by the hand and they headed for the street.

'I've never fled the scene of a crime before,' she told him. 'Do you think we ought to wipe our prints?'

John said, 'We're already in so deep, what does it matter?'

Yakamura's hospital was a ten-minute cab ride. They had cash Kate had taken out from the ATM outside the BART station. But when they arrived at the hospital, they found it an almost impossible labyrinth. The reception staff wouldn't tell them where he was. They were stranded in the foyer.

John paced up and down for a while. Kate bought a Coke

from a machine and they shared alternate mouthfuls. Finally, John said, 'Time for your doctor. I take it you parted on good terms.'

'He wanted to marry me.'

'And that's why you left him.'

'I thought you didn't need to know.' There was a touch of anger, then she relented. 'Wait here,' she said.

She went back to the desk and started asking questions. They gave her a house phone and John heard a doctor being paged. When she came back, she had the room number written on a scrap of paper.

John was leaning on a pillar as she approached, holding the empty Coke can now squeezed into a rough hourglass shape, its thin sides buckled. He stared at every movement she made. When she got close, he felt his gut tighten.

'Would you marry me?' he said. 'If I asked?'

She gazed at him in surprise. The surprise lingered for a good five seconds. Her eyes ticked on the subject.

'If you asked,' she said, 'and if you're still alive.' She tried to laugh, but he was perfectly serious.

She straightened herself and held out the paper. 'Room 2130,' she said. 'Let's get on with it.'

They had to slide past ward security, but once they got by, Yakamura was on his own. His room was standard hospital issue, but they were amazed by the splendour of its furnishings: the bed's remote control; the 28-inch TV with stereo; the grade 'A' carpet rather than tile. They took a moment to assess it all.

Yakamura was asleep. Their movements were just enough to stir him as they got closer to the bed.

'Mr Yakamura,' Kate whispered gently.

His eyes opened.

'Miss Morris,' he said, focusing, recognizing her from the interview. His speech was slurred but not incoherent. There was a certain drug-induced slowness about it. 'I'm not taking visitors,' he told her. He looked to the side and saw

John. 'You? I expected journalists. Where's your grandfather?'

'I came to ask you. I was hoping—'

'Hoping?' He connected to the word as if he had grasped it out of thin air.

'Yoshi has him.'

'I don't understand . . .'

'Kidnapped.'

Yakamura's face turned to Kate as if looking for confirmation. She gazed back, blank and nervous.

'Why would he do that?' he asked.

John said nothing and, in the silence, Yakamura nodded. 'Cold fusion,' he murmured.

'You know about it?'

'I know nothing about kidnapping. I can't believe Yoshi . . .' His voice was heavy, the words increasingly slurred as he continued. 'You should know, John, that I have nothing to do with this. I can't believe Yoshi has. But I'm afraid there is a war going on in my company.'

'In YCK?' Kate said.

'What's that to do with my grandfather?' John snapped his question on top of hers, trumping it.

Yakamura smiled ruefully. 'All wars are about power.'

'And cold fusion is a weapon?' Kate interrupted.

'In the fight for a company, technology is a great weapon. I have no power any more. Lost it with the hip. Eighty years is too long. They want me gone. They think I can't . . . Who are they? My plan was for Yoshi . . .' His words started to ramble as his eyes lost focus on the room. 'I'm sorry . . . the painkillers.' He drifted further away, then returning, he said, 'I remember I told Yoshi about your grandfather.'

'Did you know Arthur Beckett was trying to kill my grandfather?' John asked.

Yakamura's eyes opened wide and stared. 'Beckett?' he said. 'I didn't know he had anything to do with it. But then, all the Becketts are corrupt in one way or another.'

'But I met you with Joe Beckett in Singapore,' John said. 'You were his friend.'

272

'Yes, yes . . .' Yakamura seemed exhausted by the effort of conversation. His eyes began fluttering as if they wanted to close in sleep. 'You should never fight tigers. Certainly never barehanded. I have tried to make that a rule.' He stopped and took a deep relieving breath. 'You remember Mai, don't you? Weapons-gathering.'

John said in surprise, 'Mai?'

But Kate's mind worked through the riddle more quickly. She remembered the Yakamura girl who'd beaten her to a chair in Papa Joe's. 'Are you telling us you've got evidence against Beckett?'

When Yakamura didn't answer, she pleaded, 'We need it.'

'My tape library could bring down half the politicians on five continents. A company presidency is not a clean job. Though I used to think it was. The point is I never use my library . . . I told Yoshi that . . . It is better to have a friend in power than an enemy in defeat.'

He turned his head as if expecting a response.

'With the Becketts, it is far better not to stir up the tiger by showing him your weapons,' he added. 'He roams so much more beautiful when he thinks he's free.'

'OK, that's it. I don't know who you are but you're out of here!' A large white-coated man had entered, gesturing violently over his shoulder with his thumb.

'But?' John said.

'Any trouble and it'll be a security job. You damn journalists. How'd you get in here? My advice is leave quiet . . . leave now.'

John looked back at Yakamura.

'I cannot help you,' Yakamura said.

'What about my grandfather? What about Yoshi?'

'He's my son.' Yakamura nodded weakly. Seemed on the point of crying. 'He's my son,' he repeated.

273

38

They had lost the ability – or maybe the will – to calculate dangers, so they flipped a coin. Kate said she wouldn't go back to Esther's, so they decided 'heads' they risked Kate's apartment, 'tails' they went for a hotel.

It came down 'tails'.

'You want to go for two out of three?' she asked.

'No,' John said, 'I think it's best. We don't know what Beckett's thinking.'

They rented a room on Kate's credit card. The desk clerk looked at them suspiciously: two youngsters in need of a bath and clean clothes, luggage in a battered canvas bag, and waving an Amex card.

Kate smiled and offered to lodge the card to cover phone calls. The desk clerk was appeased. He held out the key on a numbered wooden key chain, dangling it as if hanging a dead rat.

In truth, it wasn't a great hotel. Upstairs in a twelve-foot square room, John and Kate stripped off their clothes and made love as much for comfort as lust. She kissed him and kissed him and wouldn't let go until she fell asleep in his arms.

John stayed for a while, listening to her breathing and watching the way the filtered street light caressed the soft hairs of her arm as it plunged through the holes in the curtains.

At last, he disentangled himself and went to the canvas bag which contained everything they had. It had once contained everything his grandfather had brought back into the world when he came to Emily's funeral. Now its main contents were a wooden chess set and a very second-hand computer.

John set up the chess set.

White moves first. Pawn in front of king. Then black. Then white. The pattern emerged. Something familiar. Something to hold on to.

In half an hour, he had completed the game. Then he started to think about the pieces of their troubles: a kidnapped king, a corrupt knight trying to make his mark, and a pawn shepherded by a black rook towards the eighth square – a soon-to-be state governor. It's strange the way, in a game of chess, the big pieces sometimes trade off against one another, so all that's left are the pawns.

Perhaps this was the escape.

He thought of those already fallen. Helen who had protected him, despite her prickly schemes. Sam the intellectual. Esther? Well, he hardly knew Esther. He had only the evidence of her scattered hardware, and her flat with its collection of bottles. It's strange what people hoard! Wine bottles!

Then he thought. Why didn't he think of this earlier? Who else did he know who hoarded everything that came her way?

Aunt Marion. Of course, Aunt Marion.

He scooted over to the bed, making sure he sat on its edge gently so he didn't disturb the sleeper on the other side. He picked up the phone and dialled. He knew Aunt Marion's number well enough, but it took three tries to crack the international code. Eventually he heard the satisfying British ring echo back up the line.

Her butler, George, answered.

'Is my aunt there? This is John.' He was almost too nervous to speak.

In a minute came her voice. 'John, happy Christmas.'

'What?'

'Happy Christmas. It's Christmas Eve. I thought you were in America. They do celebrate it there, don't they? I read about Helen . . . Are you all right?'

'I am. I mean . . . Aunt, I'm in trouble. My grandfather's in trouble.'

'Hayden?'

'Yes, listen. I know you keep everything. Did you keep any of his papers from before the war?'

'Why yes, I kept a box for him while he was ... while he was away.'

'In prison, you mean.'

'Yes, but I gave it back to him afterwards, as soon as he came out. That was years ago before he went ... before he disappeared.'

John deflated, air seeping out of his lungs as he sighed. No papers. No papers after all.

Then he remembered his grandfather's description of that last day in his college rooms.

'What about Ward?' he said.

'Oh, Ward had papers. Lots of them. He was a big writer. He had a lot of published work and his notebooks went on for ever. I used to call him my little man of letters.'

'You kept it all?'

'Boxes of it.' She paused. 'Afterwards, it was all I had left.'

'I need you to look for something. I need you to look for anything from the end of 1939 or the very beginning of 1940.'

'If I may ask, what am I trying to find?'

John hesitated. 'Anything in my grandfather's handwriting. Or any letters Ward Costello may have received from London,' he added as an afterthought.

'It'll take hours,' Marion told him.

'I'll wait. I'll give you a number. I'm in a hotel.'

'What's happened to Hayden? You didn't say.'

'He'll be all right,' he lied.

'Tell me.'

He told her, unable to stop telling her once he had started. He heard her dissolve on the other side of the Atlantic. Somehow that made it all so much more real.

When he finally put the phone down, he watched the minute hand making its slow revolution of the clock on the bedside table. Once. Twice. Three times.

The phone rang again at 2.30 in the morning.

'John, I've got something.' Aunt Marion sounding triumphant in that pluperfect voice of hers.

'What?' He was almost too tired to be excited.

'About sixteen pages in Hayden's handwriting.'

'Is it – I mean, does it make any sense?'

'Don't be silly. It's from the time you gave me, though. The pages are dated between December 15 and January 9. It's strange. The January pages are written in a different ink, but they're all equations of some sort. It's all the kind of tosh your grandfather and Ward used to speak in those days.'

'What about letters?' he asked. His pulse was rising now. He knew what the papers must be. Now, did they have something on Beckett too? Could they possibly be that lucky?

'Sort of,' Marion said.

John froze. 'What does "sort of" mean?'

'I've found a letter . . . Or rather paper in an envelope. I'm afraid that particular box is much the worst for the years – the damp has got in. All the writing is practically illegible.'

'Shit,' John said, then felt ashamed.

'I can read the postmark and half the address,' Marion offered: '7 January 1940.'

John had already sunk on to the bed, considering what to do with his grandfather's work. He had one tool now, one lever – the letters had been a long shot anyway. *The papers for his grandfather* – Yoshi would go for that. Yes, but would his grandfather? John knew all too well what his grandfather would say, what he would want. It was a trade he would never condone, one he could never forgive.

'Aunt Marion,' he said heavily, 'I have to ask you a big favour.'

'Certainly.'

'I have to get those documents out here. It's not too much to ask, is it?'

She said, 'John, my son, you should know better than that. I realize what's at stake. I knew – even back then.' A two-second pause. 'It's 10.30 in the morning here. I told George

277

if we started now, we could make the afternoon plane. It goes at one o'clock. He's just warming up the car.'

'Thank you,' John said. He thought of her effort for a moment, then something struck him. 'Do you think you'll get on a flight? Oh, God, it's Christmas Eve! Everything will be full.'

'I have cash and credit cards,' Marion told him. 'I know you would never take my money, but some things can still be bought, you know.'

'Thank you,' he said again.

'Don't thank me . . . I do not deserve it.'

39

When Zalapek passed out a third time, they left him locked in the back room and Yoshi sent Sumo Stan out to the liquor store. He ordered a quart of whiskey and a 'fruits of the sea' pizza from the take-away next door.

Soon he was drunk and falling asleep at the table. His gamble looked like a disaster. How do you make a stubborn old man talk? It was like dealing with his own father – impossible.

Yoshi picked himself up, took himself to the nearest chair and fell asleep. It was 4.30 in the morning before he woke up. His head felt terrible; his mouth like a sawdust floor. He went into the kitchen and got a glass of water. Stan was nowhere to be seen. Just as well. Time to think out the next move.

He switched on his portable computer to check the markets. OK, so it was Christmas Eve and the markets would be slow. He still couldn't let go of the hope that YCK with Suzuki at the helm would suddenly crash through the stock market floor.

The boot cycle took its normal annoyingly long time to complete. While it was whirring away, he found a telephone socket to plug into.

He typed his name. Then his password. Then waited.

The welcome screen announced the presence of three new e-mails. He went to them first. Number one was from his father, dictated to Shoyo no doubt – Kazz Yakamura never used new-fangled gadgets himself. His father was still in hospital, but wanted to know where Yoshi was. It said he'd heard a disturbing rumour which, of course, he didn't believe, but wished his son to deny in person.

The next was from Suzuki, asking him when he was

coming to clear his office. I want your key by Christmas Day, he wrote.

The last came from the account of Kate Morris. Only it wasn't written by Kate Morris; it was written by John Harringhay, full of typographic errors but translating into one hell of a message.

Mr Yakamura,
I have his papers. The ones from 1940. What you want is there: cold fusion.
By now you know he'll not tell the secret, no way. But I think more of him than that. I'll swap the papers for him.
Bring my grandfather to the top of the Glass Palace Shopping Mall tonight. I'll be there at closing time.
John H.

*

Marion Stern had sifted all the boxes, piling papers into 'irrelevant', 'relevant' and 'interesting for sentimental reasons'. The first was the biggest pile. She left that in the loft to rot. The latter two – sixteen pages and one letter of 'relevant' and half a box of things she wished she'd read forty or fifty years ago – she put in a single cardboard carton that had once held frozen waffles. Her only other luggage was a small leather Dior case, just enough for an overnight stay.

In the back of the Daimler, speeding to the airport down the M40, she opened the carton and stared at the pile of papers. Why had she hoarded them so long and never read them? Was it something to do with the way she and Ward had parted company? Not on the best of terms. She had told him about her indiscretion. She had told him about Hayden Zalapek.

She picked up the sixteen pages that had caused all the trouble. She closed her eyes. She too, like Hayden, could imagine Ward's death, only now her version was different.

They broke his ribs so he could hardly breathe. They filled a bath with water and dunked his head until he nearly

280

drowned. Then they brought before him the wife of his best friend. And they cut her face and they killed her.

And all the time he swore he had burnt the papers.

She felt a weakness in her arms; her fingers twitched across the text. Hold hard, Marion, she told herself. What was it Hayden had called her? 'A dizzy socialite who had become hardened to life?' She had held the family business together for thirty years. She had changed from the spoilt little teenager who got everything by whining and lying and pleading. It was Ward Costello and Hayden Zalapek who created that change. It was to them that she had always owed it all.

The M40 on Christmas Eve was surprisingly quiet, at least going towards London. They made Heathrow in under an hour. George dropped the Daimler in the short-stay car park and followed her into the terminal.

Airport check-ins hold an air of intimidation for most people, but Marion Stern entered on a wave. Blue-blood Jewish upbringing and a life of privilege – the dizzy socialite hardened to life. Old and rickety maybe, but you didn't say 'no' when she set her sights.

The blonde check-in girl was hardly a match for her. The old lady quaked but she would not let up.

'I know there's no room on the flight. You've said that four times already. But that wasn't my question. I asked, what do I have to do to get on?'

The blonde re-explained the situation. Marion put her hands on her hips and puffed out her cheeks as if she were some great bird trying to make itself larger.

'I'm trying to keep my calm,' she explained to the girl as if this was an act of extreme generosity, 'but I think you'd better get your supervisor down here now.'

She turned to George. 'George, you may leave me now,' she said. 'I won't be needing you. I'm getting on this flight.'

By now, the check-in girl was looking a little uneasy and furtively dialling someone on the telephone. The queue behind was starting to grow impatient. Marion showed no sign of budging.

A man with a bizarrely checked jacket tapped her on the shoulder and enquired in broken English, 'What is the problem, madam?'

'The problem is this stupid airline!' She stopped. She calculated, running through all the schemes, remembering the spoilt little rich girl of old. Then, she turned on the defenceless check-in girl. 'Look, I have to get to San Francisco,' she said. 'My little grandson is dying, for pity's sake. Cancer. I have to be there for Christmas.' Tears began rolling out of Marion's eyes. 'Look, look, I'm an Executive Club member.'

'That is a British Airways club, madam. No good for this airline. I'll say it once more: the flight is full. I have not a seat to give you.'

'Very well, I'll tell you what, I'll buy one.'

She turned to the queue, now at least twenty people long. Very loudly, she shouted, 'Who here will take one thousand pounds to fly on the next plane instead of this one?' It took all her strength to shout it.

Four back in the queue, there was a Chinese businessman in grey suit and tie. He was going home to China, stopping a few days at his daughter's home in Oakland *en route*. He had caught the gist of Marion's conversation with the check-in girl.

As it happened, his own son had died of cancer – leukaemia in fact.

He raised his hand. 'I will be honoured to help you.'

The noise of John sneaking back into the room woke Kate from the last of her slumber. She looked at the clock. It was still night time – five o'clock.

'Where've you been?' she said, sleepily.

'Out,' he told her. 'I needed a computer screen. We left the one at Esther's, remember?'

'You've been to Esther's?'

'Yes. I've got a plan. You may not like it, but I've got a plan.' He was rummaging in the canvas bag, sorting through the document they'd printed from Esther's file.

'You have? What are you looking for?'

'A telephone number. You're not really with this, are you?'

Kate stretched. 'I'm sorry. Sleepy, I guess. Have you been up all night? What's the plan?'

John smiled. 'Come over to my chessboard. I'll explain how it works.'

40

The morning was a sweet one. Arthur Beckett had wheeled his way down the lawn at the family mansion. He rested in the grand gazebo, a white lattice structure at the top of the slope leading down to the lake. Arthur liked to watch the way the sun rose across the water.

When it had nearly risen far enough to show the whole of its burning orange disc, Joe Beckett came out to meet him.

'It's a beautiful morning,' Arthur said casually. 'Are you ready for Christmas? Got little Joe Junior's present?' It took several moments for him to register the distress on his son's face.

Joe stopped a yard or so from his father, looking down at him in his chair.

'I just had a phone call – from John Harringhay.'

'You did?'

'On my private line.'

'Well, OK, spit it out, Joey, what did he want?' Arthur was holding on to his calm in his usual unruffled way.

'He says he and his grandfather would settle for five million dollars.'

'Oh, the price is going down. Does he want to sell out his grandfather as well?'

Joe moved his weight from one foot to the other, setting himself as if worried he might fall over in a sudden gust of wind.

'Be serious,' he said, 'we should consider it. Five million. He says he will guarantee both he and Hayden Zalapek disappear.'

'Horseshit! I showed the only way to handle this situation when I dealt with that nigger woman. If you want to consider something, consider this: what's to stop any of these people coming back for afters when you're in Sacramento? If it's five million now, what will it be worth then?' He waved his good arm dismissively.

'Does the date 7 January 1940 mean anything to you? He says he has a letter of yours from that date. He says it's addressed to a man called Ward Costello and that you'll understand what it is. He says he also has some papers – papers you were trying to get from Costello.'

Arthur Beckett hesitated. A muscle below his eye twitched. 'He's bluffing. He's just another bluffer like that woman.'

'Maybe we shouldn't risk it. I could—'

'Now, you hear me, Joe. What happened in 1940 has got nothing to do with today. We're going to fix it. Nothing else matters to me. I've worked too long, and I'm not going to let anyone stop you. Everywhere's full of bleeding-heart liberals and communists. It's fucked up. It needs you. It's going to get you.' He lifted his index finger and pointed, wagging it for effect.

'Father, we can pay them the five million and they'll go, I'm sure. All I've got to do is put it in a Gucci bag and take it to them, that's what he said. He'll trade the letter . . . all the papers.'

Arthur stared at him, making a lopsided attempt to shake his head. He pressed the drive on his wheelchair so it came forward until he was almost in Joe's face.

'Sometimes you're so fucking naïve,' he said.

'OK, I'll pay the money. I'm not asking you for it. I'll just go and do it on my own. I want this over.'

'Don't you understand that's what I want too,' his father protested.

Joe stepped away, skirting an iron garden table to reach the far edge of the gazebo. He stood there, face to the wickerwork, turned from his father.

Arthur said, 'All right, if that's the way you want it. We'll give them the money. Only one thing: I don't want you to go.'

'Why not?'

'You're running for Governor, for Christ's sake,' Arthur said, keeping himself under control despite the passion. 'You want to make a pay-off in a public place? Has he told you where he wants it dropped?'

'In San Francisco. He hasn't told me where yet. He's supposed to phone again. He said he'd call me at our campaign headquarters.'

'Oh, God! It's like dealing with Abe Lincoln on a bad day. OK, Joe, you go off to San Francisco. I'll have someone meet you up there.'

'I need to get the case.'

'What case?'

'The one he specified for the money.'

'OK, you buy it if it makes you happy.' His father's voice was becoming increasingly patronizing. 'I'll take a ride uptown, talk to my man in our LA bank and get him to wire the money. I don't want you picking up the cash though. Let my contact do that.'

Joe turned around. 'Thank you, Father.'

'Don't thank me. Just wheel me back to the house. I'm not sure my battery's up to it.'

Joe Beckett and his father parted as they reached the main building. Joe called the family pilot and went into the sun lounge to await the helicopter's arrival. Arthur called his nurse, put on his coat and hat, and had the chauffeur bring the car around to the front.

The chauffeur remarked how nice it was to see the old man going out again; it had been so long.

Arthur grunted and inched into the special lift that took his chair into the car. When they got going, he asked for his mobile phone. The chauffeur passed it over his shoulder into the rear of the car and Arthur shut the privacy screen.

He started making calls.

The morning of Christmas Eve may have been bright and clear, but for John and Kate it was more so through the window than in their lives.

After his explanation, John slept until ten. She watched

him sleep, read the Esther papers and watched him some more.

When he awoke he had a list of things they had to do. He showered and put on the same clothes that he had taken off. Then he said, 'We need a car. Do you think we can get a rent-a-wreck, or do we need to steal one?'

'My credit card will handle it. I've still got my licence, unless you're planning on prising open any more locks.' She smiled.

'Then we need a walkie-talkie. Radio Shack, I guess? Do you know where there is one?'

'Not a store I use.'

'OK, we'll ask someone. We also need a portable phone.'

'Then what?'

'Then we go and scout the place. We have to meet the afternoon plane. Then we wait and pray.'

Thirty thousand feet over Greenland, halfway down her pile of 'interesting for sentimental reasons', Marion found them: a sequence of papers which told her exactly what Ward had been doing on that Continental trip in 1938, the one he had returned from with such passion against the Nazis.

The first of the papers was a letter on crisp yellowed paper in an envelope marked from Zurich. Written in German, it took her a while to translate, and even then there were words she couldn't quite follow.

7 April 1938

Dearest Ward,

Your advice once again has proved invaluable. We got over the border into Switzerland just in time, it seems, on 1 March. Another ten days or so and we would have been too late.

No sooner had Austria become part of the German Reich than their army was all over the place. I understand the university has been ransacked. All Jewish staff have been removed.

I must tell you that Bernt and Lotte were not so lucky as we were. The last we heard they were still

287

somewhere in Munich. Bernt's position at the university is of course under daily threat and it can only be a matter of time. I know they want to get out, but it is not so easy now.

Also we must tell you that Heisner is dead. They put it down to a random attack, but we think it is much more likely he was a target. To be Jewish and a doctor is a sentence now. To be Jewish and a famous doctor is a red rag to a bull.

Wishing we could give you better news.

The signature was not decipherable: something that began with a 'B', but melted into a squiggle long before making a name.

There followed three copies of letters Ward had sent to various scientists in Europe, recommendations for Bernt Grebnitz. Next there was a reply, offering Grebnitz a position in Sweden. Then a letter from Grebnitz himself saying there was no chance of the necessary papers for him to leave the country.

As she dug deeper, Marion found more copies of Ward's letters. He had written to Neils Bohr in Denmark and Dirk Coster in Holland, a scientist who had recently been successful in getting another Austrian, Lisa Meitner, into his country without a passport.

At last, in August, Ward wrote to Grebnitz that he was coming personally.

Below that in the pile, there was a final letter in the sequence, signed by Lotte Grebnitz. It was not dated. It said:

Bernt has asked me to write to you. I am sure you will be pleased to know we are now in Stockholm. Safe, though the journey and the strain of everything we have left did no good for Bernt's health.

A month after we arrived he contracted tuberculosis. With his weakness and age, it has taken a strong hold.

Still, Ward, you must know that without your presence we would not have got out of Germany. My heart still beats all too fast when I think of our escape.

Thank you and God bless you.

The young Marion Stern had lived with Ward Costello all through that time. She had shared his bed. She had used her own family money to prop up the wildest of his schemes. They were in love and she told him every one of her little-girl thoughts.

And yet through all that, he had made no mention of his activities in Europe. He had not told her who he was or where he had been or who he still knew from the years before he came to Oxford in 1932. He had not told her of a single old friend in distress in the growing territories of the Third Reich. He had not told her he was part of a network of Jewish academics trying to arrange escape for those less fortunate.

Over Greenland, she asked herself how it was possible that she had loved a man she knew so little about. And yet she had. And did.

The phone on the oak desk. Ringing.

'Yeah.'

'One last time, I need your help. I've set up a drop. You understand me?'

'I don't know you any more.'

'You can "not know me" tomorrow. Please . . .'

Silence.

'I never heard you say, "Please," before.'

'I never had to.'

'Is this that "special" kind of drop?'

'They grab the boy, OK. Use him – they can get to the old man. I want this over. I want the issue dead. I don't want any of the motherfuckers coming out alive.'

The echo of presidency still lay with Kazuo Yakamura. In the drugged state he had occupied for days, he had come to one fuzzy conclusion and held to it. The conclusion was this: if he was to fulfil his duty in this time of crisis, he had to get his wits about him and he had to face the truth.

He refused further drugs. When the pain came, he simply grimaced and let it pass.

At noon on Christmas Eve, he summoned his assistant, Shoyo, and asked him to go to Suzuki and bring him to the hospital.

Suzuki was going home for the holiday. He had his bags packed and was checking out of the hotel. He had promised his Western-influenced wife that he would be back in Tokyo by the evening of Christmas Day.

Shoyo had to insist. He knew he was risking his future in the company by insisting that a new president-elect did anything, but he had been with Yakamura for many years. Loyalty in that quarter demanded obedience.

So Suzuki came. He was out of a suit and in flannel trousers when he came to Yakamura's hospital bed. He was surprised by the old man's lucid greeting and shocked by the pain that seemed to bend his face in two.

'Sir,' Suzuki addressed him, saying it in very reverent Japanese.

'Thank you for coming,' Yakamura said.

'You called; Suzuki comes.'

'Kendo, you have no need for humility now. You know you will be the next president.'

'Still I—'

'No, I give it freely to you. I am too old. I have probably been too old for the last five years.'

Suzuki shook his head in denial.

'Oh, yes,' said the old man, 'oh, yes. But now, I have but one demand and one last question for you. You must answer truthfully and fully. That is the demand.'

'I will always—'

'Tell me the truth about my son,' Yakamura said without waiting for Suzuki's assurance.

'Your son?'

'Yes.'

Suzuki paled and sat down on the edge of the bed.

290

'The truth,' Yakamura reminded him. 'Start with the China problem.'

'He was involved in that,' Suzuki said, beginning very slowly and timidly. 'All the evidence points to the fact that Yoshi had an American investigator killed in Thailand – Edward Wingate. You've heard of him?'

'Yes,' Yakamura sighed. 'I know the name.'

Suzuki catalogued a number of other stories both public and private. He saw his boss in tears as he nodded to some of the facts that he had – in the past – chosen to interpret in his son's favour. Now Yakamura heard them unrolled in a naked indictment; he could not deny them further.

And neither did he wish to.

'Tell me one last thing,' Yakamura said at the conclusion. 'Do you know if my son has kidnapped Hayden Zalapek?'

'Who?' Suzuki asked.

'So you do not know?'

'I know he's not been in the office for days. He was supposed to clean out his desk. He seems to have gone missing . . . Are you all right, sir?'

Yakamura had slipped down on his pillows. A spasm of pain from his hip made him almost pass out.

'I need to get out of here,' he said.

The bleeping phone in the campaign office. The desks strewn with paper but not manned. Everyone else at a Christmas party, a party looking forward to next year when they'd elect a Governor.

Joe Beckett picked up the phone himself.

'Joe, this is John Harringhay. Answer only "yes" or "no". Do you have the money?'

'Yes.'

'Do you have the Gucci bag?'

'Yes.'

'Good. I'll be putting the letter and the papers you want in one just like it. Understand?'

'Yes.'

'OK, I want you to proceed to the Glass Palace shopping mall.'

'I can't go in there. I'd be recognized.'

'Of course you would, Joe. During normal store hours anyway. But I'm sending you to the underground car park at closing time. Look for a blue Ford by the lifts – that's elevators to you. It's a rental car. I'll give you the licence plate.'

'Is that where we make the exchange?'

'Just get a piece of paper.'

41

Lying in a dark room on an iron bed, my hands crushed. There was not so much pain as a dull throb from the bones, no worse than on my best arthritic days. But I felt weak and empty inside as if I had been scooped out.

Yoshi Yakamura came into the room behind a burst of light.

'Don't get up,' he said. A joke. He knew I could not move at more than tortoise pace.

'I will not tell you,' I said, lips aquiver.

'I've realized.' He pointed to my hands. 'But now I have an altogether different question.'

I lifted my head with an effort. I wondered if this was the end.

'You wrote the theory down? Cold fusion?'

'No.'

'Interesting. Perhaps unfortunate. Your grandson seems to think that he has the papers. He wants to trade.'

'I don't believe you.'

'No? We shall see. Of course, whether he is bluffing or not, we will meet him.'

I didn't respond, wondering where he was driving. Then he said, 'Even if I cannot get the secret out of you, I'm sure you will not let him suffer.'

He turned briskly and walked out. My mind jumped with horrors. His briskness was almost part of the threat, the cruelty. For some reason, I compared it to those college rooms and to Arthur Beckett's Nazi smile.

When the door closed behind him, the dark returned. Back came its dark thoughts, and all I had was prayer.

More than expecting to die now, I prayed for it.

Hours passed. I don't know how many. I felt bones

grating over bones every time I moved my hands. I floated in and out of consciousness. I wondered if my prayer was about to be granted.

Then suddenly, still in my daze, light exploded once again and I was grabbed and forced upright. Before I knew it, Sumo Stan had me, leading me out of the house.

I was pushed into the back of a car with Yoshi beside me. Stan was driving.

We must have been somewhere close to Stanford University, because when we turned on to 101, we were just passing Palo Alto. Stan picked the outside lane and cruised at fifty-eight miles per hour until he reached the city traffic.

'Where are we going?' I said.

'Don't ask.'

'Is this the exchange?'

Yoshi smiled. 'That's what John likes to think.'

There was that cruelty again. I was silent after that.

We weaved through cars and lorries all the way into the centre of San Francisco. I could see that the sun was lowering in the sky – late afternoon or early evening. I wasn't sure of the times of sunset.

Unexpectedly, we made a swift left turn into an underground car park at the Glass Palace.

'Is this it?' I said.

'Shut up. We're going to go in, OK? Listen carefully, Stan has a gun in your back. Don't try anything, OK?'

I nodded, but I had no intention of going quietly. I had calculated I was dead anyway. I was only waiting for an opportunity. I thought if John was going to be in this place, I'd better choose my moment. What would I do? Scream for help? I couldn't fight them. All I wanted was to save him.

We waited at the bottom of the car park where there were three steel lifts. The first one that opened was full of customers on their way home, carrying bags marked with Christmas greetings. They looked at me strangely – my limp hands, the days of stubble growing, perhaps that smell which old men have – but they passed on without comment.

The lift took us up to the top floor. It was like walking

out into the sky. There was a large dome of glass above our heads and we were walking around on a wide marble balcony with multicoloured shops at our backs and in front of us a view down on to an enormous Roman mosaic many floors below. Christmas decorations hung like sagging coloured ropes from balcony to balcony. 'Merry Xmas' was everywhere, as were the first notices of forthcoming 'Clear-out Sales'.

Yoshi stopped in a small open area with bench seats. He gestured Stan to have me sit down. Stan nodded and as if we were one – he had an arm around my back and a hidden gun barrel pressing into my ribs – we sat on a vacant bench.

'What do we do now?' I asked.

'We wait,' Yoshi said.

'There are no papers,' I told him.

'You've already said that.'

From where I sat, I could see right across to shops on the other side. The Glass Palace was unlike any structure I had ever seen – not that I had seen much modern architecture. It was as if it had been built around a column of free space. Shops encircled it on every level with enough width of balcony for the passage of customers and the odd open area for coffee-shop tables and rest areas.

The shops themselves were beginning to close. Christmas had arrived. There were two glass-panelled lifts that ran up the opposite side from where we sat and you could see their naked mechanisms turning on the outside. I watched them ferrying the straggle of homeward-bound shoppers down through the floors and returning up empty. Lights started to go off and the shutters started to draw across shop fronts.

Soon the straggle of people had dwindled to a trickle, then a spot; then there was no one.

Stan said something to Yoshi in Japanese. It must have been something about John not coming, because Yoshi suddenly got very agitated.

'Do you think he's coming?' he asked me.

'I hope not.'

'Fuck you, he'll come. He wants to save your ancient ass.'

I tried to make a shrugging motion, but found it difficult and painful.

There was a public telephone right next to me. In my sitting position, it was not three feet from my right ear. Suddenly, it rang, loud and echoey in the now empty shopping mall. I jumped. I thought, for sure, the way Stan convulsed, that he would pull the trigger, but he didn't.

Yoshi came across and picked up the receiver.

A little mechanical and clipped and tinny and quiet it may have been, but it was unmistakably John's voice I heard whispering into Yoshi's ear. 'Look down.'

Yoshi held the receiver at arm's length so he could lean towards and over the balcony.

I had already spotted John through the iron lattice supporting the rail, standing in the now dim light by the bottom of one of the glass lifts. He had a portable phone in one hand, a dark-coloured briefcase in the other. Fear dropped through my insides like a lead weight. I had ceased to be scared for myself, but I was scared for John – he was all that was left.

'I have the papers,' I heard him say to Yoshi.

'Come up with them then. We'll make the exchange.'

'No . . .'

I couldn't hear what John said after that. Yoshi rolled away on to the other side of the telephone booth, so that he was stretching the cord and looking down on John. I could see that John had had the sense to put the side of a glass lift between himself and the line of sight.

'What do you mean "no". Didn't you come to get your grandfather?' Pause. 'Well, how do I know that? They could be meaningless junk.'

I calculated this was the moment. There were no papers. John was only bluffing and the worst thing was there was nothing I wouldn't tell Yoshi if he also had John.

I pushed myself up. Surprising what you can do when you think it may be your last act. It obviously caught Stan by surprise.

Leaning over the rail, I shouted, 'Get out of here. You don't know what you're doing.'

The words echoed in the empty mall.

Belatedly, Stan pulled me back, but I was in full cry. As Stan gripped me, I turned to Yoshi.

'The papers don't exist,' I told him. 'They were burnt by Ward Costello in 1940.'

'Really,' Yoshi said. He was still holding the receiver. I heard him say. 'Your grandfather says the papers were burnt.'

I saw John step out from behind the lift for a second. He cupped his hands to his mouth. 'Tell him Marion had them,' he shouted up.

Oh, God . . . I knew right then it was the truth.

They argued for several minutes on the phone. All that time, I thought surely someone else would come into the shopping mall, but John must have chosen the time and place carefully. No one came. I don't know whether I would have dared to call out to them if they had.

The gist of the argument was about protocol. John would not come nearer than three floors away and Yoshi kept saying he thought the whole thing was a bluff.

He came once again to demand from me an answer as to whether the papers were real. I was by then slumped back on the bench.

'I told you they were burnt,' I repeated, but hard as I tried, the life had gone out of my voice and my eyes shut when I tried to speak a half-believed truth.

Yoshi was only a foot from my face now, searching for his own version of the truth in my tired gaze. I could see his knuckles turning white on the receiver clutched to the side of his face.

'I'll tell you what,' John said, still tinny in his ear. 'I'll send you up the first four pages in this lift.'

Yoshi pulled back from me. He moved very slowly over to the rail and looked down. For five or six seconds, he said nothing. Then he said, 'OK,' with a very long 'O'.

I saw John take a wad of papers from the briefcase. He counted off the top four and placed them on the floor of the glass lift closest to him. I could see about half of each page, the rest obscured by the metalwork of the lift as it began its rise towards us. The work of all those years ago coming back to me, returning, the calendar spinning backwards. All I could do was watch and pray it wasn't true.

Yoshi hurried around the perimeter of the balcony like an excited child, arriving long before the lift reached him. He came back brandishing the papers and sounding triumphant.

'Is this it?' he said.

I looked at them. They were four pages dated 15 December 1939. The title was "Notes on Fission and Fusion". They were genuine all right, but the first four pages were only about fission. I was briefly relieved, but remembered they were part of the work I had entrusted to Ward. If he hadn't burnt these, then John was right: he had the secret of cold fusion in that briefcase.

I tried to get up again, yelling, 'Get out of here, John. Run! It's not worth it!'

But Stan was ready this time. He caught me before I'd got myself to the rail.

'Hmm,' said Yoshi thoughtfully. 'It's true then.'

42

The Mercedes with its smoked-glass windows purred through the car park entrance. Crouching in the spot John had chosen, Kate watched its shiny sides ooze past her.

This was the part of John's plan she didn't like. In fact, when he had first pushed the chess pieces up and down the board and told her how he thought it worked, she had shouted at him.

'You think Beckett'll come on his own? You think he's going to hand over five million bucks? You must be crazy. First, he's not going to come on his own. Second, they're going to come tooled up with instructions to take you, because you're their ticket to your old man. Now you're telling me that in your plan, both of you are inside the shopping mall. All he wants is you and your grandfather in the same place!'

John had smiled. He had a way of opening his hands as if his thinking embraced the world. 'Ah, but there's the beauty. There's the trick.'

He had moved a few more pieces, kissed her on the cheek, and she believed him – the most absurd things he said.

The Mercedes cruised into a spot thirty yards from the blue Ford John had carefully parked and prepared. Two large men got out. They were both over six feet, both wearing sweatshirts under noticeably bulging sports jackets. One had a Giants' baseball cap. The other was bareheaded and balding at the crown; he was carrying the Gucci briefcase.

Kate checked they were far enough out of earshot, a good fifty yards up the car park with several scattered cars still parked in the intervening spaces.

'John,' she whispered into the walkie-talkie.

A few seconds later, he returned an answering whisper. 'Yes, talk now. The first four pages are on their way up.'

'It's not Beckett, it's his men. Two of them. They're in the car park, heading for the car.'

'That's what I expected. Tell me when they're in the lift.'

Baseball Cap and Barehead circled the Ford suspiciously. They were expecting John Harringhay and all they had was an empty car. Barehead tried the driver's door. It was open. He gestured to his colleague with a finger. Baseball Cap tried the same thing with the passenger side. Open as well.

The two men now sat in the Ford, looking around for clues. All they could see was a cassette perched at the mouth of the stereo unit in the dash. Someone had affixed a yellow post-it with a message: 'Press this in.'

They looked at each other. Then Barehead, establishing himself as the more adventurous, pushed the cassette in.

From her position Kate couldn't hear the tape, but since it was her voice on the recording, she knew it pretty much by heart:

'Good afternoon, gentlemen. We see Mr Beckett has decided not to join us. That is all very well, but under such circumstances, we are not prepared to make the exchange in a deserted parking lot. I'm sure you understand this. If you would care to come up to the plaza of the shopping mall, we would be glad to do business.'

Kate saw the men exchanging words. The key question, John had told her, was whether they were prepared to move the location of the exchange. John figured they would be. Beckett's men had already tried to kill them in public once. Here they were being offered a shopping mall at closing time – no real difference from the car park.

In any case, John had said, the plan depended on getting them into the Ford before they got into the lift. It was the only way he could think of to control the direction from which they'd come at him.

The men got out of the car. For a minute, she thought they were heading back to the Mercedes, but no, they turned and headed for the nearest elevator. Why did John insist on calling them lifts?

'John,' she said, opening the channel to his walkie-talkie.

At first, there was no reply. Then he said, 'Sorry, just occupied for a minute.'

'You scared me. They're in the elevator . . . I mean, lift.'

'OK, then you get the hell out of there. Give us two more minutes, then phone the police.'

When she had called, John was occupied in the last of the negotiations. The agreement was simple enough: Zalapek would be put in one of the glass cages at the top; at the bottom, John would place the briefcase containing the papers in the other. Then they would be set off. As Zalapek descended from top to bottom, the greatest secret in modern times would pass him somewhere between the second and third level on its journey to the top-most, fourth level.

'Do we understand each other, Yoshi?' John asked over the phone line.

Yoshi was back around the other side of the balcony, looking down at John by the elevators' base.

'We understand each other,' Yoshi confirmed.

Sumo Stan had been silent for the most part. Now he said in Japanese. 'What if this is a double cross?'

'They cannot run fast with this bag of bones in tow,' Yoshi replied. Then switching to English he said, 'Come on, old man, time to go home.'

Sumo Stan led Hayden Zalapek around the balcony perimeter. Yoshi stayed where he could keep a view of both the top and bottom of the exchange.

'OK,' he said when Zalapek had been pushed into the elevator at the top, 'we're ready.'

'The briefcase is ready.'

'I want to see the papers again,' Yoshi said suddenly. 'Hold them where I can see them. Then put them in the briefcase slowly. No tricks.'

'Whatever you want.'

John dipped into the glass elevator and removed the

briefcase. He brought it out into the plaza and put it down on the mosaic floor. He opened it, took out the papers, spread them out on the floor.

'Happy?' he said on the portable phone.

'Put them in,' Yoshi commanded, still holding nervously to the receiver of the pay phone.

John closed the briefcase and replaced it inside the glass cage.

'On the count of three, then,' he said.

'My count?' Yoshi asked.

'If you like. You've got to signal your muscle man.'

'Very well. One. Two. Three.' He raised and lowered his arm in a chopping motion.

Sumo Stan leaned into the glass elevator car and pressed the button for the bottom floor. John did the reverse with the other elevator. Both had to skip quickly to get out before the doors closed.

John looked up, watching the slow progress of the two glass cages. This was his gamble in action. The next few seconds would tell.

There is no view out of a steel elevator, so Barehead and Baseball Cap were forced to watch their progress on the panel above the door.

They had pressed the button for 'shopping level one'. The display showed first their departure from the bottom-most car park level, then their arrival at 'shopping level one'.

The doors never opened.

Hayden Zalapek looked out through the dirty windows of his cage, all finger marks and smears. Rising from floor level, perhaps ten feet from him but on the other side of two sets of glass panels, was the briefcase carrying his life's work. A life's work he had thought was destroyed in 1940.

He pressed his ruined hands against the closest panel, his head falling forward so his nose touched the glass.

The briefcase lifted up level with his eyes, passed above

his head and disappeared behind the metalwork of his cage.

'What the fuck's happening? Why doesn't the door open?' Baseball Cap was yelling.

'I don't know. We've reached the floor – it says so. Maybe the doors have jammed or something,' Barehead said, attempting to be rational.

Baseball Cap had his gun out aiming at the doors. Barehead looked at him as if he was crazy.

'What do you want? We're gonna push the alarm button?' Baseball Cap said.

Slowly Barehead drew his weapon. 'I have a bad feeling about this. But I don't think you should shoot the door. I think you have to shoot the mechanism in the control panel.'

'You shoot the panel. I'm going to shoot the fucking door. Stand back.'

Yoshi watched the two glass elevator cars cross perfectly halfway up and down on their respective journeys.

Hayden Zalapek had reached the second level and was still heading for the ground, when the briefcase, on level three, suddenly switched direction and started down as well.

Yoshi looked at it once, looked at it twice.

'It's a trick,' he shouted. He gestured to Sumo Stan, but Sumo Stan was still round the other side and couldn't see what was going on below him. Yoshi drew his own gun and started firing.

The first shot was aimed roughly at John, but got nowhere near him. The next, aimed down at Zalapek's glass cage, hit the steelwork of the elevator car's roof and deflected through the front shutter of a jewellery store on the second level. All of a sudden there were a hundred and twenty decibels of store alarms going off around them.

John dipped down and rolled across the floor until he was back behind the base of the glass elevators. Somewhere behind him, he heard a rasp of semi-automatic fire. He glanced quickly, seeing great holes torn in the facing panels of the steel elevators, then turned away just as quickly. He didn't have time to check. That part of the plan had to look after itself.

'You made a big mistake, Harringhay,' Yoshi was shouting from the top. 'I'm going to come down and fuck you once and for all.'

He was waving wildly to Sumo Stan, signalling they should go for the customer stairs. Stan stopped halfway round the balcony perimeter. He had been running back towards Yoshi after starting Zalapek's descent. Standing there, he looked at his boss helplessly. He hardly had the build for a race down three floors.

Yoshi waved again, the wave conveying anger, and Stan turned and headed for the stairs in a heavy-footed run.

43

I heard the shooting break out. And then the alarm sounding. I had no idea what was going on.

I counted the seconds as I waited for the lift to stop. Finally it did and the doors opened. The first face I saw was John's. I was so glad he was alive.

'John,' I started to say, raising my voice above the alarm.

He said, 'You hear that shooting? Run towards it but avoid the bullets.'

'What? I—'

'Do it! I have to get the papers!'

He pushed me and I tottered and went blindly in the direction he indicated. I could hear the bursts of fire he was talking about, but of course I did not know who or what they were.

I turned back to see the second glass lift arriving on the ground floor. Suddenly I realized his trick, and realized why he wanted me to run. He was grabbing the briefcase as I turned again.

Limping towards the gunfire for maybe twenty yards, I reached the far wall where there were exits for three steel lifts. The doors to the left-hand exit had jagged explosions across their surface, the edges of holes erupting out like metal volcanoes. Another rasp of fire opened up more seismic activity as I approached.

The doors on the centre lift were closed, but to the right, I could see there was a lift car waiting. I assumed this was part of John's escape plan.

I got in the lift, just as John caught me up. Without speaking, he reached and pressed a button on the control panel. The doors slid closed agonizingly slowly.

I could hear the clanging of the alarm and, ever so faintly

in the background, the distant wail of a police siren. Both were muffled and suddenly cut to a whisper by the doors. The car started down and John leaned against the side, put his head back and blew out his cheeks.

'The briefcase!' I exclaimed, alarmed when I didn't see it.

John reached inside his jacket and produced the wad of papers. 'Fusion, and the Art Master's mushy letter,' he said. 'Fission, I'm afraid, is gone for good.'

'Thank God!'

'I expected you to go after these,' he said. 'In the lift, I mean.'

'How could I?' I asked.

'I thought you might figure out that if you pressed the button to "three" as soon as they set you off, you could intercept them – get out at that floor and press the call button.'

'I never thought of that,' I admitted.

'A chess player's calculation,' he said. 'I'd disconnected the button anyway.'

The doors opened in the car park basement, the same level from which Yoshi, Stan and I had started.

John led me out and we headed towards a blue Ford pointing nose outwards from the wall. He gestured me to the near side while he circled towards the driver's door. I tried to run, but he seemed to walk casually. Calm – he thought it was over.

'It's an automatic,' he said, fumbling with the keys, 'the only kind I know how to drive. Not that I've got a licence, just a history of joyriding.'

'How come you're so calm?' I asked. 'I'm still shaking. They're still after us—'

'No, no, they're not. I took care of that.'

He smiled. But it lasted less than a second. As suddenly as it came, the smile dissolved.

'STOP!'

The shout came from my right, from behind John. When I looked I saw two things.

The first was a Mercedes parked some way up the row.

There were a few other cars dotted around, but this one had its rear door flung open.

The second was a tall man in a dark suit and tie coming out of the Mercedes. His tie was pulled aside at the neck and the top button of his shirt was undone. He was holding, very unsteadily, a handgun pointed vaguely in John's direction.

'What are those?' he demanded, pointing at the papers John still held in his hand.

John looked at him in surprise. 'Joe Beckett,' he said as if his balloon had punctured and all the air run away.

'Those are the papers, aren't they?' Beckett asked, his voice trembling as much as his hand. 'And my father's letter?'

John didn't reply. I heard a police siren growing loud in the background as if it was in the street outside.

I watched the gun barrel trembling. I had to make a decision.

44

The bullets seemed to have no effect, but then the steel doors opened anyway. Barehead and Baseball Cap came out like greyhounds released from a trap.

Across the mall, maybe twenty yards away, a Japanese was bending over a Gucci case identical to the one Barehead was carrying.

Barehead didn't have to think twice. The semi-automatic hit the target clean in the chest, a rasp of bullets knocking him backwards. The body skidded face up across the marble floor, stopping only when the head struck the doors of a glass elevator. Its death slide left a ragged stripe of blood as if a cleaner had dipped his mop in the wrong bucket.

'Fuck,' said Baseball Cap, looking at the body and then at his partner.

But they didn't have time to admire their handiwork. A second, larger Japanese came panting around the elevator base. This one had his gun ready.

Barehead was still pointing at the fallen man. The panting Japanese hit him in the head with the first shot.

Baseball Cap dived to the side, taking aim as he fell. He had a clear shot at the big man's open body. It was like shooting at a barn door.

But when he pulled the trigger, the gun only clicked. All its lead had been spent on the inside of an elevator door.

Just at that moment, the alarm stopped ringing. Its last jangling sounds lingered and died against the walls of the mall.

The big Japanese laughed. He waited a few seconds while he caught his breath. Then he walked over and shot Baseball Cap where he lay.

*

Police sirens in the background. John Harringhay looking his enemy in the eye – the stare that had frozen so many over the chessboard.

'It's all over,' he said.

'Give me the fucking papers,' Beckett shouted.

'You think you can still get away with this?'

'I can kill both of you. I can kill fucking both of you.'

'OK . . .' John looked down, thinking. Out of options.

'No,' Zalapek yelled. He slid around the front of the car, stumbling into the space between John and Joe Beckett.

Beckett fired.

A hole tore through the top right-hand side of Zalapek's torso below the shoulder. The impact and his own frailty sent him spinning backwards.

John saw it all as if it was in slow motion. His plan unravelling so terribly. The booming echo of the shot stretching time.

His grandfather's head kissed the roof of the car as he fell against it and he bounced towards the wall of the car park. There was a support pillar for the roof with a fire extinguisher mounted some two feet up it. His face smashed full on into the concrete of the pillar and he crumpled, knocking the fire extinguisher off its mounting as he fell to the ground.

John saw the shooter staring goggle-eyed at the shot man's fall, the amplitude of his gun shake increasing.

It increased further as John went towards his grandfather, calling out in horror.

'Stand back!' Beckett screamed.

The blood seeping from the old man mixed with water bleeding out of the dented extinguisher. They ran together in a puddle, blood and bleeding water. They seemed to terrify Beckett.

'Give me the papers,' he said, his voice now melted down to a low whisper.

John stopped. For a couple of seconds he listened to the police sirens, but they weren't getting closer. They were above him. Going to the main entrance of the mall, he guessed. The wrong place!

'You're not going to shoot me,' John told him. He figured his last chance was to back away slowly. He couldn't hand over the papers. His grandfather had lived and died for them. Maybe Beckett wouldn't shoot him if he did hand them over, but he couldn't do it. He kept backing, feeling the nose of the car against his buttocks.

'Stop,' Beckett said again, but with no real conviction. He came forward, stopping six or seven feet from the driver's door.

John was in front of the car now. He had twisted towards Beckett, turning as he moved so he kept face to face with him. He was still trying to back away.

It was from this position he saw his grandfather rise from the floor. He was dragging up with him the dented fire extinguisher, still leaking water.

Up to chest height. Up above his head. Unsteady on his bandaged hands. His bleeding face contorted in pain and effort. He held the extinguisher cocked. Then he hesitated. It rocked briefly to one side and he pulled it back into line, but not before it had clinked against the concrete pillar.

Beckett turned.

Hayden Zalapek lunged, weapon above his head. He got within a yard and a half of Joe Beckett before Beckett fired. He fired twice. Ear-splitting. In quick succession.

John's view of his grandfather's fall was obscured by the car. He saw only the extinguisher landing on the roof. It rolled forward, bounced down on its hood and then on to the ground at his feet.

As soon as Beckett recovered, turning back to face him, someone else fired.

The shot punched a hole the size of a ping-pong ball in Beckett's cheek. He went down face first without a sound.

When John swivelled around, there were two figures standing by the car park pay station. One was Kate. The other was his Aunt Marion. It took a second to register Marion holding the gun.

'Have I killed him?' she said.

John made a move towards the bodies.

'I know it's only revenge, but I had to. He killed Ward. I've killed his son,' she said. Kate reached out and took the gun from the woman's frozen hand. She had to unpeel the fingers to get it safely loose before John could cross her line of fire.

John stepped over the first body. His grandfather was all he was interested in.

The eyes were staring up at him as he knelt down.

'Just like 1940,' the old man said in a hollow voice, 'the way Ward hit that Nazi ... Fire bucket ... Are the papers safe?'

'Yes,' John whispered, 'they're safe.'

'Good, then Pandora's box is closed.'

'You were actually going to hit him, weren't you?' John said.

He looked down at his grandfather but the old man was no longer looking up, and though John spoke more words to him, he never spoke back.

45

Two uniformed officers came charging through the fire-exit doors into the car park basement. Their guns were drawn, but all they found was a huddle of people crying and embracing. Dead on the floor were an ancient and anonymous scientist and the next Governor of the state. This was a story that was going to take some explaining.

'Fuck,' said the officer who turned Beckett over.

'Fuck,' said the officer who looked over his shoulder to see what he meant.

Reporters had started to arrive in the main mall upstairs, demanding stories and pictures. Police back-up was taping the place so no one could cross the neatly drawn police lines.

A young plain-clothes detective decided it was best to arrest the three suspects and drive them to a station some ten minutes away. He figured they could sort it out there in peace.

Sumo Stan seemed to have somehow avoided the police cordon when they had come in through the shopping mall's main entrance. The final count at the scene included five bodies. Also in the count was five million in used bills.

In the police wagon, John and Kate were silent, while Marion talked incessantly. When they reached the desk at the police station, she demanded access to her lawyer before the desk sergeant had even completed the paperwork formalities.

The station was nearly empty: a skeleton staff and seemingly only half the normal lighting. The traditional wave of Christmas Eve drunks hadn't started to arrive.

Marion threw off all attempts to restrain her, striding up and down and spouting about legal rights like an amateur lawyer. Kate and John sat in handcuffs on a bench while Marion argued.

The young detective waited patiently for Marion's tirade to subside.

'I think you better call the Feds,' he told the sergeant. 'One of the dead is Joe Beckett. There's news crews and all kinds of shit on the scene.'

'Already done, son. They should be there by now. This one's a bit too big for you, huh?'

'When do I get my call?' Marion said.

'This woman had the gun at the time of arrest.'

'That's right. I shot him. I saw him kill one man. He was trying to kill my nephew.'

'You'll have a chance to tell the judge,' the desk sergeant said. He had an air of having seen everything in the world at least once before. He probably used the same phrase half a dozen times in a shift.

'Now, why would Joe Beckett want to come down to a shopping mall to kill someone?' the detective asked, biting a little more on Marion's statement.

He stared hawk-eyed at Marion, but the response came from elsewhere.

'Perhaps I can answer that.'

Kazuo Yakamura, still plastered from toe to chest, was swinging his way on crutches, face locked in determination, Shoyo at his side.

He looked straight at Marion and smiled. 'It's been a long time, Miss Stern.'

Marion turned and peered at him in the poor light. She didn't recognize him.

'No,' he said, 'you probably would not remember me, but I remember you. It is of no consequence.' Then, turning to the desk sergeant, Yakamura announced, 'I have come here voluntarily to hand over evidence.'

'Evidence?' the desk sergeant said. All of a sudden, his expression showed that this was a turn out of the ordinary.

'I have heard what happened.' Yakamura stopped. A wave of pain contorted his face. He mastered it. 'I believe my son was among the dead,' he continued. 'You see, he was trying to blackmail Mr Beckett.'

'Blackmail? With what?' the detective interrupted.

Yakamura gestured to his assistant. Shoyo placed a video-tape in front of the desk sergeant.

'I think you will find,' said Yakamura, 'that copies have already been couriered to the offices of the major news-papers and TV networks.'

'Are you saying what I think you're saying?' the detective asked.

'The recording is old, but the contents are clear. Two very young girls, one candidate for election. What you have seen tonight is a pay-off gone wrong. A double cross, if you like. I believe these people here are the innocent bystanders. I will swear to it.'

'Do I get my lawyer now?' Marion prised her way in front of the desk sergeant.

'You have no need,' Yakamura said. 'Mine is already on his way.'

The next morning, 7.00. Out on bail. The statement made by Yakamura seemed watertight. Only a matter of time before they drop the case, Yakamura's lawyer assured them.

The TV news networks were coyly reporting the contents of Yakamura's videotape. They didn't dare show it. The newspapers, on the other hand, gave a blow-by-blow description of the action. One tabloid even published a script of the moans and the pleadings. Freedom of the press – its abuse in action.

Marion fell asleep in the taxi. She was destined for her hotel, the Stern International. She offered John and Kate accommodation, a suite, but John said they weren't inter-ested, and Kate wanted to get home.

They dropped off Marion and took the taxi on to Kate's apartment. There was no food in it, so they dropped in at a diner half a block away.

The morning was just beginning. The sleepy *maitre d'* showed them to a table by the window. It had a plastic tablecloth and a laminated menu. John entwined his feet with Kate's beneath the table; she slipped off her shoes and burrowed her bare toes on to the skin above his sock. He read the menu out loud from top to bottom.

'What do you want?' he asked her when he had pronounced the last syllable in the 'desserts' column.

'Everything,' she said.

He called over the *maitre d'* and repeated Kate's request. 'Bring us everything,' he said, 'but start with coffee.'

Ordering seemed to be an effort for him. He stopped speaking after that. Whatever lightness he had forced subsided and he slumped in the chair, staring out of the window, eyes dragging on the traffic that passed.

'There're some things I don't understand,' Kate ventured when the coffee came.

With a great effort, he turned to look at her.

'What's to understand?' he said. 'The plan failed. My grandfather's dead.'

'The part of the plan I didn't like,' Kate persisted. 'When you wanted to call Beckett. You knew he wouldn't make the drop himself, didn't you? That elaborate stuff with the car and the tape wouldn't have worked if he'd come himself. He'd never have gone up into the mall.'

'That's right,' John admitted. 'I guessed.'

'Then what was the reason for calling Beckett at all? I mean, there was no prospect he was going to leave you and your grandfather alone just because he lost another couple of thugs. Did you do it just in the hope that they'd keep Yoshi and his man occupied while you got away?'

'Something like that.'

Kate processed his answer, but it only registered as a partial one; it didn't satisfy her. She pulled her feet back under the table, leaving him alone, leaving him untouched.

'You could have trapped them in the elevator if you'd wanted to,' she said. 'You used that trick on Beckett's men, so you must have been pretty sure you could make it work. And Yoshi would have had to get in, because those three steel jobs were the only way into the car park.'

He didn't answer. The tablecloth held his gaze – chequered red PVC.

She felt bad for his pain, but she had to know. She had to know it all.

Slowly, but in one smooth movement, Kate drained her coffee. She put the empty cup down in the saucer, holding it there between the pressed tips of fingers from both hands. She looked down at it and then back at John. He seemed so horribly isolated now she'd withdrawn from him.

She said, 'You knew Yakamura had the tape, or had something. You figured the only way to make him release anything against the Becketts was if they were responsible for his son's death ... That's it, isn't it? That's how you figured it.'

He put his palms down on the PVC, feeling its coolness seeping into his blood where his veins came close to the pressed surface.

'It's OK,' she said. She stretched out her hands and placed them gently over his outstretched fingers and smiled.

'Yes,' he said at last, raising his eyes, 'that's how I figured it.'

Epilogue

When they let us, we buried my grandfather in a place I'll tell to no one. After that, I had only one thing left to do in America.

I asked Kate to drive me out to the Beckett house.

She made no argument. She got a map – or at least instructions – from some contact I didn't know. Then she gestured to the passenger seat of her dented VW and we went without a word.

During the journey, I kept my peace. The day weighed heavy and I closed my eyes and waited for my time.

Kate drove fast and silent. She knows me too well by now.

When it swung into view, the house was exactly as I had seen in a page of Esther's report, though in truth, photographs don't come out well on ink-jet printers. I guess I recognized the outlines.

Kate pulled the car up at the gatehouse and I got out. The day was surprisingly still and warm.

For a while I looked around, but there was no one. No one to stop me. I walked up the drive and just kept on walking around the side of the main house without bothering with the front door.

The place was truly enormous: the garden a country park – trees and tennis courts and a lake the size of an English county. I stood and wondered at it while I calmed my breathing.

I spotted Arthur Beckett from a distance, sitting in the 'grand gazebo', a white lattice structure at the top of the slope. I walked out on the expanse of grass towards him, my mind quite made up now.

He was seated in a wheelchair, a single fold of tartan

blanket over his knees. His face was dead, just as it had been described to me: the left side fixed like rock; the ashen skin of the right only marginally better.

I thought of a painting I once saw where life grew out of something dead as it moved from left to right. Escher. His face was like that painting.

Beckett was responsible for my grandfather's death. He had killed my grandmother. Now his son was dead too. We had been avenged, Marion and I. Now he felt the same pain.

He saw me coming with his one moving eye, and I stopped and looked at him, face to terrible face.

Within the gazebo, there was a white painted table, latticed in iron to match the surrounds. I moved so it stood between the two of us. Then I reached into the inside pocket of my jacket, brought out a wad of battered papers and dropped them, curling and yellowed, on to the tabletop. There were twelve pieces of foolscap lying in that pile, my grandfather's work, minus the four lost in the Glass Palace. They were fragile and flimsy and the writing on some was untidy and full of crossings-out, yet they were everything. All I had left of him.

I took out the mushed-up letter that could not be read and I put it on top of the papers. In the day's stillness, they all lay there and never moved.

Beckett shuffled in his seat and his lips quivered but failed to break the silence. I felt I had bound him down, even though I knew it was age and grief and paralysis which kept him planted in his wheeled chair.

'You know what this is?' I said. I neither wanted nor expected a reply.

I produced from my trouser pocket a box of extra large matches. I knew my fingers would shake too much to hold the fragile sticks and floppy folded books of the normal kind. I clumped three matches together and struck along the side of the box. The flame caught and I shielded it for a moment and then held it to the edge of the papers.

God help me, I burned my last memory of him.

The papers were halfway gone before I felt the first waft

318

of breeze. Some black and glowing embers tore away and rose on their own hot air. The white paint of the table darkened and began to flake beneath the fire.

I looked at Arthur Beckett. His good eye was crying. A big salt tear formed and burst the dam of his eyelid and cascaded down the grey cheek and on to the tip of his chin.

I think he had expected something more of me. I think he expected me to kill him. Just as Marion had killed his son. But that would have been too kind.

When I had seen that first tear drip and blot into his cotton shirt, I turned around and walked away.

Kate kissed me as I reached the car.

'He's gone,' I said.

She turned the key in the ignition and we drove away.